Acknowledgments

My special thanks go:

to the other four Voices, who know who they are and whose words comprise this entire story.

to my family, especially Bill, my husband of 54 years, for his unfailing support, his countless hours of proof-reading, and his non-directive, but helpful suggestions and to my sons, Bill, for his positive feedback, and Randy, for his help with the editing, interior design of the text and resolution of endless computer glitches, all of their help laced with good humor.

to Jeff DeMattos, for creating precisely the cover I envisioned, and to Tom Rescigno for creating and updating the DEAR VOICES, website.

to Jack Silveira, Kay and Chuck Van Damm, Maryon Hicks, Dean and Joanne Storkan, Kathy Mollicone, Jerry Hadley, Erie Mills, Gerald Preston, Sondra Orup, Lois Davis, Donna Olson, Mike Janas and Don Lundgren for reading the manuscript and giving me the critical feedback I needed to continue believing that this book was worthy of publication.

DEAR VOICES,

An epistolary chronicle of love and redemption

by

Lea Fredericks Frey

PublishAmerica
Baltimore

First printing

ISBN: 1-4137-1648-2
PUBLISHED BY PUBLISHAMERICA, LLLP
www.publishamerica.com
Baltimore

Printed in the United States of America

Dear Voices,

An epistolary chronicle of love and redemption

Introduction

It would be well for the reader to begin this epistolary biography about an extraordinary friendship by knowing something of the history and background of the story. The author and the four male participants in this exchange of letters were high school classmates, having become inseparable friends during their senior year. Virtually all of the letters are actual letters, edited of some redundancies. No surnames are used and all names of venues and people, except Joe's and Lea's are invented. Less than half a dozen letters, most at the beginning, were reconstructed from the author's memory to supply the reader with essential information, while retaining the epistolary form. In most instances, no attempt was made to rewrite the letters, except for misspellings and deletions of details, which were not germane to the story or necessary to flesh out the characters. The letters attributed to Joe and Lea, are in large part, just as written. Where there is a reference to a last name, other than, on occasion, Lea's or Joe's, " ...... " is used in its place.

Four of the writers of the letters, including the author, have long believed that this story should be told. The fifth writer contributed only four or five letters to the correspondence, but those are crucial to the denouement. The author set the story in the fictitious town of Mountmore, near Pittsburgh, Pennsylvania. It is clearly meant to be Joe's story, with the focus on him and the effect these letters from his, "Voices of the past," had upon his time in prison as well as the remainder of his life.

Some readers will be curious about what factors in Joe's life prior to his incarceration could have led to his flirtation with law-breaking. How, they might wonder, could such a basically decent, kindly, caring young man turn to a life of crime? The newspaper reported it as "armed robbery," the police describing him on one occasion as, "a gentlemanly burglar." How was the prison break accomplished? What happened during the years when Joe was at large? The reader should be aware that the intent of this book is to focus on the time of his imprisonment and all the years thereafter. This is not a story about what caused his crime; nor is it a psychological study of the causes of crime, per se. Rather, it is a story of how one man, at the very depth of his despair in prison, overcame the self-loathing and shame he felt and was able to turn his life around. None of Joe's story is concealed, and he has given us many details in these letters. If some of the readers' questions remain unanswered, it is because the author considers the answers to be less important than the evolution that took place in Joe after the uninvited reappearance of the "Voices" in his life. Perhaps even more important is Joe's professional growth in the years after his release. (See his detailed resumé in the epilogue.) In the final analysis, therein lies the importance of the story. If this book seems understated, that is intentional, since the story stands on its own—as it is—and needs no embellishment.

Readers, who have become used to swift internet communication should be reminded that e-mail did not exist in the 1960's. While such a collection of letters would be very easily obtained today via e-mail, it required considerable effort then, the writers relying on regular mail and carbon paper to distribute multiple copies of the letters to each other. The author was able to obtain directly from Joe copies (which in the beginning, the "Voices" did not make for each other) of the earliest letters to Joe, since he saved each one. It is only recently that they learned from him, that once he decided to create archives of this correspondence himself, he copied, in microscopically tiny writing, each of his own letters on small pieces of paper the size of 3 X 5 index cards, keeping them in a treasured file in his cell. In a letter from Ed (December, 1965), Joe's extraordinary files are described in more detail. These archives are among his most prized possessions today.

All five of the participants in the correspondence are known to be alive and four have remained in close contact with each other, despite their geographical separation. While it is assumed that the fifth, called Lenny in the story, is still living in Mountmore, there has been no contact with him by any of the rest, and his long silence seemed to be clearly asking to be left alone. (See Epilogue.)

The four others, however, along with their respective spouses, met in Clearwater, Florida, in January 1999, for a "Voices" reunion. Included is a group photograph taken on that occasion, along with one taken at their reunion in Virginia Beach in 1966. Included also are photos of the four as high school seniors.

Background

The story evolves within the letters, in chronological order, and the letters are not interspersed with any explanation. If some seem out of order by a day or two, it was due to the letters crossing in the mail. The reader can quickly piece the story together through the content of the letters. However, some of the history of the relationships, in particular between Lea and Lenny, will help the reader to understand the strain between them. They were high school sweethearts, clearly intending to spend their lives together, but in 1948, their romance ended. The author's original intention was to relate the details of this in this introduction. However, it became clear, that, for dramatic purposes, it would be better to reveal them within the context of the story. To preserve the epistolary form of the book, this required one letter to be constructed by the author. It is in the form of a long note from Lea to Rob, shortly before Christmas, 1965. None of the content of any of the letters, however, including that one, is fictitious. The most important aspect of the story is its authenticity and strict adherence to the truth, which needs no embellishing.

The first letter is a combination of two, which were written in the summer of 1944 to Lenny by Joe, who was called Shorty in high school. Lenny sent them to Joe in 1964, along with his first letter to him in prison. It seems remarkable that Lenny had kept them for twenty years, reflecting much about the closeness of their friendship during high school.

During Joe's incarceration, there was no limit placed on the number of letters prisoners could receive, but they could only write one letter a week. All incoming and outgoing mail was censored, and Joe's letters had to be written on one side of one sheet of lined paper, on the back of which were always printed the prison rules. Since Joe wrote to family as well, he was only able to write to one of the Voices once a month. Whoever received it copied it and mailed copies to each of the others. Likewise, each copied his response to Joe and mailed those copies to the others, as well.

Four of the five "Voices" have saved all letters from the participants, the last one in their files being dated June 26, 2003. These four continue to exchange Christmas letters to the present day. Joe sent all the Voices the final letter in the body of the manuscript some time after work was begun on the book. As soon as the author read it, it was obvious it would become the conclusion of the story. No one could have written a better one.

For the past several years, much of their contact with each other has been by telephone, and more recently, by e-mail. Communication with Lenny has been sparse for most of the past 20 years, and he remains a mystery person in many ways. He is, however, very much a part of this story, a kind of silent correspondent, occupying a tender place in all their hearts.

In early December of 1988, an audiotape arrived in Los Gatos from Joe. It was addressed to Rob and Lea, presumably a duplicate having been sent to Rob, as well. On the tape, Joe made reference to having noted the 25th anniversary of the arrival of Rob's first letter, which began this most significant phase of Joe's recovery from what he often refers to as his "fall." He described this reappearance in his life of his "Voices out of the past," as an invitation, in his darkest hour, to "come in out of the rain."

Lea Fredericks Frey, Author and editor of "Dear Voices,"

Clockwise from upper left, 1944 high school yearbook photographs of Ed, Lea, Rob, and Joe.

DEAR VOICES, RECOLLECTIONS
Summer After Graduation—1944

Fresh Air Home
Association for the Improvement of the Poor (AIP)
Warrendale, PA
Sunday, June 25, 1944

Dear Lenny,

Well, pal, here's hoping this letter finds you without your orders for the army yet. Camp life here is pretty swell so far—plenty of food, milk, sleep, and girls. However, the latter don't appeal to me too much. Rob is here working as a counselor, too, but he gives those girls a visual going-over!

Do me a favor, pal, the next time you see Ann. Take her in your arms and give her a hug and squeeze for me! I guess she already hooked another fish by now—all well and good. We quit going steady the night before I left—and believe it or not, it was my idea. Now, I'm sorry and feel like a fool, but we're all going to war, and it's best this way.

Guess I don't blame you for pepping up your leaving for the army—but it bothers me somewhat, too, for I do so want to see you before you leave. Gee, I wish I were leaving with you—we sure could have a rugged old time together when we marched into Tokyo.

How's Dude? (I called Lea that once, and something told me she didn't like it. It's your special nickname for her, and maybe she wants it to be just between the two of you. Course, whatever YOU call her will be OK with her!) Tell her I said hello. You've got a neat girl there, pal, and don't let her go without a struggle. Can't tell where in the heck you'll find one as faithful and pretty. But, I guess this is all just wasted talk, for I don't believe you need anyone's advice concerning her. Well, pal, until I hear from you—and I'd better!— I'll have to close.

Shorty

The Post–war Years
1946–1955

(Note left at desk–Columbia Hospital School of Nursing, Wilkinsburg, PA)

No date–approx. June 1946

Lea,

Just got home—still in Navy uniform—haven't even had a chance to get into civvies. I peeked in the window and saw you in the classroom. You were in the second row, near the windows, but I recognized you from the back, even with your hair in an up-sweep. The nurse at the desk said you would be in class a while, and I decided my coming was probably not a good idea. Sorry I missed you.

Shorty is home, too, and he wanted to invite you and me to a party Sunday at 6:30—just a few friends—to meet his new wife, Betty! Yes, believe it or not, he brought home a wife, and they'll be moving into an apartment in Beechview. In fact, you can see the house from the 42 Dormont streetcar as it passes over the Beechview trestle. It's a house, and they rented the second floor. (I forgot the address, but I know the house.) He hopes you can come, and I told him I'd let you know. Didn't know how to call you here, so came out instead. I will pick you up, if you want. Nothing fancy, he says. Call me at Mother's, if you can come. Too bad Lenny and Ed aren't home yet. (I hate to admit it, but in that student nurse uniform, you would look cute if it weren't for the black stockings and shoes!)

Rob

Note accompanying a high school yearbook
No date. Approximately Summer, 1948

Lea,

Good to see you again after so long. Who would have expected to see a Mountmore classmate on a streetcar going out to Wilkinsburg? I didn't even know you were interested in becoming a nurse. As per our conversation, I checked when I got home, and for some reason, I do have that extra MHS 1944 yearbook I told you about, and I am sending it to you. If yours ever turns up, maybe you can pass the extra one on to someone else who lost theirs. Ciao!

Jodi

Conneaut Lake, PA
August 2, 1949

Dear Rob,

How long has it been since I last talked to you or saw you? Months, maybe even a year? That's disgraceful. If it weren't for your mother, I wouldn't even know where you are. Thanks for the get well card. No doubt, your mom told you I had the surgery. You always could be counted on to do the "correct thing." Good old reliable Rob!

I am pretty much recovered from an embarrassing appendectomy. I am afraid it was what surgeons call, "Honeymoon Appendicitis." That's a euphemism for a false alarm. Anyway, it's an excuse to "recuperate" from this unnecessary operation at Bill's family's summer place at Conneaut Lake. Nice four-bedroom house on three lots right at Oakland Beach. The worst I can complain of at the moment is a bad case of sunburn.

I was sorry you couldn't make it to my wedding, Rob, but I was happy your mother came. The proofs just came from the photographer, and there is a nice photo of her talking to me in the receiving line. Are you still working in the summer as a counselor at A.I.P.? It seems to me, you and Shorty both worked there every summer. You both are great with kids, so I suspect you were good at it.

Nothing much to report, except that marriage is agreeing with me, and I can't tell you how happy I have been. Marrying Bill is the most colossally right thing I have ever done in my life. He is a lot like you—reliable, intelligent, with absolute integrity. Keep in touch, Rob. Good friends don't grow on trees.

Lea

Pittsburgh, PA
December 15, 1951

Dear Ed,

Thank you for inviting Bill and me to the first dinner Joyce cooked as your wife. It was a sweet way for her to meet your good friends! I am glad to be included in that number. Thanks also for allowing us to bring along baby Billy. I'm glad he slept through most of the evening.

What a great idea to have Joyce cook the dinner at your mom's house!

Please give her my compliments on a wonderful dinner. Joyce is as sweet a girl as you could find, Ed. I liked her a lot. I hope she felt comfortable with us. It's hard on a young bride to put herself on display like that, wanting to make a good impression on her husband's friends who are strangers to her. It was good to see Rob, too, and to meet Marlene. Gosh, with their engagement, it looks like we're all paired up at last, eh? Too bad Shorty wasn't in town. It's been several years now since that party right after the war—just before you came home. I seem to have lost complete track of him and don't even know where he is. Funny how our lives go in different directions after we marry, isn't it?

Military life seems to be agreeing with you. I know you transferred from the Navy to the Marines, and Rob says you were part of a V-6 Navy education program. I hear you were sent to Princeton, and afterwards, you'll be a Marine officer, right? I hope you two will be assigned somewhere close, so we can see each other oftener than every few years. Thanks again for inviting us, Ed.

Fondly,
Lea

Grand Island, NY
August 27, 1955

Dear Shorty,

Friend, your letter really came like a bolt out of the blue. I don't have the slightest idea where to start this letter because there sure has been a lot of water over the dam since we last saw each other. Note the change in my last name, for example. I had it changed to Dad's old Swedish family name while still in school.

I graduated from Carnegie Tech with a degree in Mechanical Engineering, then went on to graduate school when I was offered the chance. Stayed in grad school for three years, got my MS in psychology, and almost got my PhD. I am in the process of writing my dissertation now, and hope to get my degree this coming year.

After a year of grad school, I got married—the smartest thing I ever did. The gal was one whom I met at—guess where?—AIP camp! After all those summer romances, I finally find what I wanted, and was lucky enough to get her. By the way, my wife does have a sister, but she happens to be six-foot tall.

After two years in grad school, I took a summer job out on the west coast working for Lockheed at Los Angeles. I lived alone for most of the time, and Marlene joined me for a short time at the end of the summer. We made a flying trip to San Francisco, and I thought very much about your living in Los Gatos (at least, that was the last address I had for you.) On the map, it looks to be about 50 or 60 miles to the south of San Francisco.

Last year, I was all finished with classroom work for my PhD, and I was offered a very good job with my present company, so I left school and moved up here to start work. I am now with the Linde Air Products Co. primarily a chemical concern. I work in the Personnel Dept. as a psychologist—and find that I can help others' problems better than I can solve some of my own. Actually, I find the work very interesting, and am very happy with the job. Our finest accomplishment so far is to have a fine son, Doug, who is healthy, sleeps through the night, and is 7 months old and still going strong.

I confess, I haven't been good at keeping up with high school friends except for our close bunch. Friend, Lenny, has been a real mystery to me. He changed his name, too, why, I am not sure. Ever since he broke up with Lea, I have heard practically nothing. Friend, Lea, has at least two children by her doctor husband. I believe that he is still in the Air Force, due to be released soon. No use telling you anything about Ed, since you already know more than I do. We have both kept in contact loosely over the years, just enough to let each other know the vital things.

That's all for now. I am not sure just when I will be in town, so can't say anything about getting together at the moment. I am still working on my dissertation, in addition to my job. However, I sure would like to have us all get together some time. Let's try to work something out for some time in the fall.

Many thanks for writing, Shorty. If it weren't that I was glad to hear from you, I never would have written so soon. Take care of yourself, and we'll see each other some time soon.

Rob

ADRIFT
1962–1963

July 8, 1962

Dear Rob, Marlene, and kids,

Just a note to let you know we arrived safely. Travis Air Base is sizzling, with hot winds blowing all the time. We are staying in temporary quarters just off base—not luxurious, but it's summer, and we can make do. We'll get base housing in a few weeks, I think.

Thank you all so much for giving us a roof on our way through Indianapolis. Talk about a port in a storm! I can't recall being in a more frightening downpour—ever! We are very grateful for your hospitality and for your flexibility. I certainly didn't expect to be seeing you at all, but I felt desperate; thunderstorms always scare the heck out of me! The kids were exhausted, and Bill and I were feeling at the end or our rope when I called; I was grateful you didn't have an unlisted phone number. Your willingness to take all four of us in, feed us, and provide us with beds was heart-warming. I owe ya, Rob!!

It was almost providential, that storm, actually, since I would no doubt never have found out about Shorty otherwise. Hard to imagine he is actually an escaped convict on the FBI most wanted list. (Sounds more like a B-movie than real life!) Please let me know what you find out, if the FBI contacts you again, and certainly let me know if he is recaptured and back in prison. It all makes me so sad. I know I will want to write him, although I have no idea what I will say. But, please do let me know what you hear. My heart aches for him. I keep thinking of him as he was in high school—handsome and fun-loving, singing those darling Irish songs, so full of sweetness.

My best to all of you, and once again, my thanks for taking in four drowned rats in need of a safe haven for the night.

Fondly,
Lea

Indianapolis
October 30, 1963

Lea,

I found the letter I told you about, which Ed had sent me some time ago, with a Washington Post & Times Herald article, datelined August 31, 1962. Pertinent information was as follows:

"Joseph R. Killeen, 36, whom Alexandria police described five years ago as a 'gentlemanly burglar' was arrested for unlawful flight yesterday as he pedaled his bicycle in Denver. The FBI said Killeen was wanted for escaping from a state work camp at Baskerville, VA, on October 25th, 1960. He had served three years of a 10-year sentence for the armed robbery of a Fairfax County gas station. Police reported then that he told them he was too 'ashamed' to confess his part in a series of Alexandria burglaries. He later received concurrent sentences totaling two years on four counts of burglary and one of grand larceny. The FBI reported that Killeen had been working for a packaging firm in Denver and was starting on a bicycling vacation when he was arrested without a struggle."

Lea: This indicates Shorty's sentence runs something like this:

Original sentence–10 years (1957- 1967). Escaped and free–1 and 1/2 years. Probable release date–1969

Rob

Weston, Conn.
December 1, 1963

Dear Shorty,

This is Rob writing to you. It seems to me that it was about a year and a half ago that I was visited by the FBI and questioned about my relationship with you. It was then that I learned the trouble you were in. Shortly thereafter, I had conversations with Ed and Lenny, and the three of us decided to keep in touch with one another about you. Some time after that, Ed sent me a news clipping from an Alexandria, VA paper that told of your return to Virginia from Colorado. Ed tried to trace what had happened to you, but wasn't successful.

A few days ago, I went to Richmond to spend Thanksgiving with relatives. I took the opportunity to go to the prison and make inquiry about your whereabouts. From a guard, I received your address and was told that I could write to you. Later, I wrote brief notes to Ed and Lenny, giving them your address. You may well hear directly from them.

I don't exactly know why I am writing this letter. Perhaps some of it is a feeling of "There but for the grace of God go I." Whatever the motivation, Ed and Lenny and I agree that throughout our lives we have formed few if any friendships stronger than the ones we formed in high school. In our thinking, you are one of those close friends to all of us.

Shorty, I am not a do-gooder, and I don't want to push myself on you. I am writing as an old friend, asking you if you wish to renew our friendship via letters. The choice is yours. I don't know the kind of man you are today, any more than you know what sort of man I am. But I find it hard to believe that the boy I knew years ago could have changed so basically that I wouldn't want to call him my friend.

So, if you so desire, I will be glad to write to you in the future. I don't know what kind of letters they will be or how often they will get written. If you are agreeable about the letter writing, I am sure that Ed and Lenny (and perhaps even Lea) will be glad to join the club.

Think it over, Shorty, and give me an answer at your convenience. Whatever your decision, you know in your own mind that your old friends have not forgotten you. I hope to hear from you.

Rob

Joe Killeen, 78250
S/S State Farm, VA
December 1, 1963

Dear Rob,

My memories of those years shared with you, Ed, Lenny, and Lea, are probably keener and more alive than any of yours. Retrospection is an art I've developed during these years in prison. You "free people" aren't blessed with enough time for such meditations.

Up until now, I have been able to visit all of you via a sort of spiritual transmigration into the past. None of you knew about it; it was easy, fun—no embarrassment, no shame. Now you startle my coveted and closely guarded memory world with your immediate presence.

At the beginning of my fall, I determined to go it alone. I even refused to see my sister, until she said we were involved because we were family. I tried to draw a tight circle that shut her out, but her circle took me in. "No man is an island," so John Donne wrote. Compassion was less than half the answer when I allowed the pillars of my self-respect to crumble and crash around my frustrated life. Yet, I know it was this same compassion, by her and others, that made it possible for me to climb out of the wreckage.

An orbiting satellite sometimes breaks up into innumerable parts and thus divided and out of control, goes its erratic way through space. This sometimes happens to the human personality when it loses the fiery passion about which it revolves, and therefore it too may break up into fragments, because there is no central power to grip and hold it and swing it about itself. It's taken a mighty grasp from that something Higher to pull all my divergent elements inside together. (But how can you rely on the words of one you haven't seen or known for almost twenty years?)

You said you couldn't explain your motivation for writing, but you sought to call it "friend." I'll settle for that if you four will. It is a start. Somehow, I need all of you. (Do I sound like a decrepit mendicant? I'm not.) You can't aid my release—that's not why. It's just that the memories are too precious, too real.

Thanks for writing, for your Christmas card, for Ed's. Please tell me of Ed's mom as well as others. Write!

Joe

1964–1965 – THE PRISON YEARS
The Salamander Emerges

Weston, CT
January 8, 1964

Dear Joe,

Your very welcome letter arrived a few days ago. When I received it, I took the liberty of making copies of it and sending a copy to Ed, Lenny, and Lea. Each of them now knows your address and knows that you are willing to correspond with us.

Joe, I don't know where to start. How do we go about catching up on over 15 years? Perhaps one way is to tell you briefly what I know about Lenny, Ed, and Lea. You might be interested in knowing that it was our concern over you that has drawn the four of us into closer contact with each other. Lea and Ed kept pretty good track of me over the years through my mother, whenever they were in town. Lenny sort of drifted away, metaphorically, at least, and we lost track of him. Oddly enough, he is the only one of us who never left Mountmore.

Shortly after being visited by the FBI about you, I was in Pittsburgh and decided to try to find Lenny to talk about you. After a few phone calls, I was amazed to find that Lenny was living about a block away from my Mom and Dad in Mountmore. Needless to say, we quickly got together, not having seen each other since the early 50's. We sat down and talked for about four hours straight—and it was amazing the way all the intervening years just melted away. That conversation showed just how enduring friendship can be—even if it is not actively nourished over the years.

Lenny is happily married and has two young daughters. He is employed by U.S. Steel in Pittsburgh, working in the credit end of the business. Lea is our world traveler. She became a nurse and married a young Pittsburgh doctor. Her husband, Bill, is a real nice guy. After Bill graduated from Med. school and completed internship and a residency in internal medicine, he went into the Air Force, and I guess he must have stayed in the service for about ten years. During all this time, he and Lea traveled extensively, both here and abroad. Last year, Bill got out of the Air Force so that he could go into practice for himself. Lea and Bill are now living in Los Gatos—quite a coincidence, wouldn't you say? (You did live there, didn't you?) They have two nice boys.

Ed, of course, is also a world traveler. He is now a Marine Corps major, having stayed in the service after the war ended. He is definitely a career man, but I think that he plans to leave the Corps in a few more years after he has 20 years time in. He is very happily married to a girl from Connecticut, and they have two daughters and two sons. Quite a mob and all nice kids.

I'll try to write again within a reasonable period of time. Next time, perhaps I'll start catching you up on what I've been doing over the years.

Rob

Los Gatos, CA
January 8, 1964

Dear Joe,

I had thought to begin this letter by identifying myself, but I know now that you know quite well who I am. At the outset, let me tell you that I learned about you first a year ago last July from Rob's mother, whom I visit each time I am in Pittsburgh. I was distressed—more, I think, than you know. A few weeks later, my husband, Bill (then an Air Force physician), my two boys and I descended—in a rainstorm—on Rob and family in Indianapolis for an overnight stay en route to California. From Rob, I learned more about what had happened to you and, of course, of his shared distress. He promised to write me if he had any further word of you, your whereabouts and your condition. Ed (with whom I share only a Christmas card correspondence plus a note) was kind enough to write me still a bit more. Yet, until Rob's Christmas card this year, I had no address. And, had I had it, I'm not sure I'd have known what to say to you.

Today, however, I received from Rob copies of your letter to him and his to you, plus your address and an accompanying note. I trust you are not offended by his sending copies of your letter and his to Lenny, Ed, and me. They are good and in some ways, beautiful letters, and they explain more about you than anything else could. I know now that my doubts as to what to write were very much in vain, confirming a belief I've had all my life—that basically, people just don't change very much—at least, not in terms of what's deep inside. You're still very much the same Sky Killeen I remember—a man now to be sure, but inside the same person. That's enough for me.

I was touched almost to tears by both Rob's letter and yours. The camaraderie we all shared so many years ago was brought so sharply into focus, it very nearly frightened me. I recalled, suddenly, dozens of vivid memories—Ed's house and his sister, Ann, Ann's untimely death, Rob's house, Class Day and all of us in the rumble seat of that silly coupe you were driving, the year book and you as Morrie of Mountmore High, a party after you returned from the Navy and Rob there with me—so many memories—all crowding in! But—you might say, so what? All of that is in the past. Perhaps so, but what, anyway, composes our lives but a series of happenings all destined to become part of the past? Savor the good parts, Sky, and rest assured that we all do so, as well. You are a very definite part of the lives of Rob and Ed and Lenny, and me, and this will always be the same. I care nothing about what you have done in the interim. You've amassed a debt, and you're paying it. That is that. As to the near future, while you are still in prison, I can only offer you the same friendship you've always had. Like Rob, I'm not a "do-gooder" either. That, in fact, doesn't enter the picture at all. If you will take the hand I'm offering you in honest friendship, I would be very happy to keep in touch. Your response to this letter will be my answer. Projecting further into the future, when the time comes for your release, you have four friends you can count on. Any one of us will do what we can to help you, should you need it. But, in any case, we're your friends, and that won't change.

As a beginning, I might say that I've kept in close touch with Rob through the years. As you know, I've always adored Rob—in a special, not quite romantic way. This hasn't changed much, and in part at least, he shares the bond. Both of us are happily married to fine people.

Ed I saw last in December of 1951, when Billy (my 12 year old son) was 4 months old. He had just married a gal named Joyce and invited Bill and me and Rob and Marlene (who were then engaged) to dinner. Since then, our paths haven't crossed, but we keep in touch at Christmas.

Lenny, sadly, I never see or hear about at all, except from Rob on occasion. I broke our engagement in April 1948, for no reason except that I didn't want to get married—to anybody, then. He was terribly upset, but I felt I had to do it for many reasons I won't go into now. He refused to see or talk to me after that time—wouldn't even come to see me when my father died, and I can't say I blame him. He finally married 5 year later. And that's all I know of him. I had married Dr. Bill Frey, a sweet internist and a good man, in June 1949, and I learned from Rob that Lenny had a child. Then, in Indianapolis, a year ago last June, Rob told me in some detail about a long visit he'd had with him, how he hadn't changed at all, etc. I expressed then a desire to see or talk with him again. (So many years, I thought, are bound to heal old wounds.) But, Rob said not to. He didn't elaborate and I didn't press him. Sad. But, of course, old love affairs are different from old friendships. Love affairs burn

32

out and become ashes; friendships, fed by many things shared, often burn on—like an eternal flame.

If reading the letter you wrote to Rob and the ensuing onslaught of memories has made me near maudlin, I beg you to forgive me, Sky. I promise to be less so in succeeding letters. I'm usually a good correspondent, but of late I've slipped. I promise to answer each letter, but I can't say how quickly. You might try me and find out.

Fondly,
Lea

Pittsburgh, PA
January 9, 1964

It's strange how certain things stay fresh in your mind despite the passing years. Two things are very vivid, though you may not even remember. One time, a friend and I were talking about classical music. He and his sister had quite a collection of recordings. You know, those big old 78's that looked like they were a yard across. Well, this fellow offered to lend me a few, as a sort of introduction to the classics. He also told me much of what he knew about music and composers. I guess it really wasn't much, for we were very young, but it was very impressive to me.

Very soon afterward, the next day, I think, he brought' em over. Let's see, I still remember some. There were Dance of the Hours, Waltz of the Flowers, Voices of Spring, and I think, Waltz from the Serenade for Strings. I kept those records a long time, too long! And I played them over and over. But my friend didn't complain.

Another time, we were walking along West Carrick Ave. across from the Mountmore junction. I think we were going to or coming from the YMCA. Ed was there, and Rob and the same guy. I'd never done any serious smoking until then, just fooled around with it. So, what did my friend do? He took a big drag on a cigarette and inhaled deeply. Then, he dared me to do the same. Naturally, I did. So, I've thanked you many times for the first incident, and cussed you just as many times for the second, because I got to like smoking—

—So, hi, Joe!

You may not recognize the name, for I, like Rob, changed into something a little more comfortable. Rob sent me a copy of your letter to him. I hope that's OK with you. Unlike Rob, I can explain my motivation in writing very readily. I have a darn good friend who may need some help or maybe just my friendship. All the years that have passed haven't dulled our friendship. We certainly don't have as much in common now, but I think that we all felt deeply enough to have it last a lifetime.

I've got so many things to say to you, I don't know where to begin. I think first of all, you should know that we are not a bunch of do-gooders or butt-in-skis. Rob and Ed have been here several times and talked of you and your trouble. Take my word for it, they're sincere to the soles of their shoes in wanting to help in any way they can. I might add—me too!

I tried to picture to myself how you'd feel hearing from us after all these years. I tried to reverse our positions. How would I feel? Well, I'll tell you. First I'd be ashamed. Then, I'd be angry that my secret was out. I don't know how I'd feel next, but I hope I'd realize that there are three guys scattered around who care a heck of a lot.

I've read your letter, perhaps ten times. You know a letter has a tone about it, like a musical instrument. And, Joe, you're feeling sorry for yourself. Maybe you've got a right to. I know this; it's a good warm feeling. I feel sorry for myself, too.

You made a comment about pulling yourself out of the wreckage. To this I say, "Horseshit!" (You will excuse the expression.) You are the same guy I've always known. I don't know what psychological factors made you get into trouble, but I do know it can happen. Never-the-less, you were stupid. I can understand this because I have done some pretty stupid things myself. In my case, however, my actions never conflicted with the law. I am sure of this: given a particular set of circumstances, the time, the place and drop me into the middle—whamo! I could be in jail.

I don't judge you, Joe. Have no shame before me. When I walk, my feet touch the ground. You don't know it yet, but I think you and I are so alike, it may startle both of us. I'm sure you'll see what I mean as more and more letters arrive.

Before I close for this time, I'd better tell you a little about me. I'm married and have two daughters, Grace, who is four, and Jenny Sue, who is almost three months. I am occupationally maladjusted in a position with GMAC, whose paper this is written on, and whose envelope I shall undoubtedly send it in. We live in a pretty run down house near Bethel School. And unless I get busy around here one of these days, the Boro will undoubtedly condemn the place. We pay our bills, wait anxiously for our income tax return, put too much stuff on the charges, and hope the paycheck will cover it all.

I guess you could say we're average. But, when I take time to think about it, then I consider myself very lucky. So—I know you may not be able to write to me. Don't worry about it. Write to your family first, and, if you get a chance, well, you know—

I'll write soon. If there's anything you need that I can supply, you need only to ask.

Another voice out of the past,
Len

Quarters C-6 MCS Quantico, VA
19 January, 1964

Dear Shorty,

Rob sent me a copy of your letter as he did to Lenny and Lea. I hope that means you will be on the receiving end of some mail, and I imagine that letters are important to you. So, I am going to do my bit and bring you up to date about me. I don't expect an answer to this per se, but when you can, write to one of us, and ask that your letter be copied and sent to the others. I think Rob probably suggested the same thing to you.

I guess the last time I saw you was about 8 or 9 years ago. Joyce and I have four children, Ann 13, Paul 6, Lauren 1 and 1/2, and David 4. I made major in 1959 and will be up for Lt. Col. probably in '65. Eligible for retirement in 1967, if I want it. I plan to teach school or something like that when I retire but we don't know where now. Mom has been doing fine keeping the house going, but she will probably never recover from Ann's death. She talks about you all the time and worries about you. She still sells shoes and gets social security, and is doing OK, really. I will be able to help out some, especially if I get promoted.

I have seen both Lenny and Rob and their families in the last year; both have nice wives and lovely children. Next summer, I will be on my way to Okinawa for a year without family. I hope to stop in Los Gatos and see Lea and her family on the way to the Far East. Will probably leave my tribe in this area until I get back. Well, Shorty, this has not been a very philosophical letter, and it's short, but I hope it brings you some pleasure. I will write more and soon.

Love,
Ed

Joe Killeen 78250
S/S State Farm Prison, VA
January 24, 1964

Dear Lea,

"I promise to answer each letter—but I can't say how quickly. You might try me and find out." Those were your words to me—so consider yourself challenged.

My letters are rationed, one each week, as reverse side of this letter explains. One side of one sheet per letter. That's all. I feel confident I can write one of you each month. I trust that the one will notify and/or make copies for the rest. I honestly wish I could write each of you and more often. Everyone responded quickly—I stand amazed and humbled. I don't have the market cornered on old memories; each of you proved this to me.

Ed, as a Marine, may not be allowed to visit me, but if he still wishes, I'd like him to. Write the Superintendent, State Farm, VA and permission may be granted for some Sunday. Ed should explain the circumstances.

Lenny detected a note (or "tone") of self-pity in some of my words. Perhaps so, and if so, I must apologize. Someone once said that self-pity is a lot like drink. You enjoy it for a time when you wallow in it, but later on, you're sick of yourself. It nauseates you, and I am sure it nauseates the observer.

I have a fair background now on all of you, except Rob. He, in his anxiety to organize these "voices out of the past," failed for the moment to report on himself and his family. Nor should he fail to realize my gratitude in what he has done—this desire to present to me all of you again. It does mean a lot to me.

I lived about 6 years in the Los Gatos area, Lea. More of the time was spent in Saratoga. I attended San Jose State for about 2 and 1/2 years. May I recommend Villa Montalvo as an outstanding local scenic study? I lived there (part-time employee while attending school) for some years. It's located just off the Saratoga-Los Gatos highway. If you would love California, you must know Ordonez de Montalvo.

You spoke of pictures, Lea. I'd appreciate pictures of everyone. Wives, husbands, children, etc. I have no ready pictures of my own available—however, your various post offices may still have an old snapshot available. Uncle Sam is one of my most recent photographers and I understand that he did make plenty of copies. (Too many!) Seriously, I mean it about pictures of

all of you. (My response was more than "near-maudlin", Lea.)
Appreciatively,
Joe

Los Gatos
January 27, 1964

Dear Joe,

You challenged me, so what is one to do but perform. You may never receive an answer to a letter so quickly again, but an answer you WILL always get. That I promise you. I sent copies of your letter to Ed and Rob, and Rob will forward Len his, since I don't know his address.

I enjoy your letters, Joe. You write extremely well, in a very nearly erudite manner. I wish I did as well; but then, I'm a housewife and am not expected to, I guess. Have you ever thought of writing short stories or a novel or essays? And while I'm asking about what you do, do you read much and have you access to all the books you need or want? If not, what do you like to read? I have access through the high school to books ready for discard, and it may be I can send you some if you're interested. Let me know what type you like, and IF you would like me to look into it.

In answer to your letter, I'll do it item by item:

1. I hope Ed gets permission to visit you. I haven't seen him in about 10 or 11 years, but his notes at Christmas sound rather much the same. I hope he does get to see you, and I hope to get to see him, for that matter.

2. Lenny—nothing to comment here, since I haven't seen or heard from him since about June of 1948. I confess I was mildly distressed at his presuming to criticize you at the outset. Self-pity is something all of us indulge in from time to time. It's the old case of people in glass houses and the stones bit.

3. And dear Rob. He can fill you in on his activities over the years himself. After spending an evening with him and his family summer before last, plus a visit from time to time all through the years, I can say he is virtually unchanged from the boy we knew in high school, except that he's matured. (He seemed so then, though, come to think of it) and his hair is somewhat less red. Other wise, he is just plain brainy Rob and a very dear person.

4. And me? I can't give you an impression, since no one sees himself as others see him. I'd say I was changed some—more sure of myself, no longer a stutterer, but pretty much the same chipper, chatty, reasonably bright Lea.

(Does that give you a picture at all?) Actually, I'm pretty average—a 36 year old doctor's wife (a GOOD doctor, not a rich one, I might add) with two boys—7 and 12, who look like their father. Bill and I spent 10 years with the Air Force. Bill decided to resign last summer when he was promoted to Lt. Colonel—thus promoted right out of the hospital wards to sitting behind a desk. He's a clinician, not an administrator. So, we're in Los Gatos, struggling to get a practice going in a community pretty saturated with doctors. Bill is a specialist in Internal Medicine and Cardiology, and this is sort of a "family doctor" type of community, so it's been difficult. But we love this area and are determined to make a go of things here. We'll see. Hope we don't end up in the poorhouse!

Bill is a very quiet, sweet guy, a little socially shy, but a competent, confident physician, and a gentle person. We have a very good marriage, which is a blessing I'm grateful for. My two boys are very average sandy-haired boys, the elder a good student, a little-league catcher, a paperboy—a pretty well rounded, stable boy. The younger is a cute, bouncy, affectionate little nut—a mediocre student, a cub scout, plays the clarinet, pitches in Little League, etc. To wit—they're pretty much just normal boys—but special to me. I love them to pieces!

My activities are numerous. As you know, I'm a registered nurse, but have no inclination to return to that field. In fact, I'm, at the moment, planning on going back to college (San Jose State) and getting all I need for a teaching credential. (It will take the equivalent of about 3 years). To supplement our income now, I teach German in a private German School Saturday mornings, and I teach one class a week in German at the junior high school. In addition, I tutor problem students in German every afternoon and evening (high school students). In addition to these activities, I'm very interested in politics and am active in study workshops of the League of Women Voters. So, while I am indeed "just a housewife," I manage to keep my finger in one academic pie or another.

And that should bring you up to date on the life and loves of Lea Frey. I'll send some snapshots of everyone next time, and I hope this finds you well. Fondly,
Lea

Weston, Conn.
Saturday, Feb. 1, 1964

Dear Joe,

This is just a short note; it's one of those restful days that seem to be rather infrequent for me. There is snow on the ground, which is rapidly turning to slush. I received a short note from Lea telling me she had received my information about you and that she had written you. We will all await your comments.

I have all sorts of questions about what sort of things we should write about, but perhaps we just need to play it by ear and see what happens. I just wonder if there are any taboo subjects; do we just write about everyday things? Anything that upsets you? Let us know, so we can follow your lead.

In my daily life, unlike yours to some extent, I have little time to think about the past. My mind always seems to be filled with thoughts of the present or the future. So most of what I write will be about what I am doing in the present, keeping you informed about my doings, my travels, etc.

In my past two letters to you, I have stayed away from talking about my own life, but I think I better bring you up to date. Let it suffice for the moment to say that I am happily married (which means that my wife and I can still fight and love each other), and we have three children. Wife, Marlene, I met at good old Fresh Air Home, run by the Pittsburgh Association for the Improvement of the Poor—shades of the distant past for both of us!! I don't think that you knew her, though she, like you and me, was a counselor. Our three children are Doug, Ann, and Bill. Doug, tall and skinny, has just turned nine, and is in third grade. Ann is our talking machine, and will be four next month. Bill is the baby—just turned two. At the present, he is built like a tank. I'll write again—soon.

Rob

Quantico, VA.
5 March, 64

Dear Shorty,

Lea sent me a typed up copy of your letter, so I guess we are all caught up. I have the information about arranging a visit to you; now all I have to do is find where the prison is and figure out how I can get there before going to

Okinawa in July. If I can get permission, I will be in a position where, I can see all of the group in a matter of just a few weeks, as I will be in Connecticut in June, Pittsburgh in June, as well, and California in July. I hope to see Rob, Lenny and Lea while on my way. Joyce and the children will stay in Connecticut for the year I am on Okinawa. (I could indulge in some self-pity myself, Joe). Just hope no one starts a big one while I am out there, or I will really be stuck.

Keep your fingers crossed and we will see what happens to my request to see you. I hope it gets favorable consideration, as I would like very much to see you, but it's all up to the boss in charge now. Have Faith!
Ed

Weston, Conn.
March 16, 1964

Lea,

Here is a copy of Joe's March 8 letter to me. I am just typing it in.

Dear Rob, Problem: Should I ask Lenny to duplicate my letters? Is Ed able to? Lea seems willing but had chore last month, so you're elected again… I am anxious to meet Marlene. You went back to A.I.P. after the war. There you two met—right? All of you keep fights in the home, not the divorce court—and eleven children attest to this. You have three, Lea two, Lenny two, Ed four… enjoyed reports on your folks. My memory prompts that your Dad was in Guiian, Smar, Philippines, when I visited there; we didn't know it until later. How are your brothers? …Lea and Ed have sent pictures. I accept your excuse temporarily. Lenny and you MUST comply…Lea's Bill appears to be of quiet dignity and friendly manner. Their little leaguers are husky and healthy—the older looks like Bill, the younger like Lea. And, Lea—well—she looks just like the pretty Lea of M.H.S. days. Lea, I'm glad-happy- that you share another of my favorite memories—Montalvo. Good luck on your poet-laureate try. I love poetry, but lack training, and can only rely on intuition. I share John F. Kennedy's view, " where power corrupts, poetry cleanses." Teach me, Lea; share your poetry with me. Since 1957, I have studied mostly social and political science, general theology, and philosophy—so fire away my poet-politician. I missed meeting Ed's Joyce during Patuxent visit. Her picture speaks that she is too young and attractive for the rocking chair, but her little ones protest, as they enjoy the rocking prelude to sleep. Ed looks like John Glenn, heavyweight—though there is

more of his Dad there. And Ed's children: handsome and all blondes. Maribeth's countenance was a reproduction of her sister, Ann, and can I—or anyone—forget his first love, so tragically lost? Will I ever recover from her death—so young? Ed, contact my sister in Washington; you have her number. She can direct you here; I sure hope the visit can be arranged. Have read Lenny's first letter over and over (as he stated he has read mine). I'm humming that tune with you, Lenny. Trying to learn the melody. I like it, but it seems incomplete. One must be one's self, but I can remember wanting to be more like you, particularly in football... Being one's self is sometimes tough and awful when one tries to figure where he fits in the scheme of things. Maybe it's like the guy who went to a party, and at some point disappeared. Searching everywhere, his friends found him in a closet. When they asked him why he was there, of all places, he retorted, "Well, a body has to be somewhere." Plato called this closet a "cave" and accused us of having too much commerce with its shadows. He's right. Shadows only wrap one in night. Many about me are clothed in lonely darkness. They close their eyes tight and the metal bars and concrete floors become sticky with mud and slime. Some, but terribly few, look high and hard into the dark and find a light. The one who sees that light can claim it as his own star. It is his own, for he saw it with his own eyes; and nothing, no nothing, can stop its flicker, however bright or dim, except the clods of his own eyelids. Such darkness owes its origin to the mind of man, and yet, that same mind's eye gives birth to light. Rob, all of your letters have become important to me. Though brief has been our term of correspondence, I already care not to imagine any of you not writing. You remain, one and all, a crew of above average intelligence, and for this I shall benefit... Rob, I should offer some autobiography soon—Ill get to it in my next letter. (You failed to tell me of your work!) As Lea would say: Fondly,
  Joe

(The following letter was added to a typed copy of Joe's above letter)
Lea,
  I will send copies to Ed and Lenny. In retyping it, I have slightly altered Joe's letter—to this extent: he started his letter by saying, "problem—understanding the Lea—Lenny situation..." I will soon write to Joe and tell him that you two have been on the outs, but that I expect we all can and will send duplicate letters to the others. For your info, Lenny's address is ...
  I really feel quite lazy tonight, not in the mood to write a full-blown postscript to this letter, but I did want to make a short comment on the note

you attached to Joe's last letter.

I also was annoyed with Lenny's apparent criticism of Joe—but I am sure that there is nothing for us to do about it. Joe will no doubt be forming his own opinions about each of us on the basis of our letters to him. Enough said, I believe.

And yes, I agree that it is time for you and Lenny to bury the hatchet. I know how bitter Lenny was over what happened between you two, but I would hope that he can be more understanding after all these years. As my final note on that topic, I would say this much: I think that when you made your decision to break up with Lenny, you had come to a correct conclusion. Your summing up of the pluses and minuses within Lenny led you to conclude something about him, something which didn't ring the bell in choosing him as your life's companion. I don't think it is unfair of me to say that the years since have proven the wisdom of your decision.

Be all that as it may, or may not be, with regard to Joe, I echo your sentiment, "What a strange bond this is for five friends."

We are all well and happy. The New York rat race is just that—a rat race. But, I think that I will stick it out for a while, at least. Life anywhere has its good and bad aspects—our job seems to be to make the most of the good and minimize the bad.

Hope that Bill, the boys, and you are all fine. Especially hope that Bill's practice is doing well. Is it mostly cardiology or general medicine? That's all for tonight. Don't let Joe's comments go to your pretty (cross out pretty) head.

Rob

Joe. Killeen 78250
S/S State Farm, VA
April 12, 1964

Dear Lea,

Someone once wrote that he wasn't a category, not a thing—a noun, but a verb. A verb denotes an action. A verb wrote your, "Morning Dialog." A few words of critique, humbly, please. It is not, as you said, just subjective; it's objective, and it is both intensive and extensive. It has universality…the "yearning pain that love's about," is what life is about, or whatever it connotes to the reader. Only good poetry can do this. It's fanciful, but exact and real; it's you, your story…the metaphors tease and challenge. My mind is abuzz

42

with your plays on words, "the humid breath of a damped horn" seems to perforate. "belie" implying something personal, secretive, and "tumult" suggesting the awakening of a buried nature. Some of verse three reminds me of a young Faust—the pleasures without the responsibility of love. Verse 4 suggests the crescendo of Liszt's "Liebestraum." I see biblical references in verses 7 and 8, in them the emotive appeal of Solomon's shulamite. I like "untamed balm"…you treat "breeze" as "she". Spanish does. Does German? This correlates with Solomon's feminine wisdom" (Proverbs, OT) Verse 8 … I sense a little of the melancholy of Schiller and Goethe, have you read them?

Space stops the critique for now. Do any of my impressions come near to "Morning Dialog's" inspiration?

A word about Lenny: He suggests that he and I are alike in ways. There's one important difference. I believe he still has open sores. A guy just can't enjoy the swim of things with open sores. I'll try to help. You have no fault in this—so suffer no guilt. You're not the core of his difficulty. This goes deeper than you… I will mail you a copy—the letter for the voices on April 26th. This letter is for you and Bill alone. You entrust me with many personal reflections—I shall safeguard this honor. Tell me about your Montalvo hike. Please say hello to Bill and your Little Leaguers. (When did you write Morning Dialog?)

Joe

Los Gatos
April 30, 1964

Dear Joe,

Just wanting to let you know that I received your critique on my poem and was profoundly flattered and touched by your remarks, and was humbled by your obvious superiority with regard to knowledge of literature, philosophy, and theology. I am sorry to say, I have read only less than half of the quotes to which you refer. Yes, I've read some Goethe, mostly lyric poetry, and all in German. I know none of the books of Solomon and Proverbs. I'd hardly presume, needless to say, to compare anything I could write with these masters, but I'm flattered that you did—even in a small way.

I'm sure you have no idea how long I've struggled over that poem and I can't begin to tell you how many times it's been changed, rewritten, reworded, revamped, even the central theme has been changed since it was first written.

I began it in Germany in 1960, after the departure of a dearly beloved friend, who had returned to the states. In its original form, it was a silly, moaning, rather sappy love poem. I put it away and when I pulled it out to reread it, a year or so later, I was embarrassed to admit I'd written it. It had a run-away, undisciplined, sort of infatuated sound, and yet segments of it seemed worth salvaging. So, I've been rewriting it—off and on since, and the final rewrite was done last fall. I just threw it away last week, actually—got sick of it!. It's a funny thing having someone who really doesn't know your circumstances very well do a critique like you have done. Much of what you said is largely true. I suppose one reveals more than one intends to in poetry, as all subjective writing necessarily does. But, many of your observations say more about you than me.

This correspondence of the five of us shows no end of promise as far as "revealing" is concerned, and certainly as far as you are concerned. We are all finding out things about each other, in this funny, round about fashion, and none of us can do anything but profit from the experience. My quietly profound husband, Bill, who shares some of your letters with me (hope you don't mind!), is fascinated at the unfolding of the past 20 years by 5 high school chums. He says that YOUR letters, if quoted verbatim, would be publishable, so poetically and sensitively do you write! Best part is that they focus on the positive, with almost an absence of anything critical. (Bill is the stingiest man in the world with compliments, so you have my leave to be proud!)

I must say, that while I am a usually chipper, upbeat sort of gal, we have been having a bit of a struggle with Bill beginning a new practice and the resultant financial stress this past year. As a result, I've had some moments of stress and concern of late. For some reason, through some uncanny sense of timing, your letters arrive at EXACTLY the right time—when I need a lift. I feel at once refreshed and at peace with the world again, after reading them.

Lea

Joe.Killeen–78250
April 26, 1964

Dear Lea,
Rob writes, regarding my query on copy-letters, "I think the wisest course of action is to simply let them (Lenny and Lea) start forwarding your letters

to each other, and let them take care of the matter. I am going on the assumption that they are both willing to send letters to each other." Do you agree to this? If so, I have a suggestion. Why don't I just go ahead and mail the next letter to Lenny? I will include all of your addresses. Lenny then must decide whether he will mail your copy himself or through another. Is this agreeable to you? I will plan to write him May 17 or 24. The decision is yours.

Rob, when I read your letters, I feel almost as if I am with you, listening to your voice instead of reading your words. You have an easy, friendly manner. You're "comfortable" to be with. You always were. Please remember me to your mother and dad; I trust to their continued good health and a solution to their retirement problems. Dedicated men like Lea's Bill have given promise to longer and healthier lives for all. Ed, I wonder if you won't be reaching South Korea during a bad season. An old oriental proverb speaks that it is "better to be the head of a chicken than to be the tail of a cow." These malcontent Koreans remind me of the snake that tried to swallow the elephant... Lenny, I haven't heard from you since the first round. In your initial letter, you expressed an eagerness to write. If I am at fault, and I suspect I am, whip me in line. Let's start again. The Persian Sadi once wrote: "Two circumstances cast a shade over understanding—that of silence when we should speak and that of speech when we should be silent." It may be that the latter applies to me... Rob suggests his own personal story contains very little drama. No, I am not avoiding autobiography. Space precludes it. Briefly, in the remaining space, I shall add a few notes at least... I have a very fine wife (no children) who has stood by me most of these prison years. We had two years together during my AWOL stay. She has taught me much, particularly concerning the significance "of joy and yearning pain that love's about." (as one poet describes it!). And yet, the waiting has been long for my Doris. Loved ones usually "pull" harder time than the ones in prison, especially when there are those who insist that such a wait is futile and the love granted undeserved. Honorable absences during the war shook some marriages. How much more difficult is it for a wife when her husband is absent because of dishonor? One must experience this with Doris to understand why she may not always wait.

Joe

Weston, Conn.
Memorial Day, May 30, 1964

Dear Lea and Bill,

I realize that writing this note, brief as it will be, may well jeopardize my "world's worst letter writer" title, but I am willing to risk it. Lea, in your commentary section attached to Joe's last letter, you made the mistake of innocently asking (and I quote) "So, when are you coming out this way?" Now, I realize this is very easy to say from your sanctuary almost 3000 miles away, but this time, you've gone too far. Accordingly, I have made reservations to fly to San Francisco on Monday, June 8th.

Now, with all that baloney aside, and before you push the panic button, I am going to be in San Francisco for the week of June 8, but the company is going to require me to put in a few working hours. I will not know what my exact work schedule will be until I get there. But, by hook or by crook, with your permission, I will get together with you. That's too many miles to travel and not see friends. I will call you when I get to town and find what plans I can make.

One last comment, mainly directed to Lea, on the general topic of our writing to Joe. I have the feeling I have never been able to tell him why I am writing, although I have definite feelings on the subject. I have never been a great one for spouting my emotions, yet these deep-seated emotions are the reason I feel so deeply about writing to him.

I have not been endowed with any bent for creativity (e.g. poetry), and find it hard to let the emotions come out in any other form. Be all that as it may, I hope that Joe can find in some limited way some of my inner feelings buried below the bland sentences in my letters to him. Hope to be able to see all of you soon. Our best to all.

Rob, Marlene, and the gang.

Joe Killeen 78520
S/s State Farm, VA
May 31, 1964

Dear Lea,

Long ago, at Montalvo, on a winter's day, I started to lift an old rotted log, but it crumbled at my grip. As it fell away into its many pieces, I noticed

I had disturbed the cloister of a little salamander. He was cold and his lethargy was such that he could hardly move. I put him in my jacket pocket and the warmth therein soon increased his metabolism to where he could move about at almost his summer's peak. Then, setting him on the ground, I watched (perhaps envious) as he eagerly went forth seeking his new place in the world… In these times of my own winter cloister, I have become encased in a strange sort of carrel. It absorbs much from without but releases little from within. Some say I am reticent, another calls me retentive, but, whichever, don't misinterpret it as any intended repugnance…My memories nourish the long wait. Reading and study projects add flavor. But also, there are those of you who dare to crack the shell of my hibernation, adding invigorating warmth, much like that enjoyed by my salamander friend, while he shared my jacket's warmth… Now I find that you, in your desire to help, offer to take time from your busy schedule to write my Doris. I am indeed grateful for this gesture. (I'm not a sycophant!)… My mother, sister, and niece have tried with Doris—attempted meetings, letters, phone calls—but to no avail. She asked my mother not to write her. She wants me to write only occasionally, but never intimately… Doris, age 39, is a Christian Theologist, claiming degrees from several schools. In her profession, she is one of the most remarkable persons I have ever known. She's an effective orator, able teacher and sings in a beautiful mezzo-soprano… The stability that her public sees is but a mask, covering deep insecurity. I saw this in her eyes at the very first and she knew I had. I didn't compete against her Christ—I was already in his corner (at least philosophically). You gals can love a guy if you know that love is needed; but it is a sweeter, deeper love when that guy learns reciprocity. Then, and only then, is love electric. Marriage may not always ensue, but the memory will… Doris can't live on letters, and memories only cause her pain. Nor will my authorities permit her to visit. Divorce is topical, but not a serious one—yet!…She is an escapist. Her insecurities are now repressed by militant adventures with various right wing extremist groups (they gather up many of the frustrated). If she sincerely intends to continue this type of walk, then it must be away from me… I'm mostly a moderate: my philosophy is slightly conservative, but my political stand is liberal… I suspect what you're trying to teach me is that one must think things out, but also one must talk things out. I don't know how to talk that way. But, I've tried to in this letter. However poor I may have penned this, it can be translated as a compliment to you. I couldn't write Bill or Rob this way, but know it would be good if I could. So if you want them to read this, go ahead—but no one else.

    Joe

Pittsburgh
June 17, 1964

Dear Joe,

This is the third letter I've started to write to you in three weeks. I've been trying to explain why I haven't written, and when I finish, I know I've not explained at all. It's very complicated, and it goes back to the time before I knew all of you. These letters and visits from Rob and Ed take me back almost to that time, and it shakes me considerably.

From July 1956 until November 1960, I was going through psychotherapy trying to get things in proper perspective. Remote as it may seem, this is the reason I haven't written. It never occurred to me that you might feel responsible for my not having written. That just isn't so, and I'll do better in the future.

I'd appreciate it if you'd write to Rob, Joe. I have no means to duplicate your letters, and he sends me a copy right away. I'll send some pictures, but for now, I weigh 175 pounds, and I also wear a tire around the middle. I still have most of my hair, but I must admit there is a spot in the back there, about as big as a beanie, well, you know. I tell my 5 year old this is where I was struck by lightning. I guess you could describe me as a chubby, balding old man.

I don't know if you are permitted to receive newspapers, but I'm going to send a copy of Congressman Ronson's local paper. On the front page is an article about three good friends retiring from the faculty of Mountmore High. To me, it's a little sad. I also am sending two letters that are 20 years old. You may recognize them. You wrote them.

One thing I will ask you to do. Rather than try to answer my letters or comment on them in the letter you write to everyone, how about saving all comments until you are able to write one to me—for me. I don't care if it's next year when you are able to write it. This may seem silly, but it bugs me to have to share your replies.

Ed arrived in Pittsburgh last night for a visit before heading for Okinawa. He's like a big kid, and I admire him very much. I'm sure we'll be going out and you can be sure there will be much conversation about all of us in the good old days.

You were talking about parole. I hope when you are completely discharged, and all this is behind you, that you might settle in Pittsburgh. That would be great. Need anything?

Len

⬟

Weston, Conn.
June 23, 1964

Lea and Bill,

The top portion of Joe's letter was missing. Enclosed with the rest of the letter was the following note:

Hi, Rob,

Here's the latest from Joe. I had to censor the first paragraph myself. He chewed me for not writing. Ed's here. Hope all is well.

Len

Joe's letter is as follows:

I'm real pleased with Rob's pictures. His Doug looks a combination of his uncles Karl and Bill, if my memory images are correct. Ann reminds me of a favorite niece of mine, one of my sister's girls. Bill is just too young and precious for words. Marlene is a doll, but perhaps I shouldn't say that. Rob, Ed and I are becoming middle aged "marble tops." What about you, Lenny?…Rob, you're about an inch or two taller than I. If that is so, then you carry your 160 pounds in trim form. I've some girth on you, though—five to ten pounds worth. I refer to myself as chubby—perhaps fleshy is better; although the pick and shovel I've been married to for the greater portion of my imprisonment still holds my waist to an even 30 inches…Lea, you and Bill are gracious in your comments of me. In a practical sense, I value what you both say. You're shrewd in translating thoughts I don't write. I'm honored that Bill shares these letters. Good fortune on the July adventure. It's refreshing to know that doctors like Bill still exist. It must be insulting to see the Hippocratic become hypocritic. I shall add "Freydom" to my vocabulary. It's not a pun—it means integrity and idealism. Lea, I shall prepare a thing on verbs and direct objects soon… Ed, it is difficult to give satisfactory answers regarding my "present and future status." So much is uncertain. You may wish me more precise and less abstruse in my letters. You desire that I write of more tangible things, such as parole and discharge—but these also are abstract. I've been eligible for parole since 1959. Then, and in the year following, parole was not granted. Since my return, I have again been turned down; and in August, I expect another denial. I can be discharged any time between December, 1966 and May, 1968; depending on my keepers' interpretation of my conduct… So you see my abstruseness is reality. I fully realize the situation that I've created. It is best explained by coach Dickerhof's

old wrestling axiom: "The best way out of a hold is not to get into one." I'm not a Dadaist or a hipster, nor am I swayed off-balance by the avant-garde philosophies of today. Yet, there is a certain kind of existentialism to my environment; and it has significantly and agreeably stripped me down to PURPOSE. Pragmatism is the vessel upon which that Purpose sails. My today is not like your today, nor can I give in these rationed lines an explanation of my today; except, perhaps, to say that Purpose guides my today in preparation for tomorrow. Tomorrow is dim, imperfect to the vision, but yet so full of hope... Roughly, I might say this regarding tomorrow: I intend, upon discharge, to find some simple type of work that would coincide with a full-time college schedule. After this I shall seek some teaching position that will avail me enough leisure for further studying, writing and public speaking... Ed, I like your meaning of "help." You said, "By help I mean help you to get going by yourself, not paternalism.: I'm grateful to all of you, for not once has anyone written in tones of "pity"—indeed I'd be finished if I embraced such a hopeless monstrosity. God be with all of you and yours.
Joe

Lea and Bill, (hand written PS)

I would prefer not to write a full-fledged letter tonight, so bear with me for a few more days. I will write you when I send a copy of my next letter to Joe. I was happy to read Joe's comments on possible release dates—much closer than I thought.

I'll write soon,
Rob

Weston, Conn.
Friday, July 3, 1964

Dear Joe,

As a result of two of our letters crossing in the mail, it became apparent to me some weeks ago that it was I in a very brusque way who inadvertently informed you that Ed was not given permission to visit you. Forgive me for being so offhand in manner. I was under the assumption that you had already been told by Ed that any visit was not allowed... and I passed over the problem very quickly. Actually, I was very disappointed, for I would have come down to see you if I could. That possibility, however, now is apparently out of the question. I assume it was connected in some way with the FBI coming to make inquiries about you while you were at large in Colorado.

I received your letter to Lea. Lenny had torn off the top of the letter, explaining that he had to censor the letter in that portion where you had chewed him out for not writing to you. The date of the letter was in that missing portion, hence I know not when the letter was written. What interested me much about the whole procedure was that Lenny sent your original letter to me, obviously with the intent that I forward it to one of the others. By using this technique, he successfully circumvented having to send anything directly to Lea. Perhaps I am reading too much into the situation, but it sure looked that way to me. If my interpretation is correct, it means he still has not made his peace with Lea after all these years. She obviously wounded his ego, and he still remembers.

Let me make some comments on the contents of your letter. Your favorable comment about Marlene is much appreciated (by both of us, I am sure). I find myself more in love with the passing years of our marriage. The good and not-so-good experiences of our years together have slowly forged a real bond between us. Yes, she is still a doll.

Joe, I know the problem of your freedom is vital to you, and it is of great importance to all your friends. I believe it safe to say that we four have spent many hours in concerned thought about you. Don't forget, as the time draws near, that we, as your friends, are interested, and will want to do whatever is possible to help you see any plans you might have come true.

This brings me to some thoughts about just why I am writing to you. During my brief stay with Lea, which she has probably mentioned already, we two had a long talk about you, and all the rest of us as well. (Bill gave up gracefully after several hours of conversation, and Lea and I talked on until several hours later.) I think a great deal of my wanting to write to you is bound up with some kind of personal frustration, a feeling on my part that I as an individual am caught up in a complex world that I cannot control. I see my own life running its course, yet my contribution to society is so minimal. Yes, I keep my nose clean, I try to raise my family in the "right" way, etc. yet at the same time, I feel I am not carrying my share of the load as far as mankind is concerned. I find my thoughts caged within me. And my influence is so small and ineffective in the big matters that face us. I want to do more, yet, I cannot define more of what, and I am not sure that I am willing to make the personal sacrifice which doing more turns out to mean.

But now, in the midst of my own self-doubt, I hear that a friend is imprisoned. And here I see a way that perhaps I, by my own thoughts and acts, may be able to help out... to do something meaningful that others may not be able to do. Yes, it is egotistical, but I really felt that my writing to you could possibly give you some additional measure of inner strength, that I could extend my hand and say, "Joe, you are my friend, and as such the long years mean nothing... can I help you in any way?"

And yet, that is not the whole answer. There is another reason, and the easiest way to explain it is to turn to the Bible. Matthew, Chap. 25, "... for I was hungry and you gave me food, I was thirsty and you gave me drink, I was a stranger and you welcomed me, I was naked and you clothed me, I was sick and you visited me, I was in prison and you came to me... Truly, I say to you, as you did it to one of the least of these, my brethren, you did it to me."

Joe, I am not a highly religious man, but I do try to seek some answers. I cannot vouch for any divinity of the man, Jesus, but the words he speaks tell me that he knew the answers to many of man's problems. At the risk of sounding utterly corny, let me say that my heart was filled with sorrow and compassion when I heard you were in prison... and I was determined that I would do whatever I could do within my limited power to help you.

Joe, these words do not come easily or smoothly, for this kind of writing is not my cup of tea. Forgive me for trying to tackle this when I obviously don't even know my own mind. I wanted to tell you some of my thoughts, to share with you some of my own inner turmoil. I have done my best, so be it.

Now, let me turn to one last subject, that of my visit with Lea in Los Gatos. I can say without qualification that the visit was the high point of the trip. For some strange reason, Lea and I have had some special empathy over the years. Lea has always had the knack of understanding me. In retrospect, I am sure that in our high school days she understood me as well as or better than I understood myself. In part, I am sure that my special feeling for her was partly based on the fact that she had so much confidence in me—she was always good for my ego. Our friendship has continued over the years, mainly due to the fact that Lea had enough sense to see how valuable friendships are, and she kept in touch with me via my mother. What I am trying to say is that she is still the fine girl we used to know, and her graciousness and understanding have only increased with the passing years. I am glad that she is our friend.

As you probably know, Lea took me to Villa Montalvo, where we had a little time to walk and talk before my business took me back to San Francisco. It is a beautiful place, indeed, and I can see why your memory of it is so strong. I took some photos there and I will send some prints on to you and

Lea. Since returning home, I have received from Lea her poem, "Voices at Montalvo." It puts into words our common thoughts. My only regret is that I do not have the ability to express myself so well. I do hope that she has sent you a copy. I liked the poem very much. I also was very much emotionally moved as we walked slowly and quietly over the same paths you had known and liked. I think we both felt very close to you during those brief moments.

Don't expect another letter of this length—probably ever. I feel that I can live up to my goal of one letter a month to you, but only if I keep the letters reasonably short. I just dislike writing!

Goodnight my friend,

Rob

Joe......–78250

Note! > North Side State Farm, Virginia

July 26, 1964

Dear Lea and Rob (Bill and Marlene, too!)

"Feel where my life broke off from thine, How fresh the splinters keep and fine, only a touch and we combine!" (Browning) What is this magnet that seeks to combine us? It seems more important to retain than explain. I only know that I am the least deserving; but I shall strive equally as hard to preserve it… No doubt you are both vertical enough in your thinking to suspect my motives in my messages to Lenny. My last letter was blunt, and perhaps harsh, but it acquired its intended purpose—Lenny's response—and it was a good response. Lenny's letters are evasive but speak of a problem (though not its specifics.) He mentions psychotherapy (1955 to 1960). I believe he may desire to say more to me on this, for he prefers I write him privately. I wrote Lea in an earlier letter that she was not the core of his disturbance. Lenny, without mentioning Lea specifically, states that his difficulty stems to a time before he knew any of us. No doubt Lea's break with Lenny is involved but I trust that she is intelligent enough not to allow her sensitive nature to become confused in guilt. Also, Lea must remember that he who cannot forgive others breaks the bridge over which he must pass. Lea had nothing to forgive, yet cannot cross that bridge; Lenny must cross over to her… I have been through some things that Lenny may be suffering. It's not easy. Though analysis helps, it is a long, strange and difficult road. But once you begin, you cannot turn back. Living life is hard enough; reliving it is so much worse. One must retrace each step, relying on a memory confused by fantasy and rationalism. The analyst attempts to accompany the traveler all the way. He becomes mother, father, lover, wife, teacher, even God (and sometimes Satan). A long journey, a difficult road—yet each step of the way leads to that point of unveiling the very thing, that terrible "whatever-it-is," that one has been fleeing from. Deferments, temporizings, rationalisms are cast aside in order to force yourself forward. But finally, after seemingly endless attempts to step off the road, to stop, or to turn back, the breakthrough comes, the journey is completed… Lenny is somewhere along that road, still festering with open sores. Lea, do you remember my story about the little salamander? I can't say for sure what happened to him; but I'll wager he hooked up with another salamander. And maybe this is what Lenny is trying to do… Space defeats my hopes of commenting on the Montalvo poem and excursion—but know that I cherish both as if with you. So long for now, "Dude" and "Red."

Joe

Okinawa
Monday, 27 Jul. 1964

Dear Lea and Bill,

I said that I would write to Joe and send you a copy, but in the first letter, I felt that I should write you personally and thank you for a wonderful visit. Los Gatos is a lovely town, and I appreciated the hospitality. I wrote Joe, and then to Lenny, and now you. Tomorrow night is Rob's turn. I wrote to Lenny first to insure that the communication channel that he needs so much is fully open. I wrote both Joe and Lenny six-page letters. For me this is unheard of. Now that I have had time to sort out my thoughts of the wonderful visits I had with all of you, I am convinced that the five of us have something wonderful and tangible among us that is very rare. We can all communicate with love. Perhaps not directly to each other as in Lenny's case, but in the group there is a common channel by which messages do get through. I feel very lucky that I can fulfill such a role. Joe also acts as a sounding board for those of us who can not talk directly with each other.

I had a comfortable trip out from Travis AF Base. I had no need for the names you gave me, Bill. We left Travis on time and were in Honolulu at midnight. Some old friends met my plane there and I had a lovely visit for two hours. Then eight hours flying time to Kapena—and it was the next day. I wish they could all go by that fast.

I got a rude shock on arrival here. My job is assistant division inspector for congressional correspondence. I answer all the gripes to Senators and Congressmen. I am also division protocol officer (old big mouth Ed with the two left feet! I don't have a diplomatic bone in my body!) I also conduct the brig inspections.

My living conditions are comfortable—air conditioned office, air conditioned room, and I bought an old jalopy to get around in. Shopping is great and drink is cheap—imported beer is 15¢; all mixed drinks 20¢. I have a room cleaning girl who cleans, does all my laundry and pressing, shines my shoes, and answers the phone for $10 a month. I had to tell her to stop putting so much starch in my underwear. If she were only good looking, too, I would really be going first class.

I hope this finds you all well, and once again thank you for a very wonderful visit with your family. Don't forget to send me a copy of your letters to Joe. See you next year.

Love,
Ed

Los Gatos, CA
August 1, 1964

Dear Joe,

Your letter of July 26th arrived yesterday, and just in the nick of time. It seemed longer than usual between letters, and I had decided to wait one more day before writing to see if you had drowned in all our waves of sentimentality. I find, Joe, as do our friends, Ed and Rob, that I am awaiting your letters with increasing pleasure, enjoying each one better than the last. This can be attributed, in great part, to your beautifully sensitive style of writing. More and more, I find myself remembering things long since buried under the sundry memories crowded into the past 20 years. As you know, I had a wonderful visit with Rob in June—and last month, a visit with Ed. You, I can only visit via these letters, but these "visits" are no less real. What has become obvious to me is the very slight degree to which we have changed, with regard to basics. Rob is still Rob, and I will adore him until I die. (Marlene will, I trust, understand the platonic nature of this adoration and not want to shoot me!) Ed is like a big, sweet teddy bear—a classic big brother to me, just as he was years ago. And you, Joe? More and more I am beginning to see in your nature things I only sensed underlying the personality of witty, popular, jovial Shorty, singer of Irish songs. It is a "something" that drew me to you then and does now. I'm not sure what it is, but it is a bond that involves all of us. Perhaps it is a kind of empathy, an awareness of what is really good in people, and the recognition of this in each other that draws us together. You, more than any of us, Joe, manage to convey in beautiful language all of these things. I have carefully filed all these letters in a folder, and I treasure them as I would any other work of art, but more so because I am personally involved. I know that both Ed and Rob feel this no less strongly, and the desire to "retain, rather than explain" is no less in our hearts than in yours. Lest you feel you are coming out on the "long end," let me submit that this is not so; a great deal of old fashioned sentiment has been stirred up along with the dust and cobwebs of the past, and its warmth is spreading half way around the globe. The only unreviveable (Isn't that another word for "dead?") sentiment is that between Lenny and me; that I can attribute only to the inevitable dying of the flames of youthful passion, when nothing more durable grows in its place. Nobody's fault. It just didn't happen.

One last word on Lenny. In past letters to both you and Rob, I have been caustic in my comments on Lenny. For this I am truly sorry. Ed, bless him, explained much about Lenny and his problems (again, things I only sensed in him -without understanding—those many years ago.) I feel now that I understand his hostility (reflected) and I don't resent it anymore. Your appraisal, incidentally, is nearly letter-perfect, Joe. You have become very wise indeed these past years, my friend. In any event, I feel I owe Lenny an apology for my hasty and uncharitable criticism of him. I hope he can find peace and come to terms with himself—and with me. As you say, he is on the road. The day he sends me his copy of the letter from you directly, I will at least know it's a beginning.

Now, let's leave the past for the stark reality of the present. I am well now, but I was in a cervical collar for a month, spending most of several weeks in bed, unable to move much at all. I had daily physiotherapy all that time with fifteen minutes in neck traction twice a day for the next three months. When it became a nuisance, I knew I was on the mend, and now I am grateful to be free of pain at last. End of report.

Now then, as to my "job." Apparently, I am doing at least a satisfactory job, because I haven't been fired yet, and while I get no salary from Bill, I am saving him the expense of hiring a paid office nurse. I am doing all the office work and nursing procedures for Bill and another doctor, who is renting office space in our building. I enjoy it immensely and am gratified that it now appears I could hold down a job and support my children if the need arose. I had my doubts before. I don't enjoy being away from the children all day, though, particularly during vacation time. They call me when they wish, and I check in on them several times a day, so it's working out.

Bill left this morning for Travis Air Force Base for his two weeks of reserve duty. In his absence, I have planned an evening coffee for 40 people next Wednesday, to learn why we should vote NO on a proposed constitutional amendment, sponsored by the Cal. Real Estate Assn. It would make any legislation illegal which forbids the denial of sale or renting of property on the basis of race or religion. If this passes, it would nullify all existing laws in the field of fair housing, and preclude any unfair housing protection laws in the future. It is a shameful proposal, and I am very discouraged by what I perceive as a move toward right-wing extremism in California. The popularity of this proposed amendment is another symptom of the sickness pervading this land of ours.

I like "talking" to you in these letters, Joe, but it's late, and in a moment of weakness, I agreed to take the kids surfing tomorrow, of all things. We'll probably all drown. I'll send Rob a copy of your letter. Sorry, but I won't part with the original.

Lea

Weston, Conn.
Sunday, August 2, 1964

Dear Joe,

This was a light travel month for me, with business trips only to Buffalo, Chicago, and Indianapolis. Mother and Dad did visit with us for about a week, and it was good having them with us. As I grow older, I am aware of appreciating my parents more, and I always hope they sense this. I have never been one for discussing my feelings with others (perhaps because I don't understand myself well enough), and I rarely try to express my feelings to Mother and Dad about them. I hope my actions speak louder than my non-existent words. Dad offered to baby-sit with Billy while Mother, Marlene, and the other kids went with me to the World's Fair, since it is in New York. Before they went home, mother remarked that this was the first world's fair she had ever visited.

On the 4th of July, we had a visit with Ed's gang, our pleasure dampened some by the knowledge that Ed's year-long absence was soon to begin. We went swimming in the afternoon and finished off the day by watching fireworks from a nearby hilltop. Joyce is glad her family lives nearby, and we are only an hour away by car; we hope to see her during the coming months.

We took another trip—to Cape Cod, the trip broken up into 3 legs of 200 miles each, visiting Plymouth, going aboard the Mayflower 2, the replica ship that sailed across the Atlantic a few years ago, saw an early pilgrim site, and that night found a cabin by a lake. The next day, we traveled to Provincetown on the tip of the cape, going swimming below the Cape Cod Lighthouse. The rolling surf, clear blue-green water, and the deep blue sky combined to give that mysterious compelling pull of the sea. The rest of the trip included a visit to Woods Hole, and the New Bedford Whaling Museum, learning about the days of wooden ships and iron men. We came home happy and tired, and I hope Doug got a better appreciation of our heritage, as I did.

This is all for now, Joe. I have thought of you very much during this past month. Undoubtedly much of it is due to the fact that it is summer, and I have been enjoying the blessings of the freedom to travel and see the family growing and learning.

Good night, my friend,
Rob

Okinawa
12 August 1964

Dear Joe,

I address this letter to you, but I mean it also for Lea, Lenny, and Rob— also for both Joyces, Marlene, and Bill. Lenny mentioned in his letter, that he detected a note of self-pity in one of your early letters. If he did, relax; you have company! Anyone separated from those he loves who does not feel pangs of sorrow is more callous than I care to be. I, of course, have more personal freedom than you, but like you, it can only be lessened by a requisite amount of time. But, I have one advantage—I may write an unlimited number of letters, while yours are rationed—both in length and number. I am sure that communication is the wellspring of love. Lea and I talked about this at length. This started out as an effort to be of help to you, and we find now that it is we who are being sustained by these letters. I will respond to all the letters from each of you, which Lea sent on to me.

Let me bring you up to date first on myself. As you know, last Tuesday, the hammer was at full cock with the finger on the trigger. It's still all systems "GO" and many of my fellow officers will be gone for a while. However, there has been a definite lessening of tension, and I don't think I will have to leave this island. I have organized my job so it no longer seems an impossible task. I've applied to teach for the University of Maryland, Far Eastern Division—introductory business administration two nights a week. Pay is good, and it will help the time go faster.

Lea, my dear, thanks for calling me a teddy bear, Joyce's term of endearment for me. It's a good thing we act as brother and sister, otherwise I would find you far too distracting to talk sensibly to. Joyce and I are already planning her trip to San Francisco to meet me, and our plans will not only include you but will count on your friendship to assist in her trip and our reunion. I am glad you spoke to Joe of the warmth in these letters spreading half way around the world—further actually because I am 13 hours ahead of Eastern Standard Time. As to Lenny, even that which is lost can be found again. Don't tear down the bridge; some day one of you may decide to cross it. I am glad your neck is better.

Rob, thanks for your attention to Joyce and the kids. She is doing well, I think, and Ann is lots of company. Thanks for planning to go and visit them. It will mean a lot to both of us.

Joe, don't waste precious writing privileges on me alone. It only takes mail one day to get from Lea to me or from me to her. I can reproduce your letters and mail them to the others.

Lenny, let me hear from you, too, as Joyce wants to know about the picnic you are planning with the kids when I get home. I will have to teach you how to make pizza, like I did Lea. I will try to write again in two weeks. Hope this finds you all well.

Love from your friend,
Ed

Joe.Killeen. – 78250
N.S. State Farm, 23160
August 9, 1964

Dear Rob & All—

I am deeply concerned about Ed's present situation. He may be caught up in that sticky spider web in Southeast Asia. Ed, you must promise to keep us regularly informed. Ed, the love you humbly speak of is reciprocal, individually and collectively, in this multiple of the "five Charter Voices" and all their constituents. We have no problems within our group that cannot be worked out—we're too tight a unit to think otherwise… By now Lea must realize that we male "Voices" are concerned about what goes on in that pretty head of her's, including the pain she has so recently suffered. Since all of us have of late been prying off the tops of one another's heads to see what's going on inside, it's no wonder Lea had this strange malady. Blame me for the extra twists that have been given her neck… Lea, sometimes we don't remember to say the things we should to our special gals, but that doesn't mean we don't think and/or pray on them. Since you know you're not your own but belong to the lot of us, you must know that you're the belle of the original charter combine… I mentioned to Lea that Rob, Ed, and I were all rather light on the top now. Lenny stated he had plenty of hair, but was a bit skimpy at the crown. He described his "beanie" bald spot to his five year old as the place where lightning struck him. One day, while pulling some weeds on his terrace, his Grace brought one of her playmates up to him. Grace said, "Bend down, Dad, Missy wants to see what a bald head looks like." Lenny threw mud on them both… Lenny, I'll have that letter off to you in two weeks, I promise!!! Lea, when Goldwater stated: "Extremism is no sin if you are engaged in the defense of freedom." Your Gov. Pat Brown retorted that such a remark had the "stench of Fascism." Brown speaks my opinion. Ultra-conservative, Lea, is certainly too mild a description of right-wing extremism. But, this is only "what" they are. But, why "Fanaticism?" Let's run this down per Santayana. He describes the fanatic something like this: "The fanatic is nothing but a worldling too narrow and violent to understand the world. "Fanatics represent arrested forms of common sense—incredulous childishness, with its useless eyes wide open, and eaten up with some mischievous whim. Do you want it deeper? It's paranoia, resenter style, the cancer of the psyche… In understanding the extremist we must also realize that we are guilty of this at least in some mild form. For example, prejudice. Have you ever met a purely objective person? I never have. Somehow, we are all slaves of our environment. In plainer words, we are all wet sacks of prejudices, made up of likes and dislikes. And this is nothing more than a mask of weakness—certainly not strength. Wallace shows it as a tool of bigots; it is certainly never the device of a true moralist. It is a form of robbery, robbing the victim of a fair trial in the court of reason. (Wow! carried away again!—Anyway, Lea, I'm strong on your political views, too.) I still haven't gotten to you, Rob, or the poem, "Voices at Montalvo" Please, all of you, forgive the "left outs" of this letter. One page is all too short, but you are never left out of my mind.)

"Way out,"

Joe

Los Gatos, CA

August 21, 1964

Dear Joe,

Is it my imagination, or did your letter come a bit sooner in the month than usual? I am glad. Your letters and even the answering them has become a treat I look forward to with much pleasure. I think the idea of copies to each other is a splendid one, for which we can thank Rob. (He wasn't chosen "boy most likely to succeed" in the class of 1944 with no reason. He was always the brainiest of us all!) I trust Rob is sending copies of his letter to Lenny, as well. If this is true, Rob will, I hope, let me know what he thinks of my sending a copy of my letter to Joe to Lenny, and seeing what happens. I am certain if Lenny knew how relieved I would be if I felt the past became painless enough for him to forgive, if not forget, he would "join the club." He would benefit as much as the rest of us. I thought of writing him directly and, as tactfully as I can, ask him to rejoin us in this exchange, but I thought better of it, and I decided to wait, hoping he comes to this decision by himself. (I can, at this point, see Rob throwing his hands in the air! His exasperated comment would be, "Patience, woman, patience!) And, of course, he would be right. Stirring nearly quiet, spent ashes serves to start them burning all over again. If only Lenny could understand that the bond that has reunited us, which very much includes him, is the same bond that drew us together as youngsters—a similarity in taste, intelligence, values, and most of all basic honesty. It happens that between Lenny and me there was the deep feeling that is only present in a first love; but he must understand that romance, per se, is short-lived, in youthful love affairs or in marriage. The waning of romance from a relationship doesn't mean something else can't take its place, be it the abiding love of a good marriage, or the fulfilling warmth of a close (or not so close) friendship. Of course, there is always the possibility (and I have considered this possibility many times) that, stripped of romance, Lenny sees nothing in me he wants as a basis of friendship. If this is the case, then it is certainly his prerogative to be left alone. But, I am too stubborn in my belief that I understand human nature, to believe that all Lenny and I saw in each other was romantic. The wisdom of the ending of our relationship is shown by the very obvious fact that we both are now happily married to different people, but I also believe that we both instinctively saw in each other that which has attracted us to people all our lives. Do you agree, and do you think he might believe this, too, one day?

You know, Joe, all of us have painful memories, some of us more than others. Indeed, the memory of my high school days is largely painful, focused as I was then only on my own severe stuttering, which somehow dominated my life. Not so my senior year when all of us were close friends, after my having had a year and a half of speech therapy, which was a major turning point for me. But, as we mature and make friends with ourselves, we find we can live with all of our past. You, more than any of us, must have learned that; in fact, I know from your letters that you have. You, Joe, are the finest example of learning from adversity and turning a loss into a profit. I am glad and proud to be your friend.

Now, I'll depart from philosophical pronouncements and answer your letter and Rob and Ed's. Joe, what a gift you have for pithy expression, limited as you are to one side of a sheet of paper. You are developing some kind of micro-handwriting—smallest I have ever seen! Your obvious wealth of knowledge puts me to shame, and I love your analogies and metaphors. I was particularly amused to be part of your "5 charter voices and their constituents." I'll bet our kids never thought of being called "constituents."

As to having our heads pried off and examined, I doubt any of us minds. (Oh dear, sounds like a bad pun!) We're a pretty uninhibited crew, for the most part, Rob being the least effusive of us all, reflecting an inner reserve. Rob's blunt comments are so like he has always been with me—frank, never really critical, but very much those of a person who is comfortable with a friend, which I appreciate. It pleases me when friends know they can be blunt. Rob always has been, especially his frank appraisals of my appearance, like, "You're heavier. You're hair's getting gray. Are you wearing a new shade of lipstick?" I do agree with all your comments re: politics. Interestingly, we all seem to agree in this area, Rob being the only one of us leaning toward the conservative (except in the area of human rights, of course). I, too, have my anxieties in Ed's behalf. For his sake, as well as for the sake of the world, I hope things stay quiet in the east. A flare-up of any magnitude which could start Goldwater on a tirade of criticism could be disastrous. I am in terror he may be elected.

Ed, your letter was a delight—you write exactly as you talk. I felt like I had a chat with you. One comment: Your comment regarding tearing down bridges was pretty transparent. I hope Lenny didn't wince. But, thank you. I hope you are right. I, for one, will leave them in tact, and perhaps one day, I'll meet him half way over; that would seem fair.

Rob finally sent those pictures taken at Montalvo, with a bow-legged female blocking the view. Sorry! I took one or two with him in the foreground. Did he send you those? And did they release a flood of memories for you, as he suspected they would? I must end this letter. And, I will.

So long,
Lea

Okinawa
Wednesday, August 26 1964

Dear Joe and all,

My typing and spelling haven't improved any since my last letter, so you're going to be subjected to more of it. I was going to be a big hero and write everyone often, but two typhoons, ago I was full of rash promises. I have also found that preparing to take over a college-level course as lecturer is more time consuming than I thought. Also, we still have some involvement in the Vietnam situation, which keeps life interesting. It's still possible that things will heat up again, but I think that November is still the critical month. This latest political coup in the north has not helped our situation any. A military triumvirate is not acceptable, and whether a civilian regime can be set up there is problematical. I have to be prepared, like all of us in the Marines, for the possibility of involvement in that mess.

Rob sent me your letter of 9 August and I enjoyed it very much. I have also gotten a copy of Lea's latest to you, and that is always a wonderful end to a workday. We get our mail at 16:30 hours, typhoons permitting. I sent in my absentee ballot today, I fully intend to vote. So, I will do my bit to indicate that I am scared of Barry. I also feel a great concern over the civil rights problem and must vote against him on that count also. I recognize in myself some of the prejudices that you say we all have, but it's hard to be radical about anything but family and friends, frankly. Life is too short and full of duty at the moment.

Lea said I wrote as if I were conversing with someone. If she only knew how I must fight this infernal typewriter, she would know that this is not a conversation; it's a war! Next time, I hope she gets the carbon paper in straight, but I won't needle her; I know how much she hates to type. She never did accept getting a D-minus in typing in high school. Besides, I have to stay in her good graces, since she is going to have my Joyce waiting for my plane for me.

I will do my best to stay out of trouble, and I will try to keep you posted on how things are going out here. There are, of course, some things, which you will see in the newspaper first. So long,
Ed

Lea, this should make you feel good about your typing. I would have flunked with you!! Hope by now your neck is better. I also hope I didn't make Lenny want to break it! I fully intended that he at least try to interpret or read into what I wrote. Joyce and the kids are fine, we are sure that if all goes well, she will come west to meet me.

Love,
Ed

Weston, Conn.
September 2, 1964

Dear Joe,

Hard to believe that a month has flown by since my last letter. Today was a beautiful day, warm but a hint of fall in the air. Much as I hate to see summer fade away, I look forward to the glorious New England colors as the trees prepare for winter. Even now some of the trees around the house are changing color, and some leaves are already down on the ground. Time for me to do the touch-up painting around the house, and to get the bird feeder cleaned up for our winter guests.

Some family outings and visits during the month of August, with jaunts along the Hudson, on up to West Point, then, Newburgh, stopping at Mt. Beacon. Took an incline ride that the kids loved and had the adults holding their breath, scared to death. Good family times.

Then followed a five-day trip to Chicago, largely fruitful and a learning experience, as well as teaching classes. I spent two hours in the Chicago Museum of Natural History. On another, I attended an outdoor concert, and though I know nothing about music, I enjoyed listening to it, enjoying the evening breezes from the lake. On both trips, I traveled via the new three-engine jets (all engines in the rear). I never cease to marvel over eating supper at 30,000 feet while traveling over 500 mph, sliding along with no feeling of movement.

On Sunday, August 23, Marlene and I quietly celebrated our twelfth wedding anniversary with a family steak dinner at home. Two dozen red roses were my contribution. How those 12 years have flown by.

Had a visit with brother Karl and his bunch at Stone Harbor, N.J., a small resort town about 15 miles north of Cape May. It was a real mob scene at the rental apartment—all three of the brothers' families—8 children, 7 adults, and one dog (large!). We were sleeping all over the place, all my brood in their sleeping bags. That evening, we all took a moonlight walk on the beach. It was just like being in another world—so different from our everyday surroundings. Business took me on an uneventful trip to Washington, but before leaving for home, I took the opportunity to visit my grandmother. I had not seen her since last Thanksgiving. She is getting old and feeble, and her attention wanders at times. But, we had a good conversation, and I had tears in my eyes as we said good-bye.

The day after returning to Connecticut, we had a good visit at Joyce's. She had found a small park nearby, which proved to be a suitable place for our picnic lunch. We listened to Ed's tape from Okinawa, which was great, and then we all made one to send to him. And so passed the month of August. Now let me answer or comment on the many letters I received from our gang this month:

Joe—Hope you received the pictures I took at Montalvo. They hardly do justice to that wonderful place, but then I do not claim to be a good photographer. I thought our lady friend looked pretty good. I liked your remarks on Goldwater's stand on extremism, and I probably agree with you in the main. I submit, however, that if we consider the taking of human life as extremism, our country had indeed been guilty of extremism in the name of freedom. I actually find myself agreeing with much of what Goldwater has written in the past (e.g—"conscience of a conservative") but I find myself hard pressed to respect the man as he constantly shoots from the hip and then has to backwater out of trouble. I also cannot forgive him for selecting Miller, a political hack, for his running mate. On the other hand, I commend Johnson for his picking of Humphrey—while at the same time, I basically disagree with much of the Johnson philosophy on the role of government. I find neither candidate wholly attractive to me.

Ed—Joyce and the kids are all fine, and it was good to see them again. Your wife is a fine gal. You better slow down on your letter writing to the rest of us, or Uncle Sam will not be getting his money's worth out of you. Your letter writing really surprised me, and I must compliment you on it. Your letter of August 12 especially struck a chord within me—my hat is off to you. You and Joe and Lea are all making me feel like a clod. The phrases I want to write usually stay inside me, much to my chagrin. I find myself taking refuge in writing about current events, which are easier to handle, but are not satisfying to me. Perhaps as time goes on, I will find some changes taking place in my way of writing. One thing I know—I have never been a philosopher, and I cannot write any great philosophical thoughts. I guess that I would rather act than think. Keep on writing as often as you have the time and the inclination.

Lea—Who said you were bow-legged? Not we boys, I'm sure. Sorry the pictures of me didn't turn out so well, and the camera wasn't functioning properly. It's in the repair shop right now. Lea, you write so well to Joe that you make me feel mighty puny—but you certainly put on paper many of the same thoughts that I have and somehow, will not express. Just keep on writing for both of us (but with some qualifying statements when you start talking politics.) Hope your health problems continue to fade away. Your comment that Bill's practice is picking up is good news, indeed.

Lenny—Come on in, the water's fine, and I miss you.
Good night, friends,
Rob

Lea—What else can I say? It took me two evenings to get this typed! Joe's birthday is October 13.
R.

Okinawa
Wednesday, September 9 1964

Dear Joe, Lea, Lenny, and Rob,

So far this morning, I have handled four Congressional Inquiries. It is now noon and I will start this letter, knowing I won't finish it today. Since I last wrote you, things have stayed fairly quiet. The political situation in South Vietnam is the main thing on my horizon now, and I do not know any more about it than you do. I do feel that if they can not help themselves, there is not much we can do for them. If we do go in with force, I think it would leave me feeling a bit like Cornwallis, who tried to win such a war. If they don't want us there, I think we should go all the way to China or just get out. I get the feeling that they want our help but would rather fight each other for power than fight the Viet Cong.

This is a pretty island. If the climate was any good, it would compare with Hawaii. I drove up the west coast last Sunday and the scenery seems similar to the Italian Riviera. There are a number of excellent swimming beaches and reefs to snorkel on and I am fast becoming an enthusiast for snorkeling. The main crop is sugar cane and the whole place is a green garden. These people use chemical fertilizer and consequently this place does not smell as bad as Japan where they still use night soil.

There has been a change in colonels here in my office, which has been to my advantage and my work situation has become a real pleasure. I've been getting out of the office in time to play handball every afternoon and I can now get an occasional afternoon off. It would be a wonderful job if we had dependents out here the way the Army and Air Force do. Living conditions for dependents are excellent and many of them do not want to leave when their tours are up.

I'm having a bit of trouble with my application to teach for the U. of Maryland. They have certified me to teach public administration, but my certification to teach business administration has run into a snag, so I can't begin teaching until next semester.

This is an election year, but somehow, I can't get into the campaigns. I have been a liberal and a believer in big government since I saw my first apple seller during the depression. I guess I remember too vividly the problems my father had supporting two families and all the problems that went with it. I do admit that big government is bad if it is not responsible to the electorate, but so far, I feel that our Bureaucracy has in fact been quite responsive. I have also seen too many examples of the individual states failing to do an effective job of providing for the common good of their citizens. No need to speak of human rights here, as I think all of us are in agreement on that. Still, I don't think I can make a liberal out of Rob.

It was fun being able to hear Rob and Marlene on the tape from Joyce. Somehow it's more personal than letters and has a greater psychological impact. I got a tape yesterday with a conversation between my mother and Joyce. Mom is fine, Joe. She is still working at the shoe store, and she's hoping that the Social Security Bill is passed. She always asks about you.

Lea, I read in the paper where they are slashing the tires of cars with stickers against Proposition 14. I hope you are not involved in any acts of violence by those extremists who seem to inhabit sunny California. I know you are quite outspoken, and I hope no one takes it out on you. I am pleased that Bill's practice is growing. I note with pleasure that you haven't been fired as his office nurse yet!

Lenny, please write or I will have to make like Joe and cuss you out. I am not bothered by censors as he is, and I will really be able to use purple prose. As Rob says, "the water is fine."

Sayonara,

Ed

Okinawa
Monday, 14 September 1964

Dear Lea,

I got your letter this morning and wanted to drop you a prompt answer to your request. I remember the book very well, and I would love to have you include my name with the inscription. I have not read "The Prophet," but I know it will be right up Joe's alley—a perfect birthday gift.

I cannot predict how Lenny would respond to your inquiry. In my next letter to Joe, I will include a short personal note asking him how Lenny is holding up to the correspondence and how it seems to be reacting on him. As you know, I have, as has Rob, sent Lenny copies of all of my letters. I have not yet received an answer. I feel it might be a bit early for you to try a direct approach yet. Let Rob and me get him out in the open first.

Joyce is planning about a five-day stay in San Francisco or area when I get back. We will, I am sure, plan to spend a good part of the time visiting with you and Bill. I would like her to see Montalvo and she loves good wine. I know she would enjoy visiting the Paul Masson Winery. I hope we are able to do it as planned.

I will be anxiously awaiting your next letter to Joe. Hope all is well with you and yours.

Love,

Ed

September 14, 1964

SURVEY FORM FOR ROB
Circle the response of your choice and mail back, please:
Dear Lea,
I (would like) (would not like) you to add my name to the inscription,

which reads as follows:

"Has anyone said it better than Gibran? ...' and in the sweetness of friendship, let there be laughter and sharing of pleasures, for in the dew of little things, the heart finds its morning and is refreshed.' "

This (is) (is not) too sappy for my taste.

Ah, woman, you misjudge me! I do have some poetry in my soul—even though deeply buried. Truthfully, I never heard of Kahil Gibran—but today, I went to a bookstore and found his works. Briefly looked at "the Earth Gods", "The Madman," and the "The Forerunner," as well as "The Prophet."

I actually liked "the Prophet", brief as was my reading. Of course I would like you to add my name to the inscription.

Have Hope!

Rob

Okinawa
Thursday, 24 September 1964

Dear Joe and all,

It's about time for the letters to you to start coming in this month, and I will start mine now so that I will be ahead of the game. We have just gotten rid of another typhoon, Wilda this time. We were lucky, as it never got closer than 200 miles. Even so, we got some of the wind and rain. It was a big one and is headed right for Japan. Just in time for the Olympics, too. It has stayed hot here, and there is no indication that fall has started at all. The daily low is still in the 80's. I don't mind though; it means we can still go swimming at the beach for a while yet.

I have become an avid lover of snorkeling, which is sort of a poor man's form of scuba diving. Out here on Okinawa, there are some fabulous coral reefs and it is like being in another world to drift along over them and see all the colors. It is funny how a set of flippers, a mask, and a snorkel takes all the work out of swimming. You drift along in a sort of continuous dead man's float with no effort at all. The view changes constantly and the colors are vivid. The small fish are not a bit afraid of you and they are all colors of the rainbow. The coral grows in all kinds of fantastic shapes and the little fish dart happily in and out among the branches. I love it!

I wish I could give you some startling observations on the situation in Vietnam, but my knowledge is no better than yours. The most pertinent comment came from a navy doctor, fresh back from Saigon. He pointed out that the French did a lousy job of preparing the Indo-Chinese for self-government. He also observed that there still are a lot of French down there and they are not really on our side. In fact, they seem to be working against us. The present military situation in the area seems to be quiet, and we have relaxed considerably here, for the moment.

I am glad that things are keeping busy for me; it makes the time pass faster. I will have been here 11 weeks by the time this letter reaches you. The inquiries from the congressmen keep coming in, and in between, I crowd my visits to the Brig and other required functions. I just hope the next forty-five weeks go by as fast as the first eleven.

More after mail from the voices arrives, with comments on those.
Ed

It's a week later, and still no mail from any of you. So, I will just finish this and put it in the mail. We are getting a lot of rain now, and the nights have turned cool. It actually got down to 70° last night. If the relative humidity would go down, too, things would be quite comfortable.

Saturday, October 10

It is taking me a while to finish this letter. I started over two weeks ago, and I am still not finished with it. The weather has turned much cooler, so that we don't need air conditioning, for the first time. No chance to go to the beach, and it's rained every night for the past 10 days. Typhoon Dot has just gone by well to the south of us, so I guess fall is finally here to stay. I am also busy teaching my first course in business administration—not for U. of Maryland, though. I am teaching a course for the U. of Wisconsin under the auspices of the Armed Forces Institute. I teach twice a week, and I get 12 bucks a night. The classes last three hours and I have 25 students. All the preparation for the other classes I taught is useful for this. I have been invited to Taiwan by the Chinese I escorted this last week, and I would like to go. I also hope to get in a trip to Bancock, or is it Bangcock? (Oh, heck! I will never learn how to spell!)

Sunday morning

This is incredible! I still haven't finished this letter.

Rob, if you were worried about an uninspired letter, how about this disjointed mess which has taken me two and a half weeks to write. In a few hours you will be having a picnic lunch with Joyce and I wish I could join you.

Lea, usually you are the first to write the monthly letter to Joe. Perhaps you are so busy politicking that you have lost track of the time. Did you send Kahil Gibran's book to Joe for his birthday? If so, I know he will enjoy it.

Lenny, as you can see by this so-called letter, we need some literary talent in this circle. Every Friday night at the mess, we have beer and pizza and I think of you and the wonderful time we had in Pittsburgh when last I saw you. So please write and add your skill in English to this group. Joyce, kiss the kids for me.

Sayonara,

Ed

Joe Killeen–78250

N/S State Farm, VA 23160

27 September 1964

(written from one edge of one sheet of lined paper to the other—in microscopically tiny, but very legible script)

Dear Voices and Echoes,... Before me, spread out on my bunk, are five letters (3 from Ed and one a piece from Lea and Rob)—all unanswered! They total 9 1/2 typewritten pages. (Rob has the best typewriter, for it makes the least mistakes.) Also, there are portions of other previous Voice letters that I have yet to attend to. What's a body to do? This is the most pleasant type of frustration I've ever encountered. (Confession: I like it, and I am selfish enough to wish for more!). Ed, your frequent reports have eased our anxiety. Thanks! Continue to keep us informed on your situation. Our country must share in some of the blame for the Vietnam chaos. Oriental proverb says: "He who saddles tiger must be able to ride him." Ed, I would pump you more on your political views but understand your Hatch act position. I'm not permitted to send air-mail; how long does it take regular mail to Okinawa? Rob, your trek map of Montalvo is fairly exact- I know all the photo spots you selected. Lea's pictures owe nothing to the Montalvo background, it may be the reverse. (Lea just called me a flatterer again!) Speaking of "background", Rob, only a conservative thinker could say to Lea: "You're heavier." Ed sent me a picture that definitely is a study on legs. The girls represent the quality of the subject, but Ed (and Rob) express quantity that might be more apropos to describe as "kegs." Joyce and Lea call Ed a "big teddy bear," but he reminds me of a fair angel—the Swedish Angel...Rob and Lea: Time magazine (8/7/64, p. 70) is more gentle in their appraisal of

71

James Cozzens than was the N.Y. Times Book Review. The former describes him as an "unsmiling, non-extremist conservative." Rob, I enjoyed the August outings… I'm "drowning in the sentimentalism" (as Lea might say) of your Montalvo visits; what I might write would seem "gushy." In Lea's "Voices at Montalvo," her "silent discourse" and "unsaid words" speak better than my few. Were I privileged to carry you voices to my favorite spot of these post-war years, it would have been Villa Montalvo. But, you found it without me, yet you share it with me now… Lea, your poetry is interesting. It lingers on a rather aesthetically strange and sentimental melancholy. Your play on words continues to impress me as did, "Morning Dialog." Your thoughts—such vertical thoughts—almost stagger my imagination (but not quite). "Verdant" suggests "inexperienced" as well as "green", and this compares to the Dialog's "belie." "Silent discourse," "unsaid words," " the unsung song" are reflective of the Dialog's 7th verse. "Gone are the years" suggest the resignation of the 8th verse of "Dialog." "Yet there is much to learn" is a throwback to Verse 1 of "Dialog." What "bestirs" you, Lea?—Am I wrong to ask you this? Or am I staggering your mind with my own imagination? Is it still as you described in your answer to my Dialog critique?… Lenny is the only one who hasn't been to Montalvo. One of these years, I'd like to do something about that. Also, I wish Lenny would do something about that separate letter I wrote him on August 23rd. I warn you, Lenny, I haven't been turned down yet on my August parole hearing. If you don't write soon, you'd better hope the Board does turn me down, for I'm apt to pop in on you and cuss you out in person… I have an earnest request of all of you. If in this time any of you truly feel that I am worthy of parole, cross your fingers, and/or pray (prayer makes more sense to me), or whatever you do when you want something special. Children are the best in prayer, for they are more open and sincerely trusting in their beliefs. Those of you whose children pray—well, doggone, just tell them you know a guy who'd appreciate prayers for a very special desire he has… It will take some sort of miracle to swing this, but maybe the kids can get through for me… Ed is right, Lea, be careful; for some of your political adversaries are dangerous. Confucius offered his golden role as a guide to those who seek virtue; but of those who prefer vice instead, he said: "Rotten wood cannot be carved."

Ternura,

Joe

Entering Troubled Waters

Weston, CT
October 2, 1964

Dear Joe,

This happens to be one of those uninspired times when letter-writing comes especially hard—but I fear that if I don't write tonight, I won't find the time to do so for quite a few days. The greatest part of my free time this month was spent in painting the trim on the house. It's still not finished, and I hope the warm weather doesn't desert me for a couple of weekends. I did take a Saturday off, though, to go to a nearby state park where a helicopter society was holding a meeting; thirty or forty helicopters were being demonstrated. I thought of Ed as we watched them go through their demonstrations.

Until this week, the weather was dry and warm, but the first of the fall rains has arrived. As the weather changes, so does our pattern of living— more work, more meetings, resumption of church related activities. But, life in our family continues to be comfortable.

Last week, we were guests of Mother and Dad in a cabin in the Poconos, just west of the Delaware Water Gap. The cabin has distant memories for me. I vacationed there in the 1930's, and seven years ago, in 1957, Marlene and I were guests of Mother and Dad at the same cabin, when Doug was only three. Now in 1964, we returned again, this time with three children. The years fly by.

Joe, I just wanted to say that last month's mountain of letters has dwindled to close to nothing. Had everyone stopped writing, or what? Have my conservative political views so alienated you all that all communications have ceased? Oh, for shame! The only letter was Ed's to Joe, dated Sept. 9.

Ed, glad to hear the island has some good points about it. As you know, life is what we make of it, and there's a lot of good around if we'll only look for it. I regret that we didn't get the chance to get together with your gang this last month—most of my free time was behind a paintbrush. I called Joyce this evening, and we made a date for a family picnic on Sunday, October 11th. Hope the leaves are turned color by then. I'll take pictures.

Lea: Have you read the article in Business Week, September 26th, p 70, entitled, "San Jose discovers how it feels to be rich?" Very interesting—all about the spectacular growth in your area.

Lenny: The water is still fine. Goodnight, my friends, / Rob

(on a separate sheet of paper)

Post script to Joe, Lea and Ed,

I am sending copies of this letter to you three, plus Joyce and Lenny. This page, however, will go ONLY to you three.

A few days after sending Lenny a copy of my previous letter, the first copy I had sent to him of any recent letter to Joe, I received the following note from him:

"Hi, Rob, thanks for the letter. I enjoyed it. You can never know how I wish I could join you. Were I able, my life would have been very different. But, the water is deep—and cold—and black. Len "

I don't know what to say, but it is obvious that we have a friend in need. Please do not let Lenny know that I have passed his note along to you. If he cares to write to me in the future, I will not pass along his letters unless he gives permission. I just thought that this brief note put things in perspective pretty well as far as he is concerned.

My present plans are to be in Pittsburgh for Christmas. If so, I will do my best to talk to Lenny, and try to draw him back into the circle again. Joe, and Ed—perhaps you can turn the trick. Let's all try.

Rob

Los Gatos,
October 13, 1964

Dear Joe,

I must apologize at the outset for the delay in my response to your last letter, but I do have a reason. Bill, the boys and I took a trip to Los Angeles, combining some fun with Bill's attending an American College of Cardiology convention. The boys and I went to Disneyland—our first trip there—and what a fantastic place it is! It's a whole animated world, wired for sound, and while I have never been an amusement park enthusiast, I was a sucker for all that magic! I never dreamed I would react that way, expecting to go there and just enjoy the children's pleasure. Instead, I leaped in full swing myself, wanting to go on everything at once. I was like a kid loose in a toy store with unlimited access to candy!

Now, to answer some of your questions, Joe. By the way, Happy Birthday! As you can see by the date above, this is your birthday. Are you 38 or 39? I'm only 37, for the information of all you old guys. Joe, your compliments are a bunch of stuff,—but don't think for a minute I am suggesting you stop!! I love it, and I thank you. It's is certainly true that beauty is in the eyes of the beholder, and if I look pretty to all of you, I can only be grateful for the fondness you all have for me, which makes you see me that way.

Joe, Rob's comments and the points mentioned in the review he sent were well taken, but I continue undaunted in my admiration of the central character in *By Love Possessed*, and Rob still reminds me of him. If you have not read the book, Rob just happens to have in his possession a copy he'd be happy—in fact, eager!—to give you. I would be very much interested in your appraisal of Arthur Winner, Joe. I see him as a good man with much feeling which he, through years of habit and a very proper upbringing, manages to conceal from everyone except those very close to him. (Hello, Rob!) If Rob has, as I suggested, already used it to start a fire in his fireplace, let me know, and I'll try to dig up a copy for you (paper back, of course)!

I am glad you enjoyed *Voices at Montalvo*. I have no illusions about being a good poet; in fact, that is the only one which I honestly think says what I wanted it to, though I dare say, it would have meaning only to the four of us. As to what is bestirring me, Joe, I don't know what to say. No, certainly you are not remiss in asking. Poetry has a funny way of saying and revealing things that perhaps the writer doesn't know. I can truthfully answer, nothing of any serious import. I am perhaps a person with too much feeling for some things. But, a good friend of mine, who is a psychiatrist, once told me that my feelings would probably never threaten me, because I recognize them for what they are—only feelings. He went on to say something that has had a profound effect on me, "No feelings, no matter how bizarre, can hurt you, if they are unaccompanied by action." Does that make any sense to you? I found it a very reasonable comment and one, which has been a sort of comforting guide for me through the years. Let me say, at this point, that this is not to say that I am overly generous with my affections for people. Quite the contrary, I do not get very close to many people. But, the ones to whom I am devoted get a generous dose.

Ed: I am enjoying your letters no end. I am less concerned about your safety, for the moment at least. I agree with you that you are safe until after November. Assuming Goldwater is soundly defeated, I think a negotiated settlement may be in the wind. I can see nothing to be gained by extending the situation in Vietnam, and I am sure responsible people in government feel this way, too. If by some fluke Goldwater should be elected, then it is anybody's guess what will happen. For my part, I'll consider moving to

Labrador!

Rob: I was distressed beyond words by the post-script you added to your last letter. Lenny's comment sounded desperate. He always had an opinion of himself that was much less than he deserved. Joe is right. He needs psychiatric help. I feel quite strongly that Lenny's is a problem that none of us can help him with very much, me, of course, the least of all. In this regard, I have a confession to make. In my zeal to make our gift to Joe from all of us, I did write Lenny a short note asking his permission to add his name, saying that I knew this would please Joe. I told him I would not mail the book until the 23rd of September, allowing him time to drop me a card. In an effort to allow him to save face, I told him that if I didn't hear from him by then, I would assume he didn't want me to, or that he had some other thing in mind. I didn't hear from him, so on the 23rd, I mailed the package. Now, I don't think my writing him precipitated anything. I do think, however, that all these voices out of the past are bothering him beyond words. Mine, to which he was once the closest, and one which dealt him a blow, is understandably the most painful. Lenny, I am almost certain, feels more frustrations and feelings of inadequacy than any of us. Again, Joe, in his wisdom, has been the first to spot this. He was right when he said that Lenny is another "salamander", reluctant to stir from his cloister, regardless of how much he may need the warmth, and regardless of how genuine the warmth is. I cannot help feeling that my part in it is what's stopping him. I'd be willing to bet that if it were just you four guys, things would be different; and if all of you will be honest, I think you will agree.

And Joe, I guess this brings me to the end of this epistle. I hope you are keeping all these letters. They form a unique chronicle, since they contain all sides of this correspondence. Some day, we can all collaborate and write a book. We'll let Rob do the typing; Ed can be business manager, and you and I can be the political analysts and feature writers, like we were on the MHS yearbook staff. And mind your comments on MY typing, as I am very sensitive in that area! You know, that D—in typing kept me from competing with Rob for first in our high school class? I've been resenting that ever since! Actually, I have become a fine tipyst, *@ , not countinh thE mist%ak#s (!

Bye?

Lea

Tuesday, 20 October, 1964

Dear Joe, Lea, Lenny, and Rob,

With a letter from Joe and one from Lea to answer, I guess it is time to try my skill with a typewriter again. No complaints about the typing accepted, Joe; a letter is a letter, in spite of the typing. I know Lea agrees with me; her typing is even worse than mine. Besides, I know mine has been improving. When I get a typewriter of my own, I will be sure it is pica type, like Rob's.

My own personal situation continues to be safe and comfortable. I am getting a new boss on the first of November, which will make my job more indispensable for a while, at least. Every once in a while, I feel the urge to go south and see what is going on. But, they are sending only junior officers and I am not eligible. So, the only way I can get into trouble is if there is something big. No new visitations by the Nationalist Chinese or anyone else. The weather turned cooler, it is about like a New England summer now. Maximum temperature is about 85 with a humidity getting down to 80%. I hope it lasts a while. It never gets close to freezing out here.

Joe, if prayer can help you with your parole, you have all kinds of help. Joyce will ask the kids to remember you in theirs and you have always been in mine. You will get lots of support from the others, as well. I wish there was something tangible we could do, too. Is there anyone we can write? I am anxious for you to be back in society so we can communicate face to face, and not just through letters.

Rob, the pictures of my tribe are excellent, and I cannot thank you enough. Joyce had a good time, and she said you all got lots of exercise. The top of Sleeping Giant is quite a climb! Have to carry anyone?

Lea, I am still only 37, so you are not alone in being younger than those old fogies we write to. Anyone who could enjoy Disneyland as much as you did is still young at heart, too. I would like to take my family there some day. I agree with Joe on his appraisal of your poem. Your comments on what your psychiatrist friend said make sense to me.

Lenny, Joe wants you to write and I do, also. He and I both get lonesome, and mail from friends is a real morale booster when things become impossible. I know your wonderful wife probably prods you occasionally and I hope she can get you started soon. So, let's do a favor for the boys overseas. OK?

Joe, one final note. First class mail is flown out here from San Francisco.

So, I would get your letters about one day after Lea would. However, Rob can send them on to me via air mail all the way, and I don't mind at all getting my letters in this manner. The important thing is that we keep writing.

Good Luck and lots of Prayers!

Ed

Lea, I hope Rob's visit to Lenny does some good. I felt that he was on the right track when I saw him last, and I still think he would be helped by being a part of us. I will leave Labrador to you and take New Zealand, myself.

Love,

Ed

Joe.Killeen–78250

N/S State Farm, VA 23160

17 October, 1964

(Lea, I am sending copies of this to you and Ed only. Joe's comments sound as if he (Joe) didn't expect this letter to be seen by Lenny. I will write about Lenny in my next letter to Joe.

Rob)

Dear Voices…I give up! How? Memory? I've read *The Prophet*, but have never owned a copy… A friend, named Charlie Miller, taught me to revere Gibran. He claimed "The Prophet" can aid my life situation. On one occasion, he took a mood of my lesser angel to prove his point. It was on a day last summer. Our gang was pulling (via picks and shovels) a grade level at a construction sight. The sun was hot, the air close—suffocating, the ground dry, yielding little. It was like chipping rock. Each chip was a miniature blast, spraying fragments into faces and eyes… Nearby, a bulldozer, parked, idle, its presence teasing, its silence tormenting. Could it not do in hours what we labored days to accomplish?…Senseless labor, senseless heat, sweat, dirt, filth!…Senseless, idle, silent bulldozer…Prison: that naked truth that spells out a man's shame, and the passions of guilt that frustrate and destroy a man's right to complain. No use to complain, just continue to swing and chip! Yet, I complained to Charlie. He listened as I cursed our sad estate and the labor to which we were enslaved. But, instead of echoing my complaint, he quoted: "Always you have been told that work is a curse and labor a misfortune, but I say to you that when you work, you fulfill a part of earth's furthest dream, assigned to you when that dream was born." He then added this, "You're white, I'm black; but here, together, we're mud. Not dirt! But clay—potter's clay—to be worked, shaped. This labor you call senseless frees the mind to think, discuss, evaluate and prepare for that 'furthest dream!' No time to complain. Just swing and chip—and shape!"... Take this account as a symbol of my gratitude for, I no longer have access to my friend or his edition. Charlie is still in that gang, but I've been relocated to another area and job. (N/S kitchen clerk)... I am sensitive to the book, card and their personal messages, plus Ed and Rob's words that immediately followed... add another week to Ed's concern, Lea, and it adds up to worried voices. Are you all right? I sent you a voice letter on Sept. 27? Did it arrive?... Rob calls his moment for writing, "uninspired." Ed labels his own letter, "disjointed." Not so long ago, Lea termed her's "Wordy bit of trivia." To me, they're all a special something else. Lea's not the only letter-saver. I've not thought of parting with any Voice letters... Rob: "deep, cold, and black", author Bill Styron calls this, "drowning." When one approaches a jigsaw puzzle of a landscape, he assembles first those pieces easy to identify (trees, objects, etc.) The sky is hardest to complete, except for the clouds. One might offer Peter Marshall's view: "Sometimes God throws us into situations above our depth, then supplies the necessary ability to swim." Still, this depends on one's own spiritual unveilings... I will go to Lenny one day and do what he will not allow my pen to do. My letters reach inside him, but they cannot make Lenny respond. My person may. That doesn't mean that I or another can solve Lenny's dilemma, for one's own reason and passion are the rudder and sails of one's seafaring soul (Gibran, again). Each of us is a port that can offer harbor and rest for his long voyage. No need to stress the value of continued patience, understanding and LOVE—you all knew those well when you opened your ports to me... Lea, even with Salinger and Brown against Amendment 14—is it enough? Will it actually repeal the Rumford Act? Joe's Birth week Critique:

"What a fateful week this one has been.—
Alas, Khruschev's out and Wilson's in.
Mao Tse Tung adds an atomic rub:
While Russia orbits three in a tub.
'Quit while ahead', says manager Keane;
But fire Yogi? Why that is awful mean.
Still, all's not lost: hear that Nobel ring,
In praise of Rev. Martin Luther King!"
Edgar Allen Joe

(No date) Approximately October 15, 1964
(A note from Rob)

Lea,

Through a monumental blunder on my part, the note ABOUT Lenny in my last letter was sent TO him. I wrote and apologized. The attached letter is his reply. Perhaps my blundering has cleared the air.

His letter is open to many interpretations.

Rob

October 9, 1964

Hi, Rob,

For some thirty days, my partner here has been jabbing me in the ribs with a broom. (This in itself is unique because, normally she uses it for transportation.) She insists I owe you a letter of explanation, and, of course, I do.

Now, after the arrival of your letter from Newark, I know I must hurry this reply, because you are embarrassed, and I cannot allow that.

The only way I know to begin is, "Egad!"

Believe me, by comparison, William of Avon wrote a tragedy called The Comedy of Errors. Know this: if you had not discovered your error, you would never have known it.

When I received your letter a few days ago, I laughed heartily, because it was so like something I would do. But, a few moments later, I was shot back through time some twenty years to a date and place I do not remember. I recalled only a deep, momentary feeling. Once you and I were talking seriously about brothers and brotherhood, and you stated that we were as close or, perhaps, closer than brothers. I was startled because I had been thinking that very thought.

I have been privileged to experience this fine, warm feeling a second time. You were concerned for me, and I humbly thank you. However, I have misled you, and I apologize for it. In an effort to set things right, I'll try to tell you how things are with us. Golly, where to begin?

From the day we are born, each of us must travel a long, difficult road. For a long time, it has been a puzzlement to me whether some of us have a rougher road, or whether some of us are just less well equipped. Well,

81

whatever. This is not the time to go into that.

I started down said road and arrived at point X. Then, by a monstrous stroke of ill luck, my best friends came along at exactly the wrong time; or by the most amazing stroke of good fortune, my friends came along when I needed them most. Which? I'm not sure. I'll not go into the background of this, for it would serve no purpose now. It's sufficient for you to know that the course was charted before I met you all. I truly believe that knowing each of you helped delay the inevitable.

Ultimately, of course, there was something of a combined explosion and short circuit. Then, came the most difficult experience I've ever known. But, though I didn't know it at the time, my liberator had already been provided. Somewhere I read it's a rule of life that when one door is closed to us, another is opened. Well, when the door opened, my Joyce was standing there offering her hand. Looking back now it seems there are almost all positive results from this. The few negative ones are more inconvenient than serious. And, as you say, we learn to live with it. Over the years, I've been tested nineteen ways to breakfast, and the most disturbing revelation is that I am not able to reach my alleged potential because of little roadblocks. Therefore, I have a substantial sense of guilt about hiding lights, and bushels, and things. This bugs me considerably. But, what compensation I have—three priceless jewels and a life that fits well. Though I must admit there are times when I'm convinced we are possessed of devils. But, almost always it ends in laughter. I have been very lucky. I know so many unhappy people.

It's not easy to explain this thing about writing letters. I imagine some of it has to do with the many, many letters I wrote to Lea during the war. Remember, you all came into my life at a critical time, and she filled a great need. Also, those were times of supercharged emotion, and foreign lands, and manhood, and patriotism, and good-byes, and death. In my case, it was emotion racing emotion, side by side, down parallel tracks. Maybe it's a matter of letters plus youth plus 1944 yields—well who knows? Maybe it's all a secondary, indirect by-product of Pavlov or Pavlova or pavement.

To my mind, distance has come between us, but not time. And this is very comfortable. It's not a matter of drawing circles to close people out, as Joe suggested. Rather, it's just that the circle is getting so damned crowded with kids, and good neighbors, and good neighbors' kids, and good neighbors' neighbors, and a few dogs.

I don't know whether I've really written what I wanted to say. Stated simply, my dear friends have somehow become the enemy. And though I know it's the farthest thing from your mind, you make me uncomfortable.

This, then, is what I meant by my note, Rob. You all take me back to where I least want to go. Again, I sincerely regret having misled you. If this has caused you any anguish, I hope the pain is dulled by the great pleasure it gave to me. The standard of the 178th Field Artillery bears the motto, "True and tried." In a sense, I think our friendships are tried and true.

I believe the saying that a man can count himself fortunate if, in his lifetime, he has a friend. How wondrous to have had three. And this is reciprocal in thought, if not in action. See you.

Len

PS. Rob, Will you copy this and send it on to the others? After reading this far, you know why. I started out writing to you, Rob, but I find I meant it for everyone.

Los Gatos,
October 23, 1964

Dear Rob,

Good Grief! That is a stunt I would pull; it's totally inconceivable to me that you would. No matter! It was probably a prophetic twist of fate. Being married to a total fatalist, I suppose it was inevitable that I should become this way myself, so I can't but believe that the revelations in Lenny's letter were for the best—for him anyway. For my part, I agree with you that the air is cleared.

At the outset, consider this a "free letter." You don't owe me, nor do I want an answer, particularly. I simply feel compelled to make a few comments. I kind of hope all of you get the notion simultaneously, so that we all comment without benefit of one another's opinions. Here goes:

1) Lenny's style hasn't changed one bit in all these years. He still has a flair for expression which I can't help feeling sorry he hasn't exploited to its fullest. Still, there is less cohesion in his writing—perhaps lack of practice. (He says he has an emotional aversion to writing, which he subtly blames me for. I don't resent this; in fact I find this very easy to understand, and I am sorry.) I now understand, and I believe he is totally sincere. As I said in my last letter, these voices out of the past are bothering him beyond words. I also realize now how terribly inopportune my timing was, when I dealt him his most shattering blow by ending our engagement. The fact that it was six weeks before a fully planned wedding was inexcusable, really, and I have to

live with that. Strange. I never looked back, and I never considered what effect it would have on him. Me—the one who always considered herself kind and morally sound, incapable of hurting anyone. It's clear that he was not only hurt, he remains affected by it after all these years. As I read that paragraph, where he spoke of "supercharged emotion... foreign lands, manhood, good-byes, and death... letters, plus youth, plus 1944 yields......" I felt a little heaviness in my chest and a beginning lump in my throat. Maybe I have been suppressing some of this myself, I don't know. Or maybe I am just waking up to the result of an action of mine so long ago. I only know that it is very clear what I have suspected all along—that I am the flaw in this five-pointed friendship. Like the perfect five-pointed star in the heavens, its perfection is only an illusion. Up close, perhaps it would be better to say that two of the points are flaws, by virtue of their incompatibility. But, no matter all of this; things are as they are and all this philosophizing isn't going to serve any purpose. Still, I can't help feeling sad that I am clearly responsible.

2) Perhaps I am being overly critical, or suspicious, or just a bit female, but did you detect a subtle, ever so faint tone of condescension in the letter? This is not to say that Lenny is not perfectly sincere and truthful in the letter. He is, and I can't exactly spell out what specific words make me feel that he is being (unintentionally, I know) just a tad patronizing. Or am I reading in? I'd be interested in knowing if any of you picked this up. I think the sentence that made me feel this way reads, "If this has caused you any anguish, I hope the pain is dulled by the great pleasure it gave me." ... Sincere, grateful for your friendship. Yes, and yet patronizing. It's all part of a very familiar pattern which I recall very vividly, and one which caused me no end of frustration in the past, because then, as now, it's an intangible something which I can't point to, but which somehow I am dead sure is there.

3) Each time he talked about "you three friends, I winced. Five minus one = three, eh? Ah, me. I guess I had that coming.

4) Are Marlene and Joyce getting the enjoyment out of these letters that Bill is? He looks forward to them as much as I and more and more he is getting to know and like you fellows. His reaction to Lenny's letter was—as I would have expected- wise, unemotional, accurate. He detects the quality I spoke of in paragraph two. Interesting since much of my relationship with Lenny has never been discussed.

5) Rob, one last point. I know you well enough to know that you are too full of innate good sense to feel bad about all of this. Indeed, you did us a service, for a breath of fresh air has blown through all of this. This is an

extremely revealing letter. Some day, I shall see you again (you are making a trek out here with Marlene and the kids, aren't you?) and I shall talk with you more about this then. One thing I know for certain, however — In spite of all Lenny's compliments and warmth, he still resents YOU the most—for the many things that he sees in you and not in himself. I won't pursue it now, but I may some day.

6) I have kept a file containing all of these letters, an idea I got from you, my friend. From time to time, I sit down and read them over. Lenny's letter is another worthy bit of literary work to add to the collection. He writes extremely well, and he has a flair for the dramatic—always has.

7) And that dear Rob, is all I have to say—for the moment. I had intended to send this only to you, but I'll make some copies—just in case. I think I will send them. Good night.

Lea

Los Gatos
October 25, 1964

Dear Joe, Rob, and Ed,

Gee whiz! The penalty for being moderately reliable is that a slip up is all the more noticeable, I guess. Sorry I was so tardy the last time. I'm responding the same day, this time. I am touched by your concern, but be assured, I am just fine. My working in the office has taken away some of the financial strain of Bill's new practice, and I am so busy, I don't have time to worry (except about the election, that is). Rob, if, after the degradation of this campaign, you wind up voting for Goldwater, or even not voting at all, I think I shall have lost faith altogether. He cannot be trounced soundly enough. He should be routed, while men like Keating, Romney, Taft, etc. be reelected. The whole election process is a mess—using Baker and Jenkins to smear Johnson, exploiting recent racial strife by implying that Johnson condones riots; all of it, has a nightmarish quality. Enough! I will stop ranting and hope I don't have a stroke before the election.

Joe, I can't tell you how delighted I am that *The Prophet* was a good choice. I love it, having memorized some special lines of it. It was a lucky guess on my part, but I thought it might be something that would speak to you, too. I hope it gives you the comfort it has given me, and may you hear our Voices in the words. I am sure that Lenny not giving permission to add his name had nothing to do with you. (I have no mind to go into more on this.)

The story about your friend who quoted from *The Prophet* was touching. Much of what you say about work freeing the mind to think, discuss, evaluate is very real to me. I see your reaction to Lenny's note to Rob was similar to mine. I now believe that he will never be able to accept me in any way. It saddens me because he is also denying himself you three. So long as he is unable to face events of 20 years ago, he will not be free of fetters. On the other hand, so what? Many people have repressed pasts and lead relatively happy, productive lives anyway. Why not Len? I am for leaving him alone. That, after all, is what he asked us all to do, in effect, in that letter. Strangely enough, Bill was very impressed by Lenny. He liked him at once.

As for Prop. 14, I don't know. I am afraid it will pass, and if it does, it will repeal the Rumford Act, the Hawkins Act, and the Unruh Act, and infinitely more. Every major religion, every worthwhile social and civic organization has come out against it. We'll just have to see. Bill and I have done all we can—hold coffees, have No on Prop 14 stickers on the car, sign in the yard, etc.

Your birthday rhyme was darling, Joe. I chuckled half the afternoon over it. I am looking forward to Ed and Rob's comments on Lenny's letter and yours. Weren't we smart to have devised this clever way of corresponding?

Fondly,
Lea

Okinawa
Saturday, October 31, 1964

Dear Voices

I read Lea's comments before I started to write my own, so I guess I have been influenced by them. I have been pondering the meaning of Lenny's letter, working on my response. I am not sure I fathom his hopes or fears entirely.

This is an edited letter that I've been working on for several days. I think I have come to a better understanding doing it that way. It might also serve as a point of departure as to where we ought to go next. Rob, I am glad the accident occurred, since now things are out in the open. In the past, Joe and I have tried to force his hand, which I think may have been a mistake, which could bring about the end or the rebirth of a friendship, but, either way, it will prevent us from causing pain to one we all feel a deep concern for. Here are my observations:

Lenny attempts to open the letter on a light note. His immediate concern for you, Rob, indicates that the bond can never really die between the two of you. He becomes quite sentimental about it, but quickly wrenches away as he says he has misled you. Why does he withdraw? I guess we have to guess.

I assume point X to be high school. Lenny is referring to the period when he discovered the truth about his father (what? infidelity?), and it collided head on with his religion and his love for his mother. He then points out that we helped to delay the inevitable explosion, the breakdown we know occurred in the mid to late fifties. His references to his wife suggest she is not someone who challenges his opinion of himself. She seems to love him with a quiet acceptance, which he needs, and for this I am glad.

Then Lenny tells us the stark truth about his not accepting himself, feeling as though he hasn't reached his potential. This gives me particular pain as I have, in retrospect, been very inconsiderate of him. Old undiplomatic Ed and his big mouth has in our few meetings been quite the braggart as to how well things go with me and how well my plans for the future are laid. Lenny really feels bad that he has not made more of his life.

Actually, Rob, I feel that you cause him more frustration than any of us. Even though he feels a strong bond with you, he is envious of what you have made of your life. I think he is also a bit envious of Joe's ability to adjust to the situation he is in and make the best of it. Even Lea, though unmentioned, is probably a threat to Lenny by the way we men praise her in our letters. We make a good case for a charming, brilliant woman who might have been his wife, had he, in his opinion, utilized his talents fully.

The next paragraph is an enigma. Not only does it ignore Lea while indicating our friendship still is important to him, but it shades from happy to sad, to thankful. When he says he knows so many unhappy people, is he attempting to pull others to his own level, where he can feel comfortable, so he can rise above it? I know, Rob, that several times in my last conversation with him, he mentioned that he thought you were dissatisfied with your present state and would be happier if you were teaching.

The beautiful prose of the next paragraph is Lenny's real talent. All the pathos of our lost youth is in those few short sentences. Actually, he is right in feeling that the war catapulted us into manhood with no time for transition, and it's not hard to accept that this could hurt an already badly scarred personality. I think that all those wounds will prevent his ever being able to stand the pain of direct communication with you, Lea. You, more than any of us, bring back the pain of those old hurts; you filled the greatest need. Then, too, we don't try to avoid looking at our lost youth; its pain and its joy, in day-to-day existence. Lenny gives the impression that he does, maybe because he has to. As he says, we take him back to where he least wants to go. My question now is, can we, in the name of love and friendship do this to him, or should we listen to his strong plea to be left alone? The final point was made when he refers to his friendship with us in the past tense, "How wondrous to have had three." At first, as I read the letter, I feared I detected signs of schizophrenia, but now I am convinced I see a man torn between two conflicting desires, but not himself split. Now, I do not know where to go with this. I am tempted to write Lenny, but I won't until I have heard from each of you. And probably, I won't, anyway.

Lea, on rereading your letter, I don't think you were the cause of anything—just the catalyst. I am glad for you that you are where and what you are. I know what you mean about the patronizing tone in Lenny's letter, and I don't know what to make of it. You were closest to him, and you recognized it as something that you experienced before. I just don't know. Yes, Joyce enjoys being included in this letter exchange. She has enjoyed it, and it reinforces her desire to come to San Francisco next summer in hopes of really getting to know you in person.

Joe, you are not only of potter's clay, you have been fired in the kiln and have become a thing of beauty. What was mud is now fine china, fragile but beautiful. Don't let yourself break. The next time I write, the election will be over, and Lea will be a calm, sensible woman again. My teaching is going well, and I am as lonesome as hell for my family. Such is the life of an ersatz bachelor. Only 40 more weeks to go.

Sayonara,
Ed

November 3, 1964
Election Day

Dear Joe,

A few hours ago, I cast my vote for Goldwater. Please, no cursing, no feelings of sorrow for me, I have said very little about politics in my letters, as indeed in my daily conversations. Permit me a few thoughts about the country we live in. First off, let me say that I thought the choice of candidates this time left much to be desired on both sides. Goldwater? His choice of

Miller as a running mate was poor. Am I to like his talking against farm subsidies and yet wanting a copper price support in Arizona? What am I to think about talk of excessive government spending, but support of the Central Arizona Water Project? And I deplore his changing his stand on support for social security almost daily. Johnson? I don't like a man in government making a personal fortune in businesses which are closely regulated by governmental regulatory bodies, or who twists facts to get as much advantage as he can, as in the Lockheed A-ll story. Nor do I admire a man who tries to play the role of all things to all men. And why go with a 30-year old farm subsidy program that has failed miserably? Just what is wrong with striving toward a balanced budget or talking about the weaknesses of the whole social security set up? Neither party has any corner on the "best" plans. The liberals need the conservatives to keep from flying off into the wild blue yonder, to keep in perspective man as he is. The conservatives need the liberals so that the status quo doesn't become the way of life, so allowance is made for the fact that man can be better than he usually is. I have no doubt that I voted for the losing candidate. So be it. I will not, friend Lea, shoot myself because Johnson wins, even though I suspect I feel about him as you do about Goldwater.

And with this brilliant start, let's talk about the "Lenny fiasco." When I discovered my error, I wrote to apologize to Lenny for having been so crude in allowing him to see the postscript to you, but I did not say I was sorry for wanting to help him. I have read both Lea's and Ed's comments, but let me write some semi-independent musings:

My first reaction was to feel ashamed. How proud and egotistical of me to think that I should sit in judgment of him! In my great wisdom, I could easily see that here was a man with problems. In the same way that I brashly approached Joe, I would offer my friendship; everything would get better! But it didn't work out that way—my offer of friendship was rejected, and I sit back in stunned silence. The man I thought would want my friendship doesn't want it, and I am embarrassed and ashamed.

I try to put myself in his place. Here are four old friends; two of them are moderately successful in their business careers (probably more than he), apparently happily married. One of them is in prison, but apparently has gained some insights into life, which have made him the conqueror of his surroundings. The last friend is the one who really hurts, the one who made a dent in his personal armor, and apparently she is happily married. Just what is the incentive for Lenny to want to rejoin the group? Not much, I fear, for a man who doesn't want his past thrown up to him by our very existence. I suspect Lenny is no different from the rest of us, except in ways that we have no right to judge. All of us live with our own frustrations about decisions made and courses followed. So be it. Lenny has had to find his own solutions to his problems—by himself. Whatever the problems, and whatever the means of solution, he has fashioned his present life with the boundaries imposed by those solutions. Much as it may bother our own sense of importance, it is entirely possible that our intruding presence may not be desirable or beneficial.

So, just what are we to do? Do we force ourselves on him? Does Lea alone back out? Do we all back out? But, let me first comment on Lea's and Ed's letters on the subject.

Lea, I assume you sent copies of your Oct. 23 letter to Joe and Ed, so let me comment paragraph by paragraph.

1) Lenny writes VERY well—what a pity the talent is apparently wasted. The flaw in our friendship is not you, but is in Lenny's failure to accept us (including himself) as we are. The weakness is in him, not in you.

2) A tone of condescension in his letter? I never even thought about it. If it is there, it is a defense mechanism for him; so be it. I just hope I don't display the same attitude; I've enough problems of my own. Condescension usually masks inferiority feelings. Enough said on the subject.

3) Yes, THREE friends, designed to cut you to the quick as you read it. Childish behavior.

4) Marlene still censors all incoming and outgoing mail, and if you keep on blabbering, Lea, I won't have any secrets left.

5) Lenny still resents me? Why not Ed? or Joe? If it be so, I suspect it goes back to high school, when your half-hearted crush on me must have left a deep mark on him. That I can understand. If he resents my being reasonably intelligent, red-haired, short, and nearsighted—that I don't understand. I didn't make life's ground rules.

6) You are still very good for my morale.

Ed, your masterpiece of a letter dated Sat. Oct. 31 arrived today. It was well worth the rewriting. Let me comment on it:

Sending the note to Lenny a Freudian slip? Perhaps, but mostly it was forgetfulness during a busy workweek. I don't feel he misled us. We misled ourselves. He never tried to force a renewal of the old friendships. We were the ones in our own egotism who couldn't conceive of a real reason why he wouldn't want to be one of us again. We were the ones who assumed he had buried any thoughts about that soul-searing rejection by Lea. If there is more frustration about me, Ed, I am sure it is a combination of reasonable business success coupled with feelings about Lea's past feelings about me—which he couldn't control. Then along comes Joe, whose successful adaptation to his present painful circumstances is another twist of the knife in Lenny's mental ribs. I agree, he is in no shape to accept Lea as a friend, nor do I see this a possibility in the near future. The sore has festered too long. It could be cleaned out, but I don't know if it ever will be.

I suspect that Lenny has buried a lot of unpleasant thoughts inside himself. He has fashioned a happy, yet frustrated life, doing well in the little sphere he has built for himself. Going outside that sphere, he runs headlong into those frustrations, and he retreats to safety within that sphere. We, unfortunately, represent that outside space. Why should he want to dig up all the painful memories? If I were in his shoes, I think that I might well do exactly what he is doing, telling us to mind our own business.

But, what is to be done about all this mess? For me, the easy way out would be to write a letter to Lenny, telling him that I was now more aware of his feelings, mixed as they are, about all of us. I would then bow gently out of the picture, asking him to contact me if he wanted to change the situation, and at the same time assuring him that I would keep in touch with him. What I really want to do, however, is see him at Christmas and see if there is anything better to do than following what I just outlined.

Enough of this. Joe, I have not yet heard about the outcome of the August parole hearing. My prayers have been with you, my thoughts of you. If turned down, when is the next time? Joe, Joe, we're pulling for you.

Edgar Allen Joe, you are second on my list of favorite poets, pushed out only by that West Coast Whiz, Edna St. Vincent Frey. I hope you are aware that *The Prophet* was entirely Lea's idea, Your delight simply shows her understanding of you. I am toying with the idea of buying a copy. Quick— Lea just fainted! Did you get the transcontinental copy of *By Love Possessed* that I sent? You now owe her 95¢—it's out of my control. Talk to her about financing it.

Ed, That mess in Vietnam gets worse and worse, doesn't it? That hit-and-run attack on the airstrip shook up a lot of the brass here in the U. S. The American public is getting tired of seeing American lives just dribbling away. Something will have to be done.

Lea, Johnson has just swept the country, apparently. What more do you want of me? Down on my knees? This whole letter has been for you.

Usual travels for our family, some sadness (I lost my grandmother, whom

I visited in Washington DC recently.) I respected and loved her. Her life of 89 years spanned many of the most significant inventions and discoveries made by man, and I will miss her.

Good night, my friends.

Rob

Joe.Killeen–78250
N/S State Farm, VA 23160
8 November, 1964

Dear Voices,

"A man can scrape, scratch, hammer, and claw his way to freedom from everything but himself." This is the theme of the French movie, *Night Watch*. Check for it in your travels. The critics rate it highly... The defense mechanisms of disturbed salamanders often corrupt Pavlovian theories, to fit their own rationalizations... Ed, I agree with your Freudian slip theory. It speaks what we've always known—Rob's hero is Truth. No wedge of Truth can split the kind of friendship described by Lenny. Yet the breach is there, and we wonder why. "What might have been is an abstraction—remaining a perpetual possibility" (T.S. Eliot) If any of you had written me several years earlier, I would not have answered. If a man wants to resent himself (Lenny—"hiding bushels, and things") how does he do it and survive? Resent others, that's how! It's much more convenient and nastier. Pay no attention to Lenny's "had three," Ed. Salamander language is governed by rehabilitation, not grammar—past and future are eternally present... Lenny hopes to make Lea an "unperson" (Orwell, 1984). He's trying to vaporize her, but it won't work (even if it were possible, I think Lea has all the qualifications of a real "cloud 9")... Lenny jokes of the broom that his Joyce jabs with and rides. No matter how it reads, we see a magic wand and unfurled wings—and this is exactly what Lenny intends. Therefore, follow Ed's fine critique and see how subtle Lenny's subconscious is... Rob built that star you speak of, Lea, and he has instilled in each of us the desire to keep its points intact... Lenny's real desire is no less the same... Solution? Who knows? Time, maybe! And Lea's suggestion: let him be. This apparently is what Joyce is doing. Forward no voice letters on to him. Write him only if he writes. Yet, do visit him whenever any of you (except that "unperson") are in Pittsburgh. Lure him but don't speak on any painful subjects, unless he opens up himself... If Ed's analysis is correct, Lenny's letter may be a beginning, not an ending. Port lights may use a lot of candle-power, but never in vain… Rob, the transcontinental copy of *By Love Possessed* arrived. 95¢? What are you trying to do, Rob, make a commission? The cover says 75¢ Cheapskate! I had planned on buying up your equity—you're not as nearsighted as you pretend. Send me a bill in 1968, Lea; 75¢ represents three-days pay. I'm only 30 pages into the book, so I'll comment later… Ed, you, Lea and Rob say things that make it difficult for me to get my head through these cell doors. I need to justify what all of you say, for these are still cell doors I pass through each day. Your word "fragile" is similar to one of the multiple-uses of Lea's word "sensitivity." It's taken slow-cook to temper this crockery, but it's a lot tougher than fragile. Maybe it can be broken, but I think old age will decay it first… I'm still up for parole—but have heard nothing. My sister, Dorothy, had an interview with the board last month—they told her it would be a while before any decision is reached. "The time has come, the walrus said, to talk of many things: of ships and shoes- and Joe ……, and cabbages and kings—And why the sea is boiling hot—and whether Joe has wings." (Poor Alice, will she ever forgive me?) Political comments? No space. Dean Sayer sums up what Rob and Ed have said by calling the election a "sterile" choice. I agree. Like Ed and Lea, I still would have voted for Johnson, had I the privilege. Lea, I 'm so sorry about Prop. 14. I liked your Republican choices, except for Keating. Long live the Kennedys! Happy Birthday, Rob—I say belatedly—How about birth dates from all the Voices?

Amen!

Joe

Smoother Sailing

Okinawa
Wednesday, 25 November, 1964

Dear Joe and all,

Now that the election is over, we can drop politics from our list of things to write about. One final comment though: I'm glad Rob had the courage of his convictions. I don't think his vote puts him in the lunatic fringe, and I don't think we would all be such good friends if we didn't accept our differences. All of us have always had a social conscience all of our lives, and we all feel sorry that human rights must be subject to legislation in our country. So, for now, so long politics!

My personal situation continues good, and in the near future, I will be moving into a new BOQ, where I will have central heat and air conditioning. It will also be very convenient on the nights when I teach. I will be making a trip to Japan next week to a place called Camp Fuji, at the base of the mountain. I was there in the 50's and it should be fun to see it again. The temperature might be a problem. The coldest it gets here is about 55°, and there will be knee-deep snow at Camp Fuji. I'll have to dig up some long johns.

Friday, 27 November. The day after Thanksgiving

The turkey was good, the shrimp cocktail was fine, and I was absolutely miserable! I have a good idea what Christmas will be like! Hell, I am afraid! Joe, I know you know how I felt. You go through it every special day also. I know I have an advantage in that I have some idea of when mine will end. According to current policy, I should be eligible to go home in August of next year. As for your situation, I pray the Parole Board will report on you favorably—and soon.

I would love to go home by ship by way of San Francisco. It would be far easier for Joyce to meet me at Treasure Island as she did last time, than to have to make the trip to Travis AFB. However, I won't turn down any offer!

Rob, my Joyce has some thoughts on the subject of Lenny. She feels we should let him alone as far as the letters are concerned, but continue to send him greeting cards and call him when you are in Pittsburgh. If you do go, it is at least a starting point. I don't think it can hurt him to know we care.

God be with you all,

Ed

Los Gatos
The Day after Thanksgiving, 1964

Dear Joe,

Thanksgiving was lovely, as usual. Friends of ours drove the 100 miles from Travis Air Force Base (near Sacramento) to spend the day with us, and a young student at San Jose City College whom we knew in Germany joined us, as well. Nine around a small dining room table was a bit of a squeeze, but it was fun. Tonight, the official opening of "fat season," we had left over turkey, stuffing, cranberries,—the works, and the carcass is in a huge pot on the stove evolving into soup.

I was going to make some comments on your comments about Lenny, Joe, but I think we have exhausted that subject and ought to give it a rest. I was struck by the similarity in everyone's analysis, though, and have concluded that we have no right to force the issue. We all have wounds in our backgrounds on which we slaver balms and salves in an effort to escape the pain of "cleaning them out." If doing this enables him to function in his life, then I am for leaving him in peace to find his way. In the end, we must all seek cures for our ills within ourselves—in our own time, at our own speed, and Lenny is no exception. If that ever happens, you three will hear from him in due course. I never will, but when all is said and done, I can't say I blame him. And that is that!

Joe, I am glad Rob decided he could bear to part with his favorite book and mine, *By Love Possessed*. I have a hunch it may not be your cup of tea, either. Let me know what you think, and be honest! I would like to know what you think of Arthur Winner, the central character. I found him somewhat annoying, but in some ways my kind of man—reasonable, unemotional, but having much feeling, none-the-less, a man who quietly functions with no fanfare. He is a bit stuffy for my taste, and just a tad of a bigot (goodness, "just a tad " is ridiculous, really! Isn't that like being just slightly pregnant?)

I'm reading a very interesting book now, by the way. It is a biographical account of the friendship of Tchaikowsky and a woman named Nadejda von Meck, based almost entirely on the correspondence they exchanged during a 13 year period. The most fascinating thing about it is that they never met! Yet their correspondence was full of tender endearments, expressions of devotion, etc. it is entitled, *"Beloved Friend."*

Joe, if you have a particular book that you are simply dying to read, and it is unavailable at the library there, please let me know, and I'll get it for you, if I can. (Paper back, of course.)

Some comments to others:

Ed: I'm actually rather glad you are being kept busy over there. Maybe you will be too necessary to spare if anything explodes in Vietnam, as I fear it will, shortly. Keep well. The weeks are flying by, and I am looking forward to that visit from you and Joyce in half a year or so.

Rob: After suppressing a gagging sensation over your Goldwater comments, I turned the page and you became just the same old Rob again. I will spare you my rebuttal arguments and the blizzard of clippings I had, which I just tossed out!!! The election is a dead issue and Goldwater is a politically extinct entity, hopefully safely back in Arizona where he can tend to the store and won't have to explain his every memo. (Looks like I already commented on it, doesn't it? Sorry!) Your commentary on the "Lenny fiasco" was literate, clearly outlined and accurate. Have I ever told you that you strike heads of nails dead on? Thank you, too for all the unsaid compliments, Rob. (I read them, even though they weren't there.) What do you mean blabbering?? Moi? And Joe: Whatever decision is reached regarding your parole, we are with you. I pray it is favorable, but if it isn't, well, the world won't come to an end. We'll all feel hurt and disappointed, but we'll go on. Just please let us know. Now, I think I smell the turkey soup, so I had better go and check it, before it boils over. I already have.

Love from,

Lea.

PS The typing bears excusing. Will you? Every Achilles has his heel, as the saying goes.

Weston, CT
December 3, 1964

Dear Joe,

Do you realize that it was just a year ago that the "voices" came alive for all of us? I'm not very good at expressing myself, but I want to say how fortunate I feel to be a part of the "Voices." It has been a very satisfying thing to be part of this rebirth of friendship. I never cease to marvel at the chain of events that brought us all back together again (and I include our reluctant Lenny in the "all," for I am sure that try as he will, he will not be able to lock us out of his mind forever.)

I'm waiting for Lea's burning reply to my political wanderings, but alas, no answer. It may be that she is just too disgusted to write! My birthday came up November 6th, and I was happy to see that this year, she didn't send me a card for my "November 19th" birthday. She has had me confused with someone else for several years, which I must say, I don't find very flattering. Thanks for the card, old girl, it arrived right on time!! Next year, I will be Jack Benny's age–39.

We had our usual Thanksgiving family get together in Richmond, stopping on the way down and back in Wilmington to visit with brother Karl and his gang. The Thanksgiving in Richmond was delicious, and the warm weather a welcome change from the brisk Connecticut temperatures. Wilmington on Friday was another mob scene, this time with sixteen people and two dogs. Somehow, they found room for all of us to sleep (beds, cots, folding beds, mattresses on floors, sleeping bags) and as usual, we were well fed. Nice to be together even for a few hours. Glad we had made the trip.

I am really tired tonight, and I think I will sign off now. Ed's Joyce is bringing her gang here for supper this coming Sunday, and before I write again, I expect to have been in Pittsburgh. I hope to talk to Lenny. Take care of yourselves.

Goodnight, my friends,
Rob

Okinawa
Tuesday, 8 December 1964

Dear Joe and all,

The last letter I wrote to you all was rather miserable, and I feel I owe you a more pleasant missive. Please excuse my self-pity in those recent comments. I feel much better now, having just returned from Japan. The trip was pleasant, a much-needed change of pace, as well as climate, and I have returned refreshed and determined not to let my loneliness get me down again. I visited old haunts, camped out in a heated tent near Mount Fuji in clear, cold weather, our vistas spectacular. While we experienced a snowstorm, most of the days were pleasant, cold, but bright, and the people were as friendly and polite as I remember them.

Lea's letter from the day after Thanksgiving was awaiting me when I got back, and her calling the coming holidays "fat season" reminded me that I am gaining weight and need to watch it.

Hope this Christmas season finds you all well and happy. Joe, I am still praying that the parole board gives you a Christmas present that will make us all happy. Merry Christmas to all and to all a good night.

Sayonara,

Ed

Joe......–78250

N/S State Farm 23160

20 December, 1964

Dear Voices,

The writer of the Pentateuch describes the first rainbow as the token of the covenant of God with Noah. Some think that it had never rained upon the earth until the flood, and that the rainbow was a new phenomenon. If so, with what joy it would be welcomed whenever thereafter, showers began to fall! Thus, symbolically, the rainbow has come to be known as the "Pledge of Peace"... Suppose this Genesis account of the rainbow were true. Why then has this peace remained so elusive to the minds of men? Or, is it some sort of fairy-tale or romantic ideal that can never know reality? Could it be that the meaning of peace is too simple for man to grasp? Euripides wrote: "O peace, thou givest plenty as from a deep spring; there is no beauty like unto thee." Yet peace eluded Euripides...A multitude of angels sang, "Peace on earth..." that first Christmas morn. Years later, before his departure, Jesus left behind this legacy: "My peace I give unto you." Paul called it, "the peace that passeth understanding." Dante tried to explain peace by saying: "In thy will, O Lord, is our peace." Franz Werfel continuing that idea, gave this motto to peacemakers: "Not revenge, but expiation, not punishment, but penance."... Krishna claimed that man only attains peace when he sheds all longings and moves without concern, from the sense of "I" and "Mine." Karl Marx denounced individualism, sought to promote collectivism. Only through selflessness, thought he, could man achieve peace. Christians unknowingly go along with Marx when they teach that one should LOSE his identity in Christ. Actually, when Christ looked upon the multitudes, He saw individual souls, and He wanted each to find his identity in Him. Being a collectivist does not guarantee peace, nor does being an individualist. (Nor do the young "avant garde" souls offer concrete solution with their amoral, anarchistic, gentle, over—civilized—to the point of decadence—approach). Yet, peace must be an individual experience; coming from within, as Tolstoy might say, not from without. Its witness must be magnetic, attracting others; and thereby be reproduced, enjoyed and shared with others... Spinoza caught Christ's meaning. Spinoza wrote: "Peace is not an absence of war; it is a virtue, a state of mind, a disposition for benevolence, confidence, justice." Spinoza offers the rainbow along with Christ and Tolstoy. Judy Garland searches for the secret of the "Pledge of Peace" when she sings, "Over the Rainbow." We hum the beautiful "Moon River" and thereby commit ourselves to the same search, for "we are (all) after the same rainbow's end."... And so let these words of Giovanni be my Christmas hope and offering to all of you who are my friends: "There is nothing I can give you which you have not; but there is much that, while I cannot give, you can take... No peace lies in the future, which is not hidden in this present instant. TAKE PEACE! "

I sent the above words to my family last year—not out of any illusion of talent on my part, but rather as an expression of a tranquil heart. Christmas '63 was the first anniversary of my reunion with my family...And now, Christmas '64 is the first anniversary of my reunion with the Voices of the Past. The tranquillity of Christmas last has grown richer and sweeter as a result... I humbly thank each of you for allowing me to take additional peace in the awareness of friendships that have passed beyond the twenty-year mark... Lea, the Dimling's chocolate reminder of Pittsburgh was almost as sweet as our friendship... How I need to justify the faith you all have allotted me! I will write again soon in answer to all your letters—and I'll try to be less overwhelmed by sentimentality.

Love to all,
The Joe

Okinawa
Wednesday, 30 December 1964

Dear Joe and all,

Another year draws to a close and it is with mixed feelings that I watch it go. I have to get rid of it in order to get back to my family, just as you must see it go to get closer to the freedom you desire.

Since I last wrote, there has been a change in my situation and I am now standing by on 12 hours alert to head south to a ship in the South China Sea. If there is a big flap, I will probably go within a few hours, and before any of you know what is going on. I am going to be the G-1 (assistant chief of staff for personnel) for the 9th Marine Expeditionary Brigade which is our ready force backing up the Vietnam operation. The present address you have for me will continue to get my mail to me, so use it until I send you a new one. It's sort of a plum for me, because it is a Lt. Colonel's billet, and as you know, I am only a Major.

Meanwhile, I continue my normal work and things remain quiet.

Christmas turned out to be a reasonable holiday, and I sort of enjoyed it. We had a small office party, and I went to the Episcopal service at midnight, getting up at 10 AM to open my presents. Incidentally, Lea, I have not received the package from Pittsburgh you mentioned, but it takes six weeks for surface mail. After brunch, I took a load of troops to a leper colony that is located about two hours drive from here on the northern end of the island. We took presents for the kids and some used clothing. The children put on a little show for us, singing carols in Japanese, and I assumed these were healthy kids of some of the patients. It turns out, they had leprosy, too, whole families, and it gave me pause. Some of the kids here are separated from their families, and it nearly broke my heart. Needless to say, I stopped feeling sorry for myself and for you right then. The only good thing about it all was knowing their disease was treated in time for them not to be disfigured, but there is no cure for the disease. Maybe the future will bring one; I hope so, for the sake of those kids.

I sent Lenny a card but didn't get one in return; I'm curious if any of you did. I am anxious to know if Rob was able to see him over the holidays on his Pittsburgh trip. The weather out here has remained warm—short sleeve weather. That makes it easier on Christmas, as it did not feel like that time of year. I have a feeling it will be really hot down south. I confess I am looking forward to shipboard life, and will probably get a tan. I also need to go on a diet, and I have always been successful with them aboard a ship.

Hope all of you have a good holiday, and may you all have a good new year.

Sayonara,

Ed

New Year and New Hope
1965

Los Gatos
January 2, 1965

Dear Joe, Ed and Rob,

I sense that this will be an entirely uninspired letter, and maybe a short one. No reflection on any of your letters, which are spread out in front of me. It's just that this is the "let down" time of the year, with the holidays over and the Christmas decorations looking tired and begging to be taken down. The rain is pouring down outside onto the already soggy terrain, and the kids are scrapping from sheer boredom. I don't feel sorry for myself, but I am not ebullient, either. I must say, that in general, people take their troubles with them wherever they go, but they are easier to deal with when the sun is shining!

Joe, your Christmas letter arrived after Christmas, but what a letter it was! My goodness, my friend, you are indeed well read! I dare say, you put us all to shame. Your admonishment to "take peace" (Inner peace) will stand us in good stead for this bright new year. As to your promise to be less sentimental this year, please don't. Sentiment is all that really matters, in the end. As to there being nothing else you can give us, take account of what you have already given all of us this year- this Voice-friendship, which had gone dormant prior to the end of 1963. One thing I am very sure of—all of us are richer than we were one year ago. Joe, you made no mention of your parole. Does this mean it wasn't granted? Or have you still received no definite word? I don't want to keep plaguing you about an already decided matter, so please assure me that we will know when you do.

I am glad the Dimling's Candy arrived in time. Ed's didn't, and I feel rather bad about that. Ed sent me a lovely calendar from Japan, with an embroidered scene on it that he said reminded him of Montalvo. I saw why when I looked at it. It was a scene in a large formal garden, with a little wooden bridge crossing a stream, and lots of tall evergreen trees, and a pagoda in the distance. I took both Ed and Rob on a walk through the Montalvo estate, and we crossed just such a bridge and climbed some craggy steps to a Gazebo (represented by the Pagoda on the calendar.) As you stand facing the main house at Montalvo, Joe, this scene is just to the left, going directly past the carriage house. Do you remember it? There is an old iron gate on the other side of the little bridge. It's a perfectly lovely scene, which I will take a picture of and send to you when I go there next.

104

Ed: The above comment to Joe is, of course, meant for you, too. I loved the calendar, and surprise gifts always are a special treat. The news in today's letter about your being on 12 hours notice is disquieting to say the least. I hate to believe we mean to broaden the hostilities in Vietnam! I can't see what purpose it would serve to assure the independence of a country that has given evidence of an inability to handle its independence. Vietnam simply doesn't seem able to govern itself, and we surely can't govern IT, or worse still, create a puppet! Thanks for writing Joe, and consequently—us! And Happy Birthday, by the way!

Rob: Sorry I muffed on your birthday so often. Glad I got it right this time. I may be thoughtful, but I have not been very accurate! Does this year hold any promise of a visit to Los Gatos—preferably with Marlene?

My Christmas was fine, of course. Guessed right for the kids by getting them skateboards. They got every kid on the block working on convincing their parents they "need" them now, to do "sidewalk surfing." Best gift was from a former student—a poinsettia plant with an attached note, thanking me for putting up with him and for treating him as a person, instead of just a teenager. He said I had helped him approach the human race as a whole. Can you understand why a plant from this particular boy sent my heart soaring?

And that's all I have to say on the advent of 1965. This year holds lots of promise for all of us, for Joe, most of all. Know, that this letter, while not the cheeriest, contains a healthy measure of devotion to you all.

Lea

Weston, CT
January 2, 1965

Dear Joe,

If you and Ed will forgive me, Joe, I'd like to say that the month of December flew by for me. Travels to Rochester, Minnesota, going from Richmond with a temperature of +75° to Rochester with a temperature of—12°. Fortunately, my days and evenings were filled with business matters—meetings and classes in the daytime and discussions at night. There were other trips, football games, dinner with Joyce and her brood and sundry church related activities for me and the rest of the family, so the time sped by. Tonight, I have to admit to getting older, because I'm too tired to even want to go out—and it's a Saturday night. There has been a light snow falling since noon, and I guess there is a three-inch covering on the ground now. Good to be in a nice, warm house with the Christmas hoopla behind us.

Took a trip to Pittsburgh on Dec. 28th, over largely clear, dry roads, where I had short conversations with Ed's mother and Lea's brother. Both are well and were glad to hear from me. One of my most satisfying moments there, was when I visited with Lenny, who goes by Len now. After our Mountmore dinner with the folks, I walked over to see him. In the two-hour visit, our conversation ranged over many matters. It was quite evident that the old bond of friendship was still burning brightly for both of us. I believe that Len is leading a good and comfortable life, a life well shaped to him, as he is. He is a happy man, yet filled with some frustrations (aren't we all?)—mainly those dealing with his vocation, feeling that he could have done more to prepare for a better job. His old love of writing is still with him, but he doesn't see the opportunity to hone that skill. One very concrete thing came out of our conversation; Len asked me to forward to him copies of all the letters from the group, and he told me it was all right to mention that request to all the others. At the same time, he warned me that he has a real block about writing letters, and did not want to join in the circle at this time.

I, for one, am going to honor his request—but I would make a further request of all the circle members. It seems silly for me to have to transmit letters from Ed and Lea to Len. I would like to request Ed and Lea to send copies of their letters to Joe direct to Len. On the other hand, I think that Joe should continue to write only to Lea, Ed, and me—and whoever receives Joe's letter should send a copy to Len as well as the others.

I know this sounds like a lot of beating around the bush, but I think it should be done. I want Len back in the circle, and this is a small price to pay for a beginning. I hope that as time goes by, he will feel freer to write letters, and really join us. Time will tell how things will turn out.

Joe, I am assuming that no news is good news as far as your parole hearing outcome is concerned. As an outsider, I am at a loss for words on that subject, so I will just keep my mouth shut. Good night, my friend.

Rob

Lea, this page of comments is for you—not for the other "voices." (handwritten)

Until today, I believed I was going to have a 2-day trip to San Francisco— but my plans have changed. Now it's off to Texas. Sorry, old bean.

My conversation with Lenny was good, and I hope to have another opportunity to see him fairly soon. He certainly has his problems—he sees his limitations, but can't break out of the bonds holding him. He is

EXTREMELY security-conscious.

I believe he wants to rejoin us—all of us, including you, but he has too many internal battles to fight at present. I further believe that patience and understanding will bring us all back together—but that in Lenny's case, he will have to set the pace—we can't force him.

You may be interested in knowing that he wrote you a 2-page letter in response to your note about Joe's birthday book—and then he tore up the letter. I THINK what he was trying to say was that he disagreed with what he perceives to be your reinforcing Joe's using philosophy as an escape mechanism from reality. After he wrote the letter, he felt you wouldn't agree with or understand his viewpoint—so rather than get into an argument, he just tore up the letter.

Lea, he cares about us—very much, but he has himself to fight most of all. Sorry I won't be able to visit, as I thought I would. My best to you and Bill and the boys.

Rob

Okinawa
Saturday, 16 January 1965

Dear Joe and all,

There will be a major change next week, since I will be doing some traveling. I leave Thursday for my new job. Joyce is convinced that everything will be all right, so she has not asked me to try to get my orders modified. The new address on the envelope is the proper one to use. But, I might be at sea, Joe, so don't write to me. Write to Rob or Lea, and they will send it to me. Otherwise they would have to wait until your letter reaches me before answering.

No word yet on the result of Joyce's breast biopsy. We are both very confident the tumor is benign, and I promise to let you know as soon as I know the results. Work has been going as usual—several interesting Congressional inquiries, but I am not at liberty to tell you about most of it. You might check Drew Pearson's column. He seems to get everything even before it happens!

Joe, thanks for the gift of that beautiful Christmas letter. I didn't send you a gift, but Joyce said she was sending you cookies. Did they come? Yes, I got my box of Dimlings and it was a great reminder of our Pittsburgh days. My waistline didn't need it, though.

Lea, you can write all the uninspired letters you want to me. I know Rob sends copies of his letters to Joyce; would you mind doing the same? She is living at the Wallingford, CT. address that I think you have. She may be too busy with the kids and with her worries about the biopsy to answer, but she will enjoy the letters. I must agree with you that I don't know what we are doing in Vietnam. I am just going to that area on orders from Uncle Sam.

Rob, I agree with you about Len, and I will send him copies of all the letters as I do the rest of you and hope for the best. We will be in Hong Kong the first week in February and will make a practice landing in Thailand in March. Then, it's probably on to Singapore. I am thinking of it being like an interesting cruise.

Sayonara,
Ed

Weston, CT
Sunday, January 31 1965

Dear Joe,

Hello from the frozen northland. We have about 6 inches of residual snow on the ground covered by a layer of snow-ice, making the walking hazardous. Last night the temperature dipped below the zero mark, with more of the same to come. The only ones happy about it are the skiers and the fuel-oil sellers.

I don't know what to include in my ramblings tonight, so I will just begin and see what happens. On Tuesday, January 5th, the doctor confirmed Marlene's pregnancy, and on January 12th, at noon, Marlene called to say that she was going to the hospital under doctor's orders. I hurried home, stopping to call Pittsburgh to see if Marlene's mother could come for a few days. She did, bless her, and later that day, the doctor confirmed that Marlene had a miscarriage. That afternoon, I sat in the living room and had myself a three-minute crying jag—unusual behavior for me, and I tried to analyze my reasons even as the tears flowed. There were many elements that went into my mood, but mostly sorrow and guilt. First of all, I knew that Marlene had lost the baby. Second, I had just opened a letter from Ed telling me of Joyce's forthcoming biopsy—and I empathized with their being separated by so many miles. Third, brother Bill's mother in law had just had a heart attack. And last, I knew that the next day, I was going to be leaving for a ten-day business trip, bringing about feelings of guilt and inadequacy. . Mix all this together, and they added up to enough emotion to break open the tear ducts. The business trip went well, but my mind was troubled the entire time. When I finally was ready to head for home, the airports were all socked in under a fog that was predicted to last for the next 24 hours. Ultimately, I took a bus to Dayton and flew from there, arriving home late, and tired, but happy to be home.

Joe: first of all, please forgive me for my inadequate expression of what your Christmas letter meant to me. I never express myself to my own satisfaction, but each passing year only makes me more certain that love and concern for our fellow men is one of the few ways to achieve happiness in ourselves. I have been waiting to hear about your parole hearing and thoughts of you have been in my mind many times during this past month. Please don't let my being inept at replying suggest any lessening of respect and concern for you. I do thoroughly appreciate your letters, receiving much pleasure from them.

Lea: I received your letter of January 2nd, and I've come to the conclusion that one of us (you!) has to change his writing date. Our letters seem to cross in the mail, and we're always a month out of phase by the time the next letters flow. Your comment about receiving the poinsettia plant from the former student struck a warm spot in my heart—it is such things that really make life worthwhile. I think I know exactly how you felt.

Ed, Joyce said she would get in touch with us as soon as she knows something from the biopsy report. Nothing new yet, but I am praying for you both. January, it seems, has its ups and downs for all of us. I am glad for this circle of friends, extended as it is half way around the world, and I hope I can contribute something to it. Friendship is a marvelous, mysterious things— for which I give constant thanks.

Good night, my friends,

Rob

PS for Lea: I am going to be in Pittsburgh during the latter part of this week and will try to see Lenny, time permitting.

At sea
Saturday, 30 January 1965

Dear Friends,

Please forgive the occasional skipping of the typewriter, but the ship is rolling a bit and things get out of balance. We are on our way from the coast of Vietnam to Subic Bay in the Philippines. We left Subic rather suddenly last week when the coup took place and moved over off the mouth of the Saigon River where we would be available if needed. Our primary mission would have been the evacuation of American dependents if things had gotten out of hand. Fortunately, they didn't so we are on our way back now and should he in port by Tuesday morning.

During the next few weeks we will continue to plan the landing in Subic. We will also be ready to run back to Saigon for the evacuation mission if necessary. Chances are that one more run to Saigon will cause us to have to postpone or cancel the landing with the Thais. I am not counting on a trip to Singapore, but I think there is a good chance of going ashore at Saigon. Why anyone would bring dependents over to a combat zone is something that I cannot understand. I would not even want them in Okinawa now. Especially with me down here. This exercise in February and March is called Jungle Drum III. No word from the Red Cross about Joyce and the biopsy.

Well, it is now Sunday, and we are still steaming east so things must still be going OK in Saigon, and we can go home for a while. Next week is the Vietnam New Year celebration, and we hope it will be quiet. They call it TET, and usually the Viet Cong declare a truce during the holiday.

Lea, please don't worry your pretty little head about me. I feel safer than I would on the Los Angeles freeway and I probably am. It is doubtful I will go ashore into Vietnam, and in any case, I am in the rear with the staff group where things should be quite safe. I am too much of a coward to get myself where I can get hurt. Physically I feel great. I like my job, and if only I knew what was going on at home, things would he fine.

Aloha,
Ed

Los Gatos,
February 4 1965

Dear Joe,

This will probably go on record as the first letter I have ever answered BEFORE the letter was received! Joe, where are you? Your letter is late, and I am wondering if it got lost somewhere.

To begin with, I owe all of you an apology. After reading all your letters, I feel like an utter fool for indulging myself in the "after holiday blues," for no reason at all. I hope you will forgive me. We are all well, Randy having recovered from another strep infection of the throat, and now he is lined up for a tonsillectomy over the Easter holidays. I am still gainfully employed as Bill's office nurse, having outfoxed myself by doing at least an acceptable job there. Neither he nor the other doctor sharing the office ever mention my leaving, although I gave notice just before Christmas. I fell for Dave's (the other doctor) hard luck story and some accompanying flattery, and I'm still here. Both of them bowl me over with help when I am obviously swamped, and I admit I enjoy feeling "essential." But, I have no intention of making this a career. I still teach a class in German (9–12 AM each Saturday), and I have retained one student 2 times a week at night. Teach German—now THAT'S what I really want to do!

The days pass quickly, since I am so busy, and I find I am ready for bed by 10 PM, lying there to do my day's reading until I get sleepy. Recommended books are Hermann Hesse's *Siddhartha*, and Erich Fromm's *The Art of Loving*. (Don't croak, Rob; the title is deceiving. It's a very gentle and moral book. I am sending *The Art of Loving* to you, Joe, as soon as I finish rereading it.) I bought this copy for you, but I lent my own copy to a young friend and former student to read (the one who sent me the Poinsettia for Christmas) and I am now trying to reread this through the eyes of a 17-year-old. He calls me from time to time to chat, and he brings me his themes to read; in my last conversation with him, he said he was 1/3 of the way through the book, and he promised to call me or come and see me to tell me what he thought of it. I find myself becoming increasingly interested in the perspective of teenagers—perhaps because I have one now. (Billy will be 14 in August.) I enjoy their fresh, enthusiastic outlook and I am sympathetic with their pains of approaching adulthood, and of course, I can learn much from these youngsters which will help me help my own boys in a few years. Most of all, I get a kick out of serving a purpose in these kids' lives: I'm a listener at a time when they need to express themselves to someone they respect, but one who won't dismiss them as "just teenagers." Their problems are real to them, just as ours were when we were all in high school.

Rob, I am so sorry about the baby, Bill's mother-in-law, and of course I share your concern about Ed's Joyce. But, what got to me most of all was the mental picture of you dissolved in tears. I understood your feelings and wished I could help. Still, I doubt that, were I accessible, I actually could have helped. When all is said and done, our problems are our own and have to be handled by ourselves. Twenty years ago, the picture of you crying would have made me cry. Now, I only understand. Only the manliest of men ever admit to tears. I'm glad I know you.

Ed, just how close will you be to Vietnam? Or is that classified?

And Joe, what of you? I expect your letter daily, and being a born worrier, I immediately assume something is wrong: You're ill or you were so sick at the stomach after reading *By Love Possessed*, that you couldn't bear to write. Or will the letter arrive tomorrow? Or did you send it to Rob, and he forgot to mail me my copy? No matter, I have already answered it—or rather am doing that now!! By the way, if you want me to send you *Siddhartha*, let me know. I will. Is there a library? Are you familiar with it?

Rob, thank you for calling my sister and brother. I miss them fiercely, at times. We're all three very different, but we have always been close. I am at the end of the paper and must go. Good night. My love is with all of you.

Lea

Los Gatos, CA
February 23 1965

Dear Joe,

For goodness sake, Joe, where are you? Over two months since you wrote your last Voice letter, and I am terribly concerned. Are you ill? If you are, is there anyone there who can write to us and tell us how you are? I was joking about being worried in my last letter, but now I am nearly in a panic wondering why. Have any of us offended you? You see? All kinds of thoughts crowd into my mind, and the only thing which will dispel my worrying, is a letter from you. Make it soon!

I must write to Ed immediately, too, for I am concerned about Joyce. As I wrote last time, I was awaiting word from Ed about Joyce and the surgery. Well, before my last letter found its way into the mailbox. I got a wire from the Red Cross to meet Ed at Travis Air Force Base at 2 PM the next day. (a Sunday) Bill was already there on Reserve duty, (it's about 100 miles away) I called Bill at Travis and told him the boys and I were coming to Travis and would be driving home with him. I had a friend drive me to the airport where I caught a shuttle bus to Travis. When I got there, Bill was already at the terminal, having met Ed there. We took Ed to some friends who live at Travis, where he was able to shower, shave, and clean up (and assign me the task of sewing a button on his shirt!) and then relax and catch his breath before the rest of the trek home. He called home and got the word that the surgery went well, the prognosis was good, so some of the terrible anxiety was relieved.

Our friends insisted we stay for dinner, after which, Bill, Ed, the boys and I all drove to S. F. Airport, where we saw to it that Ed got on the next flight out, and we said good-bye.

Joe, I am sorry not to have mailed you the book yet. It will be mailed in a few minutes, and I hope you like it. Rob better brace himself; a copy may find its way to him, too, since I know how impressed he is with my taste in literature! Nothing more to say except to ask you once again to write! I MISS YOU!

Lea

Wallingford, CT
25 February 1965

Dear Voices,

First of all, an apology. I have Joe's letter which Rob left here when he came up to visit Joyce and me last week. I will try to get it reproduced and include it with this letter. The trouble has been that Rob and I have both been beset by many things and neither of us has had time to get Joe's letter out to Lea and Lenny.

Now for the important news of Joyce. I am thankful to report that the radiologist and surgeon's reports are encouraging in their estimates of what the future holds for us. The operation was a simple mastectomy with no need to go into the muscular structure at all, except for some biopsy samples. All were negative including the nodes. Based on this, she will not have to undergo long radiation treatments. They will watch her for several months, and if it seems to be indicated the radiation is still available. They did, however, use radiation to destroy hormone function of the ovaries, as a preventive measure for recurrence.

I will be returning to Okinawa in March, due in San Francisco on the 10th and will try to see Lea then. I will have only 21 weeks left to do until I can come home again to stay. We know we will be assigned to Norfolk for duty when I do come home, and this is what we both wanted. Now that the danger, pain and uncertainty are behind us, we are enjoying being together again.

Rob brought up his family last Saturday, and we had a simple supper with them. We will go down there next week, when Rob gets back from a business trip to Houston. I have a bunch of "voice" mail to answer, but I will be seeing Rob next week and Lea in two weeks, so I may keep this brief.

Joe, you know, I have never said this before, but I think it is a lousy system that limits the communication a person is allowed with the outside. I think I would go nuts if my communication to Joyce were limited as yours is. I still pray daily for a positive decision regarding your parole. Try Erich Fromm when you get the chance. I have been through "The Sane Society" several times. He has a lot to say, and much of it is very good. However, as Lea said, do not let too long a time go between letters. We count on them to keep a beautiful and necessary friendship going among us. Peace!

Ed

Joe......- 78250
N/S State Farm, VA 23160
7 February 1965

Dear Voices.

I must apologize for my late writing. In some part, my tardiness might be excused since this parole business has demanded additional writings that tax my tarried pen. I must admit that this is not the only reason. I've been allowing the suspense of the too-long parole indecision to best me somewhat. Freedom is a strange paradox. Resign a man to prison and his mind will offer him more freedom than he has ever known, but dangle the keys before him and his brain can become cluttered and confused with hopes and dreams— hibernation is disturbed: the salamander is awakened. He looks about. Is he out of season? It is still winter but he senses summer. Warm breezes of hope penetrate the cavern of his cold resignation. His mind is abuzz, restless, anxious—but the cloister prevails… The period of indecision creeps on and with it I learn much about the patience I do not have. Like another salamander, so long ago, I squiggle about in that warm pocket of promise; no longer dormant—but still enclosed. It would be easy to lapse into the despair of an Omar Khayam, save for the challenging grit of a Milton who believed, "They also serve who only stand and wait." (sic)

I have no problems, really no, not when I sadly ponder the recent loss suffered by Marlene. Rob, in grief's dark hour, we gain a strength that can only be achieved through tears. That you share the experience with us compliments the cohesion of our five-pointed star. I am confident that Marlene and you have that special balance that can say as one said long ago. "It is done."… And soon similar words may reach us concerning Joyce. Words that are in accord with our hopes, desires, and petitions… Ed, your loneliness is beautiful for it is never wrapped in cold night. Your letters bathe in the warm light of love and appreciation for that love. Your ability in handling loneliness is quite inspirational to me. Your letters relieve much of the anxiety for you, but your location continues to caution all of us not to ease our prayer vigilance. Joyce's cookies were delicious, but my colleagues here allowed me just a sample. One of these years I fully intend to enjoy, not just Joyce's but all the Echo's cooking delights. Assuming Bill does not have much time for the art of cooking, I'm quite sure that Lea can ably substitute for him. Lea, I'm not as well read as you think; but I do try. Erich Fromm is one of the many I've neglected. I have, however, an awareness of him through his collaborations with George Orwell and one or two others. I want to get into his works, but can't for the moment. For some months my workload has averaged 12 hours per day, 7 days a week. Believe it or not, I'm still trying to finish "By Love Possessed"—perhaps I shall by my next letter.

Marcus Aurelius in the lesser moments of his MEDITATIONS... wrote this passage of interest: "If the Gods took counsel about me and what should befall me, doubtless their counsel was good... If they have not taken counsel about me in particular, they certainly have done so about the common interest of the Universe, and I therefore should accept cheerfully and contentedly that fate which is the outcome of their ordinance... Whatever happens to me was prearranged from all eternity." I review what I have written and suspect I should address the envelope to myself. Lea, you are the only one who has not sent her birth date! (?)

Joe

Weston CT
March 4 1965

Dear Joe,

The month of February was filled with travel—to Chicago, Houston, and Pittsburgh, where, after a visit with Mother and Dad, I spent 3 to 4 hours with Lenny, engaged in interesting conversation about a variety of things. In between trips, where I mostly taught classes, there was a short visit to Joyce. She is quite a gal, and she was anxiously awaiting Ed's arrival. I also did some things with the family for fun and our own enlightenment, all of it pleasurable, but not significant enough to take up space in this letter. In Houston, I visited the San Jacinto Battlefield Park, the place where the Texan's routed the Mexicans and gained their independence. Very interesting. Close by is the USS Texas, the old battleship retired after World War II, which was fascinating to explore.

For Lea's information, I also spent about an hour or so in the Houston Museum of Art—still trying to get some culture to rub off on me. There was some way out art which made me laugh (I think the artist was spoofing us!) but there were also some works from earlier periods. Remington's paintings of the old West, for example, always make me stop and think.

Joe, when Lenny and I were spending those delightful hours together, we talked about many things. One of the topics was how you had earned your living. I thought it was as a tool and die maker, or as a designer of some sort. Am I way off base? If I was right, have you given any thought to resuming that endeavor, or have you switched signals altogether? Forgive my asking such questions—ignore them if you wish—but talk of parole has brought such things to mind.

Ed, I will reserve what I have to say for when you will be sitting in the very room where I am now typing.

Len, nothing more, either. Our Pittsburgh talk ranged over so many matters, that I am content to just roll the thoughts over in my mind. Don't know when I will be back in Pittsburgh again.

Lea, old worry wart, you sure made me feel guilty over delaying Joe's letter for over a week. Forgive me. Comments on your letter: *Siddhartha* I never heard of; FROMM I know only casually. PLEASE don't let the mad book-sender strike again! I'm far enough behind in my own reading without adding anything else. I always think that I'll get a lot of reading done on trips, but somehow, it never happens.

Today, I visited an exhibit centered about the life of Nehru, and the story of his life moved me. Here was a man who was thrown into prison many times—and his only crime was that he wanted freedom for his land and his people. Apparently, he came out of prison each time a better and stronger man. May each of us have in some measure, the same courage and dedication as he did.

Rob

(Handwritten note to Lea)

Really sorry about Joe's letter, but with this traveling lately, I just ran out of time. Your comments about Len in your letter were well taken. Perhaps I have written more optimistically than I have felt inwardly. I second your feelings about Len in most all respects. I feel, however, that he can make some desirable changes from his present "state of mind."

Whether he will ever really come out of his shell and accomplish things (not downgrading his present life,) I cannot predict with any accuracy. My guess will be "No." Ah, to be as perfect as we! What can I say? I like and respect Len for what he IS , not what he MIGHT be. I just happen to think that you made a wise choice in marrying Bill... it would have been a tough marriage between you and Len.

That's all for now. Ed's description of Joyce's condition tells all that I know. Joyce may have cried in private, but she's never shown that face to me. Marlene back to her old self. My best to you all.

Rob

Joe.Killeen–78250
N/S State Farm, VA 23160
28 February 1965

Dear Voices,

Biopsy, miscarriage, heart attack, falling tree, hidden light, lonely darkness—the morning of 1965 seems exaggerated with pain of body, mind, and heart. At such times, one may wish to turn his back to the sun; but if he does, he sees only his own shadow, as Gibran would say. Yet, if his despair is such that he turns away, there is a thumping on his back by those hands that knit heart to heart. No pain afflicts one part without reflecting on the whole. Responsive threads of prayer, care, and share interweave the bright threads of joy with the dark threads of sorrow. Those insistent hands continue their work—mending, repairing, and renewing strength and beauty to the pattern. Sacred tears never stain—they blend. The pattern is something to behold for it is the effulgent star of friendship... What words can I write to Joyce and Ed? How shall I explain my anxiety about them? What comfort can I afford Marlene and Rob? The expressions of my heart are too inaudible for my tongue or pen. I cannot reveal these through language. Their true unveiling lies in that cohesive star... Lea's words ease concern for Joyce's outcome; and Ed's return, even if only temporary, is an added relief... Lea, I am ashamed of my tardiness in writing—but it is nice to be missed. I did post a letter through Rob on Feb. 7th. His present conditions may not afford time for copies. It could be my letter was lost in the mail or stopped by the censor (but we are usually informed of the latter.) ...I can report nothing new on my parole except that it remains an indecision. Warm breezes tempt and stir the salamander's cloister. They can be quite disillusioning if it is still winter... Should parole be granted, I hope to return to Denver where friends and work await me. My mother plans to go with me. (The situation with Doris has magnified into a definite decision of divorce.) Two of my nieces are considering Colorado schools, thus a segment of our clan may take root in the Rocky Mountain area... Some time ago, I found these words penciled on the flyleaf of one of our chapel hymnals. No one I've talked with seems to know the writer or the source: "The wrought hand of justice has defied the beauty within,—it has slain the best within these singing men.—If heaven is an equity to this hell I live—Then, I deserve it, and all that it can give.— Poverty is a God: It destroys and it creates." If the author of these words be of this camp, I would certainly like to know him... Lea, in LIFE magazine, (p.100; 2-26-65) is an article concerning Mario Savio, one of the student demonstrators of CAL. U.—have you read it? I suggest you do; particularly his ideological attacks on the present U. S. political stand. A few papers seem to refer to Savio as a malcontent and fanatic—but I wonder? I can hear Rob's "Amens" now, if he knows that Savio is attacking certain aspects of liberalism and the present administration. His view on constitutional rights is interesting, also... Write of Joyce, Ed... Roses have thorns? No, thorns have roses—and poinsettias should always be in season!

With each of you,
Joe

Los Gatos
March 8, 1965

Dear Joe, (and of course, the rest of the voices)

Of all the people I know, you have the least need to apologize for an inability to express your feelings through language. For, I assure you, Joe, that my contact with you is only through words, and your feelings came through bright and clear. Now, I look forward to the time when we can just talk—face to face. Perhaps, one day, we can look up that little salamander at Montalvo, preferably in summer, when he is frisking about, with thoughts far from that winter cloister.

Interesting your mentioning Mario Savio in your last letter. I did indeed read the article you mentioned, and though you didn't state your views specifically, I suspect we might share those views. Initially, I had a different reaction—..."What do those students want? They should be disciplined; they have no right demonstrating about freedoms, when we enjoy more freedom than any land on earth. They should kick those nuts out, if they won't conform to campus policies and rules. etc. " And then, I began reading and talking to students and faculty at San Jose State, and slowly, I began to wonder, too. It was easy to fuss and fume about those rabble-rousing kids—Lord knows they look like a sorry bunch, Mario Savio, particularly, with his wild, unkempt hair, shabby clothes, and his cliché utterances,—"this hypocrisy of justice, etc." All of this rubs against the grain of a comfortable inhabitant of an affluent community like Los Gatos, who cannot see the reason for rebellion in a land of plenty. Gradually, however, I began to see what this rebellion is about. It's by a great mass of young people who have heard their elders—parents, ministers, teachers—saying one thing and doing another—preaching tolerance, but living by "gentlemen's agreements" to keep out minorities. I see a youth that has had the righteous, moral, peaceful image of their country tarnished by what they see with their own eyes—in Vietnam. The idiocy of our decrying the North Vietnamese training South Vietnamese Viet Cong Forces, in the face of our own (a few short years ago) having trained in Guatemala the Cuban Counter-revolutionaries for the Bay of Pigs invasion, makes me wonder if our government believes our memories are really that short! Or has it become just a way of life to live by a double standard if we believe it is in our own interest? I try to see it from the students' perspective. They have to survive in a world created for them, and they don't like the standards we've set. Frankly, when I think of the activities in Alabama and Mississippi; when I see welfare roles swelling daily with poor, disillusioned people, and I read of the decline of morality, in general, I am ashamed of our generation. I cannot say I blame these students who are crying out about injustices which exist all about them. (At this point I am sure Rob is sputtering and shaking his head over his wild-eyed liberal friend, flipping her cork again!) We all have to live by rules, but these voices on the campuses must be listened to. They are a symptom of a disease spreading throughout this land. I suspect the conservatives will have another take on it entirely, decrying the unruly "mob mentality." But the genius of America has been our ability to compromise, rather than take one side entirely. I hope we don't fail now.

Joe, I am sorry my worrying kicked up so much dust. No matter, now that I know you're OK. No more mention of books in this letter, either. Rob has insulted me by calling me the, "mad book sender," and asked me to cease and desist. So, typewriter keys are frozen! Joe, don't force yourself to wade through *By Love Possessed*; it's becoming the Voices joke! Just toss it; it's probably just a sappy chick Schtick, anyway!

Ed, I know you are headed to Vietnam, so I won't say anything more about Vietnam. The papers said that part of the 3rd Marine Division is going. I only wish I felt differently about the situation. In fact, I have decided not to send Joyce a copy of this letter, lest she find it troubling. It's bad enough to have a husband over there, without having to read a letter decrying our mission there. If you want her to have a copy, let me know, but I won't send it unless I hear from you. I still cross fingers that our reunion next summer comes to pass.

Rob, I hope you will be out this way again soon. As with Joe, I would like to talk to you about many things, politics excluded.

All is about the same with us. Randy had another strep infection in his throat, and of course, Bill was on reserve duty. With a temperature of 103° and purulent red tonsils, there was no doubt, so I went to Bill's office, got a syringe and some penicillin and he took it almost willingly. This is the third one in two months. I'll be relieved when those tonsils are out.

But, otherwise, things are well with us. Bill's practice is getting busier, and he is happier to have mostly patients who have real rather than imagined illnesses. I will have to remain in the office for a few more months, but I am already making plans to start back to school—scary thought.

My love to you all,
Lea

Danang, South Vietnam
March 25, 1965

Dear Joe,

The mail sent over from Okinawa just arrived and there are four letters from Joyce, one from Lea, and one from Father Lovejoy, the Episcopal priest from Wallingford. First the good news from Joyce. She has had her first checkup, and everything is fine; she is well. The doctor didn't think she would have to be examined again until next fall. Good news indeed.

I do not think I am in any danger here. Of course, we have casualties every day, but I feel quite safe myself. I am in a guarded compound, and am too old to be a hero. There is a certain amount of risk, but I have no premonition of anything happening to me. If all goes well, I will be leaving for home in July. I love the job; it's the most demanding one I have ever had and the most rewarding. I work 16 hours a day and this is the first night I have been caught up enough to write a letter of any length. My responsibility is taking care of personnel problems for the General. I am responsible for strengths and for the welfare of the troops who make up the strengths of the units, which comprise the brigade. My job is to get PX supplies in so that the troops have some comforts. I run the recreation program, take care of legal matters, emergency leaves, and all other personnel and administrative problems. Not exactly front line stuff, so relax, everybody. I am in no danger.

Tomorrow I fly to Saigon for a liaison visit with COMUSMACV staff members, remaining for most of the weekend. As things settle down, I will have time to write some impressions of this "dirty little war." It is dirty, and people are getting hurt. It has its heroes, and it also has its moments of comedy. The living conditions are not bad, but I dare say they would probably not be acceptable to any of you as we have to walk a hundred yards to get a drink of water, and we take malaria pills once a week, and we don't know what sheets and pillows are. But, we get clean clothes and take an occasional hot shower. We also get a cold beer before we go to bed if we get to go to bed. So, things could be worse. More later, as I want to read the rest of my mail.

Sayonara,
Ed

Weston, CT
April 3 1965

Dear Friends

This past month flew by, mostly because I was on the road so much. We had two inches of snow yesterday, but it melted by 2 PM, and clearly, the temperature is gradually inching upwards. Our first spring flowers suddenly came forth, and there are little patches of purple, yellow, and white near the stone wall. Trips were to Indianapolis, Birmingham and Atlanta. The time in the South left me with a belly full of discontent. I was in Birmingham during the week of the civil rights march from Selma to Montgomery, and I had a chance to speak with a few of the marchers. Sitting in the airport at one o'clock in the morning on the way home, a negro marcher mistakenly assumed I also was a marcher. I told him I did not have the honor to be thus counted.

What disturbed me about the South is hard for me to put into words. I was discouraged that so many of the southern whites are apparently so dead set against the negro without real cause for being so. Their minds are so closed that reasonable debate on the subject of equality is impossible. I say this with full knowledge that northern whites are generally a bunch of hypocrites in race relationships. I came away convinced that race equality in the south was not going to happen in this generation. Law may force association and compliance, but it cannot quickly win over minds. But, the strict application of the law is necessary—or else the negro would never even be given a real chance to prove himself equal. Forgive me—this is the spring of my discontent, I guess. I do want to comment on the "Voices" and their lives:

Joe, settling in Denver sounds like a good plan; I hope it works out. It's a lovely city close to wonderful vistas of the Rockies. I am sorry to hear about Doris, and the decision about divorce—there is nothing I can say further, of course.

I also read about Mario Savio, Joe, and was very interested to follow the progress of his Free Speech movement, as it advanced into the Filthy Speech Movement. I look at such fellows with mixed emotions. I admire their guts in getting up and taking a swing at authority—and they serve a purpose in making the authorities do some soul-searching about why certain things are being done as they are. On the other hand, however, I often wonder how much real good they accomplish. Many of them become professional radicals—getting their kicks about rebelling against everything. Over the long haul, I don't believe these people are the ones who really change things for the better. We need radicals to keep us from becoming too conservative, but many of the free-swinging folks go overboard with their emotions, believing that new ideas are always good ideas. The world isn't like that. Each generation falls into the old traps that sucked in those who preceded them. Sure, we need Savio—but only by recognizing that he doesn't have all the answers either.

Lea, I'm insulted. How come you say you'd like to talk to me about many things, politics excluded? Gee, I'd be happy to hear your comments about recent developments. Let's see, shall we talk about Goldwater being bomb-happy over North Vietnam? Or Johnson's current stand in Indonesia? Or Johnson's lack of campaign talk about the balance of payments problem? Or Adam Clayton Powell's role in the youth mobilization program, or the bracero problem in California and other states where those poor, unemployed Americans won't do stoop labor? Ah,

I've got a million of them, Lea!

Your comments about Vietnam were, I thought, slightly askew (You can say the same about all my comments about everything, you know!) We're in that mess up to our necks, as Ed well knows. We've gone too far to back down gracefully—we're playing brute power politics with fighting thrown in for good measure. There is no simple answer to the situation. Are we

122

wrong to be fighting a communist takeover in Vietnam? Or were we wrong in wanting to take over Malaysia? Or where do we stand in the Congo or in Angola? As far as I can see, our problem is one of being consistent. Right or wrong, the world respects power. If we don't use power to protect what we think is right, then we don't deserve either the power or the life we enjoy under the wing of that power. At the moment, I am with President Johnson.

Ed, this whole letter is for you and Joe both. If it weren't for you and those with you, the world would be a far worse place. Take care, old friend. I'm proud of you. My thoughts are especially with you. I know that I am reading more attentively all the dispatches out of your area. Yes, a dirty, nasty war not really of our choosing—but we're in it, for better or worse. I am not a super patriot, but I believe there is little else we can do that would be a better course than the one we are pursuing now.

My special thoughts and prayers to Joe and Ed.

Rob

Lea, not very gentlemanly leaving you out of my special thoughts and prayers—but all in all, your problems and mine don't amount to much do they? All of us are fine, but I miss the family too much when I am away to enjoy my travels. Can't see any California trips coming up, but things can certainly change. Trust that Bill's competence and personal traits continue to make his practice grow. Good bye for now.

Rob

Los Gatos
April 12, 1965

Dear Joe and other Voices,

Once again, I am answering a letter I didn't receive yet. This time, however, it is not because I am anxious, but because I want to answer Rob's letter, so I will probably answer your letter in a separate one. This one is mostly for Rob, as I think about it. First of all, though, I apologize for my last depressed and depressing letter. I was upset over the Vietnam situation and civil rights problems in the south, and they were magnified by my not feeling well. I had gastro-intestinal problems (esophagitis and esophageal spasm), psychogenic in origin, which caused Bill to schedule me for a first ever physical. The result showed nothing organic, but the internist said I had to cut my activities by 50% if I wished to get better. Accordingly, I handed in my third resignation to Dave (the other doctor in Bill's office), and this time he accepted it. I was appalled that there seems to be a limit to the amount of work I can do without getting sick. It was a form of conceit to think I had unlimited energy and capacity for assuming obligations, and it was a blow to discover I am not the little dynamo I am reputed to be. Since I have resigned, I am amazed that my symptoms have all disappeared and I am now left with the knowledge that I am just another member of a large club of hypochondriacs.

Now, I want to answer Rob's letter. Our letters always cross, and this time, I want to comment specifically. I find myself smiling at the familiarity of having to occupy myself by picking barbs out of my hide, a pastime I recall all too well from our high school days. It does seem that Rob and I, while we share similar philosophies with regard to moral and social responsibility, ethics, and social justice, are really pretty clearly at odds when it comes to the means to those ends.—to wit: political philosophy. And, much as you might suppose to the contrary, I REALLY am a pacifist, except where politics is involved, and the ground rules for argument are laid. Therefore, I here and now formally challenge you to a formal political debate, to be held at such time and place as is convenient for both of us (like maybe in 1992— in Heaven!!??), when I shall be happy to discuss the bracero program and fruit and produce growers who, instead of giving the welfare people an opportunity to supply them with a labor supply, responded to their panic, by UNDER PLANTING and then blaming the rise in prices of produce on the cutting back of the bracero program... and other timely subjects. (I'll defer discussion of Goldwater's policy of "good boy, Lyndon, hit 'em again, harder. Don't stop now, boy, they're not going to crawl until we really blast 'em, etc."—until that time.) I have to confess total or near total ignorance of Adam Clayton Powell's role in anything, and Johnson's role in Indonesia, and I likewise confess total bafflement over Johnson's lack of campaign reference to the balance of payments problem. But, I am willing to read up and take you on. Is it a date?

With regard to Vietnam, I respect your view that my comments are slightly askew. (Hey, that rhymes, doesn't it!?) I further respect your opinion that we've gone too far to back down. But, I don't agree entirely, any more than I agree that war is inevitable, because we seem to be drifting toward it. It seems to me that just because we are speeding toward a fatal collision we don't necessarily have to continue. We can stop, you know!! The United Nations was created for precisely the purpose of resolving conflicts, which have, in the opinions of the parties involved, "gone too far to back down from this position." I do agree that there are no simple answers to this situation, but this systematic escalation is a calculated risk I am not at all sure we should take. Nor do I believe it serves our interests or those of the people of Vietnam.

As far as asking if we are wrong in fighting a communist takeover in Vietnam and if we were wrong in trying to help overthrow a communist regime in Cuba, here again, you're asking for a value judgment. We in the U. S. judge right and wrong by what appears to be in our own interest, and I submit that this is a grand international double standard. Why should Russia's intervention to quell a revolution in Hungary arouse indignation, when we are doing the same thing in Vietnam? You can only speak of right or wrong in this if you equate right with Capitalism and wrong with Communism. In this country, in fact, we do. But, this isn't necessarily so in neutral or uncommitted countries. You may not be concerned about what other countries think, but I am. I perceive the greatest flaw in our country is our inability to see ourselves from the point of view of people in other countries. If my assertion that this sanctimonious attitude on our part—(this assurance that we are right and anyone who disagrees with it is wrong) makes me a leftist, then I suppose I am.

As to your next question, "what alternative do we have?" I don't know. Perhaps there is none—at least in the short term. But, please don't ask me to rationalize my way into believing it is a morally acceptable one. At the moment, I don't know if I am with Johnson or not, because I don't know what he is doing. If he is aiming at the negotiating table, then, I am with him.

Joe, your letter will be arriving any day, and I feel I have cheated you by writing this diatribe largely to Rob. So, my next letter will be devoted primarily to you—promise. Randy is scheduled for his tonsillectomy over the Easter holiday, and I feel sorry for him. His whole Easter break will be spent recuperating. I will have to put some ice cream Easter eggs in his Easter basket, I guess.

Ed, I feel like a bit of a heel going on so about Vietnam, when you are serving over there as an officer in the Marines. I don't expect you to agree with me, of course, but I would be hypocritical if I professed a surge of nationalistic spirit all of a sudden. I tend to have a philosophy that is not chauvinistic, but rather more in line with Thomas Paine in 1776. My favorite quote of his is "The world is my country. All mankind are my brethren." I pray that you may remain safe for the remaining months of your tour. I quietly seek communion with God (the Light inside me) in your behalf each Sunday in the little Quaker Meeting House I have been attending these past months.

I am sure He will look after you.

Rob, dear friend, after this letter, directed to you mostly, are we still friends?? I hope so. You are still my all time favorite redhead.

Lea

Joe Killeen 78250
N/S State Farm, VA 23160
April 4 1965

Dear Voices:

Cozzens writes that "Freedom…is the knowledge of necessity." If one admits that necessity governs freedom, we must also confess that necessity sometimes misgoverns it. Cozzens offers examples, particularly: "compromise assents to second best—by the abandonment of hope in the ascertained fact that what was to be, was to be…" Today, too many insist that compromise (whether it be theological, political or social) is no longer simply an idea of mutual yield. Now, it must also embrace, with special emphasis, the all-important "pacify." But it must be remembered that while "pacify" is synonymous with "allay," it is often a synonym for "appease." The loneliness of the world cannot be eased by castrating the multitudes…Cozzens wrestles with the dilemma for many pages, until he finally concludes that "victory is not in reaching certainties or solving mysteries; victory is in making do with uncertainties." It's a conclusion, but not a solution, and an ambiguous one at that, so much so that the young Savios call such ambiguity absurd. When Mario Savio says, "this is a hypocrisy of justice," he is stating that one cannot call a dismal swamp a world of emerald green… For the most part, these young people are not rebels but revolutionaries. By that I mean it is not that they necessarily wish to destroy old systems, they seem to hope to introduce better systems. They have just declared an all out war against double standards. If they win, it could be man's greatest revolution…Lea, Fromm's book arrived; many thanks, especially for your notes contained therein. My study-notes testify that I am glad you didn't allow my letter (2/7) to discourage you… Ed, I can tell you how many marines are at Danang Air Base, where they are located, how many Hawk missiles they deploy, the fact that they also employ the 5 ft. tall man-spotting radar device, which supposedly took the Viet Cong by surprise near Hill 327. I can also give you the dimensions of the air base runway, the location of the Marine helicopters, AF F-102's and sky raiders. If this is no secret to me, a man confined to a prison farm half way around the world from Vietnam, how much less a secret is it to the enemy in your immediate midst?…Do take care, Ed, and though you are busy, keep us posted as often as you can. I am happy to know that Joyce's first check-up is so favorable. And who can describe better than you and Joyce the joy of your reunion, however short. Like Joyce, we sweat the days with you, longing for your July rotation… …My parole attempt to Denver was denied. Parole itself looks slim, but is still possible. The Virginia authorities are now discussing my sister's residence in Alexandria, VA. I may now be limited to Virginia, but I'm not sure… I'm not a tool and die maker, Rob; I am a folding carton die-maker, with some knowledge of estimating and sample making in this field. I once worked for the only company that offers opportunities in this field in the Washington area. Up through 1960 they offered a parole-job. My sister is checking on this. Otherwise, I will have to find a non-skilled job in a location that is not conducive to non-skills or felons... Rob, if you, or any of the other voices have any suggestions, I'm wide open. Indeed, necessity does govern freedom…I vowed I would never ask Voices for anything!…

    With all of you,
    Joe

Danang, Republic of Vietnam
12 April, 1965

Dear Voices,

This will be a hurried letter, as there is absolutely no time for personal affairs, including letters. I will admit, though, that being busy for 16 hours a day makes the time speed by. I work hard, but I feel worthwhile, because the job has to be done, and I have more successes than failures. I have succeeded in getting a small PX opened, in two tents, where the troops can buy cigarettes, chewing gum, soap, etc.—not much, but better than nothing. Biggest triumph was the first shipment of beer—15,000 cases of it! I'm going to set up some mini beer halls and a recreation beach area, where they can get away from the dust and heat for a bit.

Got a welcome letter from Rob, and Lea's letter, but I refuse to get in the middle of an argument with Lea on the merits of this war. I only know I would rather fight it here than in California or Connecticut. I am convinced it has to be fought, and I am willing to do it. I have no intentions of being a hero, but I intend to be a professional. I refuse to accept the rationale of giving in to a society where people can't be different, and maybe I am here so that we can all continue to disagree with each other. I have no illusions

127

that our society is perfect, but I have seen enough to know that it is far better than what the rest of the world has and I want to give it a chance to mature into a better world.

Sayonara,
Ed

Los Gatos
Approximately fourth week of April, 1965

Dear Joe (and other voices, since carbons are no trouble)

This is the reply to your letter of April 4, Joe, since I jumped the gun and "answered" before your letter arrived. Had I waited for Ed's letter, the tone of mine would have been different. Not so for yours, since I sense we see things the same way; it's just that your opinions are much more delicately and tactfully expressed. This letter is almost entirely YOURS, but first I have to clarify something to Ed and Rob. Ed, I apologize for my verbosity in blabbing my feelings with regard to Vietnam. I do not apologize for my opinion, only for being so tactless as to run on so about it in the face of your presence there. It was entirely inexcusable of me, and I am truly sorry. I know that you know I appreciate your position over there as a professional military man, and in this capacity as well as that of a human being, you have my unequivocal respect. I don't presume to be anyone's conscience in any event; I have all I can do to handle my own. After all, a pacifist Quaker greets Bill when he returns from USAF Reserve duty, and sometimes I actually have the sense to keep my mouth shut! As my dear friend, you have my prayers for your quick, safe return home to your family.

Rob, even if you and Ed didn't share similar views on the subject of Vietnam, good judgment and restraint would have precluded your carrying on as I did in my last letter. I suppose I am saying this to you because when all is said and done, I CARE what you think about me. I'm sorry, pal. Please forgive me.

And now, Joe, your letter. First of all, I am as distressed as I can be that you were denied parole to Denver. I know you were hoping for its approval, but I hope you weren't counting heavily on it and that you are not devastated. What is the honest likelihood of your getting approval for Virginia?

Joe, by your repeated quotes from Cozzens, I know you did indeed read *By Love Possessed,* and since you spotted some of the best lines to quote, I am assuming you liked it—a little anyway. I hope so. Cozzens is stuffy in spots, and though admittedly a bigot, he is at least honest and rational. I agree that there is a lot to be said for the capacity to compromise. I truly believe compromise is the genius of our government, as history bears out.

In our youth, we all have glowing ideas of what we hope to find in our future. Some of us get closer to this goal than others; many never even get off the ground. No one has the right to set himself up as judge of the right or wrong of the outcomes of these dreams. But, I think the happiest people are those who are able to accept, and most important—content themselves with their lot. For my money, such a person is a successful person, as well, because he has succeeded in mastering one of life' secrets to contentment. In your letter, I had the feeling you were speaking of nations as well. Were you? (Using terms like pacify and appease, etc.) This is why I was heartened by Johnson's statement the other night, in which he said that we are willing to enter any unconditional negotiations. Prior to this time, we had stipulated conditions prior to any negotiations. Where will it all lead? And how long will it go on? I fear we are being slowly sucked into some kind of vacuum from which there may be no way out. But, enough. International politics is precarious ground. (I momentarily forgot about the carbon paper!!)

Joe, have you read any of Fromm yet? I think he is one of the sanest writers in recent years. Let me know when you are ready for *Siddhartha.* I suspect we agree about our assessment of the unrest on the campuses in the country, especially Berkeley. One only sees the Zen Kooks and the great unwashed student body on TV, and the only speech that gets the media attention is the Filthy Speech Movement, giving one the impression that all the students are nuts. I don't say all the students' demands must be granted, but I do believe they should be listened to. And I believe their cries are a symptom of a disorder in our society. Well, I don't really need to go on, do I? I am probably preaching to the choir, writing all this to you.

I heard your protestations of lack of reading time, and I am sympathetic. But, I also know that you are extremely well read. I dare say, you have probably read all the books in that prison library. You clearly have educated yourself there. I also know that, while I am a painfully slow reader (my stuttering was probably associated with dyslexia) so I only read a few pages before going to sleep each night. But, if I do this regularly, it's amazing how much reading you get done in a year—a lot!! I have tried speed-reading courses, but it doesn't seem to help much.

Joe, I am concerned about what you will do when you are released. Have you considered going back to school? Or is this out of the question? I will, too, you know. I plan to start as a lower division student at West Valley Junior College next fall on at least a part time basis. How's that for nerve? Mama goes to college! There are a lot of things I never learned, and as soon as I am no longer needed in the office, I plan to start learning. This may be sooner than I thought. Bill will be moving in with two other internists by July 1st, with an already set up office staff. Nothing would please me more. One year was more than I had bargained for in the first place. I'll be glad for Bill to be in the environment of other internists and a necessarily more medically sophisticated atmosphere.

This brings me to the end of the page, so I will say good night.

Lea

✒

Danang, RVN
2 May, 1965

Dear Friends,

Time to write again concerning life in the tropics. First, let me assure you all that I am in excellent health, and while one can never be assured of conditions being completely safe, I am in less danger than most assigned to Vietnam. Conditions in the BOQ where I live are simple, but not bad, due largely to an old man who keeps telling us we should live like men instead of like pigs. I have a bed, a chair that I bought in Danang, and a small table with Joyce's and the kids' picture on it. There are a couple of straw rugs on the floor. Cold showers are a luxury in this 90° plus heat, and the medical officer succeeded in making the water potable, so I don't have to walk across the compound for a drink of water. But, it cools off at night, enough so we can at least sleep some, and we are all getting used to the heat.

My workday has slowed to about 10-hour days, and sometimes, I even get an evening off. The job is going well, and I have a sense of satisfaction of having done it reasonably well. I even get in a bit of excitement. Last week I flew up to Phu Bai in a helicopter, and got a look at the countryside between here and there. A couple of times, I tightened the armored vest and made sure the nylon and fiberglass diapers were in place and the helmet on tight, but we got back without taking any direct hits.

The country is actually quite beautiful. I looked at the coastal rice paddies, river estuaries and beaches on the way up. The fish traps in the rivers look like a bunch of arrowheads and the junks on the ocean reminded me I was in the orient. The inland view on the way back was rugged country—hills and dense forest.

Joe, I am sorry about the Denver parole not panning out. I hope the chances of parole in Virginia are still bright. I could see you if you were in the Alexandria area, as I feel sure my orders to Norfolk will go through. I will be getting to Virginia Beach in a little over 100 days.

Lea, I hope I have a little time to argue while I am waiting for my plane headed back east. I will let you know when I am due in California and hope you will be able to meet me again. I can see holes in your arguments, but I will save that until I see you. These people don't care about anything but today. They just want to be left alone, and I am sure the Chinese have other plans.

Rob, I hope you have been able to stay in Connecticut enough to enjoy that lovely spring. Next year, when the dogwood is out, Joyce and I will run up to visit you so that I can enjoy it with you. Thanks for the comfortable words.

Write soon,.

Ed

PS (handwritten to Lea) How can one argue with a lovely, talented, charming girl? I will let you argue while I watch you!

Mirage on the Horizon

Joe Killeen 78250
South Side State Farm, VA 23160
2 May 1965

Dear Voices,

Of all the words that have recently been expressed in these Voice letters pertaining to Vietnam, Ed's words affected me most: "I cannot accept a rationale of giving in to a society where people cannot be different, and maybe I am here so that we can all continue to disagree with each other." A man who owns this sort of thoughts is more a "hero" than a "professional"... All of us agree that our country has the right to expect the president to present that guidance needed for the preservation of our desires, interests, and rights, and, although I myself have not been much of a Johnson fan, I do believe he is trying (and may be succeeding) in this guidance. I no longer question his methods, but I must confess his motives remain a mystery to me. Johnson calls himself a pragmatist; yet he's not the philosophical pragmatist I consider Ed to be. Johnson's "coat of many colors" is too prevalent in his long political career. I often think him an opportunist, a type of "Mr. By-Ends," as John Bunyan would say. Yet Johnson seems to hold the reins of government well these days. And, this, we must agree, is the essential element needed nationally and internationally...Rob, are you aware that busloads of California workers were rejected by the growers before they arrived at the farms? Lea has a point here, even though Gov. Brown may no longer agree. The California growers don't just want workers; they want more workers at lower wages. They want braceros. If the growers would hire braceros on Labor Secretary Wirtz's higher wage plan, they wouldn't want braceros. Wirtz's alternate view on using Job Corps applicants has its merits. Some sort of domestic bracero program would be better...Rob, your report on Alabama is particularly noteworthy. Your views imply more than just a sympathetic feeling toward civil rights when you say: "I did not have the honor to be thus counted." It is interesting that many young people, including Mario Savio, were counted— and honorably—in spite of Congressman Dickinson's obscure charges and Harry Truman's acid comments... Oh, boy! I'm running out of space again! Lea, I read, "By Love Possessed" twice—once for you and once for Rob. It was the second reading that caused me to allow this theme on a national and international level. I can't particularly say I enjoy Cozzens but I do feel his views are important. I much prefer Fromm (I'm a dreamer!) but will have to reserve comment until later. "A Day at Montalvo" has not reached me—if it is to be mailed yet, please include *Siddhartha* with it. Photos arrived, Lea, many thanks. I'd like more from everybody. I especially enjoyed new views of Bill. Is he really as relaxed and serene as his pictures testify? Your ski-outfit reminded me of Jackie Kennedy at Aspen. It is hard to imagine those two big fellows as your sons… Lea, I "split a gut" when you told Rob you were a pacifist! You may be non-violent, but you're an aggressive fighting spirit. Don't change! Virginia parole plan is now being studied. I have a job guarantee. School is not permissible while on parole. More on that later. Ed, Ed, Ed,—you are a VERB! PS. Please note "SOUTH SIDE" address. The dangling participle—

Joe

Weston, CT
May 9, 1965

Dear Joe,

Travel has been heavy over the last few weeks, but mostly I think that old man Spring has finally caught up with me. There was a bout with the flu, income tax to prepare, a not so hot trip to Washington DC, where we looked and acted like tourists, with mobs of people and I bet 5 million school kids on Easter break trips to the capital. My, but we do have a wonderful Capitol city, don't we? Ann and Billy did amazingly well, and Doug enjoyed it, as did his parents. Anyway, all this in search of an excuse for my tardiness. We did get to Wallingford, though, to visit Joyce and the kids, and we all made a tape for Ed.

Joe, since last writing, I received the news of the denial of your request for parole in the Denver area. Distressing is a wishy-washy word on such a vital matter. All we can hope for now is that more consideration will be given to a Virginia parole. Please send me Dorothy's address and phone number, if you will. I have no brilliant ideas about employment possibilities but I will ask my Aunt Jane in Chevy Chase if she has any thoughts on the subject.

Your comments on the subject of "compromise" (which now seem to include the concept of "pacify") were of interest to me. My three years of dealing with a labor union were instructive in that regard. And I believe that the same psychology is applied in many other spheres of activity. The use of compromise as a negotiating tool has to be based on some kind of MEANINGFUL give-and-take attitude. All too often, one or both of the parties involved goes to a negotiation with the concept of "What I now have is mine, and no longer negotiable. What we are here for is to compromise on what YOU now have and I want." Under such a situation, what is the incentive for the other side to negotiate? The same situation takes place on the national level. The "Let's negotiate what YOU have," attitude is what upsets me. I'm afraid that I feel pretty hard-nosed about such an approach. One country, for example, invades another, and at some later date, somebody calls on the parties involved to sit down and negotiate some kind of compromise. It always surprises and appalls me how "world opinion" lashes out against the invaded country if it refuses to negotiate until the original pre-invasion conditions are restored. The country being invaded somehow gets the "bad guy" label because of its refusal to bargain.... and this happens over and over again.

Ed, I still back the president in his approach—and I don't exactly know where it will lead us. I am convinced that, unfortunately, man in his present imperfect state must rely on power. I am reminded of the recent LIFE magazine article on Dietrich Bonhoeffer, which briefly told of his decision to actively plot the death of Hitler. Bonhoeffer's decision, which ultimately took him to the gallows, was in line with his basic concept of the Christian's total involvement in life. I concur with LIFE that Bonhoeffer may well be the forerunner of a renewed Christianity.

Your letters need no comment from me. We are all concerned for you, and for all the other men who are doing the job that needs to be done. Johnson's decision to go into Dominican land raises more questions in my mind than Vietnam ever did—and I must admit the move surprised me. It is quite obvious he intends to draw the line wherever possible. Those who want to stay in the game will find the stakes are a little steeper, and will think it over, hopefully, before going for another round. It's a tough world, and our adversaries are not playing for marbles—and we are put in the position of playing the "bad guy" all too often. So be it.

Lea, what can I say to you? You took a whole letter advantage over me, but I'll try to get a few thoughts back to you. Here goes. Sorry to hear the medical report, (and I didn't understand it, poor non-medical soul that I am) but we boys of the Voices could have told you that WE were getting older. Glad you took the medical advice and curtailed your activities. I do NOT accept your challenge to a political debate, because I hate to argue,—except with myself. Marlene will tell you how pig-headed I can be. Hate to tell you this, but I suspect that our views are not really that much different. I have many questions about stands I take and back, but I think that I am quicker to submerge those questions, and come to the conclusion that the hard realities of particular situations do not allow me the luxury of indecision. I think I am too smart not to see that very few situations are black or white. Glad to hear that you are in contact with the Quakers. I am not man enough to be one, but I respect them so very much. The Friends Service Committee activities, for example, speak loud and clear to me. .Thank you for all the comments in your fine letters. Something in your April 15 letter struck me especially. I suspect that we all think about what we write to each other, because we all care about what the others think about us. I know that I have that feeling. And I guess it is one of the reasons that I dislike writing, for I feel that I don't get a chance to explain myself fully enough, and I am left with a feeling of not having presented my thoughts completely enough.

My special prayers for Joe and Ed. Will try to write more promptly next month, Good night, my friends.

Rob

Los Gatos
May 10 1965

Dear Voices, (mostly Joe)

Joe, you darling! I don't know anything, which lifts my mood and brightens my day like a letter from you! This last one, (postmarked May 4th but dated May 2nd) and received in today's mail, was particularly delightful, and I felt moved to answer it forthwith.

Your response to Ed was just about like mine. The quote you mentioned was precisely what prompted me to write an apology of sorts. Big ole sweet Ed isn't just big in form. He's got a soul to match and an abundance of common sense. By now, all of you have figured out that when all is said and done, I am really just a lot of noise. (The term used by Rob was "Blabber" as I recall). I don't retract anything I said, because my feelings are the same with regard to Vietnam, (and they extend to the Dominican situation). But, Ed is over there; he is doing a good job, as he will always do in whatever he does; he believes, as I do, in the motives of our being there, and that is that. I won't go any further on the subject. (Rob has his tongue in his cheek and an "Oh, wanna bet?" look on his face!)

Ah, Joe, you write like a dream (in fact, you said you were a dreamer, didn't you?) I could cheerfully throttle the Virginia governor for limiting you to one sheet of paper. I have the feeling you abbreviate everything you want to say, and I feel cheated. Well, you won't be there forever, and I can look forward to longer letters in the near future.

I share your reservations about Johnson—always have. When Kennedy was shot, I felt my personal president had been taken away from me. I recall that I was vacuuming the living room ferociously, trying to do something to work off my fury. Suddenly, I couldn't stand it any more; I was so frustrated in my anger at the stupidity and the waste of it all, that I kicked the wall. I tell you this only to illustrate how I felt about Kennedy. The first time I heard Johnson speak afterwards, it was like adding coals to the fire of my fury. I told Bill that, as if losing Kennedy weren't bad enough, we now had the prospect of listening to that Texas twang for the next X number of years. When he ran against Goldwater, I tried to muster some enthusiasm for him because I felt that even Mickey Mouse was a better choice than Goldwater. (Sorry, Rob) As time went on, he seemed to get worse, especially in the field of international relations. As a diplomat, he barely beats out Mickey Mouse, actually! The worst of it is that no one seems to know what he is doing, and frankly, I have the feeling he doesn't either. (Oops, I am on precarious ground again. Better leave this subject, on second thought.)

Braceros! Once again, Joe, you're right on target. Recently, a grower in Orange County (that hotbed of right-wingers) ceremonially plowed under one acre of Strawberries, with media coverage, George Murphy standing by, flashbulbs popping, the whole bit. Even the most conservative papers in northern Calif. saw through the ruse. It was a showy demonstration of how, "these lazy Americans won't do an honest day's work," and as a result, all the crops are going to be lost; prices are going to go up, etc. all because the bracero program was stopped. Well, this is just so much hogwash! That grower was happy to plow under one line acre of overripe berries if it will bring back the braceros. There is an adequate supply of migrant farm workers available, and they turned out by the thousands when it became known that a decent wage was being offered. (I don't think that anyone would suggest that $1.40 an hour plus 15¢ per crate is an excessive wage for backbreaking stoop labor). I don't say that I do not understand the growers preferring a readily available labor supply which will work for a flat $1.00 an hour with no back-talk. (The braceros don't speak the language!) But, I cannot agree that we should import laborers to do the work that our migrant farmers are willing to do at a wage which is in keeping with the standard of living all of us have come to expect in America. If it raises the price of the produce I buy, well, that is something I have to accept.

One of our friends has been appointed to head that portion of the Northern California Poverty program, which deals with the plight of our migratory farm workers. He told me at our Quaker Meeting on Sunday that there is an adequate worker supply; it's all a question of what constitutes a fair wage for a day's work.

Rob, I am grateful you are my friend, but damn! I wish you weren't so conservative. You are one of the truly good people I know, and I have to admit that most of what you say makes perfect sense. It's just that we seem to see some things through a different viewfinder. I suspect it's just an alteration of perspective, seen through our respective lenses.

Joe, yes, Bill is just as relaxed and serene as he looks. How do you suppose he has survived marriage with the neighborhood rabble-rouser all these years? He is a man of very few words, but much thought. He is precisely my cup of tea.

Ed, enjoyed your last letter very much. I am relieved you're not in the center of the fighting, at least. I am reminded that you will be coming through this way before long. I will be unemployed by July 1st, so I will be free as a bird and able to visit with you and entertain you properly, this time. As to your postscript, do you really think I will fall for that kind of flattery? Boy, you haven't changed a bit!! And neither have I; I still appreciate the kind words; I liked the part where you referred to me as a GIRL the best. At 38, I'd be crazy not to!!

So, fellows, you can relax, I am now OLD—just like the rest of you! But, I won't rub it in, at least not until I come back east next year. I am already planning the trip, and it must include a reunion with all of you. More about that later.

Lenny, my best to you and your family. I hear such nice things about your wife and children.

And now, it's time to sign off—so, I will.

Love to you all,

Lea

Camp Courtney, Okinawa
Friday, 21 May, 1965

Dear Voices,

This is just a brief note to let you know what the above return address has already told you—that I am back on Okinawa safe and sound. We are here for a rest, and those of us due to be rotated back to the U. S. will probably not have to go back. I am scheduled to be the draft commander for the ship draft, which leaves here on the 19th of July and arrives in San Diego on the 7th of August. This means I will not get to visit with our unemployed female friend in the San Francisco area. I am sure she will understand, and maybe this will make her sure to continue the plans to come east next summer, so we can all see her.

I am actually referring to her in the third person, because compliments apparently get her all shook up! I will also have to be careful not to shake her further by referring to her as a "girl." Still, I don't think 38 is so old, do the rest of you? Seriously, Lea, I like to give compliments when I think as highly of anyone as I do you! Thanks for the nice letter, which came yesterday.

All is well with me. I feel like I am living in luxury here, with air conditioning, all that I need, and plush conditions in the BOQ. I have a big single room with all the conveniences and am really living! Joe, I do hope that the issue of a parole will have been resolved favorably by the time I get home. The fact that you have a job offer is very encouraging and should help the board to decide with favor to grant your application. My prayers are still with you. And, if you would be living in Alexandria and I in Norfolk, we would be not too far away. I am sure that we are going there, because the orders are in. It's what Joyce and I both wanted. I hope this finds you all well and happy.

Sayonara,
Ed

Joe.Killeen 78250
S/S State Farm, 23160
May 23 1965

Dear Voices,

Over twenty years ago, while Germany was still fumbling with V-2 Rockets and long before Russia's first Sputnik, a small satellite was launched successfully from earth. Five sensitive antennae jettisoned out from this space package, giving it the appearance of the symbolic star. Each of its antennae is channeled to a particular earth station, enabling these to remain in contact, one with the other... This is no mere communication satellite as are the more recent Tel-star and early bird. Aside from its communicating ability, the vehicle's components are able to compute, assimilate, harmonize and store endless tapes of data in its unique memory-bank. Whether a particular station responds or not to transmissions of the others, the memory-bank faithfully and continuously sends past signals which blend with those of the present. There have been long periods of time when certain stations have failed to respond to one or all of the other stations. However, no station has ever failed to respond to the seventy-times-seven signals of the memory bank... Whatever transmitting malfunctions a station might have, these are only temporary, as had already been established by at least one problem station in the past. The satellite has more than lived up to the expectations of its designer and investors. In fact, it has accomplished more than they deemed possible. None dreamed that it would be a forerunner in establishing Einstein's theory that time and space are relative; and that past, present and future are eternally present. Although this satellite remains forever just over the horizon, it is more an expanding quasar than a fixed star. Its countenance is not unlike that greater star that hovered brightly and promisingly over Bethlehem 2,000 years ago... This letter puts me one ahead of Rob and abreast with Ed and Lea (if you don't count pages). I'm still relying on the memory-bank to handle our Mountmore station. I warn all of you, I intend to write again on June 6th... Rob, the parole job has been submitted (still waiting approval however); but do call or visit my sister when you're in that area. She's well aware of our Voice letters... Ed, the Viet Cong and Monsoons are a menacing combination. Danang might be a popular target in the next two months...Have any of you read the Jerome C. Byrne report on U. C.'s recent disorders? I read the condensed report in Time (p.58; 5/21/65). It says much that some of us have been trying to say... Lea, my sister is to visit the far west for the first time next month. She is anxious to meet you and yours. Can it be arranged? You will probably hear from her by letter within the week. I'd like her to see Montalvo. I think you two might become fast friends... Nine years my senior, Dorothy is that highest person in my life, but my least communicative. To me, she's a goddess. In recent years, I've become withdrawn and speak very little. With her, I speak a lot, but manage to say nothing. It's not her; it is me. My adoration of her is higher than my ability. She knows nothing of this, I could never tell her, nor should you. It's something I have to work out by myself, and I can... you Voices have opened me up quite a lot; your letters make me respond, to even be sentimentally expressive in my filial regard toward each of you. I keep rereading Fromm; I've so much to learn—about how to love. I love all of humanity, but only a handful of humans.

With all of you,—Joe

Alexandria, VA 22304
June 2, 1965

Dear Lea,

I visited Joe on May 23 and found him in good spirits. He likes his work in the book store so much better, and it allows him free time to pursue his own readings.

And speaking of reading... he asked me to tell you that if you sent the copy of *Voices at Montalvo*, he has not yet received it. If you have not already sent *Siddhartha*, don't. The Farm has instituted a new ruling whereby inmates can only receive books/periodicals if they are sent directly from the publisher or retailer.

Mr. Gaudio, the parole officer for this area, met with me the other day. He wants to talk with Joe at State Farm before he recommends release. And this he will be unable to do until July, for he entered on a month's active duty June 1. Joe has been offered a job here on his release. I am leaving for the West Coast June 5th, and if I continue according to plan, I hope to arrive in the San Francisco area about June 15. I will call you and I am looking forward—so much—to meeting you and Dr. Frey.

The "Voices of the Past" have done so much for Joe. He feels he is very rich indeed to have all of you interested, encouraging, and forgiving.

Sincerely,
Dorothy

Los Gatos
June 4, 1965

Dear Joe and other voices,

First of all, Joe, I was moved by your last letter. Your satellite analogy was beautifully put and its message came through with clarity and poignancy. I often find myself marveling at this satisfying friendship. I cannot think of the possibility of its ending. I loved your referring to a "memory bank." It reminded me of Hesse's *Siddhartha,* in which he speaks of a flood of loved faces swimming before him, all blending together, all moving and yet being still… all fusing together as parts of one's life. Hesse is a wonderful writer, and the ideas expressed in the book reflect eastern philosophy, as one would expect in a book about the Buddah. I first heard of Hesse when a poem was read at a farewell luncheon for me when I was getting ready to leave Germany. I had completed a term as president of the German American Women's Club. It was in German, and is one of the loveliest I have ever read or heard about parting. It is not sentimental or sad, but rather speaks of parting as a new beginning and past relationships as treasures for one's memory, not affected by time or space. I hope you enjoy the book, Joe. It's in the mail.

I was interested in your comments about the Byrne report on student unrest, and you know I agree with you. I will, however, in the interest of not stirring the soup excessively, forego making comments on it. Besides, I don't know all the facts in the report and would best defer an opinion.

Joe, I am eager to meet Dorothy. Of course, I will be very happy to take her to Montalvo, and I will say nothing of your feelings about her to her although she might be pleased. I hope she comes after July first, when I will be free from office duties.

Since I began this letter this morning, Dorothy's letter arrived. She will arrive on June 15th, and, while I won't be entirely free, I will spend as much time as she has and I can spare with her. She also told me about the new regulation about books, and I only hope they return the book to me. There are good reasons why they want books only from publishers, so I understand. If it is returned, I promise to keep it for you until your release.

This promises to be a busy month—lots of graduations, one of them the boy I mentioned in earlier letters—his name is Dean—he sends me flowers for my birthday and Christmas, and I have grown very close to him. (Remember the Poinsettia?) And, Billy is graduating from 8th grade. Dorothy is visiting this month, and I have tickets to two operas in San Francisco this month. Throw in a christening, two weddings, a play and a farewell dinner for a friend, and it adds up to a full 30 days.

Ed, I am very relieved you're out of Vietnam, and much as I looked forward to seeing you on your way home, I gladly relinquish the pleasure in exchange for your safety. Still, I'm not uncrossing my fingers—yet! As to coming east, it is out of the question this year, but not entirely for next. But, there would be complications. My being in the east, doesn't mean I could lightly skip about from Connecticut to Virginia, equipped with two boys. I would be coming without Bill, and I would very likely spend about 4 weeks in the Pittsburgh area, with a trip to Washington, DC, a probability. If I do make the trip (by train?), I would let you all know well in advance. If I can't get about to see each of you, maybe you would all consider converging on Pittsburgh while I am there. In any event, it is a long time away, and I am not thinking very seriously about it at the moment.

Rob, where are you? Traveling again, I suppose. No letter from you yet this month. All I need to do is mail this one, though, and yours will arrive. It always happens.

Joyce, I hope you are well. I know you are happy this year of separation from Ed is coming to a close. Bill and I were extremely lucky that, in the 10 years Bill was on active duty in the USAF, we were never really separated for any length of time at all. I simply packed up, didn't ask for permission, and went! It always worked out. Somehow, we always managed to find quarters. I always wondered how wives stood the separation; I felt I couldn't, though I guess if it ever came to that, I'd find I would.

Lenny, I hope you and your family are well. Mountmore will always seem like home to all of us. It's nice that it is, in actuality, for you.

Lea

Camp Courtney, Okinawa
Wednesday, 2 June 1965

Dear Voices,

It was just last summer that I was here on Okinawa playing the "keep your eye on the typhoon" game, a reminder that the year is almost up and I will be going home. In fact, as of today, I have 68 days to go. The typhoons we are ducking are Carla and Babe, and the hope is always that they will miss us.

I have gotten some days of sun since I wrote and the start of a good tan. And now, I am busy shopping for stuff I want to take home to Joyce and the kids, and a shoji screen and ginger jar lamps for the house. I saved a lot while I was in Vietnam, but am spending it like a drunken sailor now. Just glad I can send it home as household goods and won't have to pay duty on it.

I hear from Joyce regularly, mostly by tape. We like this better than letters, because I can hear moods in tone of voice, etc. She is relieved, of course, that I am out of the greatest danger, and there is not much longer to wait for my return. She is doing fine, though on one tape, I could hear some blues in her voice, and in fact, she did a bit of crying, but most of the time, she is cheerful. I will be glad to get home and assume the dad role. She needs help in caring for the kids.

Lea, I feel bad that Joyce will not be able to visit with you this summer. Too many obstacles, the biggest being time and money. It's expensive to fly her out west, and it will conflict with the opening of the kids' school. Then, the arrival in San Diego was the clincher. I hope the trip east next summer for you, Bill and the boys comes to pass. We can surely all get to Pittsburgh to see you.

Rob, you must be traveling, because Joyce said she hasn't seen you this month. You have been great about going to visit them, and I do appreciate it. I hope things settle down for you in August. It would be great to get together then.

Lenny, I plan to be in Pittsburgh the end of August or early September. We still have a date to take the two Joyces out for beer and pizza, remember. Lets not go to the Toddle House. As I remember, they have no bathroom.

Joe, I hope that I can pull some strings to get to see you this time. Or better still, that the parole comes through and you are working in Alexandria. Just be forewarned, that as the days get fewer for release from where we don't want to be, they also get longer. Maybe you will just wake up one morning to discover that it's been granted. I pray so!

So, no complaints that a trip home won't cure. Hope all of you are well and happy.

Sayonara,
Ed

Weston,
Tuesday, June 8 1965

Dear Joe,
Tonight I'm too tired to even argue; don't believe I'll even challenge any of Lea's statements. The last month had been a time of too many things to do—but the sun is shining, and summer has arrived, making me want to work in the garden trying to make things grow. We have a nightly raccoon visitor who is pretty bold and a cute fellow, but he sure makes a mess. Too cute, however, to want to harm him.

Yes, Ed, your youngest does have a tendency to take off her clothes in public, as was evident several times at our last visit. Reminded me of Billy, on a late night return home from New York. Driving through Times Square at 10:30 PM, I noted that he was sitting naked as could be, trying manfully to get into his pajamas! Almost died laughing!

No comments on the world tonight. Vietnam is getting hotter and hotter, and big decisions are still to be made there. The Dominican mess is still unresolved, and no one really knows if what we did was right or wrong. The moon is getting closer and more accessible due to two brave men and all their co-workers. And America gets over-optimistic about out-distancing the Russians. Race problems just won't go away. The law says one thing; the mind says another. What a pitiful mess. Joe and Lea, I remain unconvinced about the bracero solution.

Joe, the news of sister Dorothy going west was welcome. I am sure Lea will take her to visit Montalvo. I was touched by your comments about looking up to her. It made me reflect on my own family, how lucky I am to have the parents and brothers I have. We all need to be reminded of this as the years pass.

Ed, the big news of your arrival back on Okinawa took all of us by surprise—and left us relieved. The media have more items datelined Vietnam, and the dead and wounded lists grow longer. It will certainly get worse before it gets better. The Wallingford family is well, but they want to have you back home soon.

Lea, my last letter was dated May 10th, which means ours will cross again. That letter of yours was a little hard on me—but not as harsh as you could have made it. Johnson, Goldwater, braceros, Vietnam, Dominican Republic, *By Love Possessed*—you name it; we'll argue on it. You will be interested to know that I will be in L. A. in mid July. Tried to get the meeting set up for San Francisco, but couldn't do it. I'll probably call you from L. A.

Rob

PS Sorry I won't be able to make it up to the bay area. I tried, really. I'll try to drown my sorrows by visiting Disneyland. Take care, and I'll call in July when on the coast. The dates are July 12, 13, 14.

Rob

Joe.Killeen–78250
S/S State Farm, VA 23160
13 June 1965

Dear Voices,

First Rob: Bully for Billy and his strip tease—he struck a blow for the male ego! Maybe we fellows have something to show off after all, for I read that men are still required to wear tops on San Francisco tennis courts. It doesn't matter about the women, I guess; have they gotten so skinny, there's no longer anything to cover up?... Rob, you're a real Frank Buck, facing that wild beast of the forest, armed only with an apple and a flashlight (you, not him!)—and at night, too! Keep us posted on, "Rack, the Pack," if he doesn't chomp off both your hands!... Ed, we are grateful that you are out of Vietnam; "Carla" and "Babe" may have been dangerous typhoons, but I bet they don't pack half the wallop Lea does! (Whoever heard of a pacifist tornado?) Lea, *Siddhartha* did arrive. Our Asst. Superintendent showed it to me on his desk. I might have taken it from him but we're not allowed to read in solitary confinement. It was mailed back to you last week. I wish I could return it as you suggested. (I was granted your note, though)... your next letter may include Dorothy's visit. While you have that camera busy take one of Dorothy for me. She's never sent me a photo. Also, if you get to Montalvo, capture a shot of Adam and Eve, my favorite Montalvo sculpture... Regarding my school plans, San Jose studies were in Physical Education. Now, I prefer social science, perhaps sociology, certainly teaching. Colleges are reluctant to accept "ex-cons." Virginia says no to school while on parole. At the moment, I am broke but not in debt. Who can say what my financial store may be when and if a school opportunity matures? These and other obstacles thus far do not overbalance determination... I was recently offered a spot in Christian work in Arizona. This position, with time and added schooling, could lead to the pulpit. I assisted in a particular work while on prison AWOL for several months in Tucson...But the chief obstacle in this is ME! My theology may be conservative, yet it has a certain pantheistic universality that demands flexibility and freedom... Set denominational preaching is, to me, like living in a fishbowl. One is encased by a transparent and fragile shell of traditional orthodoxy. Salamander in a fishbowl? Never! Why, the goldfish would nibble at old Sal's tail and never know what they were digesting. The eyes of the pop-eyes would really pop out the first time he ever opened his mouth. The snails would be indifferent. The angelfish would complain about the temperature. The mollies would be too busy with their own beauty or envying the colorful array of the tetras. The blown up bettas would eat Sal up… A salamander is as out of place in a fish bowl as George Wallace at an NAACP convention (or big, ole sweet Ed in a Hula skirt!) The pulpit is reserved for the High Calling of a Paul, not the existential complex of a Dostoevsky. A salamander may have the aesthetic dreams of a Gibran, but he lacks the perceptive vision of a Job. Sal's message, if he has one, is best expressed in a book or classroom. If he has no message, a pick and shovel will suffice… Anyone care to comment on the Johnson Doctrine of Santa Domingo? Or perhaps lack of attitude toward Europe, NATO, the U. N., DeGaulle, or the gospel according to Peanuts? Ed, tell me more about Ann 2. (Did I talk myself out of Arizona?) With each of you—

Billy Sunday Sartre Salamander

June 25th, 1965

Yes, I'll come and see you, Lea. Forgive the lined paper and everything else—writing this at the office. Am going on vacation early tomorrow morning and don't want to write while away Change my travel plans to the following:

Scheduled arrival at San Francisco July 14th 8:10 PM (UA, Flt. 526)

Leave San Francisco on Thursday, July 15 at 9:15 AM UA Flt. No 22.

I know that it makes an awfully short trip, but hope it will suffice. I'll call you from L. A. some evening after I arrive there to check plans. Tell Billy I won't even take his room! Best to your three boys.

Rob

PS. Still game for the travel back and forth from the airport?

Los Gatos
June 26, 1965

Dear Salamander and Voices,

Yes, Salamander suits you better than Billy Sunday or Sartre. Billy Sunday suits you least. Sartre? No, too lacking in mysticism, but possessing the freedom and humanism to your taste. Salamander it is, responding as you do to warmth and allowing for an escape into hibernation—away from the cold. I enjoyed your letter, Joe, filled as it was with allegorical commentary on yourself, laced with your wit and good spirits. I laughed at your comments about gals being so skinny now that there is no need for a shirt because there is nothing to cover up. With regard to that observation, let me fill you in with some "research" of husband, Bill, and our friend, a research physician, while we were over in Germany. They observed, after long and careful scrutiny, that there seemed to be strong evidence to support the theory that there is an inverse ratio between the bust measurement of women and their IQ. In other words, the bust size (which for clarity, we'll call the BQ is directly inversely proportional to the IQ. Think of it, gentlemen, you have the distinction of being associated in correspondence with one who is undoubtedly the smartest woman in the world!!!! The interesting part of this "research" is that within the past few months, there has appeared in the medical literature a report with precisely those findings! What Bill and our friend, Curtis, observed in jest, has actually been corroborated, proving that old adage, "He who findeth first and publisheth not, loseth." (Or something like that.)

Joe, I'll get *Siddhartha* sent to you directly from the publisher. It is exactly your kind of book! I was interested in your comments about Arizona and the pulpit. My feeling is that you have come to the realization that you would not be comfortable in the role of minister, evangelistic or otherwise—and for the reasons you cited in your letter—lack of freedom, intellectually and theologically, in an orthodox denominational faith. I think you are heading away from this type of rigid, fundamentalist religion toward a type of mystical, Universalist humanism involving a deep personal concept of God. Am I reading my own recent discovery of this in Quakerism into your thoughts? Look up the Quakers some time after you are released. If nothing else, you will feel comfortable there and you will find their form of worship unusual and interesting. And, unless I have misjudged you completely, you can't help but be impressed by the Quakers as human beings; they live their faith. And it is lived in such a way as to make no noise, cause no attention, except the observation of a job quietly done. Best of all, they don't seek converts.

For years, I have been searching for a "spiritual home," a religious faith in which I feel comfortable. Always there have been drawbacks before, either because I recognized that the dynamic speaking ability of the minister was the attraction and not the faith itself, or I quarreled with the demands that I accept a particular tenet or doctrine in order to be accepted into the faith. When I have thought of accepting a faith before, I could not in conscience do it if there were any part of the creed I could not honestly accept. There always was. But, in the Society of Friends, there is no creed. But, most important, it is a way of life. Quakers are egalitarians, were among the earliest abolitionists and prison reformers, the earliest campaigners for social justice, women's suffrage, and they are pacifists. The worship is an hour of corporate worship in silence, interrupted only by "ministry" which grows spontaneously out of the silence. It speaks to me in a way nothing ever has. After I first attended a meeting, I kept going back, not because I felt I had some sort of epiphany, but rather because I wasn't repelled. The silence isn't easy for me, but I am learning to still my mind and listen to my own inner self. Oh, dear, I am beginning to sound like a blabbing Quaker, and that is a contradiction in terms. Leave it to me to wax vociferous on the subject of silence!!! Sorry!

Yes, I will indeed speak of Dorothy's visit, Joe. I can't tell you when I was so drawn to anybody on first acquaintance as I was to your sister. What a beautiful person she is! You did not exaggerate in your enthusiastic appraisal of her, though I confess, upon reading your letter, I thought you had. I met her in San Francisco on Sunday morning, and we had a grand tour of the city, including lunch in Chinatown, tea in the Japanese Tea Garden in Golden Gate Park, and a hamburger for supper at the Hippo Hamburger Joint. I convinced her that she mustn't bypass Carmel, so she drove there Tuesday and then drove to Los Gatos on Wednesday morning. We set out immediately for Montalvo (I had gotten a substitute in the office) where we walked at some length. From there we visited the Paul Masson Winery and then headed to Big Basin for a walk through the redwoods. She was so exhausted when we got home, that she had to take a nap! After helping me with dinner, she had a good visit with Bill. They had something in common, having both grown up in Oakland, both attending Schenley High School.

I let Dorothy read some of the Voice letters, (except the one in which you talked of your feelings for her.) She seemed to have a better understanding of all of us afterwards. In turn, she filled me in with some facts that previously eluded me. For instance, I didn't know before that Doris was NOT the girl I met at your Beechview apartment just after the war. That was apparently Betty, and you and Betty lived at Montalvo from about 1950 to 1952, right? And, some time after that, your marriage broke up. Anyway, Dorothy's visit was the highlight of this year. I share your enthusiasm for her.

And that is the end of this page and of this letter. My best to all of you, especially to you, Joe.

With much affection,

Lea

Weston
July 8 1965

Dear Joe,

I echo Lea's sentiments; your last letter was by far the most light-hearted to date. I wish that I could write as well. Sorry to report that I have regressed in my relations with the visiting raccoon; he just hasn't been around of late. I think he may have found a better class of garbage.

The month of June flew by for a variety of reasons. But the thing that made June really rush by was a vacation Marlene and I took to Bermuda, made possible by Dad and Mother coming to stay with the children. I had been in Bermuda in 1947, while taking part in a navy reserve cruise. I liked the island then and always wanted to return. (I realize that Lea and Ed might consider this jaunt small potatoes compared to their travels, but for Marlene and me, it was a real treat. We rented a beachside cottage and two motor bikes, and man, did we have a ball! We covered that island from one end to another. The rule on the island is that on motor bikes, you have to travel single file, so being a gentleman, I lead the way. Ever ridden 100 miles with the feeling that Barney Oldfield was pressing in on you? I tell you, that Marlene is a tiger on that motorbike. And, eating all restaurant meals, with no kids to worry about, and whizzing around on those bikes gave us a feeling of freedom that we hadn't felt for a long time. There was so much to see and enjoy—gracious people, an aquarium, a perfume factory, an underground cavern, a lighthouse, an old fort, etc. Most fun and fascinating was renting diving helmets connected to an air supply on the surface and exploring the marvelous world of the ocean bottom and coral reef life. Super vacation!

Joe, I am planning on making an overnight visit to see Lea and Bill when I am on the coast, and I'm sure I'll hear more about Dorothy's recent visit. Keep your spirits up. All of us are hoping and praying about your parole.

Ed, nothing to say to you. You're in my thoughts even more than Joe. We will visit with Joyce soon. Your responsibilities grow as our involvement grows. I think you know my feelings well enough on the subject of Vietnam; we're there and there is a job to be done.

Lea and Bill—I'll see you soon if all goes according to schedule.
Rob

Okinawa (for the last time)
Monday, 12 July 1965

Dear Joe,

The reason for my lack of response is that I have been loading out Headquarters Battalion for its move to Vietnam. Somehow, I ended up being commanding officer of the organization. I was kept on Okinawa to be the Draft Commander of the rotation draft to Conus this month. By this time next week, though, I will be aboard ship on my way to the west coast and home. It will be a round about trip—to Taiwan, Japan, Hawaii before arriving in San Diego on the 7th of August. (Sorry about that, Lea.) I am glad to have been here, but not sorry my time is almost up, not feeling the least guilty about letting others have their turn in the barrel.

I'm enclosing a picture of yours truly and B. Gen. F. J Karch, who is pinning a Navy Commendation Medal with Combat "V" on me for my services in Vietnam. I got the whole works, parade and all, and it was quite thrilling being called front and center and then taking the salute as the troops passed in review. It's funny what men will do for a little piece of ribbon, but it is really quite satisfying to my ego to have it. I am not a bit ashamed of it as it is not for being a hero, but for meritorious service in keeping with the highest traditions of the Naval Service. I do not think that my services were in vain, and I am glad that I was able to do my part to maintain the freedom and dignity of man which, I feel that our country gives to more of its citizens than any other country on earth.

Joe, your letter was indeed a happy one, and I hope your parole is settled by the time I get home. I know that the unknown is the hardest thing of all to face.

Lea, never mind the old office stationery. I'd accept your bright and cheerful letters on the proverbial toilet paper roll if you cared to use it. I am thankful you will get to see Rob on his trip to the coast. I am more than a little disappointed that I will not get to see you on my way home.

Rob, I will be home on Sunday the 8th, and should be willing to accept visitors in a day or two. We will probably be moving on the 20th with stops in New Jersey and Pittsburgh. So, get that company of yours to modify your schedule to allow you to be in Connecticut then.

Lenny, we plan to be in Pittsburgh the week of the 23 of August, and I will call you to see if we can get together for our pizza date. Hope all is well with you. Counting the days!

Ed

Joe Killeen 78250
s/s State Farm, VA 23160
16 July 1965

Dear Voices,

First that malfeasance echo, Bill: Bill, do you realize what you have done? How could you allow this IQ/BQ survey to fall into Lea's hands? Surely, you didn't volunteer this knowledge? Just because you are married to one of the world's smartest women doesn't mean you have to ruin it for the rest of us fellows. Can't you imagine the repercussions? A man will be judged intellectual if he is seen with a skinny girl, sensual if she is an upper-story job, and pseudo-intellectual if his partner puts up a false front... It isn't fair! Why should I be judged sensual just because I'd like to design sweaters for that stupid Lana Turner? Moreover, your theory is all wet, and I can prove it! Study this mathematical formula, publish it in the AMA Journal, and I'll see what I can do about restoring you into the good graces of the men of America... (The) higher the IQ, (the) smaller the BQ. Let the symbol $>$ = the greater and $<$ = the smaller. Thus, $> IQ = <BQ$. Allow DQ = Bill's delivery quotient, LP = Lea's potential, PDQ = Paternal Delivery Quotient. If the higher IQ = the less number of children then observe: Lea's $BQ = LP + DQ$ (over) PDQ, cancel out: $LBQ = LP + DQ$ over $PDQ = L$ over $L = 1$ $BQ = 1$ (child) and since Lea has 2 children, then $BA = 1$ (child) or $< PDQ$ and $BQ = 2$ children or $>PDQ.. >PDQ = <IQ$. Thus $<IQ$ = not so smart! Hence, $L = >BQ$... Also, if $BQ = 1$, but $LBQ = 2$, which is double, thus this cuts IQ in half. Thus: $L = 0.5$ IQ... If Lea understands this formula, then all is well, for remember that sound reasoning is a convincing force against reality... If she can't understand it, all the better—it will convince her how little she does know! Blame yourself, Bill, if her vanity is hurt- you brought on this emergency. (Besides, I never heard of a vanity that couldn't be re-varnished!!)... Twenty-four hours since I wrote the above: Ed's photo and letter just arrived. "I am glad that I was able to do my part to maintain the freedom and dignity of man, which I feel that our country gives to more of its citizens than any other country on Earth..." Those words—that medal—both reflected in the intensity of Ed's face...Here I have no words, just thoughts—sacred thoughts of love and admiration. I could never speak them—nor could I describe the choking lump welled up within as I read: "I got the whole works, parade and all... thrilling being called front and center... the salute... the troops passed in review... a little piece of ribbon… the highest traditions of Naval Service." Big, lovable, humble Ed! Take a look at Major Edgar S…… USMC—our Ed! Look at those thousands of Eds who make the sacrifice and leave it to history to cross the "t's" and dot the "i's"… Bullets, guts and blood, snap, rip, bang, boom—blowie! Fighting unseen enemy bands that have neither front nor rear, that drift in and out like a vapor—quiet and deadly as dead!… Take a good look at those they fight for, that juxtaposed conglomeration of diverse Americans: the grateful, the thankless—the "egghead," the jerk—the "haves," the bums—the loyal, the truant—the worth, the punk—the saint, the damned—the doer, the spouter—the helper, the helpless—the everybody, the busybody, the nobody, the etceteras and the and-so-forths—the whole she-bang! Ed…… thank you! … In Bermuda waters, O so clear and cold." I've never been to Bermuda, but I enjoyed the verbal trip with Rob. In fact, it's been 3 years since I did any swimming. I enjoyed the splash, also feeding the fishes, and the motorbikes. Lea: I haven't heard from Dorothy since California—have you? Never enough writing space!—

Joe

Los Gatos
July 30, 1965

Dear Joe (and of course, all other voices)

Ah, Joe! How deeply you have wounded me with your mathematically straight arrow!! Bad enough it is to be stuck with a minus BQ, but now to have it mathematically proven that I have only a 1/2 IQ! This is too much! Needless to say, I understood the equation entirely! Didn't you, fellas??? On the other hand, maybe I ought to confess that things grew a little hazy after the first two steps, but Bill made it a little further, which proves he has about a 3/4 IQ. If you think I am going to try to disprove it or even to suggest an alternate bit of logic, let me put your fears at rest. I would have to accept Bill's premise and then work backwards, and since I have trouble working equations forwards, I think I'll let well enough alone. However, I have this much to say, Joe Killeen, since you're so smart! : I didn't understand one bit of your stupid equation, and therefore I summarily reject the whole thing as inaccurate. So much for men's dumb theories!!

Joe, I laughed myself to pieces over your remarkable squelch! Your wit is showing! The rest of your letter, especially the part about Ed, is echoed by all of us. I not only appreciate Ed's feelings about Vietnam, but I admire them more than I can say. That he would do an exemplary job in whatever task faced him, is no more than those of us who know him would expect. He is a neat guy, a wonderful friend, to whom we all owe a debt. My thanks, too, Ed!

A word about Rob's visit. It was too short, for one thing, since I picked him up at San Jose Airport in the evening, and I drove him to the S.F. airport at 8 AM the next morning. I convinced Rob that it was so cheap to fly from LA to SF ($14.18—one way), that he couldn't pass it up. Well, Bill pointed out that he could also fly from LA to San Jose, which is less distance. So, he did, but found out that it cost $10. more to go 50 miles less. It was great to see him, though, and I didn't mind the trips to the airports at all. You know, Rob and I have some kind of special camaraderie that has spanned nearly 25 years, and it has remained essentially unchanged. Often, those relationships, which begin in childhood and after a hiatus of years, are resumed in maturity, are a disappointment. People often find that they have grown in different directions, and that what was present in youth is now gone. In truth, I was closer to Rob than to any of you in high school. But, that very closeness made the friendship all the more vulnerable in these later years. No so, however. I still see Rob in exactly the same light I have always seen him. (Not counting the couple of months when I was 14 and had a crush on him! No explaining sophomoric idiocy!) We still spat over inconsequential things, still disagree on many issues, still have only a few scant interests in common, and it still doesn't matter! (And by now, I suppose he's thrown his hands in the air. Sentiment always made him nervous! He sat in my living room and told Bill he considered me "mushy.")

By now, Ed is aboard ship heading in a roundabout fashion for home. Let's hope this is the last separation before he retires.

Joe, I haven't heard from Dorothy either, but I am sure by the time this reaches you, we both will have. I did enjoy her visit. She's a lovely person.

Bill will be off this afternoon for 2 and 1/2 weeks of Air Force Reserve duty. I hate it when he is gone, but I am grateful that, for the time being, he is in no danger of being called up. I know he would prefer not having to go and return, having to start building a practice all over again. Among other things, I think he would rather not have to rehire me!

My wishes to all of you for continued peace of mind, and to all of you, I send my affection.

Lea

At Sea
Thursday, 5 August 1965

Dear Voices,

Right now we are about 48 hours out of San Diego and I hope about 72 hours out of Connecticut. I guess you can all rejoice with me that this year is drawing to a close for Joyce and me. I have been rereading all of the voice letters. One of the wonderful things about this whole idea of writing to Joe has been the fun of seeing Lea, Rob, and Lenny again, and I hope that Joe realizes what a wonderful gift he has given us all. It is interesting that we are approaching the second anniversary of this correspondence and there seems to be no let down on anyone's part. There has been so much interesting discussion from philosophy to politics. All of you are by nature compassionate, and the concern for Joyce and me this last year is truly appreciated. I notice that each of us has a religious affiliation now that Lea seems to have found the Quaker Meeting House, and while each may be different, they all look to the same God. I still pray that Joe's parole be looked upon by Him with favor.

I am glad it will be three more years until the next general election. Not that I mind a good argument, it's just that we will never change anyone's mind about how to vote, and the space in the letters could be put to better use. All the concern, that we show for each other is a beautiful thing. Rob's visits to my family this year have been a comfort to me, and Lea's riding the bus to Travis will remain in my heart for the rest of my life.

Soon, I will be seeing Rob and Lenny, and I will try to get pictures of everyone to send to you, Joe, so that you can see how we have gotten older over this last 18 months. I promise to write again as soon as we are settled in Norfolk and I have a new address. I will be your closest neighbor then, Joe, and will be glad to act as the relay station for your outbound letters.

Aloha means both hello and good-bye, so...

Aloha,

Ed

Weston,
August 9 1965

Dear Joe,

Another month gone by? Impossible! I have been going through old photos and slides, taken through the years and organizing them. I ran across a black and white snap of you, Joe, taken at AIP camp—remember those years?—I also found snaps taken of Ed and Joyce in 1947 during courting days at Princeton.

Only one trip this month—to the west coast, the best part of it also the shortest—to Los Gatos. It was far better than no visit at all, however. I was tired upon arriving at Lea and Bill's. I was so tired, in fact, that I gave up the ghost at 1 AM without even having the strength to argue with Lea over politics or anything else. I must be getting old. The next morning, Lea was gracious enough to drive me to the S. F. Airport early as the hour was. We arrived in plenty of time, and decided to have a bite of breakfast. Somehow, the time flew by, and the next thing I heard was the final boarding call for my flight. Poor Lea didn't even get to finish her pancakes. As it turned out, however, my tardiness was to my advantage. My economy class seat had been given to someone else, so the agent assigned me to a seat in the first—class section. Thanks to Lea's pancakes, I had free drinks and a steak on the way east, and lots of legroom.

Had a good visit with Joyce and the kids, did some sightseeing in New York, and Marlene and I saw a play at summer stock, took Doug to YMCA camp,—all the relaxing stuff of summer. And now, I am going to turn to the letters from all of you to answer.

Joe, I am not competent to respond to such an erudite, complicated formula as your BQ/IQ equation. It exceeds my analytical capabilities, and I defer to your superior scientific mind. Besides, it left me out in left field. But, I will comment briefly on your pulpit decision. What drives a man to the pulpit, and makes him think that is the way in which he can best serve? I don't know, but I have seen brother Bill struggle with his decision to go that route. If I were in your position, I would defer such a decision until after your release. I would distrust the feelings I have right now, assuming that they are tainted by my surroundings. At least, be fair to yourself. There are many ways to serve, and the world is filled with opportunities in all walks of life.

Lea, I spend a good half hour with Marlene each time before I travel out to the coast, casually assuring her that I visit you only because you like my mother—that you are just like one of the boys, etc.—and then you go and write one of those complimentary letters. Holy cow. Woman, think of my happy home. Pretty soon Marlene won't even allow me to go west of the Mississippi.

Your comment about a friendship of nearly 25 years struck home. That's a long time by our human standards—for us, about 2/3 of our lives! And I'm feeling mellow enough tonight to admit that I too am very happy that our friendship has weathered the trials of time and neglect (the neglect being on my part). In the end, life boils down to not too many fundamentals—and a lasting friendship, I believe, says much. How fortunate we all are that the Voices have become audible to all of us again.

Lea, that's about as sentimental as I intend to get for tonight. I hope my visits with your bunch will speak louder than my mumbling words. Thanks very much for all the photos. Still like very much the ones of you (alone) and Dorothy (with Billy). I don't know why you're so happy with that shot of me. Gee. I looked at that picture and wondered who that wrinkled, balding, smug fellow was.

That's all for tonight. My best to all the voices and their loved ones. Good night, my friends,

Rob

(Hand written note to Lea) Hello, Pal, Thanks for all the nice words in your last letter. The pleasure was mutual during my last visit—and I may even get to know that hubby of yours.

Rob

Joe Killeen–78250
S/S State Farm, VA 23160
22 August 1965

Dear Voices,

First Rob: Your possession of old AIP photos reminds me of a similar surprise presented to me by Lenny in June of 1964. He sent me two letters I had written him twenty years before—in June 1944. What collectors you fellas are!…Speaking of pictures, I appreciate Lea's latest of you. It allows me a closer view than any I have had in the recent past. You look good—even after 20 years, I would know you immediately. Has your hair darkened with the years? You comment about a receding hairline; I still have a widow's peak, which is slowly being surrounded by a sea of baldness... How could you fail to comprehend my simple IQ/BQ equation? An intelligent statement, similar to mine, once inspired O'Henry to write: " I am convinced that what you have uttered is what you said."...I look at Lea, especially in those pictures of her in that kimono, and wonder how Rob could dare call her "one of the boys." Come on, fella!... Lea, I can't thank you enough for the pictures, especially of my sister. In fact, I am pleased with all the pictures. Those of Adam and Eve are all good. I once spent time trying to remove pomegranate juice stains that had been smeared all over the statue (Mexican Indians use pomegranate juice for ink). I failed, but the sun eventually bleached the stone white again. I noticed there are no longer the Italian cypresses as background for the statue... Ed comments that all of us have a religion, and this is worth noting. Judging by Lea's pen, I feel I might enjoy the quiet spiritual fervor of the Friends. I know but little of Quakerism, Lea, but George Fox's central theme of, "the Inner Light" seems to embrace a kind of mystical humanism, involving a deep personal concept of God. You attribute this experience to me, but you share it as well... One's place and manner of service is not easily discerned, Rob—I must agree with you. Nothing exists without purpose. Thus my existence has a purpose. What purpose? I don't know. It is therefore not one I have chosen. It is someone wiser than I who has. I must pray that this Someone enlightens me. It is the wisest thing... You, Rob, saw my anxiety over this pulpit decision. Your inner self saw and couldn't remain silent. My play on words seems the only way I can express myself. Such unveilings are slow and I am glad you Voices are patient... Dorothy arrived home safely. Her visit, and two letters since, displays her enthusiasm for her western trip. Rob and Ed always look forward to their Los Gatos visits and now, Dorothy has had a share in this pleasure. Lea and Bill, I just don't know how to thank you. Welcome home, Edgar Theodore Bear! We all feel joy for your safe return...Lea, I've been married twice—Doris and I met in 1957, married in 1960 (in Mexico—during my escape). She was an evangelist minister who visited prisoners, and she knew of my plan. We agreed to meet 90 days after the escape in Houston, and we did, my having walked much of the way, hitchhiking or hopping freights from Virginia there. We went south into Mexico, and I married under the name of John Sherman. Believe it or not, I was able to get a social security card and a driver's license under that name in Texas. Subsequently, we went to Colorado, where we became traveling preachers for about 4 years. Ultimately, probably suffering from guilt, she told Senator Hatfield from Oregon about it, and he contacted the FBI. I was arrested as I was riding a bike, and you know the rest. I make no comment about any of this; I tell you now, because you deserve to know the truth... My next letter should say definitely one way or another if I am allowed parole. Keep those prayers in orbit.

A fond aloha—

Joe

Los Gatos
September 7 (Labor Day) 1965

Dear Joe and sundry Voices,

Bill returned from two weeks of Reserve Duty, refreshed. During his absence, I took the boys on two short trips, winding the summer up in style; now, we are all ready to dig in when school begins next week. Yes, I am all set, too—have registered, have my counseling appointment, bought my books, and am set to go. I'll be taking Psychology and Political Science. Six units are all, until I see how I can handle it. Next semester, if all goes well, I may try to add a third class, bringing my unit load up to 10. I still teach German on Saturday morning, which takes considerable preparation. So I don't want to commit myself beyond my limits.

Last week I spent winding up loose ends, so that I am relatively organized at this point. I said good-bye to one of my former students (the boy who gave me such fits, and then made up for it by giving me flowers on my birthday and at Christmas.) He is going to U. C. at Santa Barbara, leaving on Tuesday, so we had him over for dinner last night. I'll miss him. So, I get the feeling that I am running about winding up chapters and closing books. Eras do have a way of ending, and young people grow up and are on their way.

Now, to answer some of your letters:

Ed, you're home, and I am much relieved. Your letter was full of nostalgia and anticipation. I had the feeling you were reviewing the year. I was sorry not to see Joyce, but next year, if that trip east materializes, that will be remedied. I assume Joe will be released, and I plan on seeing all of you—one way or another. No more talking politics in letters, Ed? Have a heart! It's my favorite subject! Besides, I don't want to convince anybody of anything, and most of what I learn I learn in arguments! What do we substitute? Religion? Well, OK. On that subject, I have to tell you that I have indeed found that spiritual comfort zone I have been seeking, in the Society of Friends. I have decided to ask for membership, and I will do my best to live up to those high standards of behavior. Whether or not I can remains to be seen. But, I will try. My own personal life fits well into the pattern of Quaker behavior and principles. In a sense, it is an affirmation of what I already am—in the area of social concerns, in any event. I do already direct much of my activities in the area of service. Now, more of it will be within the framework of the Society of Friends. For the moment, it is enough to say that I have found comfort and pleasure in the company of these quiet and reverent people. That I have the effrontery to want to become one of them is something else again. As Rob said to Bill on his last visit here, "It is indeed a miracle that Lea could be quiet for a whole hour at a stretch!"

Rob, your letter, again, was delightful. I love your newsy accounts of your family activities. I'm happy to hear that my unfinished pancakes not only helped my spreading figure, but also got you a better seat on the plane. Gee, and they were such good buckwheat cakes, too! Sorry you didn't like your picture. I was congratulating myself so, about not having cut off your head again, that I thought it was pretty good! It was a natural picture—a good grin. And Marlene, I didn't buy that stuff about Rob's having to "explain" how platonic our friendship is. As if you needed an explanation. That Rob and I have been devoted friends for years is obvious—as obvious as the nature of that devotion, based as it is on a series of jibes, wise-cracks, and needling, like, "I'm not sure I like the darker lipstick, kiddo." or "You're getting a little chubby, pal," On the other hand, if the needling stopped, I suppose I'd worry he was mad at me for something.

Joe, your letters get better and better. Thanks for all the compliments. That hostess robe, made of towels, that you called a kimono, covers up a multitude of nothing, you know. I was in it, because Dorothy was leaving so early in the morning, and it is chilly at that hour. Her bravely making the west coast trip was partly responsible for my decision to make that trip east next year. I have already begun looking at trailers. I plan to pull one to camp in, and I want to show the boys the scenic beauty of the west—grand canyon, painted desert, Tombstone, Indian reservations in Arizona, Mesa Verde, Monument Valley, etc. and to travel through the Ozarks to Virginia. We plan to visit Williamsburg, and from there on to Washington, DC… Bill can't leave his practice a whole summer, so he may fly east and do the return driving over the northern route, via Niagara Falls, Blue Hole in Ohio, Minnesota, Badlands in S. Dakota, Devils Tower, Wyoming, and Yellowstone and Jackson Hole, Craters of the Moon in Idaho. I will have to have another adult to spell the driving, because Billy will turn 15 on the trip and not driving yet. I'll have to work on that. I plan to be away the whole summer.

Joe, I was surprised when you mentioned George Fox. You know so much about comparative religion, and you certainly have a strong spiritual base, but you are searching, like all of us. We each seem to have found, as Ed said, "a religion, but I still feel you haven't found yours, yet. Am I right? For some time, I have believed that the denomination is of secondary importance. I think the reason we have so many is not that there are many concepts of God, but that there are many ways in which people are comfortable in worshipping. For my part, I wanted no creed, no oaths, no order of worship. I wanted a form of worship stripped of all externals, simple, unencumbering, undemanding, except in so far as my own conscience demands of me. But, I realize that this is not the answer for many people. Many find comfort in familiar hymns, a familiar order of worship, in repetition of familiar old and beautiful prayers. While I prefer not to have a minister, there are those who need a minister, who need guidance or who simply enjoy the stimulating sermon on Sundays. I guess what this is all leading to is your thoughts about the pulpit. In the end, you will do what you must do. And I am certain that whatever your decision, it will be the best for you. But, I agree with Rob that it might be wiser to wait until you are released and have time to readjust to society and to learn where you can best fit into it. I rather suspect you would prefer some kind of service, as a career. I would. But, I am limited by many things,—my responsibilities to my family, which is my first love, my education, and time. So, service is now an avocation rather than a vocation for me.

Love to all,

Lea

Virginia Beach, VA

15 September, 1965

Dear Joe and all,

We are settled in our new four bedroom home in the Carolanne Farms section of Virginia Beach, about 12 miles from the office. We found it the same day our stuff arrived in Norfolk, so the move was a relatively easy one.

Arrival in San Diego was as scheduled, and I caught a commuter to L. A. with a late flight out of there to the east coast, arriving in Hartford at

8 AM, where Joyce and the kids met me. My welcome in Wallingford was wonderful, particularly at church, where Father Lovejoy has been just marvelous to us all. We spent 10 days in Wallingford prior to starting the move to Virginia, with two visits with Rob and family.

After that, we spent a week in Pittsburgh, where I visited with my mother and Rob's folks, and of course, there was a long visit with Lenny. We went out one night—just the two of us, and talked for 5 hours straight. The last 18 months has brought about considerable improvement in Lenny's outlook, I am happy to say. He even talked of coming to visit us in Norfolk. He indicated that while he will probably never become a voice letter writer, he may be able to overcome his aversion to writing enough to send an occasional individual letter to Rob or me. The two Joyces are convinced that he and I are worse than any two women when it comes to talking.

Then came the disappointing news. I found that I was passed over for Lt. Col. this year. I get another chance next year, but it hurt my vanity a bit. But, what made Joyce unhappy was my finding that I have to go away for 8 weeks to a school in Georgia—after just returning from a year away from home.

Lea, your letter was the longest you have ever written to us. Your trip next year sounds wonderful, especially your plans to come to Williamsburg, which is very close to us. And, are you aware that you wrote three pages single spaced and you didn't mention politics once? As for your interest in the Society of Friends, I am glad for you. I am one of those who finds great comfort in the old familiar prayers and hymns, though, as well as the familiar liturgy of a formal religion. I would argue with you that the religion you talk about does make demands on you over and above your own conscience! If it does not, then you are trying to be your own God, and I am sure that you would deny this. What you call your conscience may well be the prodding of a force outside of you, which I believe to be the Holy Ghost.

It is nice to talk to Joe about a life of service, but I feel that there is need for some of Ed's old pragmatism. Joe is going to have a rough road to walk when the parole goes through. American society is not perfect and we have never been real nice to people who have been in prison for any reason. A life of service requires that the survival necessities be taken care of first and Joe must look to the future with the idea of being able to provide himself with the tools to survive. He is going to need a job and time to adjust to society and society to him before he will be able to start to serve. I feel time and guts will allow him to do it in the future, but not immediately upon his release. I also feel that the evangelical circuit for Joe would not really be a life of service, but an attempt to try to atone for his past actions and he has been punished enough already. Well, enough pragmatism. My love to all. Smooth sailing!

Ed

New Suit for Sal

Arlington, VA
September 23 1965

Dear Lea,

By now, Bill is probably in full swing at his new location. I do hope he continues his enthusiasm and his success. You are engrossed in courses; the boys are back in school. Where does the time go?

I continued to postpone writing to you because I expected daily to learn that Rol (I can't get used to calling him Joe!) would be released. The word finally came from Mr. Gaudio (his probation officer) whose secretary called me and I, in turn wrote immediately to Rol. As of last Sunday, the first word came from me and the second indication was that fitting for a suit (that almost fit, he said), but nothing official at all on release or date.

Needless to say, he is joyous. He is to be released on September 28. I have written to learn of the time and place where I may pick him up. In his letter of last Sunday, Rol asked that you let Rob, Ed, and Lenny know and to tell you all that he will write the "longest letter they have ever received from me just as soon as I can focus my eyes to the bright rising sun of freedom."

I don't think Doris will present any real threat now to Rol's adjustment. Her lawyer advised her that they are not legally married and that she should "let sleeping dogs lie" and not pursue divorce. In the event she wants to marry, however, the only one who could create problems for her is Rol, if he objected. She says she loves him very much but doesn't know what she wants. She is torn by feelings of guilt.

I did so enjoy my visit with you and Bill, and I highly recommend you for personal escort service both in San Francisco and Los Gatos, Lea. There was so little time and so much to choose from, that it was frustrating. I haven't been the same since my return, wanting it to go on and on. At Yosemite, I could have remained forever. If you have not yet visited Yosemite, you must go there. It must be beautiful in the fall, and make it a camping trip for the family. I loved tenting out and would have liked to remain longer.

I have been looking for a house, a small, functional house, not too difficult to maintain, convenient to public transportation, shopping, since Rol will not be able to drive. It must be a treed lot, though.

I hope nothing alters your plans to come east next summer. I am looking forward to having all of you and for as long as you can stay. Your boys are dear. Your home is lovely. For you both, I wish many, many happy and successful years in it. You are both real assets to the San Jose/Los Gatos area.

To say "thank you" to you and Bill, Rob, and Ed sounds so inadequate, but thank you I do, for your encouragement, understanding, and love for Rol. And thank you for your most gracious treatment of me.

Fondly,
Dorothy

September 28, 1965

A Western Union night letter:

Joe, enjoy the first taste of the sweetness of freedom in the knowledge that our thoughts are very much with you. Welcome home, my friend.

Lea

Alexandria, VA
1 October 1965

Dear Voices,

The road may be rough, Ed—it is certain to offer no bed of roses—but it can still be a pathway of roses. The thorns may prick and even tear the flesh, yet a rose is a rose is a rose. No doubt, my moment is overly exuberant. The novelty of change will quickly wear off and the serious business of what lies ahead will face me squarely.

Already there has been my first taste of cold reality since my visit of the other day with the local parole office. And yesterday, I learned that my job situation won't be exactly inviting. Years ago, when I worked for this particular company, I was able to name my own salary within reason. Today, the situation is reversed. I'll be earning a much lower salary than the scale calls for. But, perhaps this is as it should be—anyway, it's a challenge I am prepared to take on.

There are other things that encourage me, such things as a family that somehow has become more united in these recent years. Discord gives way to need. My first evening at Dorothy's apartment included phone calls from Pittsburgh and New York from family. The telegram that arrived from Lea the following day was a warm reminder of the tremendous gift and inspiration offered by the Voices Five. I was treated to a reception from Dorothy and her daughter, Maureen, that would make the Biblical prodigal son's father look like a disinterested bystander. Dorothy handed me a letter, written in advance from her other daughter who lives in Nebraska, wanting me to have it on my arrival home.

Well, anyway, if Sal Salamander has no other reason to make it in this new life, the filial regards and inspirations are enough to keep him wiggling about for a long time. If you don't mind a drippy (but sincere) piece of sentiment, perhaps Galbraith's words may better express what I mean:

Not that I am strong
But that you think me so—
From need to justify your faith,
My strength and courage flow.

Maureen, who prefers to be called Gidget, has included me in just about all of her activities these past few days—driving me around in a Corvair convertible. I wondered at one moment if even my parole officer wouldn't give anything to change positions with me, riding around with this pretty young girl.

Gidget and Dorothy took me shopping for clothes the other evening, and what a BLAST, as Lea would say. I refused to render any opinions on what was purchased. I think I was too bewildered. These two gals had me trying on everything in sight, to the dismay of the young but patient gentleman who waited on us. He couldn't get over my lack of voice in these matters. Each thing I tried on, he would look to me for approval or disapproval, and I just directed him to the girls. In a word, I kept my overwhelmed mouth shut and ended up looking pretty good. The salesman didn't understand that I'm so out of time on men's styles that I felt like the Connecticut Yankee at King Arthur's court!

No need to tell you what an extreme change my life is going through right now. I promised a long letter, but so much is happening, that I doubt my powers of concentration can go much further.

One thing, however—Lea, on the eve of my departure from the Farm, I read *Siddhartha*. A fellow loaned me a copy that he just received. What better reading could I have made at such an important time in my life? Yet, I cannot, at this time, properly do justice to this book. So, add this to the other list of comments I owe. Lea, you must definitely come east next year. Rob and Ed, do either of you have any trips to Washington on your agendas in the near future? Lenny, I can't leave the area; but 236 miles wouldn't use up too much of a weekend, except, maybe all of it!

God bless all of you. Forgive my inability to keep pecking away at this typewriter, but know that all is well.

Gallopin' Sal,

Joe

Weston

October 5, 1965

Dear friends,

Joe, your freedom is something that all of us have been thinking about and praying over for two years. Let me simply say that I am so happy that you have secured your freedom. I always accuse Lea of having the corner on mushiness, and I'd hate to break out and show her that we fellows often feel exactly the same way.

Your first letter from Dorothy was a gem, and I very much liked the Galbraith quote. I am sure it holds true for all of our relations with our loved ones. The strength gained from a bond of mutual respect is a two way street, which I hoped was evident in all our writing to you in the past.

Nicest thing in the letter was the description of riding in the convertible with Gidget; it was enough to make me envious! Lea speaks so highly of Dorothy, and I am sure we will all feel the same way, once our paths cross.

The news about the job was somewhat disturbing, but perhaps not unexpected, our imperfect society being what it is. However, it's a start, and your problem now is to pitch in and prove yourself to all concerned at work. It's just as important to get your feet set on the ground and to take some things as they come—without recourse at times.

Len, just a short word in here for you. I am scheduled to be in Pittsburgh next week, I think I'm staying at Webster Hall and teaching somewhere in East Liberty. How about if I call, and we can see if it's possible to get together?

Ed, what is all this jazz about another stint away from home? What's the matter with that outfit of yours? Holy cow! Sorry about the disappointment about not being upped in grade. Let's hope for better news next time around. The enclosed pictures should bring back some happy moments. The one of you and Joyce will, I hope, be a reminder over the years of a time of renewed love.

And now, for mushy, talkative Lea. Greetings, chum (to use your expression) from part of the East Coast mob. My but that is some red-hot typewriter you have there. Are you trying to make the rest of us look bad? Three pages!! Give us a break, woman. By this time, I assume you are well into your schoolwork, and are forcing the old brain cells to function more efficiently than usual. Maybe your letters will have less volume now.

Those plans to drive to the east sound mighty ambitious, girl, but so nice. I hope we can hit the westward trail before the kids grow up too much. I envy you your proposed trip, and hope that it materializes as planned. Needless to say, our door will be open for all of you.

My west coast trip this month is firming up, but no details yet. I will arrive in San Francisco on October 24. Classes will be Monday and Tuesday and I hope that Tuesday night, I will be able to get to Los Gatos. Departure will be on Wednesday, at 10 AM from San Francisco. I hope I am not wearing out my welcome with these trips, but it is always so good to see you. I'll give you a call when I get in town on Sunday.

Weather in Connecticut has taken a wintry turn, and temperatures below freezing are predicted for tonight. Ahhhh!

Goodnight, ALL my free friends!

Rob

Los Gatos
October 8 1965

Dear Voices,

This will be a one-page letter. Rob is right. I won't have the time to write any more of those long epistles, now that so much studying is taking up so much of my life. From the tone of Rob's letter, I am sure my wordiness will not be missed.

Joe, your first letter from home was a delight, and to paraphrase Rob, a source of concern, too. I had hoped things would be easier for you. I trust that you will turn an unsatisfactory work situation into a worthwhile one, in the end. Nothing is ideal, is it? What is "ideal" anyway, but a guide? One rarely attains it. I think the way a person accepts the reality of his life constitutes a good portion of his worth as a person. I have no reason to think you will do any less, Joe. Anyway, Dorothy is there to listen to your gripes. There is a lot to be said for good listeners.

Would you like me to send you *Siddhartha*, so you can read it again at your leisure? I'll be glad to. I agree that the timing of your reading that particular book was perfect! It is a serene concept of human existence, don't you think?

Ed, sorry about your being passed over for promotion. Bill was baffled, but he predicts you are a sure bet for next time around. My opinion of you is colored by my great fondness for you, but Bill has not known you as long, is more objective, and is an excellent judge of character. Believe him!

I am glad you and Lenny had a good visit. Good for you both. Next summer, I would like to discuss my association with the Society of Friends with you if we get the chance. I prefer not launching into this in detail in a letter, because so much of one's religious orientation is personal and no concrete issues are involved—only feelings and beliefs. As to my being my own God, let me say one thing: the only aspect of God which I know about is that which is within me—the sense that I have access to the spark of divinity which I believe is in all people. Call it the Holy Spirit or the Light Within, I think it's all the same. I also believe that there is a strong drive toward Good in all people. I consider this to be that spark of God in me, and if that makes me my own God, so be it, I guess. Perhaps all this is a matter of semantics. Holy Ghost, conscience, Inner Light, what's the difference?

Rob, Bill and I both look forward to your West Coast visit, and whatever you want to do is what we will do, ranging from nothing to a whiz-bang evening on the town. We are not whiz-bangers, by nature, so that evening in the living room in relaxed conversation will be fine with us. Hey, what do you mean, "mushy, talkative Lea?" Some consider me terse! And yes, I am knee-deep in schoolwork, and it's not difficult—just time consuming. But, I love the mental stimulation, and I find it's not as difficult as I feared. Maybe I'm not as rusty as I thought I was.

Got a letter today from that former student, who is a freshman at University of California at Santa Barbara. It was full of discussion of problems in political science, philosophy, history, and asking for my ideas on these problems. (This is the same 17-year-old boy I mentioned in previous letters) He signed the letter with a statement that made me wince. It was, "See ya! Take it easy, college girl!"

And when I said this would be a one-page letter, I knew you wouldn't believe me, anyway!

Fond affection,

Lea

Saturday, October 16, 1965
Fort Gordon, GA

Dear Friends,

I am at the Army Civil Affairs School here in Georgia. Been here three weeks, with five more to go. Joyce is not thrilled with all this. I am using those tape recorders and calling twice a week, but she really resents this separation.

The school has been interesting, though. Civil affairs includes Military Government and what we call Civic Action, the military way of trying to help people in the emerging countries to help themselves to improve their standard of living. It includes international law to city management to public health and agricultural training methods. I should find it useful if I teach civics in high school some day. It includes 8 hours of class with two of assigned reading.

Joe, I am thinking we will want to arrange a reunion when Lea makes that trip back east next summer, and I was hoping for a Virginia Beach venue. I am sure Rob and I will make it down there before that, however. Joyce really liked your little poem as did I. In fact, your first letter after your release was the best letter you have written so far, I thought. Your explanation of your present situation and the feelings of being free again indicate you can be practical and yet still have faith.

Rob, we miss Connecticut, and I would not be surprised to find myself retired there some day. We like Norfolk fine, but would prefer a small Connecticut town. Hope your visit with Lenny was as enjoyable as mine.

Lea, I will venture off into world politics for a moment, but not to bait you. I am rather miffed this weekend at the young fools who are demonstrating about our involvement in Vietnam. To me it is obvious that the punks are looking at only one side of the coin and then not clearly. Granted that there is suffering and hardship involved for many, still there is much good being done, too. The average American in that country is sincerely interested in helping the people there and I am sure that there is no thought of Colonialism involved. They can use our help, by our teaching the Vietnamese to help themselves. I am proud to have had a part in that effort.

Time to go. Send any responses to the Virginia Beach address and Joyce will forward them to me after reading them herself.

Sayonara,
Ed

Arlington, VA
7 November, 1965

Dear Voices,

One should observe not only what is in words but also what words do not say. In fact, words may betray, for they may offer reasons that sound the best rather than those that are real. Most words have more than one meaning. For example, one can equivocate in the interplay of the words "kill" and "murder." Then, there is the amphibolous use of the word "genocide." These particular words are catching the attention of the various national news media these days. These, supposedly, are intended to describe those who continue to support the South Vietnam War.. It seems, therefore, more important to recognize what words conceal and what silence reveals.

No doubt there are sincere conscientious objectors among the S.D.S. and other "pacifist" movements; but their numbers are infinitesimal within these groups. The rest use it as an excuse for avoiding military service. One does not have to be a pacifist to be anti-war, anti-violence, and anti-destruction. And these attributes are not exclusive to these movements. Any man who has been through war has no desire to return to the battlefield. No parent, sister, or child enjoys the thought of a family member going off to war. Nor are we all so apathetic that we don't care what happens to the other guy. I doubt that the abhorrence of war can be more deeply felt by the sincere conscientious objector than by those who have had a first hand taste of war, resulting in that view.

The young are our greatest idealists and idealists cannot accept double standards as many of us do as we grow in age. We teach these young people about "one world," but we are too nationalistic in attitude to be universal, too sectarian to be catholic, and too bigoted to truly integrate. Yet, I cannot defend the S.D.S. and similar organizations; I do want to understand them, however. Chekhov wrote: " Man will become better only when you make him see what he is like."

Lea, I admire your notes on "that of God in me." And I endorse them! Erich Fromm, in *The Art of Loving*, interestingly defines religion into two types: Anthropomorphism, or God as the other person, and monotheism, which involves an indefinable God principle and moral activism. Sartre holds an analysis quite close to Fromm's view of anthropomorphism: "…in the infantile dependence on an anthropomorphic picture of God without the transforming

173

of life according to the principles of God, we are closer to a primitive idolatrous tribe than to the religious culture of the Middle Ages."

Monotheism, as a type of religious belief, envisions God not as an outside power to be obeyed but rather as a symbol for human moral achievement. The task of the believer is not conformity to law but actualization of an inner God principle.

People, for the most part, have become apathetic and rather sterile toward theological thinking. Religious inquiry is brushed aside with sick reasoning that claims, that what a man's beliefs really are should never be inquired into. And, still less, one doesn't ask why he holds those views. But, what good are beliefs if we remain quiet about them? How are any to know we hold them? Candles are hidden under bushels so that none share the Light. The melancholy of Job has a place here: The light is as midnight... The young are like the rush that cannot grow without mire. Spiritual reticence dims lighted doorways. A psalmist warns that without light there is but darkness underfoot and a false balance. Today, lacking direction, the wanderer is either caught up in atheistic Marxism or drowns in agnostic existentialism. For every two that have Light, there are eight who have not. And these say to the believers: " You believe in things because you need to, what you believe in has no value of its own, no function." To be without belief is to be without balance. Lack of balance is to lack morals. Today's avant garde now says, "I just think of things as beautiful or not... I don't think of good and bad." The anthropomorphic child of God is intrinsic, but only introductive; the child must become an adult. Monotheism accepts the challenge of growth and change.

(My, but haven't I gotten carried away on my own pantheistic words!!)

Lea, *The Art of Loving* has become a sort of catechistic reference to improve my limited ability in the science of Love.

Tolstoy in *War and Peace* writes:

"Love? What is love?... Love hinders death; love is life. All, everything that I understand, I understand only because I love. Everything is, everything exists, only because I love. Everything is united by it alone. Love is God, and to die means that I, a particle of love, shall return to the general and eternal source of Love."

Dostoevsky speaks of love in dreams and love in action in *The Brothers Karamazov*. He claims:

"Love in action is a harsh and dreadful thing compared with love in dreams. Love in dreams is greedy for immediate action, rapidly performed and in the sight of all. Men will even give their lives if only the ordeal does not last long, with all looking on and applauding as though on the stage. But, active love is labor and fortitude. "

In his *Theory of Man*, Ralph Harper writes, "A man cannot become the person he wants to be merely by thinking about himself, but only by doing something with himself. This requires involving himself in the affairs of others, in adapting himself to social pressures, in transforming his environment…"

An interesting demonstration of love can be found in two manila folders that I possess. They contain "voice" letters. They testify that love is simply an outstreaming of good will.

(Wow!! Now, honestly, don't you people wish I were still restricted to my one-page, censored jobs???)

Ed, your Joyce should be hearing from Dorothy about the time this letter is mailed. My sister shares my excitement about your Bethesda trip. We hope you can stay overnight.

Rob, I'm anxious to hear of your visit with Lenny in Mountmore. Perhaps in a couple of months, I might be able to visit Pittsburgh. The local officials will grant me a three-day trip. Frankly, I want to go mainly to see and talk with Lenny. Lenny, Lenny,—I am truly eager to see you!

Ed, I am restricted to the four northern Virginia counties. Of course, I work in Washington and am permitted company business jaunts into Maryland. I cannot stay overnight without official sanction.

Lea, my nieces hear so much of you from me and from Dorothy, that they look forward to meeting you. Casey lives in Lincoln, Nebraska, where her husband is working on a masters at the University. Already they are hoping you'll be able to stay over in Lincoln during your trip east next summer. Needless to say, all of us are excited for your visit to this area.

Yesterday, I moved into my own place in Arlington, which I hope to share with my mother soon. I have an unlisted phone number, which I'll attach to this letter. Lea, what philosophy courses are you taking? Keep me posted. I'm within walking distance of University of Virginia.

The past month has been one of interesting adjustment. I feel (almost) like a free-person again. I have been given permission to obtain a driver's license but am not permitted to own a car yet (which I can't afford anyhow!) Job goes well, no complaints. One good thing about having a prison background is that one has to put out twice the effort as the next guy—I like that because most of us don't put out as much effort as we should anyway.

Are you all tired of reading?—Well, I'm tired of writing. I've written most of this out in rough draft but intend to rewrite so as not to omit anything. So long for now, wonderful ones,
Joe

Lea—It may seem that I am critical of all conscientious objectors, but not so—if they are sincere. One cannot be a believer without respecting the other believer. I, in no wise, connect or confuse, the Quakers with the S.D.S. and other movements. Norman Morrison, the young Quaker who self-immolated not only his life but an important part of his own beliefs, is a victim of twisted virtue or misguided zeal. Certainly the Quakers were shocked themselves.

Los Gatos, CA
November 13 1965

Dear Joe and Voices,

Long hiatus since the last voice letter, but this one was worth waiting for. After being accustomed to your tightly crammed epistles, Joe, this one was a pleasure. Much of what you said was poetic, erudite, certainly philosophical—and from the heart. I'll make no comments on conscientious objectors, since I know how I believe, but I don't presume to judge the beliefs of others. As for draft card burning and other civil disobedience, I think that those who do this must (and most often do) expect and accept whatever punishment comes with that disobedience. I neither approve nor disapprove of what they do. I do know that there are a lot of kooks, fellow travelers, cowards, loonies, pseudo-intellectuals, phonies, among the ranks of the current rebellious groups. But, there are some sincere young people among them as well. I think it is a mistake to judge them all. Beyond that, I have no comment.

A word about Norman Morrison, the young Quaker who immolated himself in front of the White House. I agree with Joe's comments, but one Quaker doesn't speak for the rest of the Quakers. Some accept what he did, mourning the tragic loss of his life, considering that it is a reason for working harder to end the world's ills. I am not so charitable, and I said so at Meeting last Sunday. I said that, while sincere (albeit ill) in what he was doing, he was nevertheless engaging in a violent act in opposition to violence in the world. I view this as a contradiction. Quakers have always stood for non-violent social change, peace-making and constructive work. What Morrison did was none of these. I can't think of him as anything but a sick, despairing person, and for this I am sorry. You can tell by the tone of this, that the whole thing upset me. To take one's own life, it seems to me, is the ultimate rejection of God's greatest gift to us—that of life, itself. Quakers refuse to engage in killing. In my view, that includes ones self.

Joe, I am studying no philosophy at all, but I want to take some courses soon. Maybe next semester. I am glad you like Fromm's book; it has become almost my bible. Let me know if you want me to send *Siddhartha*. Have you read John Robinson's book, *Honest to God*? If not, I would like to send it to Rob (who just fainted!) The mad book sender is about to make a two-pronged strike. I'll ask Rob to send it on to you, after (or instead of) reading it himself.

No noteworthy news from Los Gatos. Delightful visit with Rob, which is always a tonic. He goes so far back in my youth, that I feel very young when I am with him. You are in for a treat when you see him. He is virtually unchanged, except for being even more mature. Enough to say, he is solid gold.

Bill's practice is going well, and both boys are pretty good students— both above average but not straight A's. These boys suit us just fine—just as they are. My school life is progressing, and I love it. My young friend who is attending U. C. refers to me in his letters as his, " old coed friend". (I don't even wince anymore!) School has always been one of my best endeavors— almost the only thing I do really well. Do you think I may become a perennial student? Will they be wheeling me into the class when I am 80?

See you all next summer; I'm increasingly sure of that.

Love to all,

Lea

Weston, CT
November 16 1965

Dear Friends,

Nothing to do but apologize to all of you. This has been a busy and lazy time. Lenny, I tried to call you several times while in Pittsburgh, with no success, and I confess, that I finally gave up. Then there were trips to Birmingham, Houston, Memphis, New Florence, and back to New York, and finally to San Francisco, where I had planned a trip to Los Gatos for an overnight with Lea and Bill. I called Lea on my arrival, confessing I had broken out my winter suit to come to the coast, finding her strangely unsympathetic. She told me that October was a traditionally hot month in

San Francisco. And, it did turn out that the town was caught in a heat wave, with temperatures into the 90's both days I was there.

After that all went well, and I did get to Los Gatos. We all talked and talked, got to bed too late, etc. but it was all worth it. They were their usual gracious, delightful selves, and it did me good to be with them again. It was obvious that Bill and Lea are living lives at a fairly high tempo, giving of themselves to family and others. I'm glad I know them both—and that's as mushy as I intend to get on that subject, Lea. Lea, by the way, ever the glutton for punishment, picked me up at SFO and deposited me there the next morning, cutting a class to do it. That's friendship, and I can only say, Thanks, pal!

November 2 was Election Day, and I confess right now, Lea, that I voted a straight Democratic ticket—a protest vote against the old guard's entrenchment in our local government. Sad to say, only one Democrat was elected.

Joe, your book length letter of November 7 arrived, and what a letter! You know, if you and Lea keep bringing up Erich Fromm and his ART OF LOVING, I may be forced to read it in self-defense. May I say, I am sorry that I can't give you any detailed report of my visit with Lea—I simply wouldn't know where to start. When we visit, we just chat on and on, some important, some nonsense, but always with the comfortable feeling that has marked our friendship over the years. The same can be said of visits with Lenny and Ed. I look forward to the time when we will have had that first conversation and you and I can also speak of those important things, those foolish things—all the things that go into that mysterious thing called friendship. It won't be long now, my friend.

Good night,
Rob

Fort Gordon, Georgia
23 November 1965

Dear Joe, Lea, Lenny, and Rob,

I have before me a pile of letters to answer, but my answers will be brief to most. First to Lea, the fairest of the bunch of you. I look forward to your trip east next year, when you will be able to explain to me something about the Society of Friends. I would love to learn something about it, and perhaps to take a course in comparative religions sometime. I am also happy you have returned to school with such ease and I know you will do well. You, having trouble with German? That's a surprise.

In regard to Roger Morrison, Lea, I wonder if his was a real protest or just an urge for self-destruction by a man who had found this world too big to cope with. We will never know, of course. However the idea of his carrying the child with him till just before the flame makes me tend to think that he was ill. Sad. And you're right, it led to others. There was another immolation in the news today. Glad you're enjoying your children, Lea, I fear mine are suffering from my year's absence from them. I want them to enjoy learning, finding that it can be fun. I found your boys well adjusted, and I hope that I do as well with mine. I am looking forward to making them pizza next summer.

Rob, I hope that all of us realize the love you show by having taken time to write that letter, reluctant writer that you are. Joyce and I continue to miss Connecticut, talking about what the future holds for us there. I wish you were going to be in Washington when I am there. It would be good to talk.

Some general philosophical remarks:

I believe that the world is wrapped up in a complete revolution, which has many aspects to it. Included is overpopulation, the eight out of ten who Joe says have no Light, and a basic struggle between two ideologies both of which claim that their goal is to give man a better life. Racial and religious struggles complicate these issues. The important thing is that it is a worldwide revolution, in which the vast majority of mankind has begun to realize that sickness, fear, and starvation are not necessary. I have had a first hand look at this revolution in Vietnam and I am aware that it also exists in Africa, South America, and in other parts of Asia and the Middle East. The have nots are not going to put up with the status quo indefinitely, and they are going to improve their lot one way or another.

The communist answer of violent revolution and afterwards, providing everyone with the necessities of life, is only one answer to this problem. Another is the American way of social revolution by the democratic process with a goal of giving everyone a good life (a chicken in every pot or whatever). Remember, that for those who have nothing, either one of these is an improvement. I of course, believe that our way is the best. It allows for a supreme being and the ultimate goal is to give a chance to all to live a better life. I admit that I would rather see the whole thing done by peaceful social revolution than by force. But, when the other side sets the ground rules, I am for playing the hand as dealt and beating him at his own game. But, the end result has got to be to have a better way of life for mankind as a whole.

Something is not right in God's world when people are starving and sick while others have plenty. Joe, you feel that it is only at the national level that power is workable anymore, but I still feel that I must try to do something as an individual or as a tool of national power. I'll write in detail after my December visit with Joe. We all have so much to be thankful for in Joe's release and our love for each other—on this Thanksgiving Day.

Sayonara,

Ed

Monday, December 6, 1965
From Ed, after a visit with Joe

Dear Friends,

The purpose of this long letter is to tell you in detail all about my visit with Joe. We talked all evening and all the next morning, until it was time to leave. Joe knows that I intend to write this letter and told me not to pull any punches. I will not, and I might as well start on myself. I was a bit frightened by the visit before it occurred. What would it be like and what would be asked of me in the way of the help I had previously offered? Could I produce the assistance Joe might need and would he accept it if I did? I should not have worried. Joe does not need our physical help at this time, as I will attempt to show you. As for the visit itself, well, it was just plain fun. It was like seeing any one of you again; Joyce and I both enjoyed it.

Joe has a nice apartment in a decent section of Arlington. It's not big or luxurious, but big enough for him and his mother. He sleeps on a studio couch in the living room, and she sleeps in a twin bed in the small bedroom. One of the parole stipulations is that Joe must show that he can live within his income. Therefore, I would advise no gifts of a big material nature until you check with him. His living environment is perfectly adequate and he seems quite happy with it and with having his mother with him. Joe has enough clothing, and Gidget did an excellent job of outfitting him. He smokes a bit, usually a pipe, and he did have two beers with me at Dorothy's, although he is purposely staying away from alcohol, having had a problem with it prior to being incarcerated. I didn't get the impression that this was a factor leading to his trouble, though.

Joe is very fortunate to have the support of a loving family—his mother, a sister and a niece in Alexandria, a brother in Pittsburgh and one in New York. If anything, they spoil him, he being the baby of the family with his mother and Dorothy treating him as such now. His job seems to be going well, and he has not had any trouble with the people he works with. He takes a bus to and from work, spending about 11 hours a day, including commute time. He is looking for a moonlighting job to help pay for the courses he wants to take at the U. of Virginia Extension. There is no degree, but he might be able to transfer credits to San Jose State later. My evaluation is that he is purposeful and capable of getting a degree in the future, but it's going to take a while.

As for his present state of education, well, let's just call it amazing! He has used his years in prison well. He has not only read everything he could get his hands on, but he has the most unusual collection of files you can possibly imagine. He kept notes on everything he read and also copies of all of his correspondence. He did this with great difficulty on any scrap of paper he could find. He wrote all these notes in a script that is just big enough to be read by the naked eye. This of course, explains how he was able to use all those quotes in his letters. He created a cross-referenced index file of quotes that is unbelievable—on 3 X 5 pieces of paper—thousands of them! Unbelievable! I envy him, in a way, as I am lucky to find time to read one book!!

I have the sense that he was entirely truthful with me, and I now have a better understanding of what caused him to get into prison in the first place. I have debated about telling you all this, but I decided I should attempt to, in order that he not have to repeat it and that you may know now rather than at a later time. Also, by knowing it, you will all be able to realize that he is in no danger of going back. First of all, Joe was the baby of his family and has been used to having roots all his life. Thus, when his marriage to his first wife (Betty) blew up in California, he suddenly found himself for the first time in his life without any real solid anchor to the type of life he wanted or needed. He got into his first scrape in Nevada, not with the law, but with a syndicate member in organized crime, and this contact led him to consider such activities himself. Incidentally, this is a fast rundown on a story it took Joe over an hour to tell me, so, I know I am leaving out a great many details.

Joe started to try a few burglaries and made it sort of a game. He indicated that he even broke into places just to prove to himself that he could get in. Sometimes he would take things and sometimes he would not. He estimated that he pulled about 45 jobs in areas from Michigan to Florida to New York to Washington.

Joe, as you know, was very close to my mother. At one point, in 1956, he came close to confessing it all to Mother, when he saw her then, and he almost told me when he saw me during the same period of time. This was about the time that he feels that he was hoping to be caught and was desirous of being punished. He did finally get caught, and he was punished for armed robbery. He was sentenced to eight years for that and two years for the other things involved.

Joe indicated that he left the prison farm in 1960 (his escape) because it was leading him to destruction either by fellow convicts or by an inability to put up with the conditions which he was living under. He hoped to live in Colorado for five years and then turn himself in to the authorities and fight extradition based on his conduct in that state. He told me that it might have worked if Doris, his second wife, had not gotten miffed at him, exacerbating her feelings of guilt, and turned him in. What her role was in his escape was not clear, and I didn't ask. But, her role in his recapture is clear. I just let him tell me what he wanted to.

Joe is convinced that the voice letters were a great help to him in securing his parole, as was the backing of his family and some of the friends he made in Colorado. He also thanks us for our prayers, which he feels were a great help. He feels we came back into his life at exactly the right time—almost providentially.

Now, for some impressions: First of all, Joe is quite well, mentally. His prison experiences have not hurt him so badly that he cannot adjust to the life he is now living. He is and will continue to be a useful member of society, I am sure of it. He will need help from us to be able to continue his way through, however, and this help can best be provided in the way we have given it in the past few years. All we have to do is to continue to give him our friendship. The nice thing about it is that we get a loving friendship in return. I feel that the voice letters and where possible, visits, are even more important now than they were during the past two years. Joe got into trouble when he lost his connections with his family and friends. This must not be allowed to happen again.

Joe hopes to come to Virginia Beach and visit Joyce and me and the kids in our home. I hope you all have a wonderful Christmas and let's all look forward to 1966 as the year we all converge in Virginia Beach for a Voices reunion—probably when Lea makes that trip east! What a blessing to look forward to in the new year!

Love from,

Ed

Weston, CT
December 12 1965

Dear Friends,

Rather than concentrate on where I have been on business, let me say that there has been less travel this month, which translates to more time with the family—always to the good. Only noteworthy trip was actually to Pittsburgh where I had a good visit with Len. We had lunch and then a visit that sped by, in spite of it being three hours long. Much of what we talked about is not for review in a letter like this, nor in general am I much for revealing private conversations on personal matters. I will just summarize by saying that I felt I know Len better for having spent these three hours together. It becomes more apparent that a lot has transpired for each of us as the years rolled by, and a few moments of conversation cannot bridge the gaps that our lives have created as we went our individual ways. Every time I leave one of you, I think I have more questions than answers.

Ed knows that Len welcomes the opportunity to see and talk with any of the male friends and this certainly includes Joe, perhaps Joe more than any of us at this time. I hope it won't be too long until Joe and Len have their first meeting. By the way, my mother reports that Len is very well liked by the people he works with in the Mountmore Booster organization. Doesn't surprise me at all, of course.

Now some comments for each of you:

Ed: Lea, Len, and I are all indebted to you for being kind enough to sit down and recount your conversation with Joe. You've filled in a few more of the gaps, which should make it easier on Joe when each of us gets the chance to see him in person. From your account, it had been a long road for Joe, and it is obviously not yet the end of that road. There is certainly much to do. I echo your feeling that this is no time to think of curtailing our friendship again. Lea and I talked about this very point during our last visit. We agreed that it was unrealistic to think that the correspondence would continue at the pace it has for the past two years. But, we also agreed that we should not slack off in the near future.

Lea, I never did thank you for the birthday card. You're right, the 39th is the last! Don't send the book, "HONEST TO GOD. " I read it, and I liked it. Your flattering comments about me were, and always are, gratefully received. Some days they are sorely needed, as I come face to face with my shortcomings. My teaching job is still enjoyable, but the range of subject matter doesn't give me the opportunity to express many of my inner feelings.

Time for my plane, and I still have to pack. Notes for you individually on the back of this page.

Rob

(Handwritten note to Lea)

Just a short note for you—short and to the point. During my visit with Lenny, I asked him if he had given any thought as to how he would react if you happened to contact him during your trip east.

It was quite apparent the question really bothered him. It was obvious that he isn't as far away from his psychological problems as I thought he was—in the area where you are concerned.

Whether the doctor (shrink variety) was the one who convinced Len you were the source of his problems—or whether Len hung the rap on you by himself, it is apparently true that Len focused quite a bit of hate toward you—which he so stated to me.

Lea, I think the feeling is still strong—and not too far buried below the surface. I believe your presence would upset Lenny very much. What I'm trying to say is that you should soft-pedal any approaches to him. It may seem silly to us that he still carries the feeling—but it's not to him. Please, don't force yourself on him. He just isn't ready for it—and perhaps he never will be. Ah, dear worrying friend, don't agonize about this. It's not your fault, and it's certainly out of your hands. This note is for you and Bill—only.

Rob

(Undated, handwritten letter to Rob—shortly before Christmas, 1965)

Ah, Rob, if I ever seriously thought of trying to see Lenny, your postscript note has certainly removed any such idea. Please don't assume I could ever do that. Good Lord, Rob, I haven't the courage; I thought you would know that. But, perhaps we both do too much assuming. For instance, I think I always assumed you knew the reason I gave Lenny back his ring. I don't think I ever actually told you. It occurs to me now that I want to tell you, so at least YOU will understand, even if Lenny never will.

As you know, Lenny and I were each other's first romance, overwhelming to each of us at 17 and 16 respectively. In retrospect, for me, he was the perfect first love—football hero, intelligent, popular, National Honor Society, honorable, sensitive, romantic, poetic. I think he perceived me as intelligent, romantic, poetic, strong, sensible, absolutely faithful. We were soul mates, the problem with soul mates being that they are too much alike to be able to fill in the gaps for each other. Some of his perceptions of me were true; I was romantic, poetic and completely faithful, but I was also overly sensitive and far from strong, with needs of my own; I needed someone strong, stable, and emotionally healthy myself. On some level, I think I instinctively knew he was none of those, but I frankly adored him, thinking that was all that was needed.

Remember, we all graduated from Mountmore High on June 5th, one day before the 1944 invasion of Normandy. Each of you guys went directly into the Navy or Army, and much of the 4 and 1/2 years of my love affair with Lenny was spent apart, Len seeing action in Italy. Our relationship was largely in the form of well over 1000 letters, written daily from fall of 1944 until summer of 1946, when all four of you returned home after the war's end. Some time after Lenny's return, though, I sensed there was something wrong. My loyalty being what it is, I may have considered it my fault, and we just drifted into an engagement, and by spring of 1948, a date had been set for our wedding. The wedding dress was made, bridesmaid dresses started, bans published in the church, invitations printed.

One night, in mid March of that year, my father and step-mother were waiting up for me to come home, sitting seriously, in bathrobes, wanting to talk to me. Kindly, but in great concern, Daddy told me that I didn't seem to be behaving like a bride who was to be married in 6 weeks. Confused and troubled, I don't think I responded, and my father gently asked, "Lea, do you want to get married?" I honestly didn't know what I wanted and replied, "I don't know." "Do you love Lenny?" I could hardly hear my own reply, "I don't know that either, Daddy," I whispered, my eyes welling up. There was a long pause, and I'll never forget my father's grave response: "Child, this is for the rest of your life. If you are uncertain, you have waited this long; you can wait a little longer. You will have to give Lenny back his ring and wait until you are sure." I was distressed about all the wedding expenses, but my father said that was far less important than that I marry when I was ready; there were tears of remorse, of confusion, of doubt, but in the end, I realized the wisdom of waiting—just a bit longer. My father suggested I give the ring back for a period of time—perhaps a month or two; then we should agree to meet again and assess how to proceed. Considerably relieved, I met with Lenny the next day to discuss our situation, recognizing how devastated he was, but determined to do what I must to be sure I was doing the right thing— for myself. We agreed to meet in one month. I will never forget how beaten down he looked as we talked in the car, parked in the nurse's dorm parking lot. He seemed to shrink into the seat. (I shudder when I think of it, even now.)

During that intervening month, I felt free for the first time in years; I began dating (something I had never done—ever!), doing actually very little reflecting about our engagement. There was no doubt that I loved Lenny, but I realized I had had no youthful flings, no "playing the field," very little just plain fun for over three years. I loved being light-hearted again, going on dates, going dancing—in short, having no one to answer to, but myself. It was clear to me right away that I was not ready to "settle down." "But, what do I want?" I wondered. I honestly didn't know. During the war, I had always been so frightened, so uncertain, so deadly serious! I had done none of the things that young girls did, and I longed to just be a girl again—not a wife— not yet.

At the end of the month, I was far from ready to go back to the way things had been. I had tasted the freedom to be myself, and it was what I wanted. There was no one else in my life. I just didn't want to get married—to Lenny or anyone else. Perhaps in a few months, I might feel differently. I tried to convince Lenny to just set me free, allow me to kick up my heels, see each other during this time, and perhaps after 6 months or so, I would find I was ready to settle down in a marriage. He would have no part of it. He felt he could not—or in any case, would not—"be in competition with doctors" for my attention. I was a graduate nurse already, and nurses met and dated doctors; he felt too insecure to be able to compete with that.

So, he kept the ring, and we parted. At no time, then—or ever—did I regret it, and I never understood what effect this would have on him. I never considered that he had lost his youth, too, and he had experienced horrors I couldn't even imagine—facing death and unspeakable tragedies that would scar him forever. I knew he was hurt, but I didn't want to think about that. It had to be done. It was a purely thoughtless, selfish decision, one of the few such I have made in a lifetime, and I never looked back—not once.

The following fall, I met Bill and knew by the third date that I would marry him. He was everything Lenny was not: stable, a medical student, self-assured, with "social credentials," and great promise for the future. We met in September, were "pinned" in December, engaged in February, and married in June. I fell deeply in love on our honeymoon, and began what was ultimately to be a very successful marriage, as you well know. I knew it was right for me, never had a doubt, and I never thought of that part of my life as anything that could touch me again. I never actually saw Lenny after that, nor did I particularly wish to. There was no contact at all, until these Voice letters began.

Rob, this has been a confession, of sorts. I have never hidden any of it, and I would probably do the same thing again, given the chance, but I am not proud of my own lack of empathy for what that hurt did to Lenny. Most of all, I cringe when I realize I was completely insensitive to his emotional stress and instability after the war. None of us can escape the responsibility for our actions—ever. It's one of life's basic truths. I hope you understand, and most of all, I hope you don't think less of me. That would break my heart. Of course, that would be poetic justice, of a sort, wouldn't it? After all, I didn't flinch when I broke Lenny's, did I?

Lea

Arlington
19 December 1965

Dear Voices,

With all due respect to Ed, the Voices will always remain Voices to me.

We began using the term in association with those earlier years shared together. However, during these two years of correspondence, the title, "Voices" has proliferated in scope. Once, in a letter to Lenny, I referred to you four as representing the better angel of my nature. "Voices" is a symbol of this representation. But, it's connotations hold greater significance to me. It encompasses the "root and all" of our association, linking the past with the present, and at the same time, expanding to include the concern, trust, cohesion, etc. of Lea's "star." So, voices you remain.

Ed has the odd experience of being the only Voice to have visited with me in person during the immediate seasons before and after my imprisonment. For this reason, his summations, expressed in his last letter, not only inform the rest of you, but are valuable to me. He has given me much to think on. Also, as Ed pointed out, he has saved me a tough chore regarding future letters and visits with the rest of you.

Local authorities have approved the visit to Virginia Beach the weekend of Ed's birthday. Gidget and I hope to make the trip together, and I'll confirm arrival time, calling at 8 PM on January 2nd.

Rob, your comments on the ministry are worth pondering. At moments you seem to agree with my own "salamander in a fish bowl" thoughts. The church is effective, but the school seems to be having the greater effect during this evolutionary period. The trend is to put more stress on the sociological and less on the theological aspects of the ministry. The ideal would be to combine them, as Christ attempted. Christmas has become a paradox. I imagine a man having a birthday party for his son and inviting everybody but his son to attend. This is what we do when we take the Christ out of Christmas. The good will remains, but Christ must go. It seems that Jesus is being kicked out of a lot of places today. Rob, I am interested in your expression "sustained commitment." I am a great believer in "free will," but since free will seems governed by time, space, and cause, then it is not absolute. Where, also, does predestination fit in? Or does it? Is purpose (one's calling) prearranged or chanced upon? Or both? In other words, what is the source of the commitment you speak of? The individual? Or that something higher? I suspect that Lea might explain her views on these things better than any of us.

Lea, I hope to be comparing school notes with you soon. Courses remain yet to be selected and will be based on a Social Science major. Congrats on those good grades—keep it up! Your school success inspires me. Perhaps we may duplicate courses. That would be fun!

Lenny, I still plan to visit Pittsburgh in March, staying with brother Frank in Greentree. Of course, I hope to see you and meet your family. Also, I want to see Ed's mom, provided she doesn't hit me on the head with the piano or something, and also Rob's parents.

Lea, I haven't read *Honest to God*, and I'm curious, especially since Rob, for the first time, agrees with you—so it must be amazingly fabulous!! I plan to add *Siddhartha* to my library, so don't send me yours. There is a story I must tell you one day about the copy of Gibran's *The Prophet*, but it will be a while before I am up to it.

I don't know if Lea will send the rest of you the same message she sent me included in her card, but it is worth repeating:

"What can I add to all we've said during the year?
Just that to all my affection and well-wishing,
I add only a Christmas prayer of Thanksgiving—
— For friends."

Isn't it truly amazing how blessed we really are here in America, in the year 1965? Sincerely, I say to all of you: Merry Christmas!
Joe

Los Gatos
December 30, 1965

Dear Voices,
Lots of letters to answer, so I will dive right in and answer each one.

Ed, your letters are always good ones, but these last two were particular gems. I like the section on your philosophy of life, for want of a better term. I would say that all of us are pretty much in accord when it comes to things of the soul. Do you suppose this is because of the time of our lives? I find myself marveling at how morally strong we all are, and how we all have quite similar values. Is this because we are all approaching the middle years of our lives, or did we all have these traits in common all along? Bill is inclined to think the latter is true, believing, as I tend to, that basically, people don't change much at all, that all of us have always been this way, that these values attracted us to one another years ago.

Your commentary on the world being in a revolution was well put. That you recognize this as a trend and want to get in and steer, rather than to attempt to buck the tide, speaks well for your practical point of view. At this point, I share many of your feelings, and I am reminded of something I read recently: it is right and proper that one should expect to obtain a fair income for his work, but in the later years of one's life, the soul needs the tonic of knowing one has helped make the world a better place for having lived down here. The concluding sentence read, " Every human being has the urge to be noble." Ed, thanks for the information about Joe. I knew most of it from Dorothy, but it will save Joe the discomfort of having to "explain." to each of us separately.

Joe, Ed mentioned something about your transferring credits (units) if you ever went back to San Jose State. Is this actually a serious consideration? If you did, we might both be there at the same time. And, if we really wanted to fantasize, we might even be in some of the same classes. I can't think of a better place to live than this area, Joe. I will hold the thought.

Rob, I have never known one to say so much in apology for saying nothing, and then to go on and say so much!! But, then, you never did rate yourself accurately, my friend!

Joe, your letter was like a lovely Christmas present! Several years ago, when I was bemoaning my worries about Bill's getting a practice started, fearing all the time that we were going to the poorhouse, I was at my lowest ebb. Then, a letter from you would arrive. Your quiet acceptance of your situation, your pleasure over little things (the things that really matter, it turns out!), made me feel ashamed of myself. Now this year, when things have improved, I was frantically running about preparing a very commercial Christmas, spending way too much money, and not batting an eye. Then, your letter came, spelling out as only you can, the real meaning of Christmas— the love of family, the joy of friendship, the pleasure of living. Again, with uncanny timing, your letter arrived as your gift, and I thank you again for unwittingly reminding me of something I didn't know I had forgotten—that WHAT one gives is less important than WHY one gives. And Ed, and Rob, thank you for your Christmas messages, too.

We have a rather unusual way of celebrating Christmas at our house. As a carry-over from Bill's mother, who used to celebrate her Christmas Eve birthday, by having an open house at their home and giving everyone who came a gift, I have had a Christmas Eve open house each Christmas Eve, too. It's a family affair, now. We invite all the people of whom we are particularly fond, and we encourage them to bring children. Our boys act as hosts and doormen, and they do a great job, carrying coats back and forth to the bedroom, serving, and generally being helpful... We have the traditional eggnog (which I make myself) and a Wine Wassail Bowl, an English hot spiced wine drink, and all the goodies, which I spend weeks making. Christmas eve seems a strange time to have a large party, but it is so much a part of our lives after all these years, that I would feel strange not doing it. I like it particularly now that the boys take part, too.

Happily, this year, my two favorite former students remembered me with gifts, something which touches me very much. This year, I got a cyclamen plant, to replace, I suppose, the poinsettia which is now deader than a doornail from the frost. From the same kid, too, by the way! (How I nursed that poinsettia, too, covering it every night! I am such a sap for flowers!!)

On that note, I will end this epistle. Keep well, all of you, and we wish each of you all the best in this bright new year ahead. Most of all, I wish us peace.

Affectionately,

Lea

Weston, CT
January 16 1966

Dear Friends,

And so starts another year, and who knows what's ahead for us all?

Letters from Ed, Lea, and Joe received, enjoyed, and about to be commented upon:

Joe, my comments about ministry requiring a sustained commitment was in reference to myself. I just never felt that I had what it takes to dedicate my life in that particular way. I am not enough of a theologian to comment except briefly on your questions about predestination. The theory leaves me cold. It goes against my grain—showing I suppose, how willful and egocentric I am. I always believed any complicated notions about predestination were insulting to my concept of man's freedom of choice. I belong to the "clean slate" school of thought which says we all arrive in life with a free mind, pure, ready to be shaped by earthly experience. I can't buy any other reasoning.

Lea, I was wishing that we could have visited your house Christmas Eve. It sounded wonderful. Christmas always brings out deep feelings within me as no other time of the year does. It's a time of joy and sadness for me, a time to think. During Mom and Dad's visit over the holidays, we four adults spent two long evenings before the fireplace, all of us wrapped up, with many secret thoughts that a fire brings bubbling up to the mind's surface. What better way to end this letter than by watching tonight's fire slowly dying out. The house is chilling off. Time for bed and readying myself for an early morning drive to the airport—with no Lea for a driver. Goodnight, friends,

Rob

(Handwritten note to Bill and Lea)

First of all, my comments about Lenny in my last letter were NOT intended to make Lea feel guilty. They were simply to say that Lenny is not currently receptive to a closer relationship with Lea. It is sad, but true. But there is no reason for us to continue to beat ourselves to death mentally because he can't bring himself back to friendship. Your life is a testimony to the wisdom of your decision. I regret the situation, but I place it on his shoulders, not yours.

Bill, I beg to differ with you somewhat in your appraisal of Lenny's attitude. In this instance, I am inclined to be more generous than you, I think. Lenny's attitude is childish, irrational, etc.—but I excuse the attitude because it is part of a wider mental and emotional pattern. He had, and has, psychological problems; his attitude toward Lea is simply a small portion, but an important part of his mental make up. I can no more damn his current feeling toward Lea than I can damn his emotional—mental problems taken as a whole. I believe he was a fairly sick man at one time—and anchoring on a dislike of Lea has been a sort of recovery crutch for him. She has been made the whipping boy for a multitude of weaknesses on his part. Good night, my favorite Californians. We are all well. Trust you are the same.

Rob

Lea, keep on sending copies of letters to him.

Virginia Beach
January 22 1966

Dear Friends,

I have had a wonderful month of holidays with my family and a nice visit from Gidget and Joe. They helped me celebrate my birthday in grand style. Joyce and I went to bed long before the New Year came in. Must be getting old.

The usual kids' activities are keeping me busy and giving me a chance to get reacquainted with them—cub scouts, school work, sports activities. I have also done quite a bit of work on things around the house, staining picture frames, fixing lamps, unpacking things still in boxes. Joyce and I are going through the period when all the furniture is beginning to look shabby. (It's the stuff we refer to as being in the style of Early Sears Roebuck.) But, things are shaping up, and we have plenty of room; any of you who get into the Tidewater area are invited to stay with us.

Sunday, we took Joe to church with us, and I tried to convert him to an Episcopalian, but I think someone has gotten a head start on us in that department, and I hope it continues to be his choice. The rector came over to meet Joe, and Joe agreed to speak to the Young People's Group during a future visit. Joe is quite concerned about the prison system in Virginia and wants to start talking to people about possible reforms, but I am not sure that this is what he will talk to the kids about. February is a big month for us—Joyce's and my 17th anniversary, the 22nd anniversary of Rob and me joining the Navy, and the first anniversary of Joyce's successful surgery for cancer.

Last week, I gave a talk at the local women's club about our involvement in Vietnam, and next week, I will be talking to the Kiwanis Club. The majority of the people here are sympathetic about our role over there. I showed an excellent film called, "The Full Blade" which is about the "civic action" of the marines over there—the real war that I know about. I've also been increasingly active in our church, going to adult discussions, working with the rector to get my lay reader's license validated by the bishop so I can write my own sermons instead of having to read one that is approved by the bishop.

Rob, I am glad you got to see Len on your last trip to Pittsburgh. My aunt is not well, so I may be back that way soon, and if I am, I will look Len up.

Lea, I think I agree with Bill. We have all been the way we are now since we were in high school. We are just older and wiser now and better able to verbalize what we feel. The idea of getting to the West Coast for your Christmas Eve party is tantalizing—but not likely. But, I hope your trip east is still on for this summer. Maybe Rob and Joe could plan to be in this area at the same time you arrive, so we could have a real reunion.

Joe, see you soon, Len, thanks for the Christmas card. Love to you all.
Ed

Arlington,
January 28 1966

Dear Voices,

"The Full Blade" is certainly informative. Coupled with the marine civic action film that Ed presented to Maureen and me, it shows the role of the marines in Vietnam, for those who have eyes to see and ears to hear, and it might clarify things to the anti-Vietnam demonstrators. For example, the barbed wire enclosures which the demonstrators call "concentration camps," to hold people in, are clearly shown in Ed's film as an attempt to keep the Viet Cong out. This is what Ed refers to as "Civic action." and it is misunderstood by some.

Ed gave a complete rundown on my trip up to Virginia Beach, and it was all he said it was. The dinner and dancing was great, but the manipulations, called "new dancing", which Maureen and Ann taught us, were daunting, to say the least. I had sore hips afterwards!!

Lea, like Ed, I want to attend one of your Christmas Eve parties some day. How do you keep such a schedule? And you, Rob, how do you manage your travel commitments? In fact, all of you lead busy, active lives, which make me marvel.

Thus far, my three-month search for part-time work (in an area where part time opportunities are plentiful) remains fruitless. So, for now, I have to skip University of Virginia courses. Perhaps September. My regular job is steady, but affords little above current expenses. Confidence lost is hard won back. But, of course, I was resigned to this and expected no easy road, but the school part is really disappointing.

Meantime, I'm finding ways to utilize my "free" time. Among the volunteers who work with the Red Cross, there is, in the Motor Service unit, a new driver. Picture Joe driving a jitney busload of Gray Ladies, delivering them to a local hospital, or a busload of Walter Reed N. P.'s on a scenic tour. Giving is something I don't know how to do—but I want to learn.

Rob, you express a strong individualism in your theology. And I would agree that this is good just so long as your thinking incorporates some of what Lea's Quakers call "The Light within" or the "God in you," and what Ed's Episcopalians call "the indwelling spirit." When we do get together, I would like to talk more of this "sustained commitment" you spoke of.

Lea, San Jose State is the quickest, and most economical route for me to obtain a degree, but just about anything I do will depend upon my tentative parole ending date of March 1967. I'm undecided at the moment. Love to all of you.

Joe

Los Gatos,
February 15th 1966

Dear Voices,

Gracious, I am remiss in not answering your letters sooner—not because you're not in my thoughts. Time is just nearly unavailable of late, but more about that later. I will respond to your letters first.

Rob, your travels are daunting. How do you do it? Your comments about your reverie with the family in front of the dying fire in the fireplace on a frigid night were very touching. I guess all of us do our share of pondering and reminiscing that time of year. And there is something about a dying fire that stirs these thoughts up. But, it's a fresh new year; and if you're like me, nostalgia doesn't last a long time.

Ed, good letter! Hey, old boy, sounds like you're back into the domestic scene, now that you have ceased for a time your "soldier of fortune" doings. (Not intended to be a nasty crack—just a little jibe from your pacifistic buddy!) "The Full Blade" does sound interesting as Joe described it. The work of our forces there in Vietnam in the areas of social work, farming, teaching, politics, first aid is commendable, indeed. I do believe that any victory in Vietnam will be on that level, and not on a military one. But, I better not launch into another Vietnam pronouncement at this point. I promised you and myself not to leap into that stew again. You all know my views, and I am not likely to change in the immediate future, nor are any of you.

Joe, I am so sorry about your not being able to go to school. When the time comes for your parole to be up, you might consider coming to California. The cost is very low compared to other parts of the country. On another subject, Joe, it is in keeping with the image we all have of you, that you should be giving your "free" time to the Red Cross. Giving is something you have ALWAYS KNOWN how to do. This I remember very well about you. If you got a little out of practice a while back, your current practice will only reinforce what has always been there. Thanks for the picture, by the way. You look the same—a bit older, a bit less hair, but the same smile—same face.

I am for planning for a giant reunion in July or August in Virginia. Everybody agreed? I'll bring the trailer; Rob and Joe can bring tents and sleeping bags, and we'll all camp out on Ed's lawn, OK, Ed??!! Well, we can work out the details later.

Bill's mom and a friend were here for some weeks and I played tour guide of San Francisco, among other things. We ate our way through that city beginning with lunch by the bay in Sausalito, dessert at Blums Cafe by Union Square in San Francisco, Tea and fortune cookies in Chinatown, before dinner drinks and hot hors d'oeuvres at the Top of the Mark, dinner on Fisherman's Wharf, after dinner drinks and European coffee at Enricos in North Beach! (For some reason, I am now on a diet!)

School is going well, and I love it! Especially the course in psychology, with a superb professor! I am learning about the important role significant others play in the lives of young people—not just parents, but teachers and other role models. One never really knows what effect he will have, for good or ill, on the life of a youngster. It is an awesome responsibility, but it is also an opportunity to make a difference—just being a role model. While it's rewarding to see a result, I also think that even if we NEVER see the result, we should not underestimate the potential good we can accomplish with young people, just by the lives we lead.

How many of you recall how severely I used to stutter? Especially if I had to get up in front of a class to talk, I would nearly go to pieces. Well, a requirement for a teaching credential is a course in speech. It will be interesting, because I have always considered my speech my nemesis. I am also taking a course in German now—Level III. It's a literature course, involving expressionistic German literature. I see my German improving daily. I am getting used to being more of a contemporary of the teachers than of the students, but I like talking to the young people, and I enjoy them tremendously. Funny how they start out calling me Lea, like the instructors, but end up calling me, "Mrs. Frey". Am I stuffy, do you think? I hope not.

Forgive the abrupt ending. My love to you all, as always.

Lea

Weston

March 17, 1966

Dear Friends,

Sure and it's a fine day for the Irish! And we are still waiting for the appearance of spring in Connecticut, the first flowers waiting for the snow to go before breaking out of the ground. But, yesterday, I spotted a few transient blue birds at the bird feeder, so it is a sure sign winter is going.

I didn't feel much like writing tonight, but Ed's comment about Joe's being with us again having slowed down our zest for writing got to me. I must admit it's true, and I'll be darned if I'll let it get in the way. But, it'll be short, I'm afraid. So, I'll launch right in with some responses. Lea your description of all those eating places in San Francisco made me hungry, both for the food and for that atmosphere of S. F. which is so wonderful; I really like that city by the bay.

Ed, your casual mention of a possible trip to Connecticut was good news. We will be here that weekend, so come ahead. I see that this is the week Ed is to go to Santo Domingo. Apparently, things are in better control there than before, but far from settled. We'll be waiting to hear, Ed.

Joe, I wanted to commend you on your work for the Red Cross. You may remember that my Dad served overseas in the Red Cross for several years during W.W. 2, and I have a soft spot in my heart for that organization. That's all for tonight. My thoughts and love to all of you and your families.

Rob

(Handwritten postscript to Lea) Lea, you don't even get a long hand written note tonight! When are you going to stop beating yourself to death over what might have been? No more postscripts like that last one you wrote. Your previous letter—just to me—I completely understand. It wasn't necessary for me to know, but I am glad I do now. Your family is among the best I know. Be happy about that—and stop badgering yourself. It isn't necessary to reach sainthood, you know.

Sorry—very sorry—I couldn't make the trip West this month, but my workload here was already heavy enough. Hope I'll be out within a fairly short time.

I do hope to see Joe soon—and then all we have to do is wait for you to come east next summer. Have you made any tentative plans yet? I'd hate to be out of town on vacation if you really do get here. Let me know your thinking.

Trust Bill and the boys are bearing up with their campus cut-up!
Rob

Los Gatos
April 14 1966

Dear Voices,

If you have given me up, surprise! Here I am! Sorry, but in a fit of insanity, I signed up for 12 units this semester, and I will never do it again. It's just too much when you have a family to look after, too. It just doesn't work—at least for me. So, next time, it will be back to nine units.

Activities of the Frey clan were varied. Over the Easter holiday, we all got into the car, hitched up the trailer and drove to Death Valley, where we had a simply gorgeous few days. We had magnificent weather (up to 91 in the day) with clear, cooler nights and a full moon, which allowed the boys and me to take a moonlight hike into the canyons. Mornings were perfect, and it is a geologist's paradise, full of scenic wonders, with a profusion of wild flowers, several ghost towns, some abandoned mining camps, and Badwater, a small salt water lake and the lowest point in continental U. S. We slept in the trailer, a sort of "trial run" for my trip east next summer.

On our return, we had a bit of a shock awaiting us, for our house had been broken into, for the fourth time. This time, again, nothing was stolen. A window in Billy's room had been forced, and (hold onto your hats!) all the damage was the same as the previous three times: NOTHING! —except for taking all my underwear—two drawers of my dresser full—and strewing it all over the house. Obviously, some sort of deviate is on the loose; the crime is breaking and entering and malicious mischief. The police, who came out to the house twice, have assured me that these individuals are harmless, but I must say that I am a bit unnerved about it. As far as the kids are concerned, it's more excitement than they have had in ages. They have blown it up into a real who-done-it. "I'll bet it's the gardener's helper!" they would say. Or, "Hey! Could it be the cleaner—or the milkman?" One neighborhood youngster commented, "I thought it was Jake Corville (a neighbor who is categorically above suspicion!!), but he was away on a camping trip. Anyway, things have calmed down now, but we had all the locks changed and windows bolted, anyway.

Rob, your trip south to see Joe sounds wonderful. Please keep notes about your visit and share it with the rest of us. Hope you got my post card from Death Valley. Joe and Ed, you would have gotten postcards, too, but I forgot to bring along addresses. Rob's is only the name, the street, and the town, so it was in my head. So, yours were sent when we got home—with a Los Gatos postmark. Sorry!

By the way, I plan to visit Washington in late July, in all probability. I will stay with our friends, the Gabriels (he is the conductor of the USAF band in Washington. We knew him and his family in Wiesbaden, Germany. I'll let all of you know exact dates as the time gets closer. Hoping for a reunion of all of us—maybe at Ed's in Virginia Beach. Excuse abrupt good-bye. So, good-bye!

Lea

Virginia Beach
Tuesday, May 10, 1966

Dear Voices,

When I say I get home every night, I guess I lied. I just returned from a three-day trip to the Caribbean, and I will be coming to the Washington area for three nights on the 19th. Joyce isn't pleased with these trips, but it's part of the job. I'll see you then. Joyce will not be coming with me. I just realized it's been two months since I last wrote, and I am ashamed of myself.

Joyce didn't get her ear operation as scheduled in March. The hospital was too full of Vietnam casualties that there is no elective surgery at this time. I hope it will happen at a later date and that it goes well. So, Joyce won't be coming along and will miss Gidget's reception. Too bad.

Rob, we have seen each other twice, so there is nothing to comment on, really. I just hope that our plans for the time of Lea's visit can come true and that you will return to Virginia Beach so that we can all be together and have a real reunion.

Now, for you, Mrs. F. If all goes well, we are hoping Rob and Joe and you and I can all get together during your stay. I would think it was wonderful if Lenny could come, too, but so far, he has not accepted my open-ended invitation to visit us. But, I continue to hope. We will definitely keep the end of July and beginning of August open, Lea. You said you wanted to visit Jamestown and Williamsburg. Well, they are about an hour's drive from here, and Joyce is a great guide and offers her services. From here to Washington would take about 4 and 1/2 hours. So, let us know when your plans firm up so we can make plans.

Your trip to Death Valley sounded wonderful and made me want to see it. The ending of the trip was a bit unnerving, though. As for me, the only way I would want to throw girls' skivvies around is with Joe, you owe us a letter, so get busy. My love to you all.

Ed

REBIRTH–REHABILITATION–REUNION

Los Gatos
May 12 1966

Dear Voices (including Dorothy this time.)

This will be a report of the state of my trip plans and to fill you in on the "Perils of Poor Lea." But, first I want to thank Dorothy for her invitation to stay with her, for a few days at least. I will be staying with the Gabriels for a few days as well. I want to see Gabe conduct the USAF band on the steps of the Capitol.

I plan to take the boys to Williamsburg and Jamestown for two days. Williamsburg might be visited en route from Washington to Virginia Beach. Rob, I hope you can get to Washington or to Pittsburgh. I rather hope not to have to drive to Connecticut, since I imagine I will have had my fill of driving by the time I am on the East Coast. But, I will see you—one way or another.

I am in the process of mapping out a trip on a huge map of the U. S. The first two weeks will be spent west of the continental divide, touring national monuments, Indian reservations, cliff dwelling ruins, National Parks, etc. Then, we will make tracks across Kansas, Missouri, Illinois, etc. to Mammoth Caves Kentucky and Lincoln's Log Cabin. That will be our last scenic stop before Pittsburgh. After resting up for a week, we will go on to Washington and historic Williamsburg.

Bill will arrive about the 16th of August. After a short visit with his family, we plan to start driving home. We're going via Niagara Falls, north to Sault Sainte Marie, the northern shore of Lake Superior, and down into the U. S. Then, on to Badlands of South Dakota, the Black Hills, Mount Rushmore, Yellowstone, and Grand Tetons, then Devil's Tower, Craters of the Moon, Lake Tahoe and then home. It's an ambitious trip, and I may never recover, but I am very enthusiastic about it. I will have a girl student as a traveling companion to spell the driving, paying her expenses, in exchange for her company and help with the driving, helping with dinner, dishes, etc. Should work out fine. She is a darling girl. I will let you know if I ever figure out exact dates. We plan to leave Los Gatos the 24th of June, and we should be home again early in September. Rob, let me know if either the final week of July or the first week in August is out for you, because I will make my final plans around that.

Now, as to further happenings around here, do you all recall my tale of the "underwear burglar?" Well, that has stopped, but now we have a firebug!!

Four fires have been set, one in our yard (a living bush!) and three directly behind our back fence. The fire department has been out four or five times. Bill came home on Monday and found the fire truck here, and on Tuesday the police. At that point, I was frantic! Then, on Wednesday, totally unrelated to any of the above, I went out to the front of the house to set a sprinkler. I tripped over a guy wire that was holding up a tree, upending myself, with my face landing on the driveway, breaking my sunglasses. With blood dripping out of my nose through my hands as I irrationally tried to catch it, I dashed into the house, leaving bloody hand prints on the white front gate, blood all over the front door knob, and big drops all the way to the bathroom. So, poor Bill arrived home, found my broken sunglasses in the driveway with a pool of blood, saw the bloody handprints on the gate, the bloody doorknob and a trail to the bathroom door. He said afterwards, that his reaction was to think, "Well, they finally got her!!" He found me looking in the bathroom mirror, as I was trying to see what damage I had done to myself and stop the bleeding. Bill called a nose and throat specialist who met us at the emergency room where he set the fractured nose, and put in six stitches. I'll have a small bump and only a minimal scar on the bridge of my nose, but I was thankful I had such an excellent doctor. This is when I am grateful for a doctor husband who will get me first rate care. Had it not been set properly and so quickly, I might have a nose like a boxer. So, no sympathy warranted. I'm fine now, except for shaking my own head at my being so stupid as to trip over a wire I knew was there.

The good news is that my injury seemed to somehow stop the incidents. If the culprit was a kid in the neighborhood, maybe he got guilt feelings and decided, "Enough is enough! I better lay off this nonsense!"

Nothing else to report...Trip is shaping up. This will be my last major correspondence before I leave for the East—except for a short note telling arrival dates. Send me phone numbers, in case I want to call.

Until July, then, be seeing you!

Much love,

Lea

Arlington
May 15 1966

Dear Voices,

Like, I mean, I am real ashamed and all that sort of stuff and like, I mean, I oughta be ashamed, what with me being truant and delinquent and neglectful and inconsiderate and Irish (begorrah!) and everything. It seems like a guy should be able to write his friends more often than—if you know what I mean and all. So, on account of because I feel sick about the whole thing and business and stuff,—like I'm going to apologize, because like I feel that's what a body oughta do—you know what I mean? Soooooo—quote—I'm real—like—sorry—end of quote. And furthermore, I am convinced that what I have written is what I have I have typed (or stolen from O. Henry).

Reminiscence to Rob: Wonderful your being here. Great to see Ed, too. Twenty years have not aged you. Good meeting Joyce and all the kids. No doubt I'll have the same attitude when I meet Lenny's Joyce and Lea's Bill.

When Rob and I parted, we both realized we had lots left to say to each other. Rob communicates other than with his mouth and words. His presence gives one a sense of comfort, and his body language conveys lots that words don't. Rob knows how to be personal without being sentimental. I don't. Never did. Sentiment just escapes all over the place from ole Joe! Must be because I'm Irish!

Word to Lea. Dorothy moves into her new house in June, and Mother and I will be moving early in July. But that won't matter. No need to change your schedule. I grow more excited about your coming with each day. Again, I warn you. I intend to dominate your time as much as possible while you are in this vicinity. Rob and Ed, beware!!

On May 25th, I will end my present employment and start with the United Planning Organization. It's a job I have been after for a long time, and I have been doing a sit-in at the UPO office. They finally got tired of seeing me, I guess, because they came up with a job. It doesn't pay much more, but I will be doing something I really want to do. It's part of LBJ's poverty program.

The poverty program is a thankless, frustrating, and often helpless task. But, like Shriver says, we may not solve poverty, but we must try. This sort of determination makes him OK in my book. Recent work has enabled me to pursue work directly with ex-cons. This means a lot to me. In Washington, some 50 % of the men in poverty are ex-cons. Some have no legitimate gripe, but most of them do, particularly those who are negro. It's hard when both a criminal background and an undesired 1/16th outer covering determine whether or not you get a chance to get a job. I will be the 45th ex-con given a position through the Washington plan. All of us, working directly in CAP (Community Action Projects) will bear watching. Only four have had to be dismissed. The national average for ex-cons returning to prison a second time is very high. Maybe UPO has the answer: use the fallen to help the fallen. But, the main help lies with society—will they look at all these things with an open mind some day?

Note to all voices: Don't give up on me. My schedule includes hopeful moments with all of you. I promise to improve my letter writing frequency. It's not a case of wanting to see all of you!—I MUST!

With feeling,

Joe

(Handwritten to Lea) A very belated happy birthday greeting. Though I let it pass by, Ed will testify that we discussed your birthday specifically for quite some time during one of his visits. What did we discuss? That's beside the point!—

Joe

Weston, CT

May 18 1966

Dear Friends,

This will be mostly a commentary about my visit with Joe. What am I to say? How do you bridge almost twenty years? The small amount of strangeness quickly melted away soon after we said hello. My overwhelming impression of him is that of a man possessed—possessed with a desire to help others. This may cause you to blush under that heavy beard, Joe, but I have to say it—I admire you! In your potent way, you make the rest of us look like we are standing still. I make reference to your MANY efforts to help others—whether it is those 10-year old wrestlers or the 40 year-old ex-cons. I think there is little danger, a fear that Ed verbalized, of your overdoing it. Just keep on doing it; my hat's off to you!

Joe, the news in your last letter of starting with the United Planning Organization was welcome. I am so glad you have a job that has potential beyond the money itself. By the way, I am considering driving down to Washington to give a lecture to some NASA personnel, and I will call you soon to see if we can set up a meeting then, if you are free.

Ed, hope the scarlet fever has run its course. I recall having it when I was 17 in the Navy! I hope there are no complications from it.

And, hello, young lady; how is the western clan? Sorry I didn't get to see you my last trip to L. A. Looks like my next west coast trip may be when you are on your summer long trip east. Good news about Bill's galloping practice. Go, Bill! Lea, those underwear and fire episodes are certainly right out of the textbooks. Attraction, frustration, acting out! Sad for the one doing it, worrisome for the recipient. Hope they have ended and that your nerves are in good shape for your trip, when you will need steady nerves. Can't recall if your original nose was anything to brag—or complain—about, but hope it's none the worse for the episode. Certainly was an eventful spring.

Lea, your trip sounds wonderful, and you know that we will find our way to you one way or another. Heaven knows when we all will have the opportunity to get together again. I'd like to think that Lenny will come out of his self-imposed shell and join us, but I don't think he will. When I am in Pittsburgh, I will have a talk with him on bended knee. But, I don't want him to come unless he comes as one of the gang, with all the things that statement implies. Good night, dear friends!

Rob

✉

Virginia Beach
May 27 1966

Dear friends,

Lea, my goodness, girl! Your past few letters sounded like something that might be an introduction to a James Bond book! I hope the arsonist has been apprehended and that you have learned to avoid your self-rigged booby-traps!

Joe seemed to be thrilled with the way things are going at UPO when I visited him last Saturday. He showed me the facility where he works, and he's clearly happy to be there. What that office is doing differs very little from what we were trying to do in Vietnam, the major difference being that those being helped are our own countrymen. Our friendship is, indeed, on the same plane it was 20 years ago.

Lea, let's firm up the idea of a grand reunion being in Virginia Beach on the weekend of the 6th of August. I possibly will see you before then, and you will get to see Joe in Washington, also. You could plan your Yorktown/Jamestown/Williamsburg trip before or after the reunion, and you could provide Joe with transportation one way and he could take a bus the other. While we are busy visiting with each other, the kids can enjoy one of the nicest beaches on the east coast. So, let's plan it that way, OK? Drive safely, and have fun!

Rob, I hope your plans for the August visit include bringing the rest of the family. If Lea has her trailer, and you bring the sleeping bags, we will have more than enough room. It would be wonderful if Lenny would come, too.

Sayonara,

Ed

Arlington
June 21 1966

Dear Lea, (handwritten)

Ed was in town, but didn't get to see him. Enclosing a bunch of addresses and phone numbers. Just keep trying them until you reach me!

My work has me all over northern Virginia. Having two apartments will be an advantage (the Fairfax Apt. involves no expense).

Am setting up my own office in Vienna, VA. Have office space but await business phone and office furniture. UPO Budget takes time to get these things. The two UPO numbers will be useful in tracking me down.

So, come—plenty of room, beds, apartments, and we're ready for you!! I hope to go to VA Beach for reunion. I may need a ride, but we can arrange that when I see you in Washington. It will have to be a three-day weekend. Can't get off during the week. My boss is off on vacation, and this will make my somewhat busy schedule a bit busier.

BUT !!!—I will definitely get off as suggested above. THE REUNION AT VIRGINIA BEACH MUST TAKE PLACE !!! So, CALL, COME. and then get ready to be overwhelmed by Joe K. and his determined monopoly machine.

Love and such,

Joe

(No date)

Well?

I've been sitting here for twenty minutes and there still isn't a mark on the paper. The trouble is, I really don't know how to begin a letter like this.

In truth, I don't know how to middle it or how to end it, either, but mostly, I don't know how to begin.

On returning from California once, Rob said something about her wanting to make peace. There is no need for it; it just doesn't make any difference.

How can I explain to her that once, when my world was sliding downhill, I put all my eggs into one small seventeen-year-old container, who, perhaps, didn't even know the eggs were there? (What an atrocious pun to add, "cracked eggs.")

If this were 1944, I could say, "Don't be sad, Small Seventeen Year Old Container. How could you know? So few summers are yet tender youth." Many years have passed since 1109 Mc Dowell Road, and the players have faded along with the old soldiers of song. Let them die. We may be seventeen for only one year.

A dark cloud remains. The small container is now tightly packed with black powder and greatly resembles a hand grenade. I don't know how it happened, but she became a symbol. She could disturb a balance I've worked very hard to achieve.

I must write and say that I know her intentions are good, but she would be doing a disservice to call. Perhaps on a future day, I hope she will understand. I suppose the best way to begin is to begin.

July 8, 1966
Mountmore, PA

Dear Lea,

(No further writing on the page)

(Postcard from Pittsburgh to Bill dated July 20, 1966)

Hi, honey! Thanks for sending me Lenny's letter (non-letter, really)— almost made me cry—for his suffering and my part in it. Of course I won't try to see him. I never planned to. I just feel sorry. Family all fine. Cissy, Mother, Rita and families all well. Boys adored the trip! I'm sooo glad I did it! Off to Washington in a few days. Fabulous trip!! Love from Lea and boys

Virginia Beach Voices Reunion—August 1966. Clockwise from top left—
Rob, Joe, Ed, Lea, Joyce, Marlene. Child at left, Rob's daughter, Annie

Los Gatos
September 29 1966

Dear Voices,

Yes, I know, it's about time! Well, where did I leave off? When Rob and
Marlene and the kids left, I guess, because that was the last time we were all
together. My impression:—like yours, I suspect—the nicest thing to happen
to all of us in years! So often, when we look forward to things, there's a
letdown, and when it happens, it's a disappointment. Not a hint of that!!!
Being with Joe again was so comfortable and relaxed; I can't even describe
it. Joe, it was like no time had passed at all since we last saw each other. The
gabbing in the car to and from Washington was the best part. And you sure
made a hit with my boys! I think we all hated for it to end! I can't speak for
all of you, but for me,—well, those two days at Virginia Beach were precious,
and they will remain forever that way in my memory. It was nothing short of
wonderful—the kids in sleeping bags all over Ed's house, the hours on the

beach watching the kids and Joe playing in the surf, chatting with Joyce and Marlene about gal stuff, and watching you guys interacting in that relaxed way, the wonderful conversations with you guys.—all of it. My pictures were Polaroid and not great, so I will appreciate prints of any of you who have "real" ones. I would love some clear, tangible evidence of those moments.

A summary of events since I left. First of all, on the way home, I had the first accident I ever had. I fell asleep—hypnotized by the turnpike in the afternoon, on a 38-mile stretch of nothing but trees to see. The policeman said there is at least one a day on that stretch, and it's always in the heat of the day. I went into the median divider, with the trailer jack-knifing all over the place. Everything stopped, and all the traffic was blocked, but miraculously, we were not hit and none of us hurt. I am just thankful for that and for the fact that it happened at the end of the trip, rather than the beginning. I am still feeling unnerved and a bit timorous about getting on the freeway.

Enough of the ONLY bad part of the trip. The rest of it was sheer pleasure. Bill got to the east coast by way of a military flight to Schenectady in New York and from there by bus to Pittsburgh. (He was a victim of that airline strike) After visits with family, we returned via Niagara Falls, then to Blue Hole near Sandusky, Ohio, through Minnesota and into South Dakota. We camped in Badlands and toured there. Then, on to Mount Rushmore, Crazy Horse Memorial, Jewel Caves National Monument, Devil's Tower Nat. Monument in Wyoming, and Yellowstone. The latter was a wonder, its reputation as our most spectacular National Park deserved. The wildlife, geysers, and pots of bubbling earth were indescribable. On to Grand Tetons, with gorgeous Alpine scenery, Jackson Hole, and the Craters of the Moon Nat. Monument. This last one was weird, haunting, volcanic country with eerie lava formations. From there, we drove into Lake Tahoe, and knew we were on the home stretch—just 5 or so more hours to home. I can say with no exaggeration, that this was the best vacation I've ever had, bar none! From beginning to end, I was blessed with good fortune of every kind, and I am grateful. More than anything, I appreciated sharing it with my boys.

Driving home from school today, it occurred to me that I don't want to take trips without the boys anymore. I realized with a jolt, that our lives are half over, but theirs are just beginning. It just doesn't make any sense to enrich only our lives, when theirs lie ahead, with so much to learn and appreciate about our country. How much better to enrich theirs along with ours!

Ed, I've already thanked you and Joyce for all your hospitality and for making this reunion possible. It was a treat, and I hope you've recovered.

Joe, well, old buddy, you didn't make it to Pittsburgh to meet Bill, though I never gave up hope you would. I never got to deliver your greetings to Ed's mom, but I tried twice. Got no answer when I rang the bell. Seeing you was an indescribable treat; it warmed my heart to see you doing so well.

Rob, I did see your mother, and I showed her the pictures taken at Ed's. She had already seen you and had news of the reunion. It was wonderful seeing Marlene and the kids. I loved them all, but I feel a special kinship with little Annie—because she is your daughter and a dear little girl. The kids were all great, weren't they? Will we see you, Rob? You spoke of a trip in the fall.

That's it for now, dear friends. We all send our love to you all.

Lea

✍️
Weston
November 14, 1966

Dear Friends,

Is it possible I haven't written since summer? Not for lack of thinking of you, but no excuses. Just remiss.

Every time I think about that Norfolk reunion being the first time we were all together after all those years, I marvel. I want to thank Ed and Joyce for making it possible by hosting it. The memory of those days together will be in my mind for years to come. The hours on the beach are especially dear—thinking of Joe swimming out beyond the rest of us, Ed buried in sand with nothing showing but his face, the gals talking away together, the boys getting dumped off the air mattresses—all wonderful moments.

With the end of summer, comes a renewal of business travel, and my many trips include one in San Francisco in December. It seems selfish to be already thinking of visiting Los Gatos then, when I realize I have just recently spent a wonderful weekend with Bill and Lea, returning to work on Monday morning with a refreshed spirit.

From time to time, I feel guilt about barging in on these trips of mine, but I always end up by inviting myself anyway. At first there was no question that my visit with the family centered about my desire to talk with Lea. Now, I notice that I am more and more interested (without any insult to Lea!) in all the family. The boys are great, and I often look at them and picture my own boys in a few years. But, the nicest part of getting to know the family is to get to know Bill better.   Lea took me for a visit to nearby Big Basin Redwoods State Park and we had a delightful walk through those awe-inspiring groves. What a beautiful place! On Sunday morning, Lea and I went to Friends Meeting. Their meditation-type of service, quite unlike the standard service I'm used to, was somewhat of a trial to me. I found that I had trouble disciplining my mind into continuous, coherent thinking. I stayed in Los Gatos later than I should have and enjoyed every minute of it. My thanks to them for making it so pleasant.

Hope to see Lenny on my Thanksgiving trip to see Marlene's mother. No trip to Mountmore this time. My mom and dad are planning a move to Ocean City, New Jersey, and they have rented a place to try out the winter months, before making the move.

And so life goes on. Kids growing, ever a source of fascination when I listen to what comes out of their mouths. Birthday card received from Lea. Thanks due, of course. My best to all. Look forward to seeing some of you soon.

My thoughts will be with the others,
Rob

(Handwritten note to Lea)
Need I add anything? Weekend in Los Gatos was fine. Thank you for being you. I am now scheduled for San Francisco for Nov. 30, Dec. 1,2. I'll call you either the 29th or 30th. Hope to be able to see you for an evening if your plans allow.
Rob

Virginia Beach
May 29 1967

Dear Friends,

I have started several letters and they never get finished and get finally dumped in the wastebasket. But, I will briefly fill you in. I was pretty definite about retiring by 1967, until I got an offer I couldn't refuse to be stationed in Washington. The Marine Corps issued me a set of orders, and if accepted, I would have to agree to remain in that job for at least a year. It was an irresistible offer, from my perspective. I am to complete schooling on the IBM 360 Data Processing System, an ideal chance to do something I have had in mind for years. I have applied to the American University for admission to work on my PhD in Management Technology.

This means buying a house in Alexandria, near Mt. Vernon. It will mean seeing more of Joe, though, which is another incentive.

I see Joe occasionally, last Wednesday, in fact. He looks good, is busy—mostly working with troubled teenagers. (I am enclosing an article about him and his work in Vienna, VA, which is very successful.) He seems to be racing to do all he can to help people, but I have stopped worrying about him now. He is doing just great!

Rob, don't know when I will be in Connecticut again. That all seems a long time ago, for some reason. But, I do hope to see you when you are in Washington next.

Lea, I see the Supreme Court did what you could not do about Prop. 14. Joe told me he talked to you on the phone not long ago. Good to know that you are well, but I'd rather hear from you via a letter. What new crusades are you off on now that you are too busy to write? My best to all. Write!

Ed

Los Gatos
June 15 1967

Dear Voices,

Ed's letter came today. Ouch! I know I'm remiss, and it may be irrelevant, but I owe letters to everybody. I call my sister and brother to try to make up for it. I may have to resort to that with you guys, too.

Ed, I am delighted about your assignment in Washington. It sounds like a challenging job with promise of rewards. Good luck! Proximity to Joe is one of them. One of the high spots of my trip was the chance to gab with Joe, particularly on the way back from Virginia Beach. The boys adored him, by the way! And speaking of Joe, thanks for the article about Joe on his work with teenagers in Vienna. But, I didn't dig that bit about Joe being a kid from the slums in Pittsburgh!!… MOUNTMORE? The slums? Now that I think of it, Joe, you moved to Mountmore in 1940, didn't you? If I recall correctly, you did move from a rough part of the lower hill district of Pittsburgh. If so, forgive my indignation on behalf of Mountmore!

Bill and I were interested in what you are doing with those youngsters, Joe. The principle is the same as the Synanon Games, isn't it, where you learn to know yourself through honest revelation of your feelings, and then face up to group opinions of your behavior? It's difficult to continue being a phony in an otherwise honest environment. Gosh, I wish we lived closer, Joe. I'd love to attend some of those sessions. I once read that recidivism is inversely proportional to the amount of knowledge of self. If this is true, then any criminal tendencies are inversely proportional to the amount of self-knowledge. Is this the idea behind this approach?

And Rob, dear friend, how long has it been now? Any trips in the offing? Bill and I feel the need of another bike ride. We've slacked off. Weather has been abominable—much cooler than normal. But, the good news is that we have a huge snow pack in the Sierras, assuring us an ample supply of water for the dry summer.

Had a huge scare with 15 year old Billy, who was rushed to Emergency with what was diagnosed as a classic acute appendicitis. Turns out, he had an intestinal obstruction, not an acute appendix, but by rushing him to surgery immediately, they were able to save that portion of the bowel. It was a case of a misdiagnosis saving the day. Had they tried to demonstrate an obstruction beforehand, he probably would have lost a portion of his bowel. He is not entirely well, but improving, and he has regained 7 of the 20 pounds he lost. Well, it's all over now. Thank God for that.

All else is fine. School ended for all of us, and I look forward to some systematic loafing, reading for fun again, instead of force-feeding textbooks.

Bill joins me in sending our best to each of you, as well as our love,
Lea

December 16, 1967
Fairfax County, VA

Dear Lea and family,

Please forgive the substitute, but Joe has been so busy that it's almost impossible to find any spare time. If phone calls were less expensive, you would have heard from him. He talks of you all the time.

Joe and I were married on October 18th. We've known each other for about two and a half years, so I have had plenty of time to decide. Ed and his wife were there, also Joe's sister, Dorothy and Joe's brother Frank.

Lots of things going on—Joe's mother is sick, and Frank, too, and I have not been feeling well, either. So, poor Joe is trying to work with all of this, and I said I would write to you and tell you of our marriage.

Dorothy is fine and sends regards to all of you. The grandchildren are beautiful. Maureen is married with two kids, and she looks like she is loaded down carrying that baby.

Hope this will help to alleviate the lack of information for now. Happy Holidays!

Catherine and Joe,

Joe calls me "Cat"

21 December 1968

Dear Folks,

Well, you see, my name is Tony. Not exactly, but Anthony Joseph is downright awful for somebody 4 and 1/2 months old; I like for my friends to call me Tony. I've got this cool blonde of a mom whose name is Cat. I don't understand this, because I am not a kitten; her real name is Catherine, but I want to call her mom.

Some folks say I am Dad's reproduction, but I don't know—I don't have much hair either, but I've got hair ahead of me at least. My dad is funny sometimes—like he hasn't come down to earth since I was born. He is still driving everyone crazy with this father jazz! And my mom's just as bad. She bought Dad a blue sweat shirt with big white letters that said, "Tony's Father." My dad heads off for City Hall dressed like that sometimes.

One thing that bothers me about my dad is that he is always busy and on the go, and he sure neglects his old friends. I mean, even Uncle Ed, who lives nearby, doesn't even know I'm alive yet, I bet! Dad and I have a ball, singing, and talking and wrestling, and making funny faces and sounds at each other.

Dad keeps telling me about his old high school friends—those "Voices" as he calls them, and the way he goes on about them, I know he is awfully fond of them. But, darn, he doesn't sit down and write them like he ought to. I know I'm a little young to take on this responsibility, but what am I to do? My dad has some of the best friends going, and he really appreciates them. I mean, lifelong friends are as rare as a clean diaper at 3 AM, right?

My dad changed jobs here last spring. Now he is working for the City of Alexandria in charge of its Community Outreach Program. He and Mom hated for him to leave the Teen Council they started, but he knew he ought to stop passing good offers by. So, Dad likes his new job, cause he is getting things done—like coordinating public and private agencies that serve the city. He is also going back to the University for a class or two, and sometimes he lectures there and at our local Northern Virginia Community College.

My dad explains that he calls you friends "voices" and your wives or

215

husbands "echoes", and that your progeny are called "satellites." So, I figure, I am a satellite, too, but I haven't been in orbit long.

So, I did the main thing I wanted to do with this letter—ask you to forgive my dad's shortcomings in the letter department, and to wish you all a very happy holiday season. This is my first Christmas, and it's fun.

Love to all,

Tony

PS. I hope you don't mind the typewriter. I'm not old enough to write yet.

Columbia MD

December 19 1971

Dear Voices,

We read Lea and Bill's report for their year that was and realize how busy and involved life is—for all of us. Christmas slows us down a bit, reminding us that, though we neglect, we never forget.

We moved to Columbia last July. We weren't too eager to, but after a year of employment with Maryland, it became sort of obligatory. We live in a planned community, which offers something for each of us.

We're a family of four now, plus the dog. Steve, our oldest guy, returned to Florida to be with his father. Betsy (now fifteen) is a sophomore at our local high school, and growing into a lovely young lady. Tony, who is three and a half attends Montessori School and is a product of Sesame Street and the Electric Company.

Catherine somehow remained a housewife since our marriage, but much of her time remains consumed with prison groups, Montessori, and a women's half-way-house. She's a busy Bahai, as I am, to boot.

Recently, Governor Mandel ordered a special commission to study the problems of Maryland's jails and prisons. The commission suggested that a six man task force be set up to implement their recommendations. The governor approved it, including my appointment as one of the six. This task force will work toward new innovations in alternatives to incarceration and community based corrections centers. It's an exciting challenge against the "big house" concept that has plagued the nation. Recidivism is still a major problem associated with our present system.

Ed and his family are close, but we haven't gotten together for so long. Ed, we'd like to change that after the first of the year.

I haven't visited Pittsburgh since 1957, so that's another stop I've got to get to. Lenny, are you there, old man? I'm going to fool you one of these days.

Rob, what's with you these days? Do you happen toward Baltimore ever?

Lea, San Jose State only came to know last January what some of us have known for thirty years—you've always been a gal "with great distinction."

Schedule didn't permit our West Coast trip last summer as planned, but my family won't allow me to stall that California trip beyond another summer. Catherine and Betsy have never been to the Pacific coast.

Merry Christmas to each and all.

Love,

Joe

(Handwritten note—attached dated 1/2/72)

Lea: You see by this date how far behind we've gotten with our holiday mailouts. A death in the family took me to Pittsburgh in December, and I took the opportunity to make that call on Lenny. He looks good, a bit gray, but still Lenny. We went into the wee hours talking, but your name didn't come up, nor did I attempt it with him. Apparently, that bridge is still a distant crossing left to the future—if at all. His girls, 8 and 13 were in bed, but I did meet Joyce, but only for a few moments. It was a good visit, a first in over 25 years, and I hope to do it again.

Miss all of you a lot, and I would like to see you this year. California is in our plans for summer—let's hope. Hello to Bill and the kids.

Love,

Joe

Connecticut
December 31 1971

Dear Lea, Bill, et al,

Post Christmas greetings from us all. The only thing we conclude from our Christmas greeting record is that we are consistent in our inconsistency—No cards in 1969, cards sent in 1970, late cards in 1971.

Christmas in Connecticut was without snow this year, which is rare. But, it was different in another way, too. Rob lost his job with Celanese Corporation after being there for about two years. Many others losing their jobs didn't lessen the trauma, and it was an ego shattering experience for Rob, but in February of this year, he started work with the Singer Company in New York City as Manager of Management Development. His office is on the 60th floor of the Rockefeller Center Buildings. Gorgeous view, but no fun if you're trapped in a stuck elevator.

The kids are growing—Doug almost 16, Annie 12, who has discovered being a girl, which in this day and age, means concern about clothes—but no boy!! Bill just turned ten, is energetic, does well in school, and is a lively, affectionate boy.

In short, 1971 started out on an uncertain note, but finished on a more positive one, and we're trying to keep our heads in this constantly changing world. Special blessings on your life.

Rob and Marlene

PS. I think I'll be in San Francisco in mid- January.

(Christmas card from Joe, 1974)

Dear Lea and Bill,

Hi! Your news from California always sounds so good—maybe it's because you folks refuse to see life any other way.

We're fine—Tony is home—we found him in Illinois after a year's search. He's well—responding well to a far more stable life. He's in first grade now, a private school—offering much needed personal attention.

Betsy (now 18) is graduated, working in a local bank, and preparing for the University of Maryland next fall.

Love to all,

Joe K.

Newtown Square, PA

Christmas 1974

(Post script at the end of his family Christmas letter. All fine in his family.)

Lea and Bill,

1. I still hate to write. Please note that we live in Newtown Square, which is close to Philadelphia. Seems I've come full circle. I spent my early childhood in this area.

2. I'm going to try to send separate cards and notes to young Bill and

Randy. (There are some things I want to say.)

3. Haven't had any word yet from Ed (but assume everything is OK) , Lenny—not even a Christmas card—EVER, or Joe. (Last communication, Christmas 73, he said his wife, Catherine, had left with the baby. Joe still in Columbia, MD, with his stepdaughter, Betsy. A mess, mess, mess!!!)

4. Our lives are so comparatively good, I feel guilty at times—many times.

5. I miss seeing you, but can't really find a legitimate reason to go to California on business.

6. Buy Scott Paper products! My job is really good, heading up Personnel Development. The work is overwhelming, challenging, frustrating, and filled with real times of joy, growth, and accomplishment.

7. I envied you and Bill your European trip in 1973. It sounded tremendous. I haven't really gotten the European travel itch yet—but perhaps some day I will.

8. The energy/economic crunch casts some doubt on our proposed travel to the west coast (San Francisco and north) next summer, but we shall see,

9. Life just rolls on—and a good marriage is getting harder to find! (Yours and ours excluded, I thoroughly hope!)

10 When I was younger, I found it difficult to write "love", but as I mature, I find it's what really does make the world livable.

Love,
Rob

⬦

Clarksville, Virginia
5 August 1983

Dear Voices,

Seventeen years since the Virginia Beach rendezvous. It was a nice time—seeing those who came—talking, enjoying—being as one with each other. The return trip north with Lea was good—extra time for more words, more enjoying. Then, later another visit—with Rob—in Arlington—later that same year, I think. Over the next few years, there were frequent visits with Ed. Somewhere during that time, I caught up with Lenny in Pittsburgh. After that, well—damn! It's 1983! Why did it happen? Could it be that I didn't need you as much as during those prior years?—Weird!—Crazy!—Incomprehensible!—Not needing you all as much is a signal to let you all slip by—out of my life? Well, I am really sorry—that's selfish, don't you think? But, I think of you—wondering how you are—and how each of you is wearing life these days. It has been a good life for me—really—in spite of the serious bumps those many years ago.

Much lighter bumps now, except in the beginning of the 1970's, when I lost my mother, brother, and a marriage (the latter completely unexpected). Divorce—bachelor father—a little boy to care for—a new respect for working moms—a lot of internal growth.

I married again in 1975, to a fine woman. We have a little girl, age six, and that little boy is now 15, and not little any more. We're a happy bunch of people—living in southern Virginia on a lake, with swimming and boating. Loving and all that neat stuff. Gail (my wife) is a writer, like you, Lea—not the poet you are—although she tries her hand at it now and then. Rather, she is a writer of children's books, including a few novels—four published so far—contracts on three more. We keep wondering where the money is that authors are supposed to make. The greatest gain is knowing she did it. It has been fun watching that happen in English, French and Japanese. Gail has helped get me up for this letter.

I'm still in Corrections—been on the proper side of this field for a long time now—a long stay in various Maryland positions—and my second year in Virginia. Thought of leaving a few times, but have given up on that—I'm hooked and assume I will stay with it until retirement.

Health wise, I've been really blessed—surgery a couple of times in the past dozen years, but feel great most of the time. I can still handle a long workday and a 5 to 6 mile jog to boot.

How are all of you? And your families? I'm open for some letters—OK? Have you all been staying in touch?

Write! C'mon, please!? I promise I won't make you wait too long for an answer. Love to all of you!!

Joe

PS to Lea,

After all these year, I'm assuming you and Bill are still at the same address. I haven't the slightest idea about Rob, so I am adding his letter to this one. Will you send it to him? You were always close to him, so if anyone's been in touch, it would be you.

Gail Radley
Clarksville, VA
August 8 1983

Dear Lea,

Joe has mentioned you many times; in fact, I have come to know you as one of the "voices" who have meant so much to him over the years. How nice it would be if these mysterious "voices" would materialize in the form of people I could actually meet. Perhaps a beginning might be to request your help in a project of mine. I am a writer, as Joe mentioned, and I am trying to build a resource file of people to whom I can turn for information, experiences, and opinions for articles I write. My current plans are for a book on family reunions, and articles on women keeping their own names, (note the heading above; I kept my own name when Joe and I married), families in which husbands went through a period of unemployment, and stepfamilies. If you have any experience in these areas, would you mind sending it to me? I will follow with a questionnaire.

I look forward to getting to know you better. With best wishes,
Gail

MID-LIFE REASSESSMENT
A fortieth High School Class Reunion—
1984

March 22, 1984

Dear Friends,

It is time for me to write a letter to all of you letting you know what has been going on. As some of you know, Joyce and I have been separated for two years, and we are in the process of getting a divorce. Despite considerable excellent counseling, we do not think we can repair our marriage now. We remain committed to our children and their children, and arrangements have been made so Joyce can live a decent life from a material standpoint.

In explanation of what happened, it is best described by what an article in the Washington Post described as, "Breadwinner Blues." It identifies something called the "meal ticket syndrome," which affects many upwardly mobile men in business and the military. It often comes as a total surprise to the rest of the family; in truth, it surprised even me.

If blame is to be placed, it could go to me for having to be the one everyone else counted on and never expressing my own needs. It made me feel I was taken for granted and that no one cared about me except as a provider. During this time, Joyce was in a chronically depressive state and unable to see my problems and help me. I must confess I didn't really understand her depression or how to cope with it, either. The more I tried to "love her out of it," the more depressed she got, and this only increased my own depression.

I know we both wish we had gotten help earlier. I suggested it, but in a way that turned her off to the idea. I didn't realize my own need for help. A dear friend of mind in California had a depression problem, and while her husband, a doctor, knew to how to deal with depression, he didn't recognize it in his wife, either. Ultimately, when she got help, she recovered. I tell you this so that if any of you suspect a depression, you might want to have the person seek help, for it's a significant illness, which requires outside intervention and treatment to cure.

The final straw was my stay in the hospital in 1980, when I was close to death. I didn't care; there was plenty of insurance, and no one really needed me anyway. Dying didn't seem all that bad compared to living. As the Post article pointed out, "The common thread for men: the feelings related to the inadequately met dependency needs, disappointments, anger, guilt, and ultimately, sometimes withdrawal and despair." The article ended on a positive note, however: "The prognosis is positive. Most of the time, it gets turned around. These people are usually good citizens with good minds and they don't usually distort reality. They just feel unloved. They must reorient themselves, reassess their lives, and decide how they want to live." That is basically what I have done. Unfortunately, this reassessment doesn't include Joyce. We both recognize that she is a dependent person, and she does better without me to hang on to.

I want you to know I now include someone else in my life. Please do not consider her to be the "other woman". For those of you who will meet Carolyn some day, please let me ask you not to be judgmental or critical. She is an IBM executive, a personnel systems analyst. She lost her husband in a drowning accident and has made her way in the world as a single parent of a lovely daughter. We will be living in the area permanently, and I would welcome any of you who wish to visit us. We hope that you all will do this, sooner or later.

Best wishes to you all,

Ed

(Handwritten postscript)

Dearest Lea,

Do not know how much you suspected when we visited you. Hope you do not mind my blind reference to you. You helped me a great deal by explaining what happened to you, when you had your post-hysterectomy depression in 1971. I was tickled to hear from Joe. He is not dead, and neither am I. Life is worth living again, and I am living it fully.

Love,

Ed

Media, PA

May 9 1984

Dear Lea,

Well, I sent in my reservation for the 40th reunion, and I am not at all sure why. Marlene isn't coming—says that reunions are for the classmates, and spouses always feel like 5th wheels. She's probably right. I called Joe, and he thinks he hasn't the courage to face possible questions about his past, thinking he would feel too uneasy. Ed is going to be married about that time, so we can't count on seeing him. I'm glad your sister is going along; I always liked Rita.

Let's just meet at the Holiday Inn. Are you and Rita spending the night at the motel? I think I will. Look for me near the pool when you arrive. I will check in early in the afternoon. We'll find each other. Maybe we can do some scouting around Mountmore the next morning. I'd like to think we could get into the school. It would be fun to see what changes we find in old MHS after forty years.

On the phone, Joe said he could drive up to Germantown, where son, Doug lives with his family, if the two of us wanted to drive down and meet Joe there. Interested? If so, we could drive directly from Mountmore, spend the night, along with Joe, at Doug's, and then drive to Philadelphia. Marlene will have dinner ready when we arrive. It would give us a lot of talking time, which I may rue the day I suggested! You could fly home to California or back to Pittsburgh from Philadelphia. What do you think? Let me know.

Best to all,
Rob

(Handwritten letter)

Los Gatos
August 24 1984

My dear Lenny,

I've just returned from a week in Pittsburgh, having gone to attend our 40th class reunion. Rob came—really only to see me, but he ended up truly enjoying it all. Joe did not come—I suspect because he was afraid his post-high school problems would come back to haunt him. In any case, on Saturday, Rob and I drove to Germantown and met Joe, who had driven up from Mechlenburg, Virginia. We spent the night at Rob's son's house and then Rob and I drove to his home in Philadelphia, where we had dinner with his wife and daughter. I flew back to Pittsburgh that evening. Ed did not attend either; he was in England on his honeymoon. He and Joyce divorced within the past year.

So, that's the skeleton outline of the reunion with respect to the original Voices in Joe Killeen's life. The only silent one was yours, and Rob and I were sad not to have at least seen you. In fact, at his suggestion, we drove past your house looking for signs of life, but seeing none, we simply continued on our little "sentimental journey" through Mountmore—i.e.. old MHS, Mountmore Park, Rob's house on Tennessee Ave, yours on Thisby, mine on Mc Dowell Road, Gordon Iller's jewelry store where Rob bought his wedding ring—all sentimental stuff. I was fearful of seeing you, not for myself, but because your utter silence seemed to be saying you wanted no part in all of this, and the better part of me wanted to respect your wishes. But, both Rob and I believe strongly that ghosts are only exorcised when you can look at them. I guess my motivation for this letter is the profound wish I have, NOT to have us go to our graves without coming to terms with one another. I don't mean covering it all up and burying it; I don't mean dredging up the past and wallowing in it, either. I think what I'd like, is to recognize that each of us played an important part in each other's past—for good or ill—and that the past is dead, but not forgotten. (What first love IS ever forgotten?) I don't presume to understand your perception of what we were—or were not—to each other, nor is it my purpose to go back to that time in any way, except to assure you that you played a very important role in my life. Your goodness and decency, your integrity and intelligence, your generous and kind spirit set the stage for my set of standards in people. I've been consistently attracted to people with those same qualities ALL my life. And, you were the primary model. But, perhaps most of all, I long to understand what I perceive to be your deep hatred for me. It's haunted me for 18 years.

I hope—have always hoped—that you would understand, that when I gave you back that ring, there was NOBODY else. Indeed, it had nothing whatever to do with YOU at all. I simply wasn't ready to get married. I had been absolutely faithful to you since I was 16; I'd had no youthful "flings," really. I wanted the freedom to just "play the field"—to act like a young girl. Whether it was the "right" or "wrong" thing to do is irrelevant—and unknowable. It's simply what is true. Nothing was erased. It's just that our lives changed directions at that point. I did not realize—because I was very young—to what extent you were hurt. For whatever hurt I DID cause, I am profoundly sorry. But, I'm not sorry for the life I've had, and I'm quite sure you are content with yours. At least, I hope so. I guess what I'm trying to say is that you had a salutary effect on MY life—because of the person you were and, I know, still ARE. I want you to know that.

You know, Rob and I had lots of time to talk as we drove all those hours for our meeting with Joe. It was a marvelous time. We laughed a lot, talked, listened, even both cried a bit. And the conclusion we came to is that we are both very grateful we have the spouses we have. Marlene is a wonderful woman—strong, warm, intelligent—all that Rob needs. Bill is strong, stable, with absolute integrity, secure enough to give me the freedom to be myself— all that I need. We congratulated ourselves on having selected our respective lifetime partners. We also recognized that we (Rob and I) have a rare, loving friendship that has survived essentially a lifetime. Neither of our spouses feels threatened by it, because both recognize it for what it is. Both of us are grateful for that.

None of us gets to be this age without trials and sadnesses, and we've both had them. Rob lost his son, Billy, in 1975, in a tragic accident, in which his other son was the driver. (Can you think of anything worse than having to help one son deal with overwhelming guilt feelings, all the while grieving over the loss of the other? I cringe to think of it.) When he called me to tell me, I could hardly stand the pain of hearing his weeping. My God! To lose one's child! It was unspeakably sad. For me, there was a profound post-hysterectomy clinical depression in 1971, which required 6 months of therapy and a two-week stay in a psychiatric ward. (You see, Len, no one is immune.) But we're both survivors, and my trauma was a Sunday school picnic compared with Rob's loss. We've both grown from our experiences, albeit in different ways.

I suppose at this point you are asking yourself why I'm writing you all of this. I guess it's an attempt to say that we've all come a LONG distance since the days of 1944, and we've all suffered losses, had joys and blessings,— and we've all come to terms in varying degrees with the limitations of our lives—the unfulfilled dreams, the disappointments. Wordsworth said it best in his poem, "Ode on Intimations of Immortality" (which I never understood in high school, because it takes the wisdom that comes with aging to comprehend these things.) He speaks about how intense and radiant everything is in youth—as it should be, but the intensity, passion, and wonder in life is for the YOUNG. His words about aging:

What though the radiance that was once so bright
Be now forever taken from my sight?
Though nothing can bring back the hour
Of splendor in the grass, of glory in the flower,
We will grieve not, rather find
Strength in what is left behind,
In the soothing thoughts that spring
Out of human suffering,
In the faith that looks through death,
In the years that bring the philosophic mind."

Lenny, in July, 1966, you wrote me a letter—a non-letter, really, which ended with the words, "Dear Lea,......" I still have it and I reread it today. I recall receiving it and weeping—over your suffering and my own—what? Guilt? Anyway, I kept it. In the letter, you said, "Perhaps on a future day, she will understand." Len, I WANT to understand. But more than that, I want to be forgiven for whatever part I had in your suffering so long ago. Can you bring yourself to do that?

I think what prompted me to write this letter is something Rob said when he dropped me at the airport. We had been pondering our unique relationship: i.e..—MORE than a friendship; certainly less than a love affair. (The most physical we've ever been in our lives is a warm "good-bye" or "hello" embrace.) I realized that it is too special to let another 6 years pass by without seeing each other, when he said, "We don't have very many 6-year blocks of time left, Lea!" Good Lord! I never thought of it in those terms.

That's the point, Len, fifteen of our classmates are already dead, and I don't want to die with this unresolved. I have no great wish to see you, just to feel better about you. Can you understand that? After all, we were each other's first love. If this cloud could somehow be cleared away, perhaps we could both treasure what we had for what it was—and be at peace with it.

I don't know if you will respond. I hope you do. Bill hasn't read this letter, but he knows how much it would mean to me to get this resolved. He has encouraged me to write, so whatever response you do make is OK.

Len, I am more fragile than you may think, in some ways. If you intend to chide me for writing, don't respond. I'll get the message, sad though it would be for me.

Now, how do I end this?

I guess with hope,

Lea

(On September 18, 1984, postmarked September 12, 1984, Pittsburgh, PA, an envelope arrived in the mail—with Lenny's return address on it. The envelope was unsealed—and empty.)

> Los Gatos, CA
> September 18 1984

Ah, Len,

How do I begin this letter to a phantom writer of non-letters? Today, in the mail, I received an empty envelope with your return address on it, stamped in red letters with the words, "Received unsealed at Los Gatos, CA," and "Received without contents at Los Gatos, CA." My initial reaction was, "Oh, my God! Lenny wrote! And the letter fell out!" I was mildly frantic! I immediately called Rob, asking what I should do. I told him I felt terrible disappointment—then wonder—then puzzlement, and finally, I concluded that, in all probability there had never been a letter inside. Rob suggested that I had gone this far and that I should go on the assumption, that there had been a letter, that it had fallen out, and I should write you again, telling you what happened.

So, on the outside chance that you HAD enclosed a letter and that it was indeed lost, I'm writing to you, in one more effort to search for understanding. If there was a letter, Len, please contact me—with another letter—or by phone. I'd be content with just the words, "It's OK, Lea. I do forgive you." But—something.

If you, however, meant to send me an empty envelope, then it was some sort of gesture meant to "say something" to me. How I wish I could interpret WHAT you were saying. Was it meant to convey, "It's OK, Lea. I want you to know I got the letter, but I simply can't bring myself to write to you?" Or was it a way of "getting back at me," in some way? (I CAN'T believe that! Vindictive you NEVER were.) Ah, Len, I WANT so to understand, truly I do, or I'd never have written in the first place.

I can understand if you want to close the book on the past, although I've found it works better for me to "make friends" with it—or if not that, at least to make PEACE with what's past. I do not intend to intrude on your life, so have no fear of that. I will simply ask you to accept that my motives are the best. Much as I desire my own peace of mind, I respect you too much to want to intrude any further. In short, you will not hear from me again.

Finally, if I hear NOTHING from you, I will get the message—loud and clear, and I would, of course, accept it. Nothing can erase you from my past; it's a part of me just as all experiences are, but this would remain forever an enigma, an unresolved question, a puzzle without a solution.

Try to face those old ghosts head on, Len. You just might discover that they evaporate. For both our sakes, I hope you do.

I've written this with considerable trepidation and thought. Please know I mean nothing but the BEST for you—for both of us.

Lea

September 24 1984
Mountmore

Dear Lea,

I would have bet the mortgage that I would never begin a letter that way again. But, by the time I finished reading your first letter, I knew I would reply. I once read of a society in the Pacific—New Guinea, I believe—where periodically, the old members of the group were led to the top of a very high cliff and were thrown off. After reading that I had mailed a letter without sealing the envelope, I can see considerable merit in that practice. I can't believe I did that! I may be ready for the cliff.

Don't read anything into it. I just forgot to seal the blamed thing. I'll try to re-write the letter just as it was. First of all, the reply was delayed by several family issues. In addition, I needed some quiet time to think about what I could tell you and how I could tell you.

I am appalled that you have been troubled by things from so long ago, and the very worst part is the thought that I might be responsible. It's not easy to get into, and it's not easy to understand.

The problem, the influence, that has touched most of my life, and dominated part of it, started long before I ever knew you. By the time I came back from the Army in 1946, I knew something was amiss. (And I don't know how to say this gently, though I don't mean it to be anything else.) I had lost trust and faith in everyone I knew—family, friends, everyone— except you. I so admired your intelligence, and sensitivity, and understanding—your strength, that it was just naturally there, that you would lead the way through that mire. Of course, it was totally unfair for me to think that. What a burden to place on your young shoulders!

Anyway, it all led, ultimately, to six years of psychotherapy and a stay at Western Psychiatric Hospital (an old landmark you will remember. You were wearing a brown, handmade sack dress when I met you there once—during your psychiatric nurse's training).

There were hard years of grueling, beads of sweat on the forehead sessions, ups and downs, sometimes near despair. At times, it seemed interminable. Then, slowly, quietly, it came to an end. It was like the sun rising on a meadow on a misty, summer morning. Beautiful sun! Beautiful day! I had gone from being unable to function, to coping. The aftermath would not be soaring with eagles, but it wouldn't be sitting looking out through a window, either. What was it all about? Why? Who knows? It involved fear, self-doubt, panic.

Perhaps I was born too sensitive. David (the psychiatrist) used to refer to me, though not unkindly, as the poet. Now that it's finished, it seems like it was a shared adventure. At the time, it was ghastly. But, enough of that.

I am retired from 25 years with U. S. Steel at a job that really wasn't very much of a challenge, though it had its moments. But, it paid the bills, put one daughter through Carnegie-Mellon University (Rob's old school) and the other through business school.

I then worked at Goodwill Industries of Pittsburgh, for three years. I tried to show ex-addicts, ex-alcoholics, ex-inmates, even one murderer, (you can't be an ex-murderer, can you? No, of course not!) how they could work in the real world.

I retired from that and went to school to learn how to drive a school bus. I think it's one of those service to the community things, but Joyce says I am just after the record for the total number of retirements. I love it!

My life has been clearly divided into three segments: before David, the David years, and then, all the rest. It is most uncomfortable for me to cross the lines. It was not easy for me to write this letter (twice!) and that is why I wish Ed, and Joe, and Rob would not call. They are fine men with good intentions, but they do not understand the total effect.

It occurs to me that of all the people I have known in a lifetime, there have been only four whom I have loved without reservation. And they are all women.

Two are our daughters, who know beyond doubt that they have their father right in the middle of their upturned palms,

One I almost married,

One I did.

How lucky I have been! We will never meet again, and that is what I want. Ah, but in my memory there is a place that is warm—and gentle—and blameless. It's YOU. I wish you peace, Dude.

Goodbye,

Len

Los Gatos,
September 25, 1984

(Handwritten—not sent to the other voices)

Dear Rob, my dearest of friends,

(And I presume, Marlene, because I sense that you have an "open letter" policy in your household, just as Bill and I do.) Bill read Len's letter BEFORE I did.

I'm enclosing a copy of Len's letter. It needs no comment from me except to say that he's given me the gift of removing a cloud from my heart. This letter allows me, AT LAST, to gently close the door on a phase of my life, which ended over 35 years ago, but which somehow never seemed to be over. Poor Len. It's not necessary that I understand all the details of his suffering. It's enough to know what he's told me in the letter and to be told that he holds me BLAMELESS. (That's the word that caused me to cry over the phone, when I read it to you.) I must have read that letter 15 times, never making it through without tears. Ah, the MYSTERY of the human heart! The letter reminded me of what I saw (and had all but forgotten) in him those many years ago—a decent, sensitive, GOOD person. I can't tell you, but perhaps you can guess, what it means to me to have this resolved. I wanted CLOSURE. He gave it to me in the gentlest way possible. I'm very grateful. I know it was hard for him to do.

I'm a person who acts on instincts, Rob. I just open my mouth and let the words roll out, just as they are, trusting I will not be misunderstood. Likewise, I write with very little aforethought. So, I'm ignoring your lack of interest in seeing my original letter to Len. A copy of that is enclosed, too. Toss it, if you want to, but on reading it, I realize it's as much about you as it is about Len—you and our lifelong friendship, for which I'm enormously grateful.

In the letter I quoted my favorite lines from my all time favorite poem, Wordsworth's "Ode on Intimations of Immortality. We talked about it a bit in the car on the way to Doug's to meet Joe, vis à vis your Billy's death, about birth being but a sleep and a forgetting—(the transcendental consciousness which exists before and after earthly existence, etc.) So, the quote from the poem is just as applicable to you as to Len. (In fact, I know I was thinking of YOU as I wrote it.

Thanks for caring, Rob, for being there (3,000 miles doesn't seem so far when you can hear a voice now and then.) But, three times in as many weeks is a bit much! Wait till Bill gets the phone bill! I'll probably hear about it.

Finally, one last comment on MY husband. Bill, I've always known, has been absolutely RIGHT for me; apart from his devotion, his superior performance as model for our sons, and his STRENGTH, he's given me the most precious gift of all—the freedom to be myself, to grow to my potential, if that's what I want. And perhaps best of all, his TRUST in me has allowed me to have one of the things I treasure most—my friendship with you— without clouding it with unnecessary and undeserved jealousy. Thanks, my friend, for being you!

Lea

Los Gatos
September 30 1984

Dear Len,

Please do not fear that this is an indication that a barrage of letters will follow. Not so. I'm not a great letter writer, normally, and beyond an annual Christmas letter/card, which I make each year, no one hears from me by mail. The voice letters have been an anomaly. It's only that it occurs to me that you know next to nothing about what has transpired in my life these last 18 years. You told me a bit about your life. I'm just writing to do the same. I'll add you to my Christmas letter list, and if you want to read it, do, but otherwise, just toss it. I'll never know.

In the 1960's, I realized, when Randy (my younger son) was about 10, that my job as a parent was going to run out. Accordingly, since I never liked nursing anyway, I decided to go back to school. I majored in foreign languages (French and German) and in 1971, I was hired to teach French and German at our local high school, which has an excellent foreign language department. I went to have a required physical, found I had a benign tumor, had a hysterectomy and ovaries removed, followed by an overwhelming depression. I can't say exactly what caused it (because I haven't had one before or since), but it's not uncommon after ovaries are removed. Still, I know I had considerable anxiety over having to "perform" in the classroom (I was hired over 250 applicants and would have to "put up or shut up!"), and I have a perfectionist personality with deep-seated insecurities. I never taught a day at that high school and had to give up the job. In any case, I had a period in the psychiatric unit (euphemistically called the "therapeutic Community." I now refer to it as "the Funny Farm.") I had a total of 6 months of therapy, probably stopping too soon, due to my own basic frugality and the need I felt not to use "Bill's money." (I also had a terrible need for financial independence.)

Afterwards, as I struggled for recovery, I contacted a friend of mine—a teacher of German at the local junior high in town—to see if she could use a volunteer aide—just to correct papers and be around kids. She was delighted, and this led to my substituting for her, and later for the French and Spanish teachers. Ultimately, I was hired to teach German there when my friend retired. A year later, the French teacher quit to have a baby, and I took over all the French classes as well. I am now an 80% teacher of French and German and I love it. I take part in the foreign language weekend camps, take student trips to Europe, organized a Belgian student exchange with a Belgian cousin who is a headmaster of a school there, but most of all I love guiding the kids through the maze of learning foreign languages.

My husband, Bill is winding down a practice. He's a good man, a good physician, but as doctors go, he is not in the high-income bracket. He's basically not terribly ambitious, probably undercharges, but this is all to my liking. We're not wealthy, but my life isn't shabby, either.

My two sons are married, have bought houses 3 houses apart on the same street, just 3 blocks from us—quite an anachronism in crazy, yuppie California. We see lots of them—do things together. In short, this aspect of my life gives me immeasurable joy. We go to high school football games together, share in local school activities. Our two grandchildren go to a school 1/2 block from our house. They go to the games to see the game; I go to be with them and watch the kids I taught grow up. I'm happy with my life and consider myself singularly blessed. My daughters-in-law are like the daughters I never had.

Young Bill is a dentist, practicing in town. Randy is a writer. He's a technical editor for a large corporation here in Silicon Valley. That job keeps body together. His soul is kept together by his 2nd job—that of sports editor for the Los Gatos Weekly paper. Randy's wife is expecting their first in January. Sue and Bill have a boy and a girl.

If there were four important women in your life, there were 6 important men in mine: my father, my husband, my two sons, Rob, and you. My grandmother was the only important woman in my early life, and you may recall that she was a gem! I still miss her, and I think I love being a grandmother as much as a mom or a teacher.

My big love is still Opera. Do you remember that I have always been an operaphile? It's my big luxury—one season ticket to San Francisco Opera.

Bill hates it, so I go alone or with an opera buddy. I don't mind; I never feel lonely in an opera house. It's a terrible indulgence, but Bill has never complained—not once. I never became involved with the "doctor's wife" scene. Too much snobbery for my taste. Just not my style.

That's really all I have to tell you. Not much—but I just wanted to fill you in. No need to respond.

Lea

October 5, 1984

Lea,
I understand. Thank you.
Len

October 15 1984
Mexico City Airport

My dear Mrs. Frey,

The next flight to Philadelphia is at 1 AM, and I have several hours to wait. I'm not overjoyed, but I brought your last letter and copies of Len's, and I am going to try to recapture my feelings of our last phone call and some insights from Len's letter.

When you called to tell me of Len's response, I had an immediate phrase run through my mind, from Martin Luther King's "I have a dream" speech. "God almighty, free at last!" I felt overwhelmingly happy for you. And like you, I also saw flashes of the old Len in his words. I saw those things that I admired—his fluency with words, his basic tenderness… But this time, I also saw the tiger waiting to be loosed—a Len still too near the brink, to tempt fate again. I think he wrote to you with love and compassion, (the old Len) coupled with an awareness of the fragileness of life for him (the current Len).

No, I don't think any of us will see Len again, but I surely do thank him for what he did for you—bless him!

You know, blabbermouth that you are, I'm sure glad you make all the efforts you do to keep our communication alive. Since our hours together back in August, I've thought on and off about our relationship. At the beginning (40 + years ago) I was absolutely too stupid to appreciate you. Then some time after the service there was a time when magic could have happened, but time passed and our lives diverged. But, it's quite obvious to me that you still are a very special person to me and I've often wondered why that feeling has actually grown and not diminished over the years. Part of it has to do with you as you are today. I admire your life with Bill and the boys; I'm proud to know you and to know about your accomplishments.

I'm convinced that some of my feeling for you rests on a very simple thing. You are the first friend I can think of who seemed to believe in me before I even believed in myself. You were someone worthwhile who thought I was worthwhile, and that was a great, undeserved flattery, which I think I've carried through my life.

I'm glad you wrote the things you did to Lenny about Bill and Marlene. I think both of us give thanks for having the lives we've had. I've never felt that there is only one person for each of us in marriage. That is to say, I think all people could find happiness with another person other than current spouses in a good marriage; there is no pre-ordained special person for each of us— but you and I certainly can count our blessings because we DO have good spouses.

You know, I think that I have always been envious of Len's ability with words. Over the years, I've become more tight-fisted, constrained with my overtness about my feelings, probably to the regret of my family. In many ways, I think I'm just beginning to feel freer about sharing my emotions. And I guess one of the real signs of my special feeling for you over the years was the always-present sense of ease I felt in discussing emotional issues with you. I may not have done it well, but at least the feelings of ease were there. And that continuous sense of ease has been a reinforcement in itself of our relationship.

Listen, I don't expect you to cry over MY letters, but then, I've tried reasonably well to communicate with you over the years (except for some things I wasn't really aware of within myself)—but I do expect you to at least give me credit for what I've tried to scratch out during this preamble to a very long night.

Just put it like this—if you weren't someone very special, I sure wouldn't have written even this much. Sorry the words come out so bare when I want them to be better. Thanks for being who you are—and thanks to Bill whose understanding has helped me to liberate myself and allowed me to end this by writing simply,

Love,

Rob

A special kind of love, but love it must be of some kind. Take care of yourself and all your brood. And I hope I don't wake up tomorrow with regret about anything I've written tonight.

Now, I'm going to slip off my watch and hunt up some attractive young thing and absolutely overwhelm her with an absolutely fluent, "Señorita, que hora es?"or something like that???

Don't write and make me feel indebted to answer!

Los Gatos
October 21 1984

Honorable Mr. L., Sir:

Your letter arrived yesterday. It was worth the wait! Yes, some communications are worth keeping alive—and you're welcome. Your friendship is something I treasure. I'm keeping that letter.

No, your letters don't make me cry as a rule; they mostly make me happy. Still, why was I blinking as I tried to read the last few lines? Yes, you are right, as you usually are; I'm free, at last!

Listen, my friend, I KNOW you. I read though, around and in between the "bare" words. Your gentle feelings and kind thoughts—and yes your affection—get through in spite of yourself.

The special love I feel for you and your family is alive and intact, as it has been for as long as I can remember.

Lea

PS. I called Annie yesterday. She had called—just to chat! What's more flattering than a phone call for NO reason? I said I hoped she's been thinking about that trip out here and she is actually talking about next December. I'd love for her to come. Not having a daughter of my own, I will enjoy spending time just gabbing with yours!

By the way,—this is definitely not a response. So please do not respond, or I will get confused as to whose turn it is to non-respond next time.

L.

Los Gatos
October 28 1984

Hi, OLD buddy!

Happy birthday! Now, you are OLDER than I again. I'm still 57! Called

Joe yesterday, having vowed to keep in touch with you two guys by phone, since the reunion. He said our mini-reunion at Doug's caused him to reflect on the passage of time. You know how sentimental he is; it's one of his best traits, I think. He said, by the way, that he wiped away tears for quite a few miles after saying "good-bye" to us. (Guess I'm not the only one who went "round the bend" over that reunion, fella!) It was good to hear his voice.

Had a wonderful dream about you last night. In Jungian dream interpretation, the only one who can interpret it is the dreamer. So, let me tell you about it and give you my interpretation:

I dreamed you sent me two presents. One was a large sack of rich topsoil and the other was a smaller package of kindling. They were delivered to our house, and I was very pleased with them. Bill and I spread the topsoil over a large portion of our front yard, and we both planted young ferns in it. Both he and I stood there and admired them. I don't know what we did with the kindling, but we have a wood-burning fireplace insert, so it was obviously to start a fire there. That's it. That's the dream.

My interpretation:

The presents represent your contributions to my life: your down to earth, basic goodness, your practicality, your affection which is always predicated upon my long term best interest and that of my home and family. In short, that dream tells me I perceive you as one who gives me warmth (the kindling), but above all, you are someone who makes things and people grow (rich topsoil). Interesting that Bill and I were both planting the ferns, indicating that you meant the gift to be for both of us.

I don't think you have ever given me a present—ever! But, never mind; you couldn't top the ones I got in the dream, anyway. So, now, have a Happy Birthday, Rob! (This is not a letter—or a response. You owe me NOTHING! Relax! I just felt like writing!)

Lea

Intimations of Peace

(Note inside the cover of a 1944 Mountmore High School yearbook.)
Not dated, but received October 18, 1987

The old lady died in the spring, the part of the year she loved the most. I've always wondered if she would have wanted it that way, or if she resented it.

Her home and all its contents were divided among her eight surviving children. Piece by piece, her treasures, collected through a lifetime, were carried away.

At the end, only a few boxes remained on the living room floor. (How sad that empty house was. My eyes kept returning to the corner where the Christmas tree stood each year.)

None of the children really wanted the last boxes. They contained only unimportant papers and cards, and a few books. A daughter took the boxes to her farm home in Washington County and placed them in the attic, to be inspected at a later date. Many years passed, and the boxes were forgotten.

Then one day, my telephone rang.

Los Gatos
October 18 1987

My dear Len,

The yearbook arrived today and inside it, your note. It's somehow inadequate to write a simple "thank you" note. In the obscurity of my memory, I only dimly recall that we had only bought one, assuming that one would suffice for both of us. But, whose was it, Len? Yours or mine? I've forgotten. I haven't thought about it in a long time. Odd, once—years ago—after we happened to meet on a streetcar headed to Wilkinsburg, Jodi Morrison sent me a copy. I had told her I hadn't seen my yearbook in years, and she kindly sent me an extra one she had. Then, when that one disappeared, once again, I was without one. No matter. What is important is that you have given THIS one to me, and I am grateful; it is a kind and generous gift.

Len, you ARE indeed a POET! In fact, my first thought was that this must be a selection from some well-known prose, with which only I was unfamiliar. Then, at the mention of Washington County, I KNEW you had to have written it. I wondered who the "old lady" was—your mother? I thought not, and then it came to me. Suddenly, I understood; you were talking about your

242

grandmother. Then, came a flash of illumination, revealing a torrent of memories flowing over me from out of nowhere: a yellow brick house on Marlin Drive—the Christmas tree in the living room, not far from the stairway leading upstairs—Christmas dinner in the big dining room. (At least it seemed big to me, because the family gathering was so big.) I remember your grandmother, busy getting dinner ready, several of your aunts helping in the kitchen, and your granddad sitting in the living room. How sweet they all were to me. I remembered the kitchen and drying dishes, and a kitchen table and a plate of sautéed mushrooms. (I think of you every time I sauté them for myself now; that was the only time I can ever remember anyone fixing a special favorite food—just for me—and for no particular occasion!) I saw a big front porch with a glider and some chairs and—need I go on? It was as though someone had unlocked a door and a whole closetful of memories came tumbling out—all wonderful ones. I suddenly remembered a Christmas Eve midnight mass at an orphanage, the church dark, and the choirboys' faces shining in the glow of the candles they were carrying in a procession— a long forgotten scene brought suddenly into focus. I could even hear the organ and those cherubic voices singing the Ave Maria.

Lenny, it was as though your eloquent words had somehow let in fresh air and sunshine, wrapping those days in the glow of a light and warmth they deserved. They were, after all, the best part of my youth.

I know how difficult it was for you to cross those time lines that divide your life into segments, and that difficulty makes your gift very precious. I hope this kind of contact will not always cause you discomfort. We will never see each other again, and that is OK.. But, I earnestly believe that "crossing those lines", if you risked it often enough, would eventually stop causing you unease. I guess I am saying that I hope you could come to trust me and my motives, as I know you trust your own.

Each of us has had a good life, a family we treasure, and a good marriage. And none of these are threatened by allowing healthy light to illuminate these past memories, so that they can be enjoyed for what they are. Personally, I treasure them all, though it is probably my style to focus on the positive ones. I wish you could. The radiance Wordsworth spoke of is, indeed, gone forever, but let it be replaced by a soft patina, golden and blurred with age perhaps, but with a beauty of its own. The yearbook and your note were a start.

No matter what ensues, Lenny, the only REAL purpose of this letter is to say a simple—and profound—

Thank you!

Lea

✉

(A simple birthday card mailed to Lenny on August 8, 1988, with the following message:)

        8 / 8 / 88
        A singular, once in a lifetime date!
        Mailed on time, but arriving late
        Shouldn't detract from a fortuitous fate.

Len,

I saw this date in the bank, written as it is above, and I realized it was the birthday of someone I knew very well in the past. I think it was you. The Chinese believe anyone having a birthday on this date will have a particularly fortunate day. I hope that was the case for you and for all of your family.

If I am wrong about the date, and your birthday is actually in December, I hope you will attribute it to early Alzheimer's and thus will have the charity to forgive me.

Lea

✉

(Postmarked August 25, 1988, Mountmore, PA) on a lavender thank you card

Lea,

You are quite right. Your memory is as good as I remember it to be. I was very pleased to receive your good wishes, and I send my own to you, multiplied by ten—along with a small bouquet of violets.   No signature.

(This is the last communication exchanged between Lenny and Lea.)

✉

                         DeLand, FL
                  December 18 1989

Dear Friends at Christmas,

"Friends are like the gentle whisperings of a love divine," a poet one wrote; and this is a season when we listen intently and savor those whispers that are forever recorded deep within.

I hope these days are full and special for all of you, as they are for me. High school friends, Lea, Rob, and Ed are well. When the October 17th earthquake struck the San Francisco area, with the epicenter in Los Gatos, it took me a day or so to reach Lea at her Los Gatos home. Great was my relief and joy when I did hear her voice. No injuries, and, although things were tipped over, broken, or otherwise in disarray inside their house, it was structurally intact. "Even our serious cases of jitters are improving as the aftershocks lessen in number," she wrote recently. Rob and Marlene's holiday letter is an enjoyable one that describes travels to Costa Rica and Africa. They are becoming the best traveled friends I have—even managing a trip to Los Gatos to see Lea and Bill—that for sure was a special trip. Ed and Carolyn write from New Milford, Connecticut, and are doing well and are happy. There is a nice coincidence of which they may not be aware. Ed's stepdaughter, Melinda, is in her second year of studies at Stetson University, which is about a half dozen blocks from our home in DeLand. We encourage the New Milford folks to let Melinda know about our being in town-- we'd love to get to know her.

Florida living is nice, but very busy. Working with affordable housing programs for moderate and low-income people, including the homeless, takes a fair share of my week. Florida ranks near the bottom in offering social services to the needy. Gail and I also have gotten involved in preparations for January 15th Dr. M. L. King celebrations, plus the New Year's eve U.N. Peace Vigil, and other social concerns. Tony and Jana are both involved in theatrical ventures, and Gail continues writing and working as a librarian.

This holiday season, I leave you with a thought from the Itza-Maya Central American Indians, recorded in the 16th century:

"Listen! It is not too late to listen! A new wind is blowing, a wind of change....

Listen no longer to those who divide you; listen to the Lord of Love who would unite you.

Love not just your people, but all people; love not just one religion, but all religions; For they are all one!"

Joy, peace, and unity embrace you all from Joe and all the Radley/Killeens of Florida.

Orlando, Fl.
May 9, 1990

Dear Lea,

Alas! The time slips away—January since you wrote—four months. I'm looking through the class reunion packet you sent me. You're great, you know that? All that cutting, gluing, photocopying—all this to provide me an enjoyable view of the participants. I've leafed through them, and the names and faces are familiar, but the memories are limited. You have held fast to so many memories; I've let too many slip away.

You mention maybe going to the next one. Hmmm...maybe if I had a guarantee that you and Rob never left my side, I might do it, but I wonder if it would be an ordeal. I don't handle the past well—I'm better with the present. No promises, though, OK?

Mountmore was a comfortable time in my life; it was like a temporary shelter in a troublesome storm, because pre-Mountmore was not comfortable. Mountmore was calm—not healing—but calm. Rob was comfortable and you were. So were Ed, his sister, Ann and their marvelous mother. But, a lot of post-Mountmore was not comfortable. Post- Mountmore was, in fact, VERY uncomfortable. Post-Mountmore didn't become comfortable again until the early 60's; then it was like being born again—like getting another crack at life—and everything falling together neatly—comfortably— particularly these past years with Gail. We're soon to celebrate our 15th year together. Wow! 1990 is so comfortable!

There is a special trip Gail and I (and maybe Jana) might take in 1991— the West Coast! We were thinking about a month long trip by car—seeing some special sights along the way. Of course, Montalvo and you would have to be a highlight, as well as a visit in Pennsylvania with Rob and Marlene, and maybe a stop in Pittsburgh. Let me know when you fashion your 1991 schedule.

Our current times remain busy. Gail is back into her writing mode. She's in the process of contracting her latest book, another children's novel—should be in print by the end of the year. In addition, she is negotiating a poetry anthology and a biography, both geared, of course, to kids.

My own days are still involved with housing needs for the homeless and other low-income people. Florida is a place of extremes—with a terrible disparity between wealth and poverty. It occurs to me that the right to lifers, with whom I sympathize morally, are difficult to support, when our country doesn't seriously reach out to the homeless and other impoverished children that are overwhelming us in numbers. It's a troubling situation, coming to terms with moral principles that don't entirely jive with the realities.

Cognizant of the high mobility of America's families, I think you and Bill Are very fortunate having your sons and their families living three houses apart on a street about 3 blocks from your house. Amazing! I trust you are both terribly spoiled by it; you clearly love it—and you even get to have a grandchild in your class! I gather that, by now, last year's earthquake is fast becoming more of a frightening memory.

Lea, there are a lot of people that I've admired and respected in my lifetime, and I've been blessed with a lot of good friends. Yet, outside of my own immediate family, there are only about a half dozen men and women that I've learned to love and cherish deeply. Three of those have passed on, and maybe one or two others will bless my life before I pass on myself. Somehow, it is important to me that you know that you are one of those very special people. How to explain this—I'm not really sure, but the answer lies in a certain poet's *Voices at Montalvo*. I would love to walk through the gardens of Montalvo some day with you and Rob—those beautiful gardens that are second only to the Bahai Garden of Ridvan in my mind's eye. My favorite fantasy is sitting on that expanse of lawn in front of the main house, stretch out on the grass, and have you read it to me.

Whoops! Another of those sentimental moments just slipped by. Enough said; I'm out of here! Love from all of us to all of you.

Joe

Los Gatos
September 20, 1990

Dear Joe,

It occurs to me I never answered your last letter, and I am sorry. You asked me what my schedule is for next summer, and I must tell you that I am currently planning a trip to Europe for just family and close friends, which I will lead (after a fashion). I've already begun making the arrangements, and we will leave in mid July returning about the second week of August.

I earnestly hope you and Gail will make that trip to California in June or early July. Please, PLEASE come! We will both be terribly disappointed if you don't. It's about time you meet Bill, and it certainly will be easy to make your fantasy of stretching out on the Montalvo lawn a reality, since it's a scant 4 miles from our house... And, since I no longer stutter, I can manage a reading of *Voices t Montalvo* then.

As you requested, I am sending you my latest version of that often rewritten poem. Take your pick among the versions you now have, and just hand it to me. I'll do my best to read it. That I will do so with sincerity is a given. This is my favorite version, but it is written for you, so you pick the version you want me to read. Love to you, Gail, Tony, and Jana from

Lea

VOICES AT MONTALV0–1964
(Rewritten June 1990)
Summer and early morning's beaming face
Deny the lingering buds and dew
Of spring. We walk and talk of you
And Mountmore and the days when love and laughter
Bathed our lives in youthful grace.
Dear friend, how came the circumstance
That bound you then in walls of grey?
Or need we sound the distant drums
Of why, but send instead what comfort comes
In joyful sparks of memories grown,
The rest of little consequence?
We all inhabit prisons of our own.
Sleeping salamander, dared we enter
The confines of your winter cloister
Then and risk intrusion
On the chance that we might warm
The penetrating cold of your seclusion?
Past dry ponds, a century of plants and jagged twists
We stroll, heads only slightly bent,
Reminded that the years are spent,
And yet, the splendid pale green fern persists
In you and us, and overhead a hawk planed
The treetops of this Eden, as though it knew alone
That Adam and Eve are only made of stone.
The love that splashes at the statue's feet
Awake the memory of Irish songs and rumble seat
And chocolate phosphates in Dickson's drugstore.
They cry, too, the shrubs, their blossoms scattering
In the morning breeze for all of us, shattering
The dreams of you, who always loved this place
And walks with us now with more than just a trace
Of yesterday.
Written June, 1964 and sent to Joe September 1990 with love from
Lea

Los Gatos, CA
Christmas letter–1991

Dear friends,

This has been a year of multiple events, most of them good ones, one causing us all some anxiety, but all with good outcomes. Last May, Bill had open-heart surgery for a congenitally defective aortic valve. Thanks to a marvelously gifted surgeon, who juggled his full schedule to accommodate Bill, the human valve replacement was done promptly and successfully, and we were able to take our trip to Europe as planned. Bill has renewed energy since the surgery, and we are grateful it is behind us.

Highlight of the year was my European swan song, my dream trip. I spent over a year planning it, planning the itinerary, making all the hotel and meal arrangements, (even choosing menus) hiring a bus and driver, and pre-paying everything in three different currencies. It was a monumental task, but one I did with love, since the eighteen people in our bus were son, Bill and family, my sister, Rita and her neighbor, friend Rob and his wife, Marlene, and the rest other special close friends. We visited Belgium, France, and Germany, focusing on charming, out of the way places and spending the night in three medieval towns, Rothenburg, Bruges, and Riquewihr (one each in Germany, Belgium, and France). To my amazement, everything happened as I planned it, with no delays or organizational problems of any kind. We visited Paris, staying in a small hotel across from the Sorbonne, the Loire Valley, the Mosel valley, Bruges, St. Georges, and Brussels in Belgium, Riquewihr and Strasbourg in Alsace, Baden-Baden, Rothenburg and the Romantic Road, and winding it all up in Garmisch in the Bavarian Alps. My German cousin, Hilde, had all 18 of us for coffee and Kuchen in her park like garden in Aachen, and in St. Georges, Belgium, we were all guests for dinner in the home of my cousin, Charles. Their warm hospitality added a wonderful dimension to the trip.

In October, Bill ended his medical career. He has not regretted it, and he is enjoying the luxury of doing projects at his leisure and having time to play in about six bands. He has become proficient on the clarinet, bass clarinet—alto sax, tenor sax, flute, and electronic keyboard, all of which greatly impress his musically unproficient wife.

I continue to teach foreign languages, enjoying for the fourth year in a row, the presence of a grandchild in my French class. Craig, Sue, and I have become a legend of sorts, since we make up the first three-generation family at Fisher School. This may be a mixed blessing to Craig, but it's a joy to me. We still consider ourselves among the singularly blessed people of the world, with all of us living in the same community, sharing pumpkin festivals, pony league and soccer games, and holiday celebrations.

To those of you whom we see frequently or infrequently, we are grateful for your friendship. To those from whom time and distance separate us, we think of you no less and wish we could see you now and then. And so, in this season when people don't hesitate to speak of love, we remember all of you and the times when our lives touched, however long ago it was. We wish for all of you a holiday season enriched with sentimentality, which, in the end, is what sustains us all. Happy Christmas and good health in the new year!
Lea and Bill

P. S. (to Rob) Interesting that there are references to two of the Voices in this Christmas letter—you and Joe. Lenny's silence is a given, but we seem to have lost track of Ed. A remarkable year in all events, however. Since we finished those three weeks of close daily contact, still thinking kindly of each other, I hope we can try a trip again in a few years. So what do you think? I am thinking of Italy and Greece. Any interest? If you say yes, I will be encouraged. Happy New Year to you, Marlene, and Annie.

L.

West Chester, PA
March 22, 1992

Dear Mrs. F.

Of course I am interested in another trip. Let's keep an eye out for one in a few years—to Greece, preferably, maybe including a side trip to Ephesis and Istanbul. Any ideas of how soon? Maybe after you retire. I'd rather not go in the middle of summer, when it's scorching hot.

Annie is well, starting a new job. I am thinking retirement, but not seriously yet. I think they call it being scared.

Love,
Rob

DeLand, FL
9 / 7 / 93

Dear Lea,

Thanks for "Charlie's Victory". What a wonderful book, and what wonderful models are Charlie and Lucy Wedemeyer. I knew they lived in Los Gatos, but I didn't know you knew them. Michael Nouri, who played Charlie in the Television Movie of the story, stated that Charlie faced the choice of whether "…to hold on or to let go. And he has chosen to go on." I think he probably holds a record as one of the longest survivors of ALS in history. As you knew it would, it sent my memory back some thirty plus years to a time when I was forced to make a choice—to wallow in the bottom of that barrel or to struggle my way out. It was not a choice as noble or courageous as Charlie's, but it was most important to my moral and spiritual well being—and what a difference it has made in the latter half of my life.

Charlie could not have made it alone. There was Lucy, marvelous Lucy. She made her decision and anchored that decision to her spiritual beliefs and values—and these are what brought Charlie through. There were their children, significant others, family, siblings, friends, and in the end, an entire community. In a way, it's about the town of Los Gatos, and having lived there once, it touched me greatly.

For me, about 1962, my mother sent me her old prayer book with a note inside, "This old book picked me up when I was down. It'll do the same for you." Perfect loyalty came to me in the form of sister Dorothy. Then, those special "Voices of the Past" rallied around me. Their compassion was demonstrated by a wonderful friend, whose *Voices at Montalvo*, manifested that caring friendship especially with her, Rob and me. There were others, like brother, Frank, a special niece, and of course, for the past 18 plus years, my wonderful Gail. What she brought to my life is not unlike what Lucy brought to Charlie and what you bring to Bill. It's what brings meaning to the expression, "The human family." I loved Charlie's words: "Tomorrow is not promised to anyone. We're all terminal."

Yes, Lea, I did finally read, "Charlie's Victory. I did not see, "One More Season" on PBS or "A message of Love and Hope," but I did see the TV Movie, "Quiet Victory." I like the book better than the movie. It's very moving. Thank you for bringing me close to Charlie and Lucy; and when you see them, thank each of them for being the kind of people they are.

252

Had a good letter from Rob. He seems excited about learning more about his Irish roots. He described the itinerary he and Marlene have planned for their three-week stay between Northern Ireland and the Republic. Rob says he can still remember some of the words and tunes of the many Irish songs I used to sing in high school.

Son Tony is still in Germany, his entertainer aspirations seeming to bear more fruit there than here. Jana is now a sixteen year old licensed driver, flitting back and forth to school and her part time job.

Gail continues at Stetson, and her writing career is doing well. She seems to be hitting her professional stride, publishing two more books, two of which should be released some time in 1994. It's fun to watch her career evolve from that first picture book eighteen years ago.

In spite of my communication delinquency, I miss you—A LOT! I miss the conversations with you and Bill I had in my 1991 visit—the trek along the California coast—and that special day at Montalvo stretched out on that huge lawn. Take care, and write to me when the spirit moves you.

Love to you, Bill, and your family from all of us,

Joe

Los Gatos.
December, 1995

Hi, Joe and Gail,

This is to let you know the die is cast—Bill and I have signed up for an Elderhostel trip to be held at Stetson University in DeLand. I don't have to tell you that we chose it less for the course content than for the venue. We look forward to lots of time with you—either before or after the Elderhostel courses. Will we be able to see Manatees then? And alligators? Do I sound like a tourist?

Great trip in October with Rob and Marlene and their daughter, Annie and a gal friend of hers to Greece, Ephesis, the Greek Islands and Istanbul. We sent you a bunch of crazy postcards. Did you get them? We all had a super time together, and I really got closer to Marlene this time than ever in the past. What a great lady she is. Rob and I did a lot of talking on the trip, and we are now talking about meeting in Sarasota, where his brother Bill and wife live. Ed and Carolyn have a place in Clearwater, so that area may be an alternate spot for another Voices reunion, a repeat of our 1966 Virginia Beach caper—only with no kids, and this time, including all the spouses. Gail,

Carolyn, and Bill will be new to this one. Maybe in 3 or 4 years would be a good time. Let's think about it and make some real plans. I'll write to Ed and suggest it. It's about time, don't you think? It's been almost 30 years since the last one. And, we are all still alive and in good health. That won't last forever, you know.

I know no one ever hears from Lenny. I assume he is still alive, but I have no way of knowing if that is true. I continue to send him my Christmas letters as I do you, Ed, and Rob. Rob says he will do so, too, until he is told to stop. It's hard, though, with no feedback at all. Communication that is one way is very unrewarding, and it requires a commitment to continue it. I am betting he gets something out of hearing from us in spite of himself.

Sorry to hear about your joint and heart problems. Getting old ain't for sissies! Love to you and your family, my wonderful friend. I look forward to DeLand in March—and to YOU!

Lea

Harmony for Four Voices–Reunion 1999

West Chester, PA
November 29, 1998

Hi, Bill and Lea,

OK, here are the plans for the Voices grand reunion in Clearwater next January. It seems to me, as I calculate a bit, that this is just about 35 years from the time it all began—January, 1964, although I don't think as these plans materialized, anyone ever bothered to count. When we last talked on the phone, you never brought it up, anyway.

Marlene and I will be going a few days ahead, staying with brother, Bill and wife, June in Sarasota. We can drive to Clearwater from there, staying at a motel nearby, if need be. Joe and Gail will be driving up from DeLand. Ed felt you two should stay at his place, since you are coming the furthest distance.

The dates are firm, then—from the 7th of January until the 10th. Since you will be going to DeLand first, you and Joe and Gail can work out how you will get there—with them, or borrowing Bill's brother's car, as you suggested.

I see on the map, that with his brother living in Deltona, your driving from there to DeLand will be a piece of cake, so it should be pretty easy to have a visit with both beforehand.

Marlene and I are looking forward to seeing you both. The weather should be pleasant. Maybe we can all converge on brother Bill in Sarasota at some point. At the very least, we can share one meal, anyway.

Love,
Rob

Taken atJanuary, 1999 reunion in Sarasota FL.
Left to right: Joe, Lea, Ed, Rob

De Land, FL
26 June, 2003

Dear Voices and Echoes,

Since Lea has started the Voices writing project, (and indeed the chronology of over 60 years is quite an involved task), I've had the wonderful pleasure of spending special time on the phone with her. Pulling out those old letters is producing indescribable reminiscences within me. I'm overwhelmed! Why? Why have I been so truly blessed with having your friendship? That precious bond that you've allowed me to share with each of you these many years is humbling, indeed. It's a bond that began for me when my family moved to Mountmore in 1940, and I cringe to think that I jeopardized those friendships in the late fifties when I chose my criminal actions.

Yet, when you discovered me in prison late in 1963, and I was at the bottom of the barrel, convinced I had squandered my life, that my future was hopeless, you immediately came to me with your letters of loyalty, love and

257

forgiveness. I often wondered, in those early years, why you would grant me any attention at all—so undeserving did I feel. But, you never expressed any anger or disgust—you never asked why or how it happened; you simply came quickly to me with open hearts and sincere concerns. You all would have come to me in person, had the prison authorities allowed it, but a recaptured escapee knows he has sacrificed many privileges and has to live with the consequences.

I was overwhelmed by your determination to be there for me, as time progressed and your continuing letters so beautifully testified. Despite your busy lives—families, careers, so many interests and responsibilities—you were always there. I had many moments of grateful tears then and I'm having to wipe away a few now, as I write. You kept those abundant letters flowing for the remainder of my prison days; and the letters (though none of us now write as frequently) are still coming and going. And, Gail and I have gotten together with three of you in person, several times, despite the geographical distance between each of us.

As I think about those years so long ago, I realize that there were others as well, my wife of those days, Doris, my mother, my sister, two brothers, and one or two special others. I am not sure I ever really talked much about Doris. She and I came to a parting of the ways when she realized that I wanted to work with people, but not as a Christian minister. She is a gifted theologian who had dedicated her life to Christian teaching. Through her, and with the guidance of the Bible College she represented, I obtained two Christian Study degrees during my prison confinement. I did pastor in a Christian church for several months (during my escape period); but later I realized my need to be a part of direct community involvement. I felt I had to jump into the trenches of the War on Poverty and later the prison system itself.

I had become pretty much of a drifter after I left California around 1950. My contacts with family and friends were rare until I was incarcerated in 1957. This could not have been easy for my mother; but there she was, full of forgiveness and love which she showered upon me in her own quiet way. She continued to live with me after my marriage to the mother of son, Tony. Somewhere about 1969, Mother went to live with sister, Dorothy and her two young daughters at their Springfield house just down the highway from where I lived. In 1970, her health began to fail, and in March of the following year, she passed on. I was so glad, in retrospect, to be a part of her life again during her final years and to be leading a much more productive life in which she could find more satisfaction. God knows, she must have experienced enough shame on my account.

Dorothy, nine years older than I, was very special to me. Our father wasn't always there, as is the case in many Irish families. Mother had to work as a waitress in order to provide for us. This kept her away from home between 3 PM until 1 AM every day except Sundays, so I rarely saw her during the school year. I was the youngest brother and Dorothy was the oldest sister in a very large family. Even though we were quite poor, Dorothy guided and cared for me faithfully until shortly after I entered high school. World War II had started by then, and she moved to Washington D. C. where she began a long career working for our government. To this very day, (and she is 85), she holds a special place in my heart—being more than a sister, not quite a mother, and I have wonderful memories of her modeling of what character meant.

And, of course, there is Gail, whom you all have gotten to know. Next month, she and I will celebrate our 28th anniversary. She raised Tony from the time he was six—he'll be 36 this year. Jana, now 26, is the daughter born to Gail and me. Gail has been the epitome of a perfect friend and mate—my soul mate—my good angel. I honestly believe that God sent her to me as a reward for my turn around in life—a turn around in which you all were active participants. Your respect for me helped give me the time and confidence that I needed to forge ahead in life after those incarceration days. Gail, as my life partner, has been with me through every twist and turn. What a contented Joe I am.

Just a few days ago, after talking with Lea, I pulled out the old resumé of my post-prison years, because she asked me to send it to her. I am grateful for the opportunities presented to me during these past years. How many people are blessed with so many chances for atonement? How many ex-cons could ever dare to even dream of them? How many ex-cons are appointed by the governor to a special task force on prison reform? How many ex-cons are asked to speak before the U. S. House of Representatives? How many ex-cons are asked to appear on the Today Show? Who is this guy, anyway, who not only dared to dream but fulfilled those dreams, as well? Are you people aware that this ex-con could not have done any of this were it not for those Voices of the Past, his wife, and those loyal members of his family? You all taught me that I could overcome my past misdeeds—that my life was not over. You gave me the courage and confidence—in your respect, your trust, your unspoken faith in me. You made me feel important! And you've backed it up with decades of love.

God made sure that there were people like you in my life, who He knew would have the sticking power to remain in my life. Watch what you say, now! I know what I'm talking about. My hefty tears that are spilling over as I write this attest to that.

A prayer just found it's way into my heart: "Oh, God, thank you, thank you! Thank you for those Voices of the Past. And especially, God, thank YOU!"

Sorry Gang, I've got to stop now. These expressions are long overdue; they are not easy, and they tug at my heart as I send my

Love to you all,

Joe

Dear Voices,
Epilogue

After receiving the copy of Kahil Gibran's *The Prophet*, Joe tells the "Voices," in his letter of October 17th 1964, about a fellow prisoner, an African American named Charlie Miller. Charlie had quoted from the book during a work detail, explaining that hard work often sets the mind free. They were apparently very close friends. In his letter of December 19 1965, Joe mentions that something had happened in connection with *The Prophet*, but he felt it would be some time until he "would feel up to talking about it." He never told anyone why, nor did he ever clarify that sentence. It wasn't until 38 years later, that Joe, in a phone conversation, revealed what it was that had troubled him all those years ago, which he couldn't bring himself to discuss in that 1965 letter.

On the day of Joe's release from prison, dressed in his newly fitted suit, and as his sister, Dorothy, waited to pick him up, he made his way into the cell block where Charlie was housed to say goodbye to him. Just as he walked into the cellblock, he observed an altercation between two prisoners, one of whom had a knife. At that moment, Charlie intervened, trying to break them apart, and in the ensuing scuffle, Charlie was stabbed as Joe watched, stunned. Rushing to Charlie's side, he held him in his arms, as the blood from his pierced heart poured all over Joe. Fatally wounded, Charlie died in Joe's arms in just a few minutes. The prison got Joe another suit, and devastated, he did leave that day, meeting Dorothy outside the prison as planned. He never talked about it, so unspeakable was the trauma of that experience. It seems astounding, that it took him until 2003 to share the story with the author, and it was only because she asked him to clarify that comment in his letter of December 1965. There was strain in his voice even then, all these years later, when he described the incident.

Since 1988, there have been only scant letters exchanged by the Voices, except for family Christmas letters. Ed, Lea, Rob and Joe have, however, never been out of contact with each other, mostly by phone and personal visits. Joe's third marriage to Catherine ended in divorce, with the custody of their son, Tony, given to Joe. This leads one to conclude that his history of being an "ex-con" was not sufficient to deny him custody of his son, once Joe located him in Chicago. Tony studied theatre arts, and he has pursued a career in stage acting, with considerable success.

Joe's spiritual evolution during his time in prison was toward liberal rather than fundamentalist, pacifist rather than martial, universalist rather than dogmatic. It's not surprising, then, that soon after his release, he found the

Bahais, a universalist religion that gives worth to all faiths, honoring prophets in all religions. It is a religious community in which he and his wife remain active today.

Joe came to Los Gatos on two different occasions, once in 1991 alone, at which time he met Lea's husband, Bill, for the first time. He was able, then, at long last, to fulfill his favorite fantasy, that of stretching out on the vast expanse of lawn at his beloved Villa Montalvo. Joe handed Lea a crumpled piece of paper with the words of her poem, *Voices at Montalvo* written on it. His eyes as damp as the ground, he lay back on the cool grass beneath a century-old live oak and gazed up at a cloudless summer sky, listening as Lea read it to him. It became a memory, forever warming the heart of each of them.

Several years later, he returned, spending several days in Los Gatos, this time with his wife of 28 years, Gail Radley. Her name is perhaps known to librarians and readers of children's books, she recently having published her 20th book for children. One of her books, *Golden Days*, was made into a movie, called *The First of May*, with Mickey Rooney, Julie Harris, Charles Nelson Riley, and featuring Joe Dimaggio, in the only screen role he ever played. Joe and Gail are happily married and in good health at this writing. In retirement, Joe became actively involved in projects addressing peace issues and social concerns, among them one to house and feed the homeless in Daytona Beach, Florida . Gail is a professor of English at Stetson University in DeLand, where they live.

While attending an Elderhostel at Stetson University in 1996, Lea and Bill learned in detail about Joe's extensive and highly successful career in corrections, including having served on Governor Mandel's task force on prison reform in Maryland. His efforts in that state and in Virginia involved his serving as operations officer, assistant warden, and warden of various prisons in both states. Most significant for prison reform, was his serving for six years as operations officer and administrative assistant to the Warden of a maximum security prison in Mechlenburg, Virginia. Mechlenburg Prison was held up as a model for prison reform in Virginia, housing only the worst of the worst criminals, all serving life sentences. Prisoners were sent there because they had been constant troublemakers in other prisons, and they were housed on their arrival in cells which met the bare minimum requirements allowed by law. The goal at Mechlenburg was to teach these intransigent "lifers" to modify their behavior in exchange for improved living conditions and other privileges. This model prison had an 85% success rate in rehabilitating prisoners sufficiently, so that they could return to the prisons where they were serving life sentences and maintain their cooperative behavior. Unfortunately, despite it's success, Mechlenburg was recently closed, having been described by critics as the "Country Club" of the Virginia prison system, and a "waste of taxpayers' money." Many of the reforms instituted in Virginia and in Maryland by the Task Force on Prison Reform, however, remain in force to this day.

Tragically, Rob's youngest child, Billy, was killed in an automobile accident just a mile from his home, as he and his older brother were embarking on a week long camping vacation. He was just 14, and Rob and Marlene have never quite recovered from that loss. In retirement, however, Rob finds time to tutor, on a volunteer basis, fifth graders in math and first graders in reading and math three times a week. Once a week, he volunteers his time at the local Y, teaching handicapped children how to swim.

Ed and Joyce divorced, and Ed remarried in 1984. Retired from the Marines after 25 years of active duty, he taught Business Management and Computer Science at the community college level for many years. Lea is retired from 25 years of teaching French, German, and English to Middle School students in Los Gatos. Always a lover of opera, she then began a career as a German and French diction coach for opera singers, entering her tenth year in the fall of 2003 as the language coach for Opera San Jose. Lenny remains a mystery to all of them, jealously guarding his privacy, presumably, preferring it that way. However, Rob and Lea, not wanting Lenny to hear of the publication of the book from another source, worked together on a letter, telling him of the book's pending release. To the surprise and pleasure of both of them, he wrote right back, congratulating Lea on the project. "You done good, girl!" he wrote, "I wish you the best of luck and will be watching the New York Times Best Seller list for it. Your cup must be full! Thanks for letting me know!"

Perhaps the most remarkable aspect of this story is the salutary effect the relationship has had on all the Voices, and most notably on Joe. He has, on many occasions, alluded to the appearance of the Voices in his life being a turning point, injecting a feeling of hope, acceptance, and unconditional love into his life at the time he was at his lowest ebb. He has expressed his happiness to the author that this book consists only of the letters, which tell the story by themselves. Although the perspective of the story is hers, since she is the editor of the book, in all other ways, this is a story about Joe, about how essential it is to never give up on anyone—to go the extra mile for a friend.

Most important of all, Joe's life is a testimony to the possibilities for overcoming adversity, and for redemption through reaching out to touch the lives of others. Redemption came, after all, not just to Joe, but to all the Voices, for, as Lea wrote in *Voices at Montalvo,* "...we all inhabit prisons of our own!"

Although Joe's path to redemption had begun before the reappearance of the Voices in his life late in 1963, their letters served to affirm and strengthen his resolve to atone for his past transgressions. No one can say for sure what course Joe's life might have taken without them, but it is clear that the lives of all the VOICES were affected as a result of this remarkable half century of friendship. Nothing speaks more simply of Joe's redemption than his resumé, compiled in 1992, the last one of his post-prison career in corrections. It states clearly and succinctly the most remarkable ending of this chronicle. Readers should note especially the section headed, "Related Professional Activities." An appendix with his resumé follows this epilogue. What more fitting way to conclude this story of a man who turned his own, self inflicted adversity into an opportunity to contribute to society? This contrite, humble man deserves, more than anyone this author knows, the comment made by her soft-spoken husband when he first met Joe, "He is the most impressive man I have ever met."

Lea Frey —Author/Compiler/Editor
February, 2004

Appendix
Resume–compiled 1992

Joseph Roland Killeen
DeLand Florida 32724

PERSONAL DATA
Born- Pittsburgh, PA, Honorable Discharge–U. S. Navy
Married, Father
EDUCATION
University of Maryland, School of Social Work, Baltimore
Course in Field Work Supervision–1978
American University, College of Continuing Education, Washington D.C.
Courses toward Master in Correctional Administration–1968
Courses: Clinical Counseling, Case Study,
Criminology, Parole, and Probation
Sacred Scriptures Institute, Oakland, FL, Majors in Soteriology and
Eschatology. Unaccredited degrees (1958 to 1960)
San Jose State University, San Jose, CA, incomplete Major in
Physical Education and Recreation (1948 to 1951)
TRAINING
"Performance Appraisal and Evaluation"–16 hours
Department of Corrections, Region III, Virginia
"Group Facilitation–20 hours–Community Education Project,
George Mason College, Fairfax, VA
"Sociodramatic-Psychodramatic Role Play Techniques"–48 hours
St. Elizabeth Hospital Psychodrama Theater for U. S. Parole and Probation
Office, Washington, D.C.
"Unmet Mental Health Needs for Northern Virginia"–8 hours
Northern VA Pilot Project in Community Education–VPI
"Job Coaching and Counseling–40 hours
Community Ed. Project, George Mason College
Fairfax, VA
"Volunteer Aid Training"–120 hours Community Ed. Project,
George Mason College, Fairfax, VA
"Community Organization and Development"–80 hours
Institute for Research Development, Washington, D.C.
"Jobs for Hard-Core Unemployed"–80 hours–Northern VA–Pilot
Project in Community Education,–VPI (Virginia Tech)

"Personnel Management For Supervisors and Managers"–40 hrs.
U. S. Civil Service Commission, Baltimore, MD
PUBLICATIONS
• Community and Regional Correction Centers, Maryland
Co-Author, Community Corrections Task Force, Maryland Division of
Correction, Baker-Wibberly-Cole-Burger and
Associates, Hagerstown, MD Curtis and Davis Architects and Planners,
New Orleans and New York (July 1972)
• Training Techniques featured in How to get Things Changed,
Bert Strauss and Mary E. Stowe, Doubleday & Co. (1974)
EXPERIENCE
• Piedmont Court Services, Farmville, VA (1/88 to 1/89)
DEPUTY DIRECTOR of the program for the court services.
Community Divergence Incentive Program for non-violent misdemeanants
and felons.
Alcohol Safety Action Program sentenced Driving Under the Influence
(DUI) offenders needing alcohol abuse counseling.
• Virginia Department of Corrections, Div. of Adult Institutions,
Mechlenburg Correctional Center, VA–(7/82 to 1/88)
OPERATIONS OFFICER.   Administrative assistant to warden.
• Virginia Dept. of Corrections, Div. of Adult Institutions,
Headquarters, Richmond, VA (10/81 to 7/82)
CORRECTIONS SPECIAL INVESTIGATOR.–Overall administrative
functions (investigations, field surveys,litigation preparation, budget
preparation, planning, research, policy development.
• Maryland Dept. of Public Safety and Correctional Services, Division of
Correction, (2/79 to 8/81)
WARDEN (unit manager) -
• Maryland Dept. of Public Safety and Correctional Services, Division of
Correction, (2/75 to 2/79)
OPERATIONS PLANNER/COMMUNITY COORDINATOR–design
overall systematic plan for community corrections.
• Maryland Dept. of Public Safety and Correctional Services,
Division of Parole and Probation, Towson, MD (8/70 to10/71)
COMMUNITY AWARNESS COORDINATOR
• Alexandria Community Mental Health Center, Alexandria, VA (4/68 to
10/70)
GROUP THERAPIST–develop and conduct forensic psychiatric program

RELATED PROFESSIONAL ACTIVITIES
• Guest appearance on the NBC Hugh Downs "TODAY SHOW" 3/24/71
• Past member–Interstate Drug Task Force (Maryland–Pennsylvania Parole Departments–1971)
• Past member–Board of Directors for "Threshold, Inc., an ex-offender half-way house for female ex-offenders. (1971-72)
• Trainer–Baltimore Division of Maryland Department of Juvenile Services in Drug Counseling (1972)
• Guest instructor–Law Enforcement and Corrections School, Penn State University (1970–1981)
• Guest instructor–St. Mary's Theological Seminary, on Counseling the Delinquent (1972)
• Guest Instructor–American University Institute for Corrections (1968–1970)
• Guest Instructor–Johns Hopkins Medical School of Psychiatry, Dr. Jerome Frank, reference (1971)
• Guest Instructor–Catonsville College for Correctional Casework (1970)
• Information consultant to the Select Committee on Crime, U. S. House of Representatives, Chairman Claude Pepper (1969)
• Information consultant–Virginia Crime Commission (1969
• Past member–Advisory Board–Lorton Regional Training Academy for Correctional Personnel (MD, D.C., VA, NJ, DE, WV, and PA.)
• Past member–Corrections Advisory Committee–Northern Virginia Community College Police School (1970–1972)

Author's note:

Fifty percent of the net proceeds from the sale of this book , will be donated by the author to FRIENDS OUTSIDE, a charitable organization dedicated to supporting families of people serving sentences in prison.

Printed in the United States
19978LVS00004B/223